Vital Ties

Vital Ties

A NOVEL BY KAREN KRINGLE

spinsters book company
san francisco

First edition.
10-9-8-7-6-5-4-3-2-1

Cover painting by Carmen Goodyear

Spinsters Book Company
P.O. Box 300170
Minneapolis, MN 55403

This is a work of fiction. Any similarity to persons living or dead
is a coincidence.

Printed in the U.S.A. on acid-free paper

Poem by Ann Bradstreet reprinted by permission of the publishers from *The Works of Ann Bradstreet*, edited by Jeanine
Hensley, Cambridge, Mass.: The Belknap Press of Harvard University Press, Copyright ©1967 by the President and Fellows of
Harvard University.

The Spinsters Book Company desktop publishing system was
made possible by a grant from the Horizons Foundation/Bay
Area Career Women Fund and many individual donors.

Library of Congress Cataloging-in-Publication Data

Kringle, Karen
    Vital Ties : a novel by Karen Kringle
        p. cm.
    ISBN 0-933216-90-4 : $10.95 (acid free paper)
    I. Title.
PS3561.R557V5   1992
813'.54—dc20   92-26958
                                          CIP

To my partner Grace, my mother Gladys
and in memory of my father Leonard–
good farmers, all.

I

PRELUDE

Dawn on the morning of Clare Lewis' marriage to George Hansen came in hot and humid and sticky. Sweat trickled down Clare's face as she fed and milked her thirty cows. Flies gathered in swarms that buzzed angrily when disturbed. The cement floor of the barn glistened with slippery moisture. Clare stepped carefully as she urged her reluctant cattle out to pasture.

She spent more time than planned on the task of briefing the man she had hired to milk and care for her cows while she was away on her honeymoon. It was nearly noon by the time Clare, her clothes and hair wet with sweat, could turn her attention to the task of preparing herself for the wedding ceremony at two.

A shower and a hasty sandwich eaten as she dried and set her hair consumed the time. This is my last time alone here, she thought with a sharp pang of regret. When I come back, George will be my husband and this will become our farm. He used to be so shy, so interested in the farm, but now... I just hope this works. Of course it will. She spoke the last words aloud, trying to sound more certain than she felt. Just wedding jitters, she decided.

Then her mother and father were at the door, her mom in a dressy peach outfit and her dad in his best suit. Clare felt almost detached as she allowed her mother to fuss and flutter over the fitting of the white wedding dress. She submitted patiently to the trembling-fingered rearranging of her hair, the inspection of her wedding bouquet.

Her dad stood off to the side, a calm look on his face. Only the constant checking and rechecking of his wristwatch betrayed his nervousness to her. "We better get going," he said finally. The three of them got into her folks' car and drove the short distance to the tidy white country church in a familiar and easy silence.

Already cars were beginning to fill the church's small parking lot, spilling out onto the shoulders of the highway. Clare and her folks squeezed their Ford into the far side of the lot and walked across the gravel surface to the side door.

They went to the basement where the rest of the wedding party was gathering. Not the groom, of course, or his attendants. They were already upstairs in the sacristy, wiping sweat from their foreheads, sweat from the humid heat of the day and sweat brought on by the excesses of the bachelor party the night before.

In the basement the yellow-gowned bridesmaids fluttered back and forth adjusting yellow veils and recombing already perfectly combed and styled hair. The minister appeared with last-minute instructions for the wedding party and a quick prayer. Clare's brother Marsh materialized to wink at her encouragingly. She thought he looked handsome in his dark usher's suit. His grin was a comfort in this twittering yellow mass of nervous females. With a flourish Marsh took hold of his mother's arm and escorted her up the stairs, down the aisle and into her seat.

Clare and her father lined up behind all her attendants out in the narthex and waited while the organist played on and on. She felt calm as she watched the flower girl shift from foot to foot and listened to nervous giggles from her bridesmaids.

At last. The grand moment was announced with soaring musical notes, and Clare and her dad moved slowly down the aisle past the now-standing congregation. Her father gave her arm a reassuring squeeze as they reached the front of the church. Clare's eyes met George's as on cue the groom and his attendants moved into place and the minister strolled to stand in front of Clare and her dad.

"Who gives this woman in marriage?" the minister asked solemnly.

"Her mother and I do," Ed Lewis said in a voice unaccustomed to public utterance.

It seemed to Clare that it went so quickly, this event that had been planned for so long. She moved through the rituals of the vows and the exchange of rings without any error. She noticed the sheen of sweat on George's forehead and felt sweat trickling down her own back. George's formal peck of a kiss felt like a sticky exchange of sweat.

"I present to you Mr. and Mrs. George Hansen," the minister said triumphantly. The marriage was completed, Clare realized with amazement. The organ music rose high in celebration as she and George strode with brisk steps down the aisle and out the big church doors. They stood outside with the hot sun beating down on them and accepted handshakes and hugs.

"It was a perfect wedding," Eleanor Marshall, the minister's wife, assured them.

But it was not quite so perfect.

"What's the queer doing here?" George muttered to Clare as they waited for the next hand to shake.

"I didn't see her," Clare said, showing no outward reaction to the news. Inside she felt a tight leap of excitement. Lee had come to her wedding. But why?

"She's here," George assured her. "Why did you invite her?"

"I didn't," Clare protested. She smiled automatically and accepted a hug from her neighbor Stella Grimes. George smiled graciously at Orrin Grimes and shook his hand.

"Lovely wedding," Stella said.

"It's a hot day for it, though," Orrin added, grinning as he wiped off sweat with a handkerchief.

"Sure is," George agreed. He was sweating profusely. His hangover was still strong. Even sleeping until noon had not done much to remove its effects.

"Here she comes," George alerted his bride.

As Clare shook the strong hand of her neighbor Lee Collins, she tried to see what there was about Lee that upset George so. Lee was short and compact and quiet-looking. She was going gray at the temples and the grayness in her short dark hair added to her appearance. Clare thought she was striking in her deep green pantsuit with a bright yellow blouse peeking out tailored and trim. She supposed Lee did stand out in this crowd of women in dresses and men in suits. But she knew it was not Lee's appearance that upset George.

"I won't offer you congratulations," Lee said quietly to Clare. "But I do wish you good luck." She released Clare's hand and moved on to George.

George, aware of where they were, was jovial. He shook Lee's hand, hard. Clare, watching, saw her slight wince. Only she was close enough to hear George's words as he used one of his huge hands to pat Lee on the back.

"Guess the best man won, huh?" He grinned at Lee.

Lee smiled sweetly back. "I doubt it," she said in a low voice. She walked away and Clare saw the annoyed anger start in George's face and then disappear as he remembered where they were.

Automatically Clare shook more hands but her eyes followed Lee's progress across the parking lot. The free-moving stride was so familiar that it brought a pang. She watched Lee shed the top to her pantsuit and casually brush a hand through her hair before she climbed into her car. There was a freedom to the motions that struck Clare like a physical blow. As Lee's car left the churchyard, Clare felt suddenly abandoned and bereft.

There was no time to worry about the feeling. She was engulfed in a hot enveloping hug. Jowly cheeks trembled against her face as George's mother planted a wet and sweaty kiss on Clare's cheek.

"So nice to have a daughter-in-law, after all those sons," Mabel Hansen said loudly. She moved on to her son and fondly patted his cheek. George laughed and Clare noticed for the first time that he was developing jowls just like his mother's.

When the last photograph had been taken, the wedding party climbed into cars and headed for the reception at the Vets' Club in town. Once alone, George returned to the subject of Lee.

"How come you invited her?" he asked.

"I didn't," Clare insisted. "Maybe Marsh did."

"You didn't invite her?"

"No, I really didn't."

"I guess it's all right she came," George decided. "Make her realize you're married now. To me."

"She *is* my neighbor."

"Our neighbor," George corrected. "And that's all she'd better be. I still want to know if she ever tried anything with you."

"Nothing. She tried nothing," Clare said, knowing this was the answer she had to give and also aware it was not quite accurate.

"I don't believe you."

"It's true," Clare insisted. She wished George would just drop the subject. She wished.... Oh, never mind what she wished.

But as they were surrounded at the Vets' Club by well-wishers, Clare knew what she wished. She wished she had not gotten married. The moment she'd looked over at George in front of the altar at St. Paul's she had known this marriage was a mistake.

It was too late to back out now. And what would people have said in this small Wisconsin farming community if she, on taking a good look at her groom, had run screaming from the church? It would have been the local sensation of this hot and humid summer. It would have made the rounds from bar to feed mill to church ladies' group to grocery store and beyond. Clare knew she could not have faced the knowing looks, the amused stares if she had done what she'd wanted to do: run.

Instead she took another deep drink of her Seven and Seven. She smiled and ate food she did not taste. She stood with George for more photos, stood with him to cut the cake and stood with him again at the long table loaded with gifts and cards. Together they opened them and Clare did the right and proper thing: exclaimed over the gifts and was enthused. George carefully pocketed the cash.

She and her dad danced the first dance together. Ed Lewis chose that time to give his only daughter a piece of advice. "Let George make the decisions on the farm now," he told her. "Let him be the boss."

Clare said nothing in reply. But as she danced the next dance with George, who had been liberally applying the hair of the dog to his hangover, she wondered: why did I think this marriage would work? I'm twenty-eight years old. I've been my own boss on my own farm for eight years. Why did I go ahead with it?

George dropped his arms and swayed away from her, making his unsteady way to the men's room. Clare moved to the side of the dance floor and looked around. The band was playing. People were dancing. Other people were propped up at the bar. And there at one end of the bar was her neighbor Lee, talking with Clare's brother Marsh. Clare watched the two of them laughing together, chatting like the old friends they were. She, the bride, was the outsider now, alone.

Lee saw her staring and waved. Without meaning to, and knowing what George would say when he found she had done it, Clare cut across the crowded dance floor to Lee at the bar. Marsh moved off before she got there, claimed by one of the bridesmaids for a dance.

Lee watched the tall slender figure dodging gracefully around dancing couples, holding up the skirt of her white wedding dress. Lee felt the familiar pleasure the sight of Clare always brought her and then a painful stab at what that dress signified. She managed what she hoped was a warm smile as Clare sat on the next bar stool.

"You came," Clare said, drinking in the warm smile.

"Yes. I did." Lee was aware that she was staring too intently at Clare, but she couldn't help it.

"I didn't invite you because I...didn't think you'd want to come."

"Marsh talked me into it," Lee said. "I hope it goes all right for you with George."

"Thanks," Clare said awkwardly. There was silence between them in the noise of the hall. "It was a mistake," Clare said softly. "I shouldn't have."

"Why did you?" Lee asked the question, but she already knew the answer.

Clare shook her head. She looked miserable, and Lee felt sympathy for the younger woman trapped now by the conventional life she sought to fit into.

"Your eager groom is coming," Lee murmured, aware that the sarcasm in her voice was not helpful to Clare but unable to keep it out.

George, solid, handsome and tall, stood possessively next to his nearly as tall bride. His glance at Lee was not friendly.

"Time to go," he said to Clare.

A drunken Air Force buddy claimed George's attention and into the moment of his distraction, Lee said softly to Clare, "Hey, I'll still be around when you get back."

PART ONE

1955-1968

CHAPTER ONE

C lare Lewis was fifteen years old when her neighbor Lee Collins did the unthinkable for a woman and bought a farm.

"You'll never believe what I heard today," Ed Lewis told his wife at supper. "You know old man Larson's place? Been vacant just since his death. The Collins girl bought it."

"You mean Lee? She isn't married, is she?" Eve put the hotdish on the table and sat down.

"Who'd want her?" Clare's older brother Harry put in. "She's a..."

"Strange girl," Eve said quickly.

Harry snickered. "Just like Clare. Weird." He dodged his sister's kick under the table.

"Cut it out, you two," Ed ordered impatiently. "Yeah, I heard down at the feed mill, Lee Collins bought that farm. They say she's gonna farm it herself."

"What are Charles and Lydia thinking of, letting her do that?" Eve wondered.

"Yeah, girls can't farm. They're too dumb," Harry put in. "And weak." He smirked at his sister who glared back. Sometimes Harry was just too much, Clare thought. She wanted to hear more about Lee Collins farming.

There wasn't much more for her dad to tell. "Chuck isn't too happy about it. The girl is sure different enough as it is, but she's twenty-three and she got financing somehow. Let her get it out of her system, I guess. She'll see soon enough she can't do it."

At his dad's words Harry looked triumphantly at his sister. She resisted the impulse to throw her pudding at him. It would just end in a lecture for both of them. She did not know Lee at all really but she knew about her from the local gossip mill. Clare's interest was high simply because she had never thought about a woman being able to farm before. She loved the farm but it hadn't seemed likely she would have a chance to do more than help with chores. Her dumb brother Harry was the chosen one. She and her younger brother Marsh knew that already. It made her mad to think of Harry taking over, he was such a jerk. She sure hoped Lee would prove everyone wrong and do a really good job on her farm.

Lee Collins didn't have to buy a farm to get the gossips wagging. Even in high school she'd shown defiance by wearing blue jeans and men's work shirts when other girls were wearing skirts and sweater sets. She'd been denied admission to the agricultural courses in school but had obtained the course materials on her own. But the real head-shaking started when Lee, after high school, went to work at the local wood products factory, on the line with the men.

The other workers gave her a wide berth. Oh, she was good at her job, all right, but she was just too different from other women, too self-contained, too independent. She was short, slender, quiet, not much given to smiling. She drove her own car and kept it serviced and clean. She still wore blue jeans and men's blue work shirts, with the sleeves rolled up her arms. With her short hair she was sometimes mistaken for a very short man. Lee herself didn't much care about the gossip or even being mistaken for a man. Mostly she thought being female was a burden. She felt no kinship with the chattering giggling young women who would drop a female friend flat if some hulk of a male even glanced their way.

Lee found the wood products factory dull but bearable for two reasons. First, she wanted to save enough money to buy a farm. And then there was her friendship with two men on the line. They lived together and were regarded with suspicion by everyone in town. Les drank too much sometimes and was hungover at work. Wade, shorter and slimmer than Les, fussed and worried.

They provided amusement for the other line workers, but beyond making an occasional joke, the other men left them alone. There was still enough of the independent pioneering spirit left in rural Wisconsin for the different to be, if not accepted, at least not actively harassed.

Still, without Les and Wade, Lee knew she could not have continued at the wood products factory. Her folks gave her no support at home, prodding her to do something more ladylike.

"Why do you stay here?" Les asked one day at lunch. The three of them were outside, eating home-packed sandwiches together. "You could leave home and get a job in a city or something."

Lee shook her head. "I want to save my money and buy a farm," she said, pausing for the laughter that always greeted this remark. "If I left home, I'd have to spend more of my pay to live. This way I help out some at home and they let me stay."

Neither of the men laughed. "You must really want to farm bad if you stay at home," Wade said. He brushed sandwich crumbs from his neat work pants. "I left as soon as I could get out. I'd never go back. There's just my sister now and she's a bitch."

"I came back home," Les said. "But I came when my folks died. They wouldn't have wanted me back when they were alive."

Lee felt sad when she heard them talk like that. She loved her parents and didn't understand why their acceptance of her became more conditional as she grew up. She knew that differences were not appreciated in most families, and she knew she was about as different as she could get. At nineteen, she didn't have a name or a label to put to that difference.

She worked on the line at the wood products factory for five years, wondering when she would ever escape life at her parents'.

Then in 1955 the Larson farm came up for sale. Old Lars Larson had died suddenly, falling over in the barn one morning. His daughter, who had long ago fled the farm for Minneapolis, wanted a quick sale. It was costing her money to have one of the Hansen boys milk the cows and she wanted the cash the farm would bring.

"It would be perfect," Lee told Les and Wade after work one day. "But I don't have enough money saved. She wants all of it right now and I only have enough for a good down payment."

"Can't you get a loan?" Les asked.

Lee shook her head. "They said at the bank that they make it a policy not to lend to women. We're too unstable or something." If her father had been willing to cosign, the bank would have given her a loan, but Lee knew better than to ask her dad to do that.

"You can't farm. Get the idea out of your head," he had said the last time Lee had hesitantly mentioned her dream.

"I'll cosign," Les said suddenly. Lee looked at him to see if he was serious. "I could even put up my house as extra collateral. I know you'll pay it back."

"I couldn't ask you to do that," Lee protested, feeling touched and deeply grateful.

"You didn't ask," Les said gruffly. "I volunteered."

"Take it," Wade urged. "He means it." The atmosphere among the three of them was full of unspoken solidarity. Lee felt tears touching her eyelids. She blinked them back. "Thanks, you guys. Thanks. You're the best friends I've ever had."

She moved onto the farm in the spring of 1955. Les and Wade were there to help, of course, and the biggest surprise of all was the presence of her folks and her reluctant brother Dan. She watched with hidden amusement as her mother Lydia tried to be polite to Wade who was fussing in his pseudo-serious way as he helped her hang some kitchen curtains. Later, Lee and Les and Wade would remember that day and laugh but at the time it had been a serious business, this mixing of family and friends.

Lee had eighty acres of cropland and pasture, with a trout stream running through the back pasture. On either side of the farmstead, level fields stretched out to the road. A line of old oak trees in the front yard would provide shade if she ever had time to sit and enjoy it. Her dad kept insisting she was going to be busier than she could handle. The fields rolled and dipped a little toward the back of the land, and the pasture was steep and hilly, with maple and elm trees and a grove of small pines that old man Larson had planted.

"She should at least have seen to it the house was cleaned up," Lydia complained as she mopped and swept the kitchen floor. She had grudgingly decided that this Wade character was a good worker. He was dusting the old-fashioned floor-to-ceiling kitchen cabinets and doing a thorough job.

Lee's excitement over owning the farm was contagious. It kept her dad from making derogatory remarks about the buildings needing work or about the old machinery that came with the place. "Cows look okay," he said of the fifteen Jerseys munching hay in the barn. "You got enough feed here to last them to spring pasture?"

"I'll need to buy some," Lee admitted.

"We can let you have some hay, I guess." Chuck Collins said the words grudgingly but to Lee it was enough that her father said them.

Over the first few years of her farming career Lee was not aware that her progress on the farm was watched with more than casual interest by a young girl on a farm not far away. Lee knew the Lewis family, as she knew everyone in the neighborhood, but she had finished high school before Clare Lewis entered it.

Clare was the only girl taking agricultural courses in school, a situation that brought her some ribbing. "What you taking ag. for?" Harry asked in his older brother voice that grated on Clare. "You can't farm."

"I like it," Clare replied.

"I bet you just like being the only girl among all those guys," Harry decided. "Either that or you're gonna be just like Lee Collins."

"What's wrong with that?" Marsh, their younger brother, wanted to know. At thirteen he was usually Clare's ally.

"I'll tell you sometime," Harry promised. "You're too dumb to figure it out for yourself."

"I'm not dumb, you're dumb," Marsh insisted. "I get better grades than you ever did. Mom said so."

"Who cares about grades? I don't need all that junk they teach. I'm gonna farm with Dad when I get done." Harry said what they all knew was true. He would finish high school that spring of 1955 and farm with Ed. There would be no room on the Lewis farm for either Marsh or Clare.

But Clare listened for information from the adults about how Lee Collins was managing on her farm. It seemed important that she do well.

"Oh, I guess she must be doing okay there," Clare overheard her mother saying on the phone. "Chuck and Dan help her out some, I hear, but they say she's getting more milk from those cows than Old Man Larson ever did."

Good, Clare thought.

"I know," Eve Lewis said into the phone. "If she just wouldn't walk around like that. Those men's shirts and the short hair. And I saw her down at the grocery store, wearing men's work boots too. Bold as you please. I tell you, I sure wouldn't want my kids around her." Eve chuckled reluctantly. "No... She wouldn't bother the boys, I suppose. But I sure wouldn't want her around..." Her voice trailed off as she realized Clare was listening, but Clare got the message.

Clare soon learned that you did not wear green clothes on Thursdays. That was Fairy Day. You were a "fairy" if you wore green and that wasn't a good thing to be. The not-so-subtle social order in high school rated dates above good grades, especially for girls. Clare did not have Lee's ability to ignore the social pressure. So she dated, often with her friend, Marsha, who seemed to have an endless supply of spare, gangly, boring boys to pair Clare up with.

It did not take Clare long to realize that Lee Collins had gone against the accepted social order by farming on her own. Women were supposed to marry farmers, not be farmers themselves. But Clare had the same yearning Lee had, to farm, to be the farmer, not the farmer's wife. Every word of Lee's success was useful to Clare as she took agricultural courses instead of secretarial.

Her parents laughed at her. "How will you farm?" Eve asked. "You don't have any money. You need a man to farm. Wait and get married. Get a job for a couple of years until you find the right man."

Finding the right man was the thing for a young girl just out of high school to do, but Clare couldn't imagine herself doing that. She did agree about getting a job. "Couldn't I work here?"

"You know we can't afford to pay you," Ed said. "We're paying Harry. You can live here and help out until you get married."

Clare protested. "You've always paid Harry. I've worked hard too. Harder than Harry sometimes."

"Harry has agreed to take over the farm, so it's different with him," Ed said. "What you do pays for your food and clothes. Harry—"

"Harry is a jerk. He's lazy. Who cleaned all the calf pens this week when Harry just had to go fishing? I did. Who gets up and helps in the barn when Harry stays out too late drinking? Me, that's who."

"Help is what you do," Ed pointed out. "You don't know the first thing about farming. Ag. courses don't replace doing it, you know. Harry's learning how to do it, but he's young yet. Needs some time to himself. Needs to find himself a wife."

Clare snorted. He'll sure find himself a wife fast out on Cedar Lake fishing, she thought. But it was useless to argue about it. Her dad had chosen Harry. She might as well get a job in town and save her money.

Clare lived at home and worked in a grocery store in town as a checkout clerk. The pay wasn't great but she didn't have many expenses living at home. She watched sale bills and real estate ads for farms. Then in 1959, the Peterson place came on the market.

Clare, on her own, inquired about the price. She chose Thanksgiving dinner as the time to mention she wanted to buy it. The Lewis family had guests for dinner and Clare thought perhaps the presence of her uncle Martin and his wife Sal would keep her folks and brother Harry from ridiculing her idea.

"Oh, for God's sake," Ed said. "I thought you gave up that nonsense."

"You've got a good job in town," Eve said. "That's all you need."

Martin leaned across the table toward his niece. "What's all this? You want to buy a farm?" Martin had no children but he did have a soft spot for this tall gangly girl of his brother's. It was funny too, because he felt so much resentment toward Ed sometimes that he could hardly stand to come and visit him on his farm. His farm. Should have been Martin's farm, but no. While Martin had been overseas during WW II in North Africa, Ed had been safe at home on the family farm and able to buy it cheap when their dad died in 1944.

He listened to Clare's eager description of the Peterson place and watched as Ed continued his objections. "Don't go telling Martin about your nonsense. You can't buy a farm."

"But I've got almost enough for a down payment," Clare said. She could see she should have kept her mouth shut. "I just need you to cosign because I'm...too young yet to get a loan on my own."

"Too female and dumb," Harry put in.

"She's not dumb," Marsh said. "You're dumb, Harry."

"Shut up, you two," Ed said. "You ever hear anything like it, Martin?"

Martin couldn't understand why his brother felt so strongly. He looked at things differently than Ed, he guessed. He had built a good business in St. Paul after the war; he could call himself wealthy, really. Sort of made up a little for Ed sneaking the family farm out from under him. "Might be a good investment for her, Ed," he said. "Land is going to keep going up in value. It's a good buy now."

Ed snorted. "Well, somebody's got to work the land. I sure can't see how a young girl could do it."

"I can do it," Clare insisted. She kicked Harry under the table before he could start making his usual smart remarks.

"Well, you know I bet you could," Martin said, looking his niece up and down. "Hire some help for the hardest work. Management is what's important in any business. Farming shouldn't be an exception. How about showing me this farm, Clare?"

"Don't you go encouraging her," Eve protested. "I don't want my daughter farming. What will people say?"

"I don't care what people say," Clare said, but that was only partially true. At the moment she didn't care; later she would.

For now it was exciting to have her Uncle Martin interested. She took him there in the old Ford pickup she'd bought. In the end, he surprised and angered his younger brother by offering to put up the money needed for Clare to buy the place. She could pay him back monthly, on easy terms.

Her mother was horrified. "I just can't believe anyone would offer to set up a twenty-year-old girl on a farm. What's your brother thinking of?"

"He's nuts," Ed agreed, angry at Martin's sudden generosity to his daughter. "I could see it, if it was for Harry even, but not for the girl."

"Well, I just won't stand for this. I forbid you to try this," Eve said to Clare. "What will people say when you set up there? Don't you even care?"

"People around here gossip too much," Clare retorted. "I don't care what they say."

"Well, you will," Eve said. "Someday you will. You know what people say about that Lee Collins. My god, Ed. She's bought the farm across the road from Lee Collins. You're not to have anything to do with her."

Clare sensed victory. Her mother had just gone from forbidding it to recognizing it. "I'll be too busy to have anything to do with anybody for awhile," she said happily.

"You sure will," Ed said. He still couldn't believe it. His daughter had just bought a farm.

CHAPTER TWO

When Clare first moved in across the road, Lee was twenty-eight. She had been on her own long enough for her own folks to have given up on her ever marrying and settling down. Her dad had turned the family farm over to her younger brother, Dan, and was partially retired, although he still helped out. Her family lived close enough so she still saw them frequently.

"I wish, if you had to have male friends, you'd at least pick some that weren't so different," her mother said at one Sunday dinner. She was referring to Les and Wade again.

Lee sighed. "They're my friends, Mom. I like them."

"As though that excuses anything. They're also homosexuals." Her mother managed to get the word out, although her lips struggled with it in distaste.

"So?" Lee said, her voice sharper than she had intended. It wasn't that she hadn't known really, but neither Les nor Wade had ever brought it up. She'd heard the rumors and she guessed they were true, but to have her own mother bring it up brought it into focus for Lee. She didn't think she cared, but it was a shock to hear that word applied to Les and Wade, her good friends. The word suggested wickedness. She knew them as loyal, caring men and saw in their faces the genuine affection they had for her and for each other.

"So you'd better be careful," her mother said. Lydia had struggled with her thoughts on this subject for a long time. She half-knew that her daughter probably was one, too, but it was not a subject a mother wanted to have to discuss with her daughter. She could not bring herself to go any further with it and ask Lee outright.

Lee could not have given her a direct answer anyway. Despite her scorn for the frilly behavior of other females or her friendship with Les and Wade, she had not made the connection about herself. Oh, there had been vague stirrings of interest for a couple of female high school teachers but she could dismiss that as simply liking women who were sensible and intelligent. There had been no light crushes, no feelings of love stirring in her. Until she met Clare.

Years later, Lee could still remember exactly how she felt when she first met Clare. It was a spring day in 1960, not long after that Senator from Massachusetts and his attractive wife had passed through town, stumping for votes in Wisconsin's presidential primary. Lee had been to the public forum where John Kennedy had spoken. She thought she might vote for him.

The day was cold and gray when Lee, coming out of the barn after morning chores, noticed smoke rising from the chimney of the house across the road. She knew somebody had bought the place. Rumors at the feed mill suggested that it was Ed and Eve Lewis' young daughter. "Bound to fail" was the prediction of the feed mill pundits. Lee thought the girl's name was Clare. Lee stood in her farmyard and watched the old Ford pickup being unloaded at the back door by one lone person. Looked like a female, all right, Lee decided. She strolled across the road and into the farmyard where she was greeted by a friendly mixed-breed dog.

"Get down, Caesar," a light and pleasant voice commanded. Caesar got down reluctantly and allowed Lee her first good look at Clare Lewis.

She saw a young woman in faded blue jeans and old winter coat. A red stocking cap hid her hair but Lee could see strands of light brown peeking out here and there. Clare was tall, much taller than Lee and still almost gangly with her height. Something about Clare's open young face caused a twisting in Lee's chest. She could not think of anything to say and finally, as the silence lengthened, Clare broke it.

"You're Lee Collins, aren't you?"

"Ah...yeah...that's right. I'm Lee." Lee knew she sounded like a half-wit. Self-consciously she held out her gloved hand to be shaken. Drew it back to remove the barn glove. Held it out again.

Clare shook the offered hand. She looked the shorter woman over with hidden surprise. So this was the Lee Collins everybody gossiped about. She'd seen her, of course, around the area. It was too small a community not to see most people at one time or another but Clare had not wanted to appear to stare at Lee like her mother did when she saw her. It seemed rude to do that.

Clare thought Lee looked, well, nice. She was much shorter than Clare had expected her to be, up close like this. Somehow all the gossip had made Clare expect her to be bigger than life. Her gentle face with its soft brown eyes was appealingly open. Clare looked Lee over in all the detail she could manage before one of them would need to speak again.

The Levis Lee wore were what Clare's brothers wore. The flannel shirt peeping out at the neck of Lee's denim barn jacket was a man's shirt. The work boots were men's. Lee looked comfortable, capable, competent. Clare regarded her own ladies' jeans and old ladies' coat, the thin snowboots on her feet. She decided right then and there that at least for chores, some men's clothes might be a good idea.

"Could you use some help?" Lee asked, surprising herself by making the offer. She'd just been going to say hello and then go home, but the offer had popped out of its own accord.

Clare looked at the boxes and pieces of furniture still in the truck bed. "Thanks. Some help would be nice." Here she was, moving in all alone. Her dad was still mad about the farm purchase and it had taken all her resolve to leave home this morning without some parental blessing.

Her mother had not wanted to see her only daughter go off alone but Ed had been very stubborn. "Let her do it herself," he ordered. "Let her get set up and get them cows to tend all by herself. She'll give it up fast enough, wait and see."

He had not been able to prevent Eve from sorting through her linens and towels and finding some furniture she could send off with Clare. He had not known about the boxes and bags of food Eve had had Marsh load into his sister's old truck.

Marsh had been the only one of her family to see Clare on her way. "I'd come and help if I could," he assured his sister. "But you know what Dad said. He thinks you'll be back because you can't do it. I sure think he's wrong."

Clare was touched by his support. She gave him an awkward hug before she left home. It felt like she was going a lot farther than the mile and a half to the Peterson place. Her place, she corrected.

Now, as she accepted Lee's offer of help, she was almost glad her family wasn't here. Almost, but not quite. It was exciting to be moving here, but it was scary, too, and her dad's dire predictions of failure echoed in her head. Oh, heck, I can do it, she thought. I hope.

Lee, now that she was actually carrying in boxes and maneuvering the few sticks of furniture through the back door, was wondering why she had offered to help. What would happen once the moving-in was done? What would she say to this very young woman? She didn't think she could make conversation very well. She could talk to Les and Wade but they were old and familiar friends.

Lee need not have worried. Clare, in her excitement at being in possession of her farm, talked enough for both of them.

"I never thought I'd get this place. My dad..." Clare shook her head. "Well, he didn't approve at all of me farming. Said I couldn't do it. But my uncle lent me the money."

So that's how you got it, Lee said to herself. Neighbors had been wondering, herself included.

"It took so long for the papers to go through and everything. And the old owners...did you know them?" Lee nodded. "They didn't want to move until the end of the month. I got ready to move in as soon as I could after they left."

Lee had seen the large moving van when it came for the Peterson's possessions. They had never been close neighbors. Mrs. Peterson, it was true, had made the usual country gesture of bringing a plate of cookies over to welcome Lee. But it had seemed to Lee that Mrs. Peterson was less interested in being neighborly than in looking Lee over. Olive Peterson's eyes had darted around Lee's small kitchen. She had craned her neck to see into the next room. Lee had watched in amusement. She'd been noncommital in replying to Olive's probing questions, and finally the woman had given up. She had not repeated the visit.

As she and Clare moved in the last of the boxes, Lee looked around the ex-Peterson house. I'm as bad as Mrs. Peterson, she thought. The house was nicer than her own, and it was clear that Olive had left it very clean. She would, Lee thought. It was a matter of pride. The kitchen was large and light, with south-facing windows over the sink. The white walls looked newly scrubbed. The old linoleum gleamed under a heavy coat of wax. There were built-in cabinets and lots of counter space, something Lee did not have.

The Petersons had left their old combination wood and electric stove. Clare had a small round wooden table from her mother. Two mismatched chairs completed the kitchen furnishings.

"I won't be able to afford a 'fridge for awhile," Clare said cheerfully. "But I can keep stuff in the old milkhouse out back. It's got an old milk can vat in it. I can just run some cold water in that and submerge my food in jars for awhile. Maybe quite awhile," she added with a frown. "I don't know..."

Cold feet? Lee wondered. She remembered all too clearly her own worries when she had started farming. She felt sympathy for this younger woman who was trying to do the same.

"I'm going to make some coffee. Want some?" Clare offered.

Lee nodded. "Thanks."

She watched as Clare struggled to master the old stove. Tactfully, she did not offer to help. Better to let her figure it out for herself, Lee thought. Instead she wandered through the solid swinging door into the dining room. The room was large and high-ceilinged like the kitchen and had polished oak flooring.

Beyond the dining room through a large arch was the living room. A faded blue carpet, not the new wall-to-wall variety that was becoming so popular, had been left in place on the floor. More polished oak flooring showed around its edges.

Clare had one old wooden rocking chair to place in her new living room, plus an old standard floor lamp with faded blue daisies on a yellow shade. Her two pieces of furniture sat there now in solitary splendor.

Lee's boots echoed in the empty space as she walked on bare wood floors out of the living room through an open door into a large hallway. The front door was just ahead of her down the hall. Off to one side was the staircase. On that same side was the door leading to the downstairs bedroom, which now held Clare's own single bed, a simple iron frame with a mattress and unboxed spring.

Lee did not go in, although she had been in earlier to help Clare assemble the bed. It seemed too personal a room to just casually wander into. And, Lee was conscious of a deeper reason for avoiding it. It shocked her to realize she was visualizing Clare in that bed. She walked quickly back across the hallway through the door leading to the kitchen.

Clare was rummaging in boxes. Triumphantly she placed two cups on her small table and gestured toward one of the chairs. "Sit down. I got the stove working so we can have some coffee soon. Hey, I just realized. You're my first guest in my own home."

Lee smiled and sat down.

"There's so much to do." Clare took the other chair. She had removed her coat and stocking cap so her long light brown hair tumbled around her shoulders. She pushed it back away from her face. "I think I need to get this cut. Your hair is so much more sensible." She studied Lee's short dark cut with such attention that Lee felt herself blushing.

"But your hair's so pretty," Lee surprised herself by saying. "Seems a shame to cut it."

"Oh well, it's kind of a nuisance this way." Clare wasn't used to compliments, especially from this woman about whom she had heard too many rumors, too much innuendo.

The coffee pot quit its perking noises. Clare filled their cups. "I've got to get some wood. It'll save money not to be using the electric part of the stove. I won't get milk money for awhile and I just don't have that much to start with. I've got some savings left, but I've got to buy feed for the cows. Maybe I shouldn't have moved in so soon." Clare knew she was chattering too much, but it seemed hard not to.

Lee calmly sipped coffee and thought how familiar Clare's words sounded. She had faced the same dilemma five years ago. Luckily, she'd had Les and Wade to help her until the steady milk money started coming in. And her folks had helped too. It didn't seem like Clare was going to have even that.

"My dad thinks I'll fail," Clare said bleakly.

Lee nodded. She couldn't think of anything to say about that. "When do your cows come? If you want, I can let you have some hay from my mow. I got a good crop last year. You can repay me out of the field when summer comes."

"I can't let you do that," Clare protested, shocked and surprised at the offer.

"It's no problem. You'll need your money to buy some grain, get the cows off to a good start." Lee was wondering why she had made the offer. There was something so vulnerable and touching about Clare that somehow the words had just formed of their own accord.

"Well, it's awfully nice of you. Thanks." Clare smiled her gratitude, and Lee felt again that unfamiliar twisting pang inside.

"They're coming in three days. Friday. I got Bert Olson's herd. He's retiring."

"How many cows?"

"Twenty cows and five springing heifers. The heifers are due in about a month, Bert says. The cows are all bred back and in mid-lactation. I think I can get more milk out of them than Bert did." Clare talked enthusiastically.

"I've never been in the barn here," Lee said. "There must be about thirty stalls for cows?"

"Thirty-six. And four pens for young stock. There's a barn cleaner and I got a used manure spreader at the Allis Chalmers dealer in town. The barn looks very clean. I haven't turned on the water yet, but the pipes and bowls look okay."

Lee had expected Peterson would leave the barn in good shape. "There'll probably be some rust in the pipes," she said. "The water bowl valves may stick at first."

Clare nodded, grateful for the advice. She had not thought of that. "Do you want to see the barn?"

"Sure." Lee put on her denim jacket and followed Clare out the back door and across the yard to the barn. It was a hiproofed building, painted white, with the lower story constructed of cement blocks and the hayloft of wood.

They entered through a vestibule that connected the milk house with the barn. "Well," said Clare with pride, "here it is. There's a separate feed room for the grain and a silo room over there. It's going to be handy."

"It's a nice barn." Lee thought it was better than her own which only had twenty stalls and room for a dozen head of young stock.

"I think so, too," Clare said, pleased at her neighbor's response. "I think I got a good deal. But I need so many things. A scraper. Barn brooms. A feed cart. A silage cart. I guess I'll need a wheelbarrow."

She frowned as she thought of how much all this would cost. "Maybe I'll get that first. I can haul the grain and silage around in it for awhile."

"How about bedding? Is there any straw in the mow?"

"Just some chaff. I guess I need to get some straw too."

"I can let you have some," Lee said. The offer was another spontaneous gesture. She was surprising herself by making them, but it seemed to be what she wanted to do.

Clare protested again, but gave in with obvious relief. She truly hadn't planned this very well.

Lee saw the uncertainty in Clare's face. She felt memory tugging at her again. She'd been uncertain like that, too, and she'd at least had some good support. Clare seemed to have none. "You'll do fine," she said reassuringly, warmly.

Clare looked at her, surprised. She was not accustomed to having her thoughts read. "Thanks," she said. "Thanks."

Lee found herself blushing. She could not have explained why. "I better be getting back home," she said quickly, anxious to leave and sort out her confused thoughts and newly awakened feelings. "You come for that hay and straw when you get time." She started back out of Clare's barn.

Clare followed her, bewildered by the older woman's sudden need to leave. "Thanks for the help," she said to Lee's back.

Lee stopped and turned. "Thanks for the coffee." With a wave of her hand she was gone, walking quickly out the driveway and across the road to her own farm.

CHAPTER THREE

Clare was busy for the next three days getting the barn set for her cows. On Friday morning as she watched the large cattle truck back slowly down toward her barn, she decided she was as ready as she could be.

The day before, she and Lee had loaded Clare's old pickup with hay and straw, making several trips to bring enough to last until the pastures were ready. Lee had calculated what she thought Clare's cattle would need.

"This should get you through until pasturing time," she said. "Unless we get a late spring. Then you'll have to buy some because this is all I can spare."

Clare was grateful. She had not realized how expensive it would be to get set up. Her uncle had lent her money for the farm and the cattle, but there were so many little unexpected things she needed. Her savings were evaporating, and she still needed to buy more grain. She had purchased a ton of grain mix at the feed mill, but that wouldn't last until the first milk check.

She would be starting to send milk to the creamery the next morning, seven days into the month. It would not be until the first of next month that she would receive any money, and that check would be a "guess", representing twenty-five percent of the money owed her for the first month of milk. She would not receive full settlement for that month's milk until the twentieth of the following month.

Once the farm was operating for awhile, this method of payment was fine. But a beginning farmer like Clare did not have credit established with any of the local businesses. She had paid cash for her feed at the Farmers' Union mill. Had she checked, she would have discovered that as a new customer, she would need to pay cash for her purchases for the first ninety days until she established credit. It was not a policy designed to help beginning farmers.

The trucker finally had his rig backed in close to the barn door. He set out a wooden-sided ramp and opened the door into the cattle rack. With a whoop and a holler he began whacking cows, urging them down the ramp. Clare winced as one of them slipped and almost fell under the hooves of her startled herdmates.

"Git in there," the man yelled at the last two cows coming down the ramp. They were older girls with low-slung udders that bounced back and forth as they moved. One of them was limping. Clare had looked the cattle over carefully when she agreed to buy them. She was certain neither of these had been part of the twenty she had seen. It would be difficult to prove, so she said nothing.

"Be back with them heifers soon," the trucker told Clare as she stood uncertainly at the barn door. Was it her imagination or did he seem to smile slyly at her, triumphant that he had switched two of her cows?

She was thankful to be rid of him as she went inside to deal with her new herd. The cows were milling about in the central alley, huddled together in confusion. Some of them had gone over the side alley barriers and found the hay Clare had placed in the mangers. Not one of them had taken a stall.

"Need some help?" Lee's voice offered behind her.

"Yes, I do." Clare turned in relief to see her neighbor leaning in the door. Lee had never extended herself like this before, but it seemed to be something she was getting in the habit of doing for Clare.

"I see you got Chuck to haul for you. That damned fool is a menace to cattle. Most of the others aren't so bad."

"I didn't know," Clare admitted, feeling right then as though there was too much she didn't know. This was the kind of information her dad would have given Harry by not her. "I thought one was about like any other."

"Nope. Chuck likes to torture cattle a little."

"I noticed. He spooked them a lot."

The cows found Lee's presence soothing. Clare watched in admiration as Lee coaxed and soft-talked the cows, calming them down. Soon she and Clare were able to guide them into stalls, where they settled quickly to munching the hay in their mangers.

"What do you think of them?" Clare asked, looking with some pride of ownership at her new girls.

Lee examined them carefully, going down the middle alley to stare at each cow. "Mostly they look pretty good. They could have been fed better maybe, but they're solid and healthy. Except for these two old girls here." She pointed at the last two cows to come off the truck. "That one needs some foot work. She's pretty lame. And I don't like the udder on this other one. Looks lopsided. I bet she's got one quarter that won't milk very much."

"I'm pretty sure I didn't buy those two," Clare said. "I don't remember them at Bert's."

Lee nodded. "Could be Chuck did a switch. He's been rumored to do that. If the cows were registered then it'd be easy to prove it, but with these grade girls, you're out of luck." She suddenly felt very protective of this younger woman who looked so downcast. "Hey, they'll still milk for you," she said reassuringly. "Get the vet out to look at that lame one, and she'll be okay. The other one, well, see if she's bred. If she is, you can still get a calf from her."

Clare was grateful for Lee's words. She knew if it had been her dad, or her brother Harry, they would have taken pleasure in making fun of her. "Well, I sure won't use Chuck again," Clare vowed.

They could hear Clare's dog Caesar barking out in the yard. Chuck had returned with the heifers. Clare held her breath as the five pregnant young animals came off the truck, and Chuck raised his cattleman's cane to whack at them.

"They don't need to be hit," Clare found herself saying. She knew she could not prove Chuck had switched cows on her but darned if he needed to beat on them. The trucker lowered his cane and shrugged. His eyes did not meet hers when she paid him. At least he knows I know, Clare thought.

"Heifers look good," Lee commented once the five animals had been settled into a freshly bedded pen. "Feed 'em decently and when they freshen, they'll milk well for you. I'd give them all the hay they'll eat and as much grain as you can spare."

Clare cringed at the thought of putting grain into animals that were not paying in, but she knew it made sense. They never did it at home but it made sense. The heifers were the future of the herd.

"You all set for milking tonight?"

"I think so." She had purchased two used Surge bucket milkers from the local dairy equipment dealer. She had also needed to buy two stainless steel pails and a strainer to strain the milk before it went into the modest-sized bulk cooler in her milkhouse.

"I think I forgot to buy strainer pads," she admitted, feeling foolish, feeling that Lee was having to look out for her too much and correct her mistakes.

"You can use some of mine. Order some from the milk hauler tomorrow. That's the cheapest way."

"I'm using too many things of yours," Clare protested.

Lee shrugged. "Well, you can't remember everything. Come on over with me and I'll get you some pads."

Clare followed Lee across the road and into Lee's milkhouse. She looked around with interest. There was a bulk cooler about the size of her own. The white painted walls were spotless. The stainless steel of pails, strainer, and milker units gleamed. She was impressed. Lee sure kept things tidy and neat, much more so than they did at home.

"Want to see my barn while you're here?"

Clare followed Lee into the smaller barn. "You've got Jerseys. I didn't know that." She had been too absorbed in filling her pickup with hay the other day to even wonder.

"Yeah, the stalls in here are too small for the bigger Holsteins like you've got. I don't get as much milk, but I think I come out okay with the higher butterfat."

"They're pretty girls," Clare said, stopping to pat a willing head. "You take good care of them, I can see. They look great."

"Thanks. Yours will look better once you've been working with them for awhile."

"I hope so. I just hope I can make it."

"You will." Lee put as much reassurance as she could in her voice. Then she asked hesitantly: "You want something to eat? It's nearly noon. I've got chili cooking."

"Thanks. That's really nice of you," Clare accepted with some hesitation because, while she was coming to like Lee and appreciate her many kindnesses, she was still wary. She didn't want to be seen going into Lee's house. But it's okay to take her help, her hay and straw, even her strainer pads, she chided herself as they walked toward the house. You haven't noticed the Grimeses from down the road offering help, have you? Or the Hansens either. Or your own folks. And you know why. Because you're just a girl, doing something a girl shouldn't try to do. You're just like Lee when she set up farming.

The tiny back entry was crowded with a washer and freezer. There were hooks to hang barn clothes on, and Clare carefully removed her barn boots and set them next to Lee's. She followed Lee into the kitchen, her stockinged feet cold on the linoleum.

"I'll get you some slippers," Lee said. "Make yourself at home."

Clare protested but Lee had already left the room. While she was gone, Clare took a chair at the kitchen table. It was a round oak table, the kind her grandmother had and which her mother had scorned in favor of something modern in chrome. The wooden chairs matched the table.

The kitchen walls were painted off-white. Gauzy blue curtains hung at the small windows. Lee's counter space was small compared to her own, but it was tidy. The stove was electric and new. The refrigerator was older but looked in good shape. Floor-to-ceiling cabinets held kitchen supplies.

"Here. Put these on." Lee held out a pair of soft wool slippers.

"Thanks." Clare was embarrassed to accept them, remembering the unkind words of her parents and the jibes of her high school friends about this woman.

"I'll just get things ready," Lee said. She appeared ill-at-ease herself.

Clare wondered why. Maybe I'm being a nuisance, she thought. But Lee did invite me.

"I like your house," she said. "It's comfortable."

"Take a look at the rest of it while I get this together," Lee invited.

There wasn't all that much more of the house to see. Lee's bedroom opened off the kitchen in one direction. Clare took a hasty look in the open door and passed on by to the next open door which led into what Clare assumed was the living room. It looked more like a library. Shelves of books lined two walls. There was a desk. A padded rocking chair looked as though it was often used.

"You sure have a lot of books," Clare commented, coming back to sit again at the table.

"I like to read," Lee said briefly. "Borrow some, if you like."

"Thanks. I will," Clare said. "I don't think I'll be getting a television for a long while."

"It'd be nice to have one," Lee admitted as she set bowls of chili on the table. "My friends Les and Wade have one, but they're expensive."

"Yeah, I know," Clare said, wondering who Les and Wade were. "This is good chili. I'd better get your recipe. One thing I never did learn was to cook. I took ag. courses when the rest of the girls took home ec."

"Lucky you. I couldn't take the ag. courses. Never took home ec. either," Lee said smiling. "But cooking's easy. Didn't you help your mother with it at home?"

"As little as possible," Clare admitted. "I'd rather have been in the barn."

Later, Lee saw her new neighbor out the door with an armful of books. She went back inside and cleared away their dishes, thinking it'd been nice to have Clare as a guest. She hoped it would happen again, because she liked this new young farmer, was attracted to her. She felt such pleasure in Clare's company, such a sensation of having found in Clare the someone she hadn't even known she was searching for. Lee wanted to know her better, much better.

CHAPTER FOUR

In 1955 when Lee began farming, milk from the farm brought the farmer a return of $3.30 per hundred pounds sold. By 1960 when Clare began to milk cows, the price had risen slightly, to $3.40. Lee had paid $10,000 for her eighty acres, complete with cattle and machinery. It had cost Clare $15,000 for her bare farm of 120 acres, plus another $5,000 to buy the cattle she needed.

It was a lot of money to owe, Lee thought, what with interest rates at eight percent and the price paid for milk never going up much. She worried about making her monthly loan payment of $150, especially in the fall, when sometimes her entire milk check for a month was not much more than $200. But she was managing it. By 1960 she had paid off nearly half the loan and she was pretty certain she could pay it all off in another five years.

For Clare, just starting out, there were no guarantees. So much would depend on her management of the cattle. An equal amount would depend on sheer luck. If Clare was lucky, the cattle would stay healthy. They would not develop mastitis, hoof rot, hardware disease, ketosis or pneumonia, and the heifers due to calve in a month would have easy calvings, not requiring the services of a veterinarian.

The first few milkings Clare was not certain she had purchased wisely. The amount of milk in her cooler was disappointingly low. She chalked that up to the stress of moving and being beaten by the trucker.

The next two milkings were equally low, and the next two. Simple arithmetic told her that with production like that she was not going to be able to pay her $250 mortgage payment, let alone buy feed or seed and fertilizer as spring planting time came. The cows seemed gentle and easy to handle. They ate eagerly, cleaning their mangers of grain, not leaving much hay. Clare could not understand their low production and finally on the fourth day, she went to consult Lee.

Lee was sympathetic in her low-key way. She stopped what she was doing and came across the road with Clare. Together they looked at the cows.

"They look fine," Lee said. "Healthy. But I wonder if you're feeding them enough. It's only nine in the morning and they're already almost out of hay. When do you feed again?"

"They get grain again at four-thirty. I feed them more hay after evening milking. How much do you think I should feed?"

"I'd give them each about half a bale of hay, morning and night. I'd come down around noon and redistribute it. Make sure they have as much as they want. They're big animals. They need a lot of food."

"Maybe I'm not feeding enough grain, either," Clare admitted. She was embarrassed. She should have known it was because she wasn't feeding enough. What had she been thinking of? She'd been so concerned about saving on feed and not spending money that she'd been cheating her cows. She said so to Lee.

"It's hard to keep feeding when nothing's coming in," Lee said. "Can you manage until the check on the first? Are you okay for money?"

"I hope so." Clare did not sound at all certain. Her newly opened checking account held less than fifty dollars. The savings from her grocery store job was nearly gone, put into a used tractor to go with her used manure spreader. And she needed to buy gasoline for the tractor. If she filled the storage tank, it would cost her forty dollars, leaving just ten dollars to last until the first of next month.

"Well, if you get in a bind, let me know, okay?" Lee could see the panic in her young neighbor and her heart seemed to reach out in sympathy. She wanted to, well, put her arm around Clare's shoulder and just reassure her. Or something.

"Thanks," Clare said, looking gratefully at Lee. "I'm sorry to be so stupid."

"You're not stupid," Lee said with feeling. "It's hard to start farming alone. You'll be all right once you get that first check."

"I hope so." Clare was not feeling confident. She could already hear her dad saying, "Told you so. I knew you couldn't do it."

Over the next few weeks Clare discovered ruefully that it had been one thing to help out at home on the farm and to read and dream about farming. It was something else entirely to be in charge of a farm with no back up money and no real experience. There were so many things she did not know. When her heifers started calving she was terrified. She had never assisted at a birth alone.

The first heifer, a stocky placid creature, was now lying on her side in a pen, her breathing labored. With a feeling of total inadequacy, Clare watched the heifer kick and thrash and moan. Finally, she went across the road to Lee, thinking it was becoming a habit to go to her for help, but relieved to know she was there.

Lee came willingly. She observed the thrashing heifer for a moment and then sent Clare for a bucket of soapy water. After washing her hand and arm she went slowly into the pen. She got down on her knees and carefully inserted her hand into the heifer's vagina.

"She's dilating okay," Lee observed. "I can just feel some feet. Let's give her a little time to do it on her own. I think it's a normal birth, so she should be okay. There's room for the calf to come out if it's the right way around."

Clare felt foolish again. "I was worried about her," she said lamely.

"Sometimes they do make a lot of noise and fuss." Lee grinned. "I guess I would, too. Let's leave her alone for about an hour. You could fix me a cup of coffee?"

"Would you settle for a glass of milk? I'm out of coffee and I can't ..." Clare's voice trailed off in embarrassment.

"You can't buy any until the first," Lee finished for her. "Well, the first is tomorrow. I think I'd still rather have coffee. Come on over to my place and I'll make us some."

The heifer had made some progress when they came back to check. Both front feet and part of the calf's head were visible as the heifer strained to expel the entire calf. Lee grabbed a couple of pieces of baler twine. She attached a piece to each of the feet and after inserting her hand into the cow again, settled down to help the heifer. She gestured for Clare to join her.

With each of them holding a twine, they pulled on the feet in unison with the heifer's straining pushes. The calf's head suddenly slid free and Clare watched as the eyes blinked. She felt a leap of joy. Her first calf was alive.

After the head emerged, the shoulders came stubbornly out, and then the rest of the calf slid free in a gush of amniotic fluid and placenta. Lee dropped her twine and quickly cleared the calf's nostrils of mucous. The tiny black and white animal sneezed and began to breathe on its own.

Lee lifted one of its rear legs. "You've got yourself a nice healthy bull," she said. "A heifer would have been nicer, but you can sell the bull in a week or so for some extra money."

"Or keep it and raise it as a steer," Clare added.

The exhausted cow was lying on her side, breathing easier now but tired from this new experience. Her head came up slowly as Clare and Lee dragged the slippery calf around to her. With a mighty heave she sat up and began licking her calf as though she had done it many times. Within minutes she was standing again and with rough swipes of her tongue, urging her calf to try standing, too.

"It would be good if she would let you take a little milk from her," Lee suggested. "The calf will be better off if you can get some milk into him soon."

Clare nodded. She knew that from her reading. Her dad had never bothered with it, leaving it up to the cow and the calf to figure it out. Sometimes, the calves did not learn to suck from their mothers and then Clare's dad lost some of them. The first milk, called colostrum and rich in protein and anti-bodies, was essential to a new calf's health.

With a new galvanized calf bucket in hand, Clare carefully approached her new cow. When she ventured out a hand toward a teat, the cow jumped in surprise. But her main interest was in her calf, and she allowed Clare to milk a small amount from each quarter.

The calf sputtered and resisted when Clare attempted to lower his head into the pail. His instincts suggested he should raise his head in search of a teat, but, finally, with some forcing, he allowed his head to be lowered into the foamy yellow colostrum. With Clare's fingers in his mouth he figured out how to suck up some of the rich liquid.

"He did well, drinking," Lee commented, watching with amusement and a feeling of affection as her younger neighbor seriously went about the business of feeding the new calf.

"Yeah, he did, didn't he?" Clare felt a rush of pride. There was something in Lee's voice that suggested she thought Clare had done well feeding him, too.

CHAPTER FIVE

Spring was coming on fast, with warmer days and balmy breezes. As the days lengthened and the ground thawed, Clare thought eagerly ahead to her first planting. She would need seed and fertilizer but she had some money put by now. The cows were milking better, and she was making her loan payments with cash to spare. The big problem now was that she needed more machinery.

At Easter she had gone to church for the first time since she started farming. She had gone hoping that perhaps her dad would unbend from his position of having nothing to do with her. Maybe, she thought, he'd see she was doing okay and be willing to let her borrow some of his machinery, just for this spring, because buying it was going to be expensive.

Her whole family was in church: her mother looking bright and springlike in a pale green suit with matching hat, sitting beside her dad and her two brothers. She hesitated at their pew and then sat down next to her mother, who smiled and gave her hand a welcome squeeze. Clare felt tears prickle in her eyes. She had missed her family.

After the service, she talked eagerly with her mother, relieved to be able to share some of what had been happening in her life. "And the new calves are doing great," she told her. "I've got three nice heifers and two bulls. The cows aren't due to calve until fall."

"Are you eating enough?" Her mother asked in concern. "You look thinner to me."

"I'm fine, Mom. I'm even learning to cook. I've been using the cookbook you sent along."

Her dad turned his attention from visiting with Orrin Grimes, who smiled at Clare and her mother and went on down the church steps. "I see you finally made it to church," he said. "Suppose you probably need some help."

"Well, not exactly, but I was wondering if maybe I could borrow the grain drill this spring?" Clare thought she'd better start out asking for one piece of machinery at a time. She watched his face closely, hoping to see acceptance in it.

He shook his head. "You wanted to farm on your own, remember?"

"Ed, surely we could help her with the spring work?" Eve said in a low voice, her eyes roaming around to make sure they were not being overheard.

"Don't see why we should," he said stubbornly. "I thought you'd be throwing it in long before this," he added. "Surprises me that you haven't."

"I'm not going to quit," Clare said firmly, even though she felt dismay at her dad's attitude.

"Suppose you could come for dinner today," he said gruffly. "Your mother misses you."

"So does he," Eve told Clare. "He just won't admit it."

Clare mostly enjoyed the good baked ham dinner. The food was great. It was just that she found Harry and her dad very irritating.

At twenty-two, Harry was handsome, but his attractiveness was ruined for Clare by his superior attitude. With uncanny radar, he seemed able to zero in on Clare, picking away at those things she felt most uncertain about. "I can't believe you're still trying to farm," he said as the family ate Eve's ham and sweet potatoes. "The little girl farmer. You should just hear what people say about you."

"I really don't care." Clare pretended indifference.

"Oh, sure. I'll bet. But you wait. You just wait until you get into the real work of it. Putting in crops. Haying. You'll be home crying real fast."

"I don't think so," Clare said, but she knew her voice lacked conviction.

"She already asked me if she could borrow the drill," her dad put in. "I told her no. We ain't got time to do her work for her. She wants to farm, she does it herself."

"Ed, I really think that's unfair," Eve said more loudly here in their own home. "She's doing well with her cattle." Harry snorted in disbelief. His mother frowned in his direction. "Can't we help her out? You'd do it if it was for one of the boys, I know."

"That's different," Harry said. "Isn't it, Dad?"

"Why is it different?" Marsh asked. Clare looked gratefully at him. At eighteen he was slighter in build than Harry but with a much more pleasant disposition. He had given her a self-conscious hug at church. "I don't see why it should be different."

"Girls don't belong in farming. That's why it's different," Ed said.

"Why don't they belong?" Marsh persisted. "If they can do it and want to do it, why shouldn't they, just as well as any guy?"

"Listen, Mister Brain," Harry started out with his usual scornful reference to Marsh's intelligence. "You're so busy with books and junk, you don't know nothing about it."

"The word is anything," Marsh pointed out.

"Who cares?" Harry glared at his younger brother.

"Come on, you two, enough," Eve said. "I've made lemon pie for dessert. Let's enjoy the food."

It had not been the most pleasant meal, Clare decided as she drove home. But at least she'd made some sort of contact again with her family. Not that it solved the machinery problem. It had been foolish of her to think her dad would have come around. She guessed she would have to go to Lee again, but she decided it was time to repay her neighbor before she asked for any more favors.

"Sure, I'd love to," Lee said, pleased, when Clare invited her to a noon meal.

After morning chores, Clare began nervously to assemble the food to make this a special meal, something that would say how much she appreciated Lee's help. Plus, she wanted Lee to be impressed with her cooking skills, though she had to admit they were still limited.

Clare had decided on a beef roast with gravy, mashed potatoes and fresh asparagus from the bed she had discovered in the back yard. She would make baking powder biscuits, too, and have a homemade chocolate cake for dessert.

The cake turned out not too badly and she put in the roast, with onions sliced on top of it, just like the cookbook said. Soon the rich smell of cooking beef filled the kitchen as Clare struggled with a chocolate frosting.

The biscuits needed to be made yet, and the frosting did not seem to be thickening like the recipe said it should. She stirred and impatiently rechecked the recipe, realizing she should have put it in cold water once it boiled. Well, no problem. Maybe it had boiled a little more than it should but never mind, Clare thought.

She was just patting out the dough for cutting into biscuits when Caesar's bark told her someone had come. She went to the door with floury hands.

"Shouldn't you be in school?" she asked her brother Marsh as he let himself in the door.

"It's spring," he grinned at her. "I'm playing hooky today." He pointed at her hands. "You seem to be playing in something, too."

"I'm making a meal for my neighbor Lee. She's been great to me. I owe her more than just a meal."

"Oh?" Marsh's tone encouraged her to explain.

Clare filled him in eagerly on her days of farming and Lee's help. "Sounds like she's a great neighbor," Marsh said. "You know what they say about her, though, don't you?"

"I guess." Clare was having trouble getting her biscuit circles transferred to the cookie sheet. "But, she's nice, Marsh, really nice."

"Can I stay for dinner and meet her?" he asked.

"Sure," Clare said, disappointed somehow that it would not be just her and Lee. "You can also peel some potatoes." She handed him a knife and with his engaging grin, he accepted the task.

"It's not like you to play hooky," Clare said.

"No? Well, I didn't get a chance on Easter to tell you my news, and besides, I wanted to come see you. I got the car this morning to go to school, so it seemed like a good time."

"So tell me your news," Clare urged.

"I'm class valedictorian," he said, smiling broadly. "Plus, I got a full scholarship, four years, to Eau Claire. Dad always said he wouldn't come up with any money if I wanted to go to college and now he doesn't have to."

"Wow," Clare said. "That's great! I'm really glad for you."

"Yeah, old Harry thinks it's all a bunch of junk, of course."

"Harry would. Bet he's just jealous."

"Maybe, but Harry's too busy thinking he's a great farmer to be very impressed with anyone else."

"Well, I'm impressed," Clare assured him. "Darn. Something's happened to this cake. ...It sank in the middle."

"It sure did," Marsh agreed. "Maybe you could sort of cover it up with frosting."

"Maybe." Clare went to stir her frosting. "This stuff is sure getting hard fast. I'd better try and spread it on the cake right now." She regarded the frosted cake with dismay. "It really doesn't look very good, does it?"

"It's lumpy," Marsh said honestly. "It'll taste fine, though."

"Yeah, but I wanted this meal to be really nice. I hope the roast is okay." She opened the oven. "Looks okay yet. Well, we better cook the potatoes next."

By the time Lee arrived, the roast was done and the biscuits baking. At first she had felt dismay at the presence of Clare's younger brother, but that changed to enjoyment as Marsh displayed his friendly charm.

She and Marsh talked books while Clare struggled with the final meal preparations. The gravy wasn't doing what the cookbook said it should. The lumps wouldn't go away. Clare brushed at her hair with a hand still sticky from the frosting. She quickly opened the oven door. Smoke rolled out. "Shit," she said aloud. "I burned the biscuits."

"Oh, don't worry about it," Lee said. "They aren't too bad."

Clare was regretting her impulse to cook this meal. She regarded the food she had just placed on the table. The meat hadn't sliced very well and was mostly in big chunks. Lumps floated in the gravy. Her potatoes had scorched slightly and mashing them had not disguised it much. The asparagus looked limp and sickly instead of slightly crisp and green. And the biscuits were black on the bottom and very hard on top.

"I guess we can eat," she said uncertainly. There was an awkward silence.

"Well, go ahead," she said. "I hope it isn't too bad." Clare was standing. She still had only two chairs in her kitchen. "I'll just eat at the counter," she said.

"I'll go get your rocker," Lee said. "You should sit, too."

They settled again at the table. "Well," Marsh said. "This all looks ... good."

"It certainly does," Lee agreed gamely.

"Oh, shit, you two. It does not. It's awful," Clare said, looking as though she wanted to cry. "I'm sorry. It didn't turn out like I wanted it to."

"Hey, that's okay. It will be just..." Lee started to speak and stopped, unable to go on. She had just met Marsh's gaze across the table and suddenly was finding it hard not to laugh.

He was having the same trouble, but with less success at disguising it. Finally he snorted and gave in. "I'm sorry, Clare, I can't help it."

Then she was laughing with them, too, and it was okay that the gravy had lumps and the biscuits were burned. Suddenly the company and the talk was just what she'd wanted and needed to make her big old house feel more like a home.

Later, when the cake with the hard frosting had been eaten and coffee was being sipped, Marsh asked his sister about the farm.

"How is it really going?"

"Okay, thanks to Lee and all her help and advice," Clare said. "But I wish Dad had been willing to let me use the grain drill. I need to buy a lot of machinery, and it's expensive at the dealer's."

"Maybe you could get used stuff at auctions," Marsh suggested.

"That would be cheaper," Lee put in. "And some things you can hire done. Orrin Grimes would probably pick your corn when he does mine. He'd combine your oats, too, and my brother Dan might chop your corn for the silo. He does mine, for a price."

"I'd still need tillage equipment and a baler..."

"True. But, you could use my grain drill and corn planter," Lee offered. "So what you'd have to buy this spring would mainly be a plow and disk. Maybe a drag. And some hay wagons, a rake, and the baler."

"If I got it at auction..." Clare mused. "Maybe I could swing it."

"I'll go with you, if you like," Lee said.

"Wish I could go, too," Marsh sighed. "But, I suppose I'd better not skip school too much. Although it certainly was worth it today, just for the meal." He grinned mischievously at his sister, who pretended to be angry.

Clare wasn't, of course. She could never stay mad at Marsh no matter what he said. As for Lee, she was grateful for her offer of support at an auction. "I'd love to have you come, both of you. Marsh, she's really the perfect neighbor."

Lee felt herself blushing. She was not used to compliments and one from Clare, while welcome, touched too closely for Lee on the growing attraction she was feeling for Clare. That attraction could not be described as just neighborly.

At least to Les and Wade the nature of her feelings for Clare was obvious. They had begun to tease her good-naturedly about it.

"How's the love interest coming?" Les asked on one of their visits.

"What love interest?" Lee knew exactly what he meant.

"Don't be coy," Wade said knowingly. "We can tell what's going on."

"Nothing's going on," Lee retorted.

"No? But you sure wish it would, don't you?" Wade pressed.

"Yeah, I do, sort of," Lee answered honestly. She had few secrets from these two men who had befriended her when no one else would.

"Just sort of? Come on, Lee..." Les snorted.

"She's too young and too...too..."

"Too straight," Wade finished for her. "Probably so. She comes from a pretty four-square family. Although I've seen that younger brother of hers and he could swish, I think."

"Oh, come on," Lee protested. "I doubt it."

"Doubt away," Wade said airily. "I have good radar for that sort of thing."

"Yeah, he does. He picked me out," Les said with an indulgent grin for Wade. "You should get off the farm once in awhile, Lee. Get into the Cities. Try the bars. Get your mind off your neighbor."

"You could ride in with us some weekend. It would be fun," Wade said eagerly. "We could shop and then go to the bars. Maybe you'd meet somebody there. We always do," he said archly.

It was a bothersome thing to Lee that her male homosexual friends could talk so blithely about their weekend pickups in the Twin Cities of Minneapolis and St. Paul. They played the gay bars on Saturday nights, each looking for a likely body. Lee couldn't understand why they needed to do that when they so obviously had each other.

Plus she was not certain she would want to be part of the female side of that. It sounded too sterile, too unfeeling. On the other hand, she sensed that this yearning after her neighbor was likely to go nowhere. Clare liked her, she thought, but the liking was nonsexual and would probably stay that way.

"Maybe I'll go in with you some weekend," she found herself saying. "I'll get somebody to milk the cows for two milkings. I haven't had a vacation in five years."

"Good girl!" Les said. "We'll show you a good time."

Lee nodded, thinking that at least it might show her what to do if she ever got up the nerve to approach Clare. Because even if Clare did someday ever feel the way Lee felt, Lee did not have the least idea how she was supposed to proceed.

CHAPTER SIX

A week or so after Easter, Clare asked Lee to go with her to a farm auction being held out south of town. Lee agreed readily, quickly catching Clare's enthusiasm. They agreed to pack a picnic lunch. Not that you couldn't buy food at the auction, but Clare was feeling concerned about money. She was always concerned about money these days, and the thought of spending it by bidding at an auction was scary.

The day of the auction was warm and almost breezeless, a perfect day to bring crowds of bidders. Clare and Lee arrived early to look things over. The farm was neat and tidy. Its owners were retiring, and their machinery, while old, was in good repair and had been kept in a shed when it wasn't in use.

The bidding started at an old hay wagon on which the auctioneers had piled a jumble of small items. The main auctioneer was a local celebrity of sorts, well-liked and much in demand.

Clare found herself mesmerized by the man's staccato patter. At first she had trouble making out the words or understanding who was bidding. As the pile of small items on the wagon dwindled down, she began to catch on to it, but the idea of actually bidding scared her. She said as much to Lee.

"You need to jump in," Lee urged. "Try it on the wagon. When they get through with the small stuff, they'll most likely sell it. Be a good hay wagon if you can get it for no more than thirty dollars. Set a limit on what you're willing to bid and don't let the auctioneer talk you into going over it."

Clare nodded nervously. She wanted to ask Lee to bid for her, but decided she'd better do it herself. When the last small item was gone the auctioneer rapped on the wagon rack with his cane. "And now the wagon," he said. "Who will give me twenty-five?"

There was silence. "Offer him five," Lee urged.

"The little lady bids five," the auctioneer rasped. "Who'll give me ten?" More silence. "Come on, boys. You ain't lookin'. I gotta have me ten."

"$7.50," a bidder on the opposite side of the wagon said.

"Aha!" Fresh blood always brought out a triumphant cry. "And now who'll make it ten?"

Lee nudged Clare. "Nod at him. He'll see you."

"The little lady bids ten. I got me ten. Now fifteen, gotta have fifteen." He gestured to the bidder who had come in at $7.50. The man appeared to be considering it carefully. Finally he nodded.

"I got fifteen," the auctioneer rattled. "Gotta have twenty. Who'll make it twenty?"

"Wait just a little," Lee said. "Then nod."

"I got me twenty. Now twenty-five. Come on now. You got a good wagon here. You gonna let the little lady have it?" he asked the other bidder. The man shrugged. "Hey! Come on, somebody. I got me twenty. Gotta have twenty-five. Twenty-five," he appealed. "And the little lady gets it for twenty. Give your name to the clerk, honey. Old man send you to bid today?"

Clare shook her head.

"Boy, you better be sure he knows how you're spendin' his money," he joked. The crowd laughed good-naturedly and followed the auctioneer and his clerk on to the machinery. Clare took the pink bidding slip from the clerk. Her hands and legs felt weak and shaky. The bidding had been scary and now she was not liking the auctioneer much for his jokes. I couldn't just be bidding on my own, she thought. Oh, no. I have to be doing it for some male.

"Don't pay any attention to what he said," Lee said, sensing her anger. "Let it go. You got a good deal on the wagon."

The auctioneer was selling an old McCormick Ten-Twenty tractor. They passed by the crowd around it and moved over by a three-bottom plow.

"Your 'M' would pull this nicely. Just what you need. I'd go up to a hundred on it."

Clare nodded and took a deep breath. The auctioneer was on an old silo filler now. The plow was next.

"Allllll riiiight. I got me a dandy three-bottom John Deere trailer plow here. In real good shape. Been shedded all the time. Who'll give a hundred to start 'er off?"

Silence. The auctioneer had established what he wanted for it. "All right. Let's see if we can start 'er off at fifty."

"Twenty-five," Clare said firmly.

The auctioneer looked startled. "The little lady again. Must be you got money to burn, honey. Well, the little lady says twenty-five. Boys, you gonna let her steal it from you?"

"Thirty," a male voice offered.

"Thirty-five," Clare came back with quickly, angry at the auctioneer's condescension. She felt Lee touch her arm, reminding her to stay detached about it.

"Forty," the man across the plow said.

"I got me forty on this here plow. Who'll go fifty? Let's move this along here, boys. Time's a-wastin'. We got us lots to sell yet." He was ignoring Clare, assuming she would drop out when it got to the serious money.

"Fifty," Clare said in a loud clear voice.

The auctioneer swiveled around to her, pointing his cane. "And the little lady is still in at fifty. She wants to spend a fifty dollar bill on this here plow. What you gonna do with it, honey? Hitch your old man to it?"

Clare's face reddened amid the general laughter.

"Come on, boys, you gotta save her old man from the poor house. Who'll go seventy-five?" He was deliberately increasing the bidding increments, hoping to scare her off. Women bidding on machinery made him nervous.

"Well, then, sixtee, gotta have sixtee dollars. Nobody?" He pretended to be horrified. "Boys, you gone to sleep in the sun." He shook his head sadly. "Sold. For fifty. To the little lady. You sure you want a plow, honey?"

Clare nodded, too furious to speak.

"Let it go," Lee murmured. "You got a good deal."

"I know, but..." Clare broke off, still too angry to speak.

The auctioneer was relieved to be able to sell the disk to a man. But damned if the young woman wasn't back in there again bidding on the drag. He sold it to her for twenty dollars. He relaxed again as he sold an old Gehl chopper, another plow, and some horse machinery, all to men.

As he moved on to the baler, the nicest piece of the auction, there she was again. Surely, she wasn't going to bid on the baler? She was. Sighing, the auctioneer acknowledged her starting bid of seventy-five dollars. He had a feeling she was going to get the baler, too. Cheap. The men seemed reluctant to bid against her. They were letting her walk away with the stuff. He'd wanted the baler to go for around five hundred dollars but here they were stuck down at two-hundred-fifty with the woman holding the bid. He worked awhile, cajoling, extolling the baler's features, but nobody came up with a higher bid.

"The little lady gets it," he intoned. "You got a steal, honey. What you gonna do with all this stuff?"

"Use it," Clare said stiffly. The crowd laughed. It had been the right answer.

So far Clare had spent three-hundred-forty dollars and had a lot to show for it. She was feeling the euphoria that came from being the successful bidder. Auctions were fun, she decided, if you could just ignore the auctioneer...

She passed the haymower by. It looked in tough shape. She bid on the hay rake and didn't get it. Remembering Lee's advice about setting a limit, she quit when it was reached on the rake. This time the auctioneer found himself trying to urge her to bid more.

"Come on, little lady," he cajoled. "Take the rake home for your old man. It's only his money you're spending."

"It's my money," Clare retorted. "The rake's too high."

She was right. It was, the auctioneer agreed silently. He signed it off to a male bidder.

"You sure you can pay for what you bought?" he asked her. The crowd laughed.

Clare's face reddened in humiliation. She felt about two inches tall. She managed to nod, thinking the auctioneer would never ask that question of a man.

"Hope you can, honey," the auctioneer drawled. He patted her shoulder familiarly in passing.

"Let's get out of here," Clare muttered.

"I guess it's time." Lee was right at her side. "Hey. Take it easy. Men just can't handle women doing things they don't expect them to. I don't think it's a personal thing, you know?"

"Men are dumb," Clare said through clenched teeth.

"Can't argue with you there. Come on. Let's go and get you paid up. We've got a good picnic lunch to eat and I'm hungry."

"Well, I did get some machinery. I guess I did okay."

"You sure did."

Clare wrote a check for her purchases and they walked back down the driveway to her pickup. "We could eat right here, I suppose."

"We could," Lee agreed. "But there's a nice grove of trees down the road a mile or so. Let's eat there. We can come back later and get your machinery."

"Okay. Let's go." Clare's spirits were recovering. It was a lovely day. No need to let some dumb male get her down. Who needed them anyway?

CHAPTER SEVEN

Trilliums, small wild violets and last year's rustling dead leaves made a colorful carpet in the grove of trees Lee had chosen for their picnic. They added an old blanket to sit on in a spot of sun right at the edge of the grove. Lee dragged over the cooler in which she had brought her share of the food.

Clare carried a cardboard box containing the cake she had baked and dishes and silver and cups for the thermos of coffee. She watched as Lee carefully set out potato salad and cold fried chicken.

"Looks great," she said. "I guess you didn't trust me enough after my last dinner to suggest I make chicken?"

"Well," Lee admitted, "I did think it might be safer to take that on myself." She smiled to take the sting out of her words.

"I think I'm improving," Clare said. "The cake turned out good, if I do say so."

"Didn't sink in the middle? The frosting didn't harden too soon?" Lee teased.

"Nope." Clare helped herself to chicken and salad. "I'll get this cooking thing down yet." She bit into a chicken leg. "This tastes great. My favorite picnic food."

"Thanks." Lee filled her own plate and settled back to enjoy the meal. As they ate and then lounged back on the old blanket, Lee allowed herself to study her young neighbor. Clare had cut her long hair. The short pageboy style made her look even younger than twenty, Lee thought, young but attractive with her very open and expressive face.

Clare's eyes were closed now as she leaned back on her elbows, long legs stretched out, relaxed. As Lee gazed at her, she felt a twinge of longing and desire stir inside. She wanted in the worst way to simply lean over and caress Clare's smooth face, hold her close and feel Clare respond. She wanted to kiss Clare.

But Lee held herself away. It took some effort on this lovely relaxed spring day. She knew that all the desire she was feeling must be in her face and her eyes as she allowed herself to continue to stare at Clare. That she could not control.

Clare opened her eyes and was immediately aware of Lee's intense gaze. In that first instant, she allowed herself to stare back, knowing somehow that her own response would control the situation, sensing that this was an intimate moment.

Her eyes dropped. She could not hold Lee's searching look. Confusion stirred inside, along with other feelings she had never known before. The confusion won out, and she sat up.

"Guess we better go pick up my machinery," she said, not able to look again at Lee just yet. She busied herself picking up the remains of their meal.

"Yeah," Lee agreed. She folded their blanket, shaking off the feelings of desire. Clare was too young, too naive, not enough aware of herself to be approached as Lee wanted to approach her. So much so that it was an effort now to make conversation. Bleakly, she acknowledged to herself that Clare might never be ready.

❧

Spring work rushed in on them after the auction. Clare bought a used disk at the machinery dealer's and was soon out on her "M" using her auction plow. As the furrows of rich dark soil were turned to the sunlight and the birds followed the tractor in search of newly exposed earthworms, Clare gloried in her work. She relished the new shoots of green everywhere, the tiny leaves on the trees at the edge of her fields, the grass coming back in her yard. It excited her as much as it did any farmer, this fresh start in the fields in spring.

Before she was through with her plowing, she was visited by her parents. Their coming was unexpected but not unwelcome.

Clare felt a moment of hope as she invited them in.

"I'll make some coffee," she said.

Her mother looked around her daughter's kitchen and sighed at the dirty dishes in the sink, the unswept floor. "I wish you'd keep your house clean," she said. "This place is a pigsty."

"I've been busy in the fields," Clare said sharply, her hopes for a peaceful visit fading. She tried to ignore her mother's theatrical sighs.

"Saw you out there yesterday, trying to plow," her dad said, sitting down on one of Clare's two chairs. Her mother carefully perched on the other, after inspecting it for dust.

"It's going well. I got the plow at an auction and it's really a good one..."

"Yeah, we heard you went to the Ackerman auction south of town," her dad said. "Suppose you paid too much for it."

"No. I don't think so. Lee said she thought I got a good deal on all the stuff I bought."

"Lee? Lee Collins?" her mother queried. "I heard she was with you at that auction. I thought you promised us you wouldn't have anything to do with her."

So that was the reason behind this visit, Clare thought. She was amazed at how quickly gossip had been delivered to her parents. Amazed and appalled. "She's my neighbor," Clare pointed out. "She's been very nice to me, very helpful."

Wrong thing to say, Clare realized as soon as she said it. Her dad pounced on her words. "I'll just bet she's been helpful."

"She has," Clare said, defending Lee from what she wasn't sure. "She lent me some hay. She's helped when I needed advice about a heifer calving. She..."

"What will people think?" her mother inserted. "You know what they say about the Collins girl. They're going to say the same thing about you."

"I don't care," Clare said, caring all the same. She had noticed the way Lee looked at her on their picnic. At the time she had been intrigued and drawn, wishing Lee would say or do something, she didn't know what. Now she was disturbed by her own response that day. Her mother's words sank deep. What were people saying about her?

"Well, you should care," her mother said. "I saw your friend Marsha Henderson in church Sunday. She said she hadn't seen you in six months."

"I've been busy," Clare protested, thinking it was true she hadn't been in touch with any of her friends lately. There had been no time and being with Lee had been all the socializing she wanted to do.

"It's too much for you," Eve said, her worry about her daughter very visible. "I wish you hadn't gotten this farming bee in your bonnet. Why couldn't you just be a normal girl, with a job in town and a boyfriend?"

"Because..." Clare started out and then didn't know how to tell her mother that farming was important to her. More important than being seen as "normal"? she asked herself. "I'll give Marsha a call soon," she said instead.

Her mother looked relieved. "Ed, she shouldn't be working so hard here she has no time to do anything else. I'm sure that's the problem."

"All right," Ed said, conceding points to his wife in what had obviously been an on-going argument between them. "I'll let you have Marsh and one tractor. That's what we can spare. I suppose if you're going to keep on with this farming nonsense, we should help you."

"But you have to promise us you won't have anything more to do with Lee Collins," her mother insisted. "I know she's your neighbor. You can be polite to her, of course, but just don't be seen in public with her."

Clare nodded. It was easiest to agree. Her feelings were confused enough right now without trying to argue about Lee with her folks. She liked Lee. She really did, no matter what people said about her. Maybe, a small very quiet voice inside her said, maybe you more than like her. Clare hushed that small voice. Better to do some dating and get people off her back. She would be friendly and polite to Lee. There was nothing to worry about.

᠊ᡒᢞ᠊

One good thing to come of her parents' visit was the arrival at odd times of her brother Marsh to help. He came after school and on weekends.

"It's a lot nicer working with you than being at home these days," he confided. "Harry is unbearably in love with himself. He's got a girlfriend." Marsh strutted around the yard imitating their brother's way of walking. "I don't know if she's in love with him, too, but he's got enough ego to think any girl should be."

"Well, you'll be off to Eau Claire in the fall," Clare pointed out, thinking how much she would miss him when he went.

"Yeah, thankfully. Oh lord," he gestured theatrically, "can I stand it at home until that blessed time?"

"Be brave," Clare said, laughing.

"I will," Marsh promised. "Hey, forgot to tell you. I'm doing chores for Lee this weekend."

"Oh?" Clare said, thinking that Marsh, in addition to helping her, had been spending a lot of time over at Lee's, too.

"Yeah, she and some friends are going to Minneapolis tomorrow. I'm milking her cows, but I can still help you in the fields."

Clare knew Lee was done with her spring planting of oats and corn. There was no reason why she shouldn't be taking a break, was there?

She had not seen much of Lee since the auction, just glimpses of her out working in her fields on her Ford tractor. Clare had been too busy herself to do more than wave. She was out in the yard on Saturday morning when the car containing Lee's friends drove slowly down Lee's driveway.

Clare could see the friends were male. She felt a twinge of pain and confusion. So Lee had men friends, knew them well enough to go on trips with them? Part of her, the part her mother had schooled, thought that was disgusting. Good girls didn't go away with men. And she'd thought Lee didn't like men much. Another part of her felt disappointment and envious jealousy.

From her position in her own yard, Clare was close enough to watch as Lee came out of her house carrying a suitcase. Lee looked carefree as she waved to Clare from the car as it left her driveway.

Clare felt a wave of dejection. She could not go traipsing off like that. She still had ten acres of corn to plant. Her dad had lent her his planter after he and Harry had finished with it. Well, she thought, I'll get it done today, with Marsh's help. Then maybe I'll just call up Marsha and see if she wants to do something. In fact, I'll call her right now.

Marsha expressed surprise and delight. "It's been a long time. I thought you'd forgotten about me."

Clare heard the hurt feelings and reassured her. "Nope. Just been busy."

Later that evening, tired from corn planting and evening milking, Clare found herself in the backseat of the Henderson family car. Marsha and her current boyfriend were in the front seat. With Clare in back was the date Marsha had rounded up for her. Clare knew him from high school, but not well.

His name was George Hansen, one of the Hansen boys from the farm a couple of miles west of her own. He was taller than Clare, with light blond hair that waved thickly and attractively above a pleasant face. He did not have much to say as Marsha's boyfriend piloted the Henderson car through town and out to the drive-in movie.

Now, as darkness came on, he and Clare sat stiffly apart in the back seat. They were sharing a large tub of buttered popcorn. In the front seat Marsha and Floyd had foregone the popcorn in favor of more intimate sharing. Little moans and kissing noises drifted to the back seat.

Clare shifted uncomfortably, aware of how tired she was and how achy from her hard work. The main feature was unreeled dully on the large screen. She yawned. Obviously, the movie was not the attraction for most of the people here.

Finally, she quietly opened her door and got out of the car. She heard George's door close behind him, too.

"The movie isn't much good, is it?" George said as they walked together up to the lights of the concession building.

"I guess most people don't mind if it isn't." Clare smiled shyly at him.

George smiled back. "Yeah, I know. The old passion pit. I guess I'm just not very good at that sort of thing."

"Me, either," Clare admitted, finding it easy to talk to George now that they were alone.

"Want a Coke and a hot dog?" George offered.

"Sure. Thanks." Clare realized she was hungry. There hadn't been time to eat any supper and still get ready to go out.

"I saw you out in your corn field working today," George said, once they'd found a bench outside the concession building. "How do you like farming?"

"I love it," Clare said. "It's hard work, though, and I wish my family wasn't so disapproving."

"Well, at least you got a farm. I envy you," George said but without any malice in the words. "I guess I'll just keep working in town at the gas station, but I'd like to farm."

"Can't you farm at home?"

"Nope. I'm the youngest of eight boys. Everybody else is off somewhere except me and Nathan, and Nathan is going to be the farmer."

"Sort of like my brother Harry," Clare nodded in understanding. "My folks picked Harry to carry on. Marsh and I always knew it."

"Yeah. That's familiar." George grinned shyly at her. "I guess we have a lot in common."

"Maybe so. Don't you like the gas station?"

"It's okay, but, well, you know how it is. When you want to farm, it's just there. That urge. Maybe if I save my money..." George's voice trailed off into a private dream which Clare understood.

By the time the movie ended, Clare and George were still talking farming. Marsha came in search of them.

"Here's where you guys went," she said. "Want to go out to the Green Parrot for some beer now?"

Clare refused politely and was surprised when George backed her up. "She's had a long day," he told Marsha. "I'd be tired, too, if I'd done what she has today."

Marsha looked totally uncomprehending, which was not surprising. She lived in town and spent her days leisurely. But she did not push the issue. Soon, Clare was at her back door. George got out of the car and walked her to the door.

"I had fun tonight," he said. "Maybe we could do something again? Take in a real movie or something?"

"Sure," Clare said. "I'd like that. Some night next week?" she found herself saying.

"Okay." George hesitated. Clare thought maybe he was going to kiss her, but instead he just held open her door for her. "I'll give you a call or else stop in."

Then he was gone and Clare, undressing for bed, thought: he's nice. I like him. She did not let herself think about Lee at all.

CHAPTER EIGHT

The drive into Minneapolis was filled with good-humored chatter and joking. As Highway 8 carried them closer to the city, Lee began to relax and enjoy the feeling of actually being on vacation.

"Let's eat lunch at Jay's," Wade instructed Les, who was driving.

"That truck stop," Les said dismissively.

"It's got great food and it's cheap," Wade insisted.

"You just like to look at the truckers," Les countered, but with affection. "Okay, Jay's it is."

They lunched on huge hamburgers and wonderful fries, or so they seemed to Lee. The bustle of the large restaurant brought her a feeling of excitement. They were actually going to Minneapolis to visit gay bars. She wondered what the friendly waitress would say if she were told that. Probably wouldn't be so friendly, she supposed.

The traffic picked up after they crossed the St. Croix River into Minnesota and it was slower going through the little towns, but finally the hazy silhoutte of the Foshay Tower loomed over them.

Les drove skillfully into downtown Minneapolis, passing large buildings, taking them past Donaldson's, Dayton's, Powers', the Leamington, the Curtis, the Sheridan and other landmarks.

"We get a hotel room," Les explained. "Usually we don't use it."

Wade chuckled. "So you can have the room in case you need it." He looked Lee over critically. "I'll bet you won't. The girls in this town are gonna love you."

Lee felt uncomfortable. She had never done anything like this before, and she was not certain she could be quite so casual about it as Les and Wade were.

They were a couple at home but that didn't stop them from sampling the livestock at the bars. From the way they had described it to her, Lee thought they split up and each had their own sexual encounters. She decided that sounded too bare and starkly physical for her. Surely the women weren't like that too? She hoped not, thinking, I'll go along this once. I can always retreat to the hotel room.

Their room was in a large impersonal hotel on Sixth Street. It was warm with steam heat, too warm on this late spring day. They carried in their suitcases, and immediately Wade was ready to leave. "Let's go shopping," he urged. "We've got the whole afternoon. I want to go to Dayton's."

"He always wants to go to Dayton's," Les informed Lee. "Luckily, he doesn't buy much. Too expensive."

"You two go ahead," Lee told them. "I want to just wander around downtown. Window shop. Maybe find some books."

"Well, be careful," Les instructed. "This is a big city. It's not your cow pasture, you know."

She grinned at him. "I know. Go on, you two. Meet you back here later."

"If you're sure..." Wade said. "You could come with us."

"I'm sure," Lee said, wanting to wander the shopping area alone. She joined the crowd of well-dressed shoppers bustling on Nicollet Avenue, feeling underdressed in her slacks, blouse, and loafers. Nobody noticed her at all, which suited her just fine. She enjoyed the bustle and the pleasure of looking in store windows and going inside to browse.

Lee had brought more money along on this trip than she usually set aside for her own pleasure. So far, Les and Wade had not let her pay for anything, saying the weekend was their treat. Now, as she gazed at the harvest of books in Dayton's book department, she decided to splurge.

Usually her book purchases were made at an old junk shop in town. Choosing from the new hardcover and paperback books at Dayton's, the bill was high compared to what she usually spent, but it was fun to be carrying a dozen new books in a Dayton's bag as she window-shopped her way back to the hotel.

Les and Wade had suggested she might want to return to the room first and get herself ready for the evening. Lee quickly took a shower, thinking how useful one would be on the farm. Sometimes she was just too tired to go to the bother of running a bath.

She changed into clean slacks and a fresh tailored oxford cloth shirt, put her loafers back on and settled eagerly into a chair to examine her purchases. She felt secure handling the new books, but the thought of the evening ahead and where it might lead made her heart beat faster.

Lee realized she did not know what to expect at a gay bar. It sounded exotic, exciting, frightening to her. She shivered, suddenly feeling homesick and wanting to be back in the barn with her cows.

She thought how strange it was to be sitting idle at this time of day. For five years she had been busy every single day at this time, milking and feeding her cows. There had been no money for time off. Maybe I shouldn't have taken the time now, she thought. Maybe I should have stayed home. Maybe...

Her thoughts were interrupted by the arrival of Les and Wade, who were in high spirits. Wade waved a Dayton's bag.

"I got a new vest," he said. Eagerly, he brought it out of the bag to show her.

Les shook his head. "He's obsessed with clothes."

"Well, clothes make the man," Wade retorted.

"Not so I've noticed."

"Oh, you, that's all you think about," Wade said, pretending to be disgusted, but not succeeding. There was an air of suppressed sexual excitement about him. The two men changed quickly and joined Lee in the lobby.

"Boy, have we got an evening planned for you," Wade said, giving Lee an impulsive hug. He looked clean-cut and handsome in neatly pressed slacks with his new sweater-vest worn over a pale pastel shirt and matching tie. His casual loafers gleamed with polish and care.

"Don't you two look handsome tonight," Lee said, regarding them both. "How did I get so lucky to have such charming companions?"

Les snorted. "Flattery will get you a limited distance with the two of us," he said, grinning. "But it will sure get you a good meal."

"Yeah, we're treating you to Chinese food tonight," Wade told her as they left the hotel. "I'll bet you've never eaten Chinese."

"Nope. I never have."

"You'll love it, I know." Wade was in high spirits, hardly able to wait for the other two as they walked along more sedately after him.

It was impossible not to be infected with his good humor. Lee felt her earlier apprehension and homesickness evaporate as they moved along the street. Tonight she was here to have fun, she decided.

"Not quite the same as Rex's Diner, is it?" Wade said with a comical lift of his eyebrows as a dignified waiter seated them at the Nankin.

"Sure isn't," Lee agreed. "Do you think they'd have a hamburger here?"

"You're not going to have..." Wade said. "Oh, you're kidding me!"

"I'm going to have the family dinner," Lee decided. "It's got lots of different dishes. I wonder what Szechuan Beef is? Egg rolls sound good, too."

"Order anything you like," Les offered. "Except maybe the Peking Duck. I don't think I can afford that."

"Let me treat you guys," Lee said. "You've paid for everything so far."

"It's our treat," Les insisted.

Lee gave in and settled back to enjoy the food. The novelty of a very different meal was probably fitting before embarking on the rest of the evening.

"Let's go find a bar," Wade urged even as the waiter brought them fortune cookies.

Les nodded. "Better look at your fortune first." He split his cookie and removed the tiny slip of paper. "Huh. Mine says I'm going to meet a fascinating woman."

Wade chuckled. "That'll be the day. Well. This is good. 'Fortune will smile on you.' What does yours say, Lee?"

"I'm not sure I want to look." She removed the paper just the same. "It says: 'Time will bring you happiness.'"

"Cryptic," Wade said. "Well, time we were moving, if any of us is going to get happiness."

Lee felt a leap of fear. Now that they were actually proceeding down the street heading for a bar, she was nervous. She wanted to hang back. She almost claimed she didn't feel well. She could picture the safe warmth of the hotel room and the familiar security of her newly purchased books. Instead she allowed herself to be pulled along by Wade.

"I think you'll like this place. We do," Wade said.

"She won't be looking for the same thing," Les said drily.

"Oh, that's right. I think some women come there. Don't they?"

"Not very many."

"Oh, great," Lee said aloud. "Maybe I should just..."

"No, you shouldn't," Les said firmly. "We'll look after you. Don't look so frightened. It's just a bar."

Maybe so, but Lee could not push down her fear. They were walking into a less respectable area now. Dark buildings, even darker alleys, and loud noises from bars greeted them. It all looked derelict and dangerous to Lee. She would not have wanted to walk alone at night in this seedy area.

They proceeded down Hennepin, crossed Washington and continued on Hennepin for another block. The Burlington Northern Railroad Station was only a block or so away and beyond that was the Mississippi River. Not the best area of town, Lee thought. Wade led them onto a side street and they walked down it for a couple of blocks to a bar called the Dugout. It proved to be just a bar, as Les had said. Nothing exotic. Just a bar with stools, a jukebox, and some tables. They sat at a table against the back wall.

"This is a good spot," Wade said approvingly. "You can see everything from here."

"And everybody," Les said. Lee was beginning to realize that Les was much less eager for these evenings in Minneapolis than Wade.

She watched Wade eagerly scan each newcomer. No women had come in yet. It felt strange to her to be the only one. She never drank much, so she had allowed Les to choose for her. The screwdriver he had bought her tasted okay, but she could feel the vodka already. A few more of these, she thought, and I won't care what happens.

By the end of an hour and two drinks each for Wade and Lee, three for Les, Wade decided they should move on.

"This place is really dead," he said. "That's unusual for a Saturday night."

"It's still early yet." Les held open the door of the Dugout.

"Yeah, but just the same..." Wade's voice trailed off. He had spotted an interesting man on the street. "I wonder if he's going where we're going?"

The man turned down Hennepin toward the railroad station. "Shucks," Wade said.

"Oh, come on. Let's keep moving," Les urged. Wade had stopped on the sidewalk to stare.

After some discussion the men decided to take Lee to what they had heard was a women's bar. They trekked back to Hennepin, crossed Washington, and turned off Hennepin onto Third Street. The area was still seedy, and Lee was wondering if she really wanted to go to this Trocadero they were mentioning. But Les urged her on with a gentle hand on her arm.

They found a table in the Trocadero and brought drinks to it. Lee sipped on her third screwdriver.

"I see some women," Wade said excitedly. He pointed across the room to a table near the jukebox. Lee stared at the four women. They looked ordinary, like herself. She felt disappointed. Somehow she had been expecting exotic creatures, not ordinary women talking over drinks.

"I think they're all together," Les pointed out.

"Yeah, I guess so," Wade said, disappointed. The Trocadero was even less lively than the Dugout had been. But probably the Dugout was picking up by now. Wade thought maybe he wanted to go back there, but until Lee was set for the evening he couldn't just leave.

Les seemed to read his mind. "Go ahead. Go back if you want. Lee and I will be okay here."

"Are you sure?" Wade tried to keep the eagerness out of his voice.

"Go ahead," Les said gruffly. Wade left with a casual backward wave.

Lee, with three screwdrivers in her, asked: "You don't like this nearly as much as he does, do you?"

Les smiled ruefully. "Is it that obvious? I try. But I'd rather it was just him and me. Oh, once I've had some drinks, I'll go and do the same thing," he admitted. "It's better than sitting by myself knowing he's off with someone."

Lee nodded, though she didn't understand. It certainly wasn't what she wanted for herself. Bar hopping and farming were incompatible, anyway. You couldn't stay out late at night drinking and hope to rise early and alert.

"That woman over there is watching you," Les said with a slight smile. Lee's eyes followed where Les indicated and, sure enough, a woman sitting alone at the end of the bar was staring at her. Lee's heart sank. The woman looked bold and, well, tough. She had short blondish hair brushed back from her face like a man's. She sat almost arrogantly on her barstool, a lit cigarette in her hand. She blew smoke out one side of her mouth and continued to stare boldly at Lee.

"She frighten you?" Les asked.

Lee nodded. The woman did frighten her, but at the same time Lee found herself intrigued by her. Lee let herself look back at the woman, although she did not think she was doing it very boldly.

"What should I do?" Lee asked Les. She did not want to sit here eternally, staring at the woman.

Les chuckled. He tapped Lee's hand lightly. "Go buy her a drink. Either she says yes or she says no. What have you got to lose?"

What indeed? Lee thought quite a lot was riding on this one as she forced herself away from the safety of their table. She walked on shaky legs over to the woman at the bar. As she got closer she could see that the woman was older. There were some wrinkles around her eyes and some of what had seemed blonde from across the room now showed itself to be gray among brownish hair.

Lee sat down on the bar stool. "Hi," she said, wishing her voice sounded more assured and less scared.

The arrogance of the woman's earlier staring was gone, replaced by something else. Lee could not decide what it was, except it looked a lot like disbelief.

"Hi," the woman said back in a low voice. She averted her eyes, the boldness gone.

"What are you drinking?"

"Just beer," the woman mumbled, her eyes on her beer.

"Can I buy you another?" Lee asked, quickly before she panicked and retreated to the safety of Les at the table.

"I guess so. Thanks." The woman's voice was uncertain. Lee was puzzled. The woman had been so sure of herself in her staring. Lee gestured to the bartender for refills. The woman next to her continued to stare down at her glass. Her only movement was to raise her cigarette to her lips for a puff.

The bartender brought fresh drinks. Lee paid for them. Silence reigned. Lee gestured back at Les: Now what do I do? He shrugged his shoulders and grinned.

Perhaps it was the effect of a fourth screwdriver. Perhaps it was that elusive thing called intuition, but suddenly Lee knew that, for whatever reason, this woman was as shy and uncertain as she was. This was an unexpected discovery. Lee had assumed that women she would meet in this large city would be sophisticated, able to show her things. But, here she was, seated at this bar, next to an older woman, and it looked like it was up to her to get things rolling.

"I'm Lee," she said. "And you are…"

"Oh. Ah…Marion," the woman managed.

"Would you like to bring your drink over to my table? I'm with a couple of male friends. One of them has gone off already and the other will probably do the same. We can talk?"

"Oh. Sure." Marion picked up her beer glass and her cigarette pack. She fumbled for her lighter and dropped it on the floor. Lee picked it up for her.

They moved to the table and sat down across from Les. Marion said hello, then she fastened her eyes on her beer glass again. Lee and Les exchanged glances, and Les rose.

"I'm going to go sit at the bar," he said.

"You don't need to," Lee protested, wishing that he would not. It seemed safer to Lee somehow to have Les at hand, but he left. His parting glance told her she was on her own now. "So," Lee said to the silent woman next to her. "Do you live in Minneapolis?"

The woman nodded.

"I'm from Wisconsin myself." Lee wondered if she was going to have to make all the effort at this encounter. "I've never been in a bar like this before."

That got Marion's attention. "Never?"

"Nope. I'm twenty-eight, and this is my first time." Lee tried to give out that information as though it was unimportant.

Marion nodded. "That explains why you'd bother with me," she said matter-of-factly.

"Oh? Is there something wrong with you?" Lee asked with a smile.

"Just that I'm older. The women in this bar go for the younger ones."

"Why?" Lee was curious. She thought that Marion was nice looking, nicer now that she wasn't trying to be so arrogant and bold.

Marion shrugged. "That's just the way it is in the bars." She sipped her beer, lit another cigarette. Then she turned to Lee. "What do you want with me?"

It was such a bald question that Lee did not know how to answer. "Well, to talk, I guess," she said, not knowing if she wanted anything more from this woman or not. And I sure wouldn't know how to say so if I did, she thought wryly.

"Talk," Marion repeated. "Yeah. That figures."

"Isn't it all right to want to talk to you?"

"Honey, most of the women that meet in here don't come looking for someone to talk to. You ever been with a woman?"

"No," Lee said honestly, hoping Marion would not laugh or be scornful. "I've thought about it a lot. But, no."

Marion did not laugh. "Small-town girl?"

"I run a dairy farm."

"By yourself?" Marion was looking interested and intrigued. "With cattle and crops and everything?"

Lee nodded.

"You farm by yourself?" Marion appeared fascinated by the oddity of it.

"Yes, I do. It keeps me busy. This is the first time in five years I've been away from it overnight."

"Five years," Marion repeated. She regarded Lee with an expression that softened the lines on her face. "Well, you must like it a lot, then."

"I do. But sometimes it's lonely, too."

"There isn't anybody for you back near your farm?"

Lee shook her head. She thought of Clare. "There's this woman across the road, but I think she's interested in men."

Marion nodded sympathetically. "You like her, though, right? Happens to a lot of us."

"Yeah, I guess I do," Lee admitted. "But there's no way I could say that. She's a lot younger than I am. Just twenty."

"That's young. So you came to the big city to try your luck."

"Something like that. I mean, I came because Les and Wade kept urging me to, but I don't know what I expected."

Marion laughed. "And here you are, talking to me. An old lady of fifty-two the girls ignore. I stare at them and they look away. At least I can still look."

"I didn't look away," Lee reminded her.

"No. You didn't." Marion regarded her thoughtfully. "Twenty-eight is old to be looking around for the first time. You want another drink?"

Lee started to refuse. She was starting to feel the four screwdrivers she had drunk. But then she thought: why not? One more won't hurt.

Marion took their glasses and went up to the bar. While she was gone Lee pondered with semi-drunken sadness what Marion had said. Marion was regarded as old. At twenty-eight, Lee herself was almost too old.

"Here you go," Marion was saying. She sat down again and raised her fresh glass of beer. "Cheers."

"Cheers." Lee was surprised when the word wouldn't seem to move past her tongue.

Marion looked at her and chuckled. "You don't drink much, do you? Maybe you shouldn't have that drink."

"Oh, why not?" Lee said recklessly. "I may never have the chance to get here again." She took a gulp of the screwdriver. Marion's hand took the glass when Lee set it down.

"I think maybe some coffee would be a better idea. You don't need the kind of hangover that stuff gives."

"Coffee. Where?"

"At my place?" Marion suggested, meeting Lee's eyes, holding contact, offering what Lee had come for.

Lee nodded, knowing that Marion was taking the supreme risk of being turned down. They put on their coats. Lee stopped by Les at the bar. "I'm going home with Marion."

He smiled. "Good. I don't think we'll see you again until morning, will we?"

"No, I don't think so." Lee blushed.

"Meet us in the hotel lobby before noon," he directed. "And have fun."

They left the smoky warmth of the Trocadero. The night was chilly for late May, and Lee was glad of her jacket. The cooler air was reviving her, although she felt dizzy from the drinks.

"Where do you live?"

"It's a ways to go. We could take a bus if we could find one, but I think maybe the walk would be a good idea. You need to work a little of that alcohol out of you."

Lee had never walked in a city at night before. The street lights did a good job of illuminating their way, but there were shadowy areas she would have been frightened to pass alone. The streets felt safer once they were a few blocks away from the area of the Trocadero. It was also quieter now than Lee had expected.

"That bar is in kind of a seedy area," she said.

"What did you expect? The Flame Room of the Radisson?" Marion asked. "Our kind of bars are always in seedy areas. Nobody checks too closely for age or anything. So we get the young kids now and then, the ones who want to drink when they're under age for it. I suppose it gives them a thrill coming to places like the Trocadero. Slumming with the queers."

"Oh." Lee did not know what to say to the bitterness in Marion's voice.

"Don't mind me. The Trocadero's okay."

They walked for a long time, mostly in silence, Lee absorbed in her thoughts. It was exciting and frightening to be going off on such an intimate involvement with a stranger. Lee knew she would never have dared this at home. Here in the city it seemed possible, maybe even inevitable.

Marion led the way into a darkened building, and for a moment in the dark entry Lee had a moment of fright. She tripped following Marion and wondered if perhaps the woman had lured her here to do her an injury.

Then Marion flicked on a light. The dark disappeared to reveal a simple entry hall with doors off it to the left and right and a stairway straight ahead. Marion began to climb the stairs. Lee followed her up into a city apartment.

"I have this whole floor," Marion said. "It's comfortable. Here. Give me your coat. I'll go make some coffee." She took Lee's coat and bustled off, leaving Lee to wander around the living room, filled with magazines and books. The sight reassured her. She sat for awhile on the sofa and then restlessly wandered into the kitchen. Coffee was perking cheerfully and Marion was bringing out cups.

"You should probably have some food, too," she said.

"I ate quite a big meal at the Nankin."

"Well, you know what they say about Chinese food. It fills you up, but you're hungry again in an hour. I'll make us an omelet."

An omelet late at night in this apartment sounded like exotic fare. Lee sat down at the kitchen table and watched Marion work.

"What do you do?"

"Me? Oh, nothing so exciting as farming. I'm a secretary downtown at one of the banks. Been there forever."

"You must like it, then."

"It suits me," Marion admitted. In her own home she did not seem at all like the challenging woman Lee had first set eyes on. Here she was relaxed and pleasant, a comfortable woman to be with.

They ate at the kitchen table, sipping coffee, talking with ease, getting to know each other. Behind it all was a sense of anticipation. They both knew they were going to end up in Marion's bed. For Lee fear was mixed with the anticipation, fear that she would not know what to do, and that Marion would laugh at her or find her unacceptable.

Finally Marion rose and came to stand behind Lee. She touched Lee's shoulders and brought her hands up each side of Lee's neck to rise gently over her ears and into her short dark hair so she could massage Lee's head.

Lee stiffened for just a second. She immediately relaxed, but Marion caught the stiffening. "You don't have to do this, you know," she said.

"I want to." Lee turned in her chair to bury her face against Marion. Her arms went around Marion's waist.

With a sigh Marion pulled her to her feet. "Come on," she said after awhile, breaking their embrace. "Let's go to bed."

In the early morning Lee woke and wondered where she was. For a moment she felt panic that she had overslept and not milked the cows. Then she remembered. She sought out the woman sleeping next to her, touching the warmth and softness, feeling the curve of her breast under her hand. Sleepily she remembered the newly discoved pleasure and wonder of loving a woman. Smiling contentedly, Lee curled into Marion and went back to sleep.

Later when they were both awake and pleasantly satisfied again, Lee said: "This is wonderful. I feel great."

"No hangover?"

"None."

"Nothing like a little exercise in bed," Marion said with a soft chuckle. She regarded Lee with a look of intimate fondness.

The feel of soft warm flesh against her own naked body was both intoxicating and comforting to Lee. She felt intimately connected with this woman and wondered if Wade felt any of this with his men. She somehow doubted it. Wade simply went from one male body to another. She never wanted to part from this woman. In fact, she was not at all eager to ever get out of this warm bed.

"I suppose I should feed you again," Marion said. "I wish you didn't have to go home so soon."

"Me too," Lee agreed. "I wish you could come back home with me."

"I wish I could, but I've got to work, too."

"I know. Maybe you could come and visit?"

"Maybe," Marion said doubtfully. She was certain that once Lee was home again, she would forget all about her.

Lee was equally certain she would never forget this woman, even if she never saw her again.

Marion made breakfast. For the first time in her life, Lee felt at home in her own body, comfortable with herself now that lovemaking was no longer something mysterious and frightening. She said something of this aloud.

Marion smiled both ruefully and affectionately at Lee. "It was your first time," she said. "I'm glad it was with me. But you'll go on and find some younger woman, maybe even the one you said lived across the road."

"No," Lee protested. "I don't want anyone else."

"You will," Marion said sadly. She liked this younger woman who had been brave enough to approach her in the bar, but she was realistic enough to know there would be other women for Lee.

They walked back downtown to the hotel, the Dykeman. In later years she and Les and Wade would chuckle together when they thought of staying in such an appropriately named place.

Les was waiting in the lobby. "I packed your stuff," he said. "Wade's waiting in the car. He's sick this morning. Wants to get home."

Back to reality. "Well," Lee said, "I guess I need to go."

"I'll walk you to the car." Marion felt an odd jolt at this parting.

At the car Wade raised his head feebly from the back seat and managed a weak wave. Les was already behind the wheel and had the engine running.

Lee looked at Marion, feeling awkward. "I'll write," she promised. "You have my address, too."

Marion nodded. She waved until the car disappeared into traffic and Lee's eyes followed her until she was out of sight.

CHAPTER NINE

Aware that she owed Lee a good-sized part of her own first crop, Clare watched anxiously as the spring rains brought the hay fields back to life, hoping that the seeding was good. Lee stopped by early in June, right after the Memorial Day weekend. Clare greeted her eagerly, proudly offering coffee and homemade brownies.

"Very tasty," Lee pronounced, grinning at Clare. "You seem to be mastering cooking right along with farming."

"Thanks. I keep trying. Marsh never lets me forget my first efforts."

"I'm sure he doesn't. He's a tease."

"Yeah, well, what can you expect from a younger brother?" Clare poured them more coffee. She'd been feeling tired from cleaning calf pens but Lee's unexpected visit had vanquished the tiredness, replacing it with a pleasant stirring of excitement inside her.

"I'm going to start cutting my hay tomorrow," Lee told her. "The forecast is good for a few days."

"So soon?" Clare had not planned to start her own haying yet. "I thought I'd start mine in a couple of weeks."

Lee nodded. "I just wanted to suggest you start soon, too. You'll get better quality hay if you do." She went on to explain that she had discovered a couple of years ago that hay cut early in June was much better feed for her cows than the stemmy mature stuff most farmers cut.

The idea made sense to Clare. She mentioned it to her dad and brother the next day at the Co-op feed mill.

Harry scoffed at her. "You're nuts. Wait until it grows some. You won't get enough off them fields to see your cattle through the winter."

"Let it mature," her dad advised. Other farmers nodded their agreement. Clare was torn. She had fed enough of Lee's hay to know it was good. But these were seasoned farmers, with the exception of Harry.

She wavered on it for a day or two while Lee got into cutting her own hay. Finally she decided to go ahead and cut, reasoning that Marsh would be available to help her with the bales if she did it before her dad and brother did theirs.

"Harry says you're crazy," Marsh told her when he came to help. He picked up a handful of the early-cut hay. "I think you're not so crazy after all. This stuff looks and smells great."

In the days that followed Clare and Marsh harvested field after field. The rains came before they had time to bale the last of it.

"We were so close to being done," Clare lamented to Lee on the second day of steady rain. She had gone across to Lee's to borrow a book, wanting something to take her mind off her soggy hay. "Wish I'd started the same day you did. I'd be done now, too. My last five acres are ruined."

"Maybe," Lee said. "But I think it will still be good feed for your heifers and dry cows." She regarded Clare with affection, still feeling that old twinge of desire. Even Marion hasn't been able to erase that, she thought wryly.

"I'd better go, I guess," Clare said. "Thanks for the coffee and the book and for listening to me gripe." She stood awkwardly by Lee's table. "I guess you've been going into Minneapolis a lot lately," she said with a question in her voice.

"Yeah. Thanks to Marsh doing my chores. I don't know who I'll get when he goes away to college this fall. You're going to miss him, too." Lee did not know how to interpret Clare's interest in her trips to Minneapolis. She had managed two more visits to Marion on her own since her first trip in with Les and Wade. Both visits had been, well, wonderful. But how was she supposed to explain that to Clare? "I've been enjoying the city," she said briefly.

"Wish I had the time to go sometime, but I don't. Not that I've got the money either." There was still an unspoken question.

Well, I sure can't invite her to go in with me, Lee thought, imagining such an event just the same. Wouldn't that be interesting, Clare meeting Marion? She saw Clare to the door and watched her dash on long agile legs across the road, splashing through puddles as more rain came down.

In the weeks that followed, both Lee and Clare had reason to be thankful for their early haying efforts. The weather stayed unpredictable. Showers of heavy rain drifted across the area every other day or so. In the feed mill the other farmers lamented the poor haying weather.

Lee's brother Dan, who had helped her with her own haying, was worried enough by the delays to call on his sister to help bale when the weather was good. He was getting married soon and it was beginning to look like haying would extend over into the time he and Linda, his fiance, had set aside for their wedding and honeymoon. He didn't offer, however, to pay Lee for her help, and this rankled.

"I pay you to help me," she told him. "I pay you to combine my oats. Why shouldn't I get paid when I work for you?"

"That's different," Dan said. "You're a woman."

"What's that got to do with it, for Pete's sake?"

Dan shrugged. "You should help at home for free."

"Why?" Lee was getting angry. "That's totally ridiculous."

"Don't guess I have to combine your oats, if you feel that way."

Responses such as this left Lee speechless. "All right," she said. "I'll find somebody else. Get somebody else to help with the rest of your hay." She left him standing in his hay field next to the baler ready to gobble up twenty acres of dry hay.

She was still invited to his wedding and a shower for the bride. She and Dan might fight, but he was still her brother. She went to both events, pondering the strength of family ties. Lee wanted her family's love and approval, however hard it was to get.

Clare was dating George Hansen that summer. Her parents definitely approved.

"He's a nice polite young man," Eve said over a Sunday dinner of roast beef.

"Yeah, he's okay," Clare said, nonchalantly.

"He must be dumb," Harry observed. "Who else but a dummy would date Clare?"

"Must be he's smarter than I thought," Marsh put in. "If he's dating Clare, he's got pretty good taste, I think."

Clare sent a grateful look his way. "Well, it isn't any big deal. We just go to movies and stuff."

"It's the 'and stuff' you have to watch out for," Marsh teased.

"Really, he's just a nice guy," Clare insisted. "We talk farming and he helped me fix my fence last Saturday when he wasn't working."

"Well, you be careful," Eve advised. "I'm glad you're dating but there's no need to rush into anything." "Anything" meant sex, which Eve felt embarrassed to be discussing even in so veiled a fashion with Clare, especially with the boys around. Not that they were exactly boys.

It worried Eve that Clare was alone over there in that big old house of hers, with no one to supervise when she had a date over.

"Like I said, it's no big deal." Clare repeated, thinking that George was probably an ideal date, from her mother's point of view. He had never so much as offered to kiss her, which she thought was sort of strange. Marsha and her current boyfriend, Floyd, seemed to spend a lot of time kissing. Among other things.

Clare thought she might have liked it if George would have kissed her when he brought her home from movies these days. In fact, their times together were fun. They laughed and talked easily now, establishing a comfortable relationship.

"Boy, I sure wish my dad and Nathan would try early haying," George had said after Clare showed him some of her first crop.

"This is nice stuff." He paused and then went on. "It made me kind of mad, listening to those guys down at the feed mill. Maybe I shouldn't tell you, but some of them sort of make fun of you, like you couldn't know what you're doing because you're a girl. And the stuff they say about Lee Collins..." He didn't finish.

"I know what they say about her," Clare said.

"Are they right?"

"I don't know. Maybe...How's the new pickup?" she evaded

"Want a ride?"

"Sure. You must do okay at the gas station."

George shrugged. "I bought it on credit. That's the only way to do it." He grinned. "I'd be ninety-three if I waited until I'd saved enough to buy this, like my folks wanted me to."

Between dates with George and a lush second crop of hay, the first summer on her farm passed quickly for Clare. August was warm and dry, the weather bringing on her oats early in the month. Clare talked to Dan Collins about harvesting them for her, but he turned her down.

"First crop didn't go well," he said. "I got married, too, you know. Now I've got all my second crop and my regular oat customers. Try Orrin Grimes."

Clare knew Orrin and his family from church and encounters at the feed mill. Some of their land bordered hers but she only waved across the fenceline as Orrin or his wife Stella worked in their fields. Their only child was a boy of four, Orrin Jr., called Butch. His freckled face and carrot-top hair were already a familiar sight to Clare. He was often out with one of his parents in the fields.

She stopped in one morning after chores, looking with envy at the neat yard and the newly painted big barn and sheds. Wish my place looked this good, she thought. I wonder where they get the energy to keep this place so neat, milk fifty cows and still do custom work in addition to their own crops?

Stella was in the milk house washing and sanitizing bucket milkers and gleaming stainless steel pails. She was older than Clare, in her early thirties, with dark auburn hair and bright green eyes that sparkled with good humor.

"I didn't recognize you at first," Stella said. "How's it going over there on the old Peterson place?"

"Pretty good."

"Well, I'm glad. It's not easy to start out farming on your own, but you look to me like you can handle it." Stella wiped her hands on a paper towel. "If I was a betting person, I'd put some money on you."

"Thanks." Stella's warm words were welcome ones.

"Who's betting money?" Orrin Grimes poked his head in the milkhouse door. Orrin was not a handsome man, with his large ears and wide-toothed smile. He was short and stocky, with long muscular arms that gave him a slightly monkey-like appearance. What he lacked in looks, he made up for in good humor and charm.

"Don't get nervous," Stella said. "I'll let you know if I bet the farm or something. I was just telling Clare here I'd bet on her doing okay on her new place."

"Oh, well. That's different. Bet ahead, then." He grinned at Clare. "See you beat us with your second crop. We're still working away."

"It was a good crop," Clare said. "Maybe you wouldn't have time to harvest my oats if you're still on your hay?"

"Oh, I think we could fit it in," Orrin said. "Got about twenty acres, don't you? We're getting Lee's, so we can get yours, too. You're so close."

"What he didn't mention," Stella added in a conspiratorial voice, "is that we bought a new Gleaner combine, self-propelled yet, and we need to pay for it."

"You bet we do," Orrin agreed.

"Wow," Clare said. "Those machines are expensive."

"Tell me about it," Stella said, with a wink. "We buy much more of this shiny new stuff and I won't be able to sleep nights worrying about the payments."

"Our custom work is what makes it possible," Orrin explained, chuckling at his wife's words. "Don't worry. Stella always sleeps like a log. Although I guess logs don't exactly snore like she does."

"How would you know if I snore?" Stella retorted good-humoredly. "I'll tell you, sleeping with him is like sleeping with a diesel bulldozer."

Clare laughed, enjoying the banter. "Well, gee, if you need the money, maybe you'd be willing to do my corn, too?"

"We sure would," Stella said. "Got to keep the banker happy. I don't want to have to sell myself on Main Street to pay for the equipment. Oops. Hope that didn't shock you. I get carried away sometimes."

Clare shook her head. The Grimeses at home were certainly not what she had been expecting, but she found herself liking them both very much. "I can see it's going to be fun having you do my crops," she said.

"It's nice to see some other women out there working at farming," Stella said. "Sometimes I feel like I'm the only one around here that gets out and works with her husband. Gives me a good feeling, seeing you and Lee, too, over on her place."

"You hate it in the house," Orrin reminded her.

"I sure do. Housework stinks," Stella said. "I do as little of it as I can get by with."

"Yeah, if I have to wash the kitchen floor again this Saturday, I may go on strike," Orrin said soberly.

"Poor thing. He'd be a perçfect husband if he could only cook."

Clare went home still chuckling. The warmth and humor and genuine acceptance she had felt from the Grimeses stayed with her all day.

ॐ

The holiday bustle was in full swing. Lee hadn't bothered much with Christmas in recent years, beyond gifts for her family and Les and Wade. This year, she was looking forward to the holiday.

Lee had been very persuasive on one of her visits to Marion and Marion had finally yielded. She had some vacation days coming. "Might as well use them up," she said, deciding on a five-day visit.

Lee drove into town the Friday before Christmas to meet Marion's bus on a cold night with snow flakes drifting slowly down. The cafe was warm and crowded with folks waiting for the bus to arrive. Lee sat quietly at the counter, listening to the good-natured talk around her, enjoying the warmth and the cheerfulness, eager to see Marion again.

A stir over by the door announced the arrival of the bus. Folks gathered up their coats and a general exodus occurred, with Lee among the crowd that gathered just outside the cafe door to watch the bus pull in and stop with a hiss of its air brakes.

Marion was third off the bus. She looked anxiously around until she spotted Lee and then her face relaxed into a wide smile that made Lee want to hug her tightly. Other people were hugging their passengers, so Lee threw off caution and put her arms around Marion briefly, too.

It was not until they were back in Lee's house that Lee allowed herself to fully welcome Marion. "It's so good to see you again." Her voice was muffled in the collar of Marion's coat. She raised her head and their lips met in a kiss that started softly and grew in intensity.

"Phew," Marion said at last. "You sure warmed me up. Let me take my coat off."

"I'm really glad you're here." Lee took Marion's coat and hung it up while Marion looked around at the house.

"I like your place. It's cozy." Marion moved into the living room. "My gosh. Books everywhere. Somehow one never thinks of farmers as being great ones to read."

"A lot of us do," Lee replied, already defensive. Marion held some patronizing views of rural people that irritated Lee.

Lee had planned simple activities for the two of them: putting up a Christmas tree, sharing the opening of gifts and eating a good Christmas dinner with Les and Wade. Now she was wondering if Marion was going to be bored.

She needn't have worried. On Saturday morning when Lee had finished her barn chores, she took Marion out to the woods at the back of her property. The two tramped up and down in the small woodlot, considering various trees until they finally picked the perfect one. Lee cut it with ease, her sharp axe biting neatly through the trunk.

They set up the tree in the living room and were in the middle of trimming it that afternoon when someone knocked on the back door. Lee put down the decorations she was sorting and went to admit an unusually shy and hesitant Clare.

Clare had seen Lee out in the yard that morning with someone, bringing in a tree. She had seen, with a twinge, the closeness between them. Now, Clare took in the partly trimmed tree and the woman in tailored slacks and oxford cloth shirt and knew with a certainty that was painful that Lee was involved intimately with her.

Unwelcome and unreasonable tears threatened to overwhelm her. She blinked rapidly, trying to digest her feelings. It hurt to know this woman was someone very special to Lee, yet she also knew it was stupid to feel as though her own friendship with Lee had been displaced. She felt like a total bumpkin, ungainly and ugly, as she stood in the doorway. "I didn't know you had company," Clare managed to say, feeling her tongue trip over the lie. She now regretted the curiosity that had made her come with a gift so she could get a closer look.

"Marion came in on the bus last night. She's here for the holidays. At least she's here for Christmas but then she has to go back before New Year's," Lee babbled uncharacteristically. In her excitement at finally getting Marion to come visit, Lee had not anticipated having to introduce Clare to her. Now she nervously invited her neighbor in.

Clare couldn't think of any reason not to come in, although she wanted very much to throw down the gift and the box of cookies and run home. Instead she stepped inside and took off her winter coat.

"This is Marion," Lee said unnecessarily to Clare.

"Hi," Clare managed to say as she shook the older woman's outstretched hand. She felt clumsy in her heavy Levis and flannel shirt. Marion's perfume reminded her that she hadn't washed her hair lately. I probably smell like a cow, she thought.

"So you're also a farmer," Marion was saying to her.

"Ah, yeah... I am." Brilliant conversation, Clare thought, wishing the woman did not have such a penetrating gaze.

"I...ah...brought you these," Clare said to Lee, handing her the gift box and cookie tin she had so eagerly prepared.

Lee admired the wrapped package and opened the cookie tin. "These look really good. Your cooking's come a long way," she said, touched that Clare had thought of her, embarrassed that in the excitement of Marion's visit, she had not taken time to get Clare a gift.

There was a lengthy silence. Lee broke it. "I'll just go make a pot of coffee and we'll try some of your cookies," she said. She escaped from her own living room with relief, leaving her lover and her neighbor to get acquainted.

"Well," Marion said after she had lit her cigarette. She was both amused and irritated. So this was the girl back home that Lee cared about. Clare looked so uncomfortable and miserable that Marion lost her irritation and set out to put Clare at ease. "It's nice to meet you. Lee has talked a lot about you."

A slight lie, Marion thought, but only slight.

"I guess you must be who Lee goes to see in Minneapolis."

Marion nodded. "She manages to get in to visit fairly often, given her farming schedule. I imagine your own farm keeps you pretty busy. I think it's quite amazing that the two of you should end up right across the road from each other. I'm sure it can't be all that common to have women farming alone."

"No, it's not," Clare agreed, relaxing slightly. She did not think she liked Marion much, but she knew part of her dislike came from an unwelcome knowledge that she did not want Lee to be involved with this woman or with any woman, for that matter. She wanted... What the heck do I want, anyway?

While she struggled to answer Marion's efforts at small talk, Clare's mind was busy digesting the news about Lee. Well, it wasn't really news, was it? It was just that the actual presence of Marion in Lee's house made avoidance of the knowledge impossible. Lee was a queer, just like people said. She did with women what you were supposed to do with men.

Not that I've done it with anybody, Clare thought, man or woman. That made her feel even younger and more naive, as she nodded at something Marion said to her. Pay attention, she chided herself.

Lee edged quietly back into the living room and saw with relief that Marion and Clare were talking easily. "Coffee's ready," she interrupted. "Come and sit down."

The three of them sat at the kitchen table and ate Clare's cookies. Clare accepted their compliments. "Thanks. I made a bunch of them. I'm giving them to the mailman and the milk hauler and also to George. George is sort of my steady boyfriend," she found herself saying.

"I didn't know you were seeing anyone," Lee said, startled. A hollow empty spot inside her got larger.

-73-

Marion hid a smile. The atmosphere changed subtly after that. Clare soon rose to leave.

"I need to get over to the Hansen's yet, before chores," she said. "To give George his gift." She didn't know why she was making such a point of that when all she had to give him was some cookies.

"I see," Lee said. "What are you doing for Christmas?"

"Going to my folks, mainly." Lee glanced at Marion, suddenly very thankful for the warmth of her companionship. Her brother and his new wife would be at her parents' house. Dan was insufferable these days. His wife was already pregnant. Of course, Lee's folks were overjoyed and not a little relieved.

"Well, it was nice to meet you," Clare said politely to Marion.

"Nice to meet you, too," Marion murmured.

Lee escorted Clare to the door. "Thanks for the present. I didn't get you one. I should have."

"There's no need," Clare assured her. "Well, I better go." She felt awkward around Lee now. "Have a good Christmas." She made her escape with relief.

Lee shut the door and came back to the kitchen where Marion was having another cup of coffee.

"Good cookies, actually," Marion said as she helped herself to another one. "So that's the girl next door. Interesting. Very interesting."

Lee sat down and sipped some coffee. It was cold but she didn't really notice. Clare was dating George Hansen.

"What did you say?" she asked Marion. "Sorry, I wasn't paying attention."

"No, I can see you weren't. Your face and hers were a study in emotions. If you could have seen them..." Marion shook her head. "I definitely felt the charge between you. Talk about feeling like an intruder."

"I'm sorry. I didn't think she might come over."

"No need to be sorry, honey," Marion said gently. "I think your neighbor was shocked to find you had someone. I think she thought you were hers."

"That's ridiculous. You heard her. She's dating George Hansen."

"And you're 'dating' me," Marion pointed out. "Just the same, the fact remains clear. If she so much as crooked a little finger at you, you'd come running. Wouldn't you?"

"Of course not," Lee protested. "She won't, anyway. She's dating..."

"I know. George. Lee, I'm not blind. I care about you a lot, but if you two ever figure out how to get together, I'll understand."

"For Pete's sake, Marion, let's drop it." Lee was feeling disoriented enough without needing to think about Marion not being in her life. "I want us to have a good Christmas together..."

Marion reached out her hand to caress Lee's shoulder and neck. "We will. Don't worry, we will." Her face softened into a look of affection and need. "Meantime, let's finish the tree."

CHAPTER TEN

In the spring of 1961 Clare passed into her second year of farming. She felt more settled that spring, more capable of managing her cattle and crops. The milk price stayed above $3.45, even climbing later that year to $3.56. With her cattle milking well on her early-cut hay, she was able to make her loan payments and pay her regular bills.

"It's not easy," she told George one day in May when he had come by to help out with corn planting. "I wish I didn't have to be so careful with my money. Then I could afford to pay you for your help."

"I just like helping," George dismissed her offer. "I couldn't take your money. Nobody offers to pay me when I help at home, so why should you?"

"But I know you need extra money, too," Clare pointed out. "You've got your pickup to pay for."

George shrugged. "I think I'm going to just let it go back to the dealer, or whatever happens. I haven't told anyone else yet, but I joined the Air Force this week."

"You... joined the Air Force?" Clare stopped adding fertilizer to her dad's corn planter. "Why?"

"Well, what else is there for me here? The gas station job isn't going anywhere, and there's no place for me at home. I can't afford to buy my own farm." He smiled. "Something tells me you wouldn't want me around on this one all the time, either."

Clare did not protest that, but she did feel as though everyone was deserting her. Lee had Marion and Marsh was too involved with college to be around much anymore. Now George was leaving, too.

"I'm going to miss you," she said honestly.

"Well, we've had some fun together, haven't we?" George looked at her shyly. "I guess I wish I didn't have to leave you behind but I really can't stay around here and feel like I'm getting nowhere."

Before he left for basic training, George took Clare out to eat at Morgan's, a local night spot that was expensive but served good food. In the dim light at their table, he passed over his high school ring. "Something to keep me in mind while I'm gone," he said casually. "You'll write to me, won't you?"

"Of course." Clare felt the ring, warm from being on George's finger, and heavy in her hand. "I ... thanks. Are you sure you want me to have this? You might meet somebody..."

George's hand covered hers. "I know I'm not very good at this, but I don't think I'll ever meet anybody like you. You're so different from some of the girls. They just seem empty-headed and you're smart. You know what you want. Somehow you got it and no matter what people around here say, I think that's neat. Maybe some day if I can save my money in the service, we could... you know, like, get married?"

Clare allowed George's large hand to cover her own. It was the first time in their dating that he had been physically demonstrative. He's shy, she thought. That's why.

That evening when George dropped Clare off at her door, he finally worked up enough courage to plant an awkward kiss on her lips. She returned it eagerly, knowing she was actually going to miss this quiet Hansen boy.

Clare's folks were delighted that George had given their daughter his class ring.

"I suppose you'll be getting married one of these days," her mother said when Clare had shown her the ring she kept on a chain around her neck. "I don't want you rushing into marriage. There's plenty of time."

"I know, Mom. I'm young yet," Clare said, thinking that her mother sure could be contradictory.

"Yes, you are. Too young to be farming alone like this," Eve said, indicating Clare's tractor and the Lewis corn planter she had just returned home.

"You better hope George doesn't make a career of the service," her dad said. "If he does, you'll have to sell your farm and go with him God knows where. Martin will get left holding the loan on it when that happens."

"George and I aren't planning to get married," Clare said. "We're ...well...we're really just good friends."

"Not too good, I hope. If you've been intimate with him, you'd better be careful," Eve said, regarding her daughter with new fear.

"Mom, you really worry too much about me."

"Well, you certainly give me plenty of cause."

"I'm very careful," Clare said reassuringly. She could see that her mother was genuinely concerned. "Anyway, George isn't going to be around for awhile. That's one less thing for you to worry about, right?"

"Your mother will think of something, you can bet on it," Ed Lewis told his daughter gruffly.

꒰꒱

The early years of the 1960's were static years for dairy farmers. Milk prices stayed steady, varying only by a few cents. Prices for feed and equipment held fairly steady as well. For Clare those years were static in ways that had nothing to do with prices.

Clare wasn't sure she had many friends anymore. Her girl friends from high school bored her with their talk of dates and clothes and who was getting married or having another child.

She wished sometimes that Lee wasn't so involved with Marion. Most weekends Lee was gone, off to the city while a neighbor boy milked her cows. During the week she was busy, just as Clare was, with farm work.

She missed Lee, missed the good talks with her, the exchanges of farm information where she was an equal in the discussion. The men of the area still looked down on her, so talk with them at the feed mill or machinery dealer was never very satisfying. Her own dad still would not admit she was doing okay, though sometimes she thought maybe he thought so. He was too darned stubborn to say anything, even though he couldn't help but compare Clare with her brother Harry.

It pained Ed Lewis to realize that his oldest son, chosen at an early age as the farming heir, was not cut out for it. Harry had married in 1962, to a city girl who had no interest in the farm. She had a job in town at one of the beauty shops. Nothing against Diane, she was a good worker, kept the trailer house she and Harry lived in neat and cooked good meals.

Ed, in honest moments, had to admit that his son just wasn't much good at farming. But Ed had been farming and milking cows for forty years already, and he didn't want to be doing it for another twenty. Besides, he'd bragged Harry up too much to just kick him out. But there were more and more days when he was tempted. Harry milked his cows whenever he felt like it. He was the same way with the field work, always behind on it, so Ed had to get out there more than he wanted to just to keep things moving. He had to admit to himself he sometimes wished Harry was gone and Clare was home doing the farming. Not that Ed ever admitted this aloud, even to Eve. He certainly never said it to Clare.

ક

And then came the assassination of John Kennedy in November 1963. Clare heard the news on her barn radio as she did afternoon chores. Like others all across the country, she stopped what she was doing and turned up the volume. Like others, she felt a sudden need to talk, to share the horror.

Without hesitation she went quickly across the road to Lee's. "Did you hear it?" she asked.

Lee nodded, her face wearing a blank look of disbelief and grief. "I voted for him. I thought he was going to be a good president. I can't believe it."

"It's horrible."

"I know." Lee led the way into her house. "I've been watching it on my new TV. I know you don't have one yet."

That entire weekend, between necessary chores, found Lee and Clare planted together on Lee's old sofa, watching the black and white image of history in the making. The shock of such a tragedy had wiped out almost three years of distance between them dissolved it completely.

In an unspoken but totally natural way, Clare found herself early in the viewing, edging closer to Lee on the sofa. Lee's physical presence, the obvious grief on her very familiar and suddenly very dear face, brought out in Clare a need for the comfort of physical contact.

Their hips touched. Lee, absorbed in the events on the screen, jumped slightly when Clare's warmth pressed against her. She sat up and casually draped her arm over the back of the sofa, coincidentally, of course, over Clare. Clare did not pull away when Lee's arm slowly descended from the back of the sofa. Instead she snuggled into it with a sigh.

It felt like coming home to sit this way, Clare acknowledged to herself. I just want to be held and comforted, she thought. It doesn't mean anything. I've got a boyfriend. My boyfriend is in the service, she reminded herself. And actually he's never touched me as intimately as I'm touching and being touched by this woman.

But it's all perfectly innocent, she defended herself. Lots of people are probably seeking comfort all over the world. What could be more natural than to need comfort at a time like this?

What indeed? Lee, later that night, talked with Marion by phone. "Oh ho," Marion said, once they had covered the topic of the assassination and the murder. "So your little neighbor is with you."

"She's gone home to bed," Lee said, needing to let that be known.

"And she'll be back tomorrow, I bet. Interesting that she sought you out at a time like this."

"I just happen to be handy."

"Oh, sure. I think I probably should be jealous." Marion did not sound particularly jealous, but Lee blushed and was glad Marion could not see her.

Much as she cared about Marion, she had to admit to herself at least that her feelings when close to Clare on the sofa had little to do with comfort, and a whole lot more to do with an inner excitement that left Lee hopeful. When Clare came back the next day and they settled in on the sofa, Lee wished she had the nerve to invite Clare back into the circle of her arm.

When Clare kept a slight distance, Lee felt disappointed. But the disappointment was tempered by the knowledge that some restraints between them had vanished. There was an easy friendliness coming again from Clare. It had not been there since that first Christmas when Clare had found Marion was in Lee's life.

Even after the assassination weekend was over, the new ease persisted. Clare was back to visiting with Lee, stopping by on impulse to share farm news, borrow a book, have a cup of coffee. Clare could not have explained, even to herself, why it was suddenly okay again. It just felt right. She had missed the comfort and support she felt from Lee, missed it a lot.

She knew that people still talked about Lee, enjoying a good gossip at her neighbor's expense. The talk just made Clare feel uncomfortable. Her own girlfriends, on the rare times she was with them, attempted to pry from her further details of Lee.

"I hear she has women out there," Marsha Henderson Parker said. "What are they like? Do you see them?" Her face was avidly curious.

"I really wouldn't know," Clare said, thinking she did know but feeling as though it would be disloyal to Lee to say anything.

"She sure acts like a man, even dresses like one. Do you know, I saw her in Farm and Fleet last week, trying on men's boots," Marsha said in a hushed voice, as though to wear a pair of men's boots was right up there at the top of the sin list.

Clare smiled faintly. She thought of her own men's boots, purchased at Farm and Fleet. Her friends sometimes seemed oblivious to the fact that Clare farmed too, that she herself wore men's clothing around the farm. George's ring on its chain around her neck was evidently good protection.

George came home on extended leave in 1964. He had been home briefly, after basic training, before being sent to West Germany. But this was a lengthier visit, one granted to him because he had just signed on for another of duty; he would be starting it in January by being flown to Vietnam.

Although he and Clare had exchanged dozens of letters and talked sometimes on the phone, Clare was acutely aware of a change in him. Gone was the shy younger George who hesitated to even kiss her. In his place was an older, physically mature man, with hard muscular arms, and a forceful manner that made him seem like a stranger to Clare.

He was good-looking in his Air Force blues, with gleaming shoes and a snappy cap, his handsome face accented by the neatly trimmed mustache he now wore. Clare felt a twinge of pride at being with him as they entered Morgan's and people's heads turned in their direction to stare at the serviceman.

The pride changed to discomfort as George launched into a one-sided conversation. Where he had once been interested and supportive of her farming, now he ignored it, interested only in himself and his years in West Germany.

"Boy, I saw it all," he said. "I took as many trips as I could. Some of those jerks never left the base. It was safer, you know, not to. But I got to Spain, Greece, Italy. I even skiied in Switzerland. We weren't supposed to do it, but I got over into East Berlin and into East Germany."

"It must have been interesting to do all that traveling."

"Sure was. Now, Denmark was great. Most open people I've ever seen. The porn you could get there, incredible. And the women, too. But the best were on the Rieperbahn in

Amsterdam. This whole street of women, sitting in lighted windows, waiting."

"Oh."

"Boy, we had some good times," he smiled to himself, remembering. "The beer and the wines. German beer so strong it makes this stuff seem like cow piss."

"Well, this stuff is plenty strong for me," Clare said smiling at George, but inwardly puzzled by how much time he spent talking about women he had known in Europe. It made her feel small and inexperienced to listen to him.

"Hey, isn't that your neighbor over there?" George pointed to a table across the dining room. "Who's the woman with her?"

Clare turned to look. "Yeah, that's Lee. Her friend is from Minneapolis."

"So it was really true what people said about her, that she's queer. Must be. Look at the way they're looking at each other. Makes you sick, doesn't it?"

Clare did not reply. Briefly she had a mental picture of the two of them sitting on Lee's sofa during that strange weekend after the assassination. She remembered the warmth and comfort of Lee's arm around her shoulders.

"You don't see much of her, do you?" George asked. Something in Clare's silence was bothering him.

"Not too much, we're both busy," she said noncommitally.

"Yeah? You talked about her a lot in your letters. She ever try anything with you?"

Clare shook her head. "Did you go to Paris?" she asked, hoping to distract him.

"Ah, Paris. An Air Force buddy and I went over there for a long weekend. Incredible. It was in the spring and we picked up a couple of girls at some sidewalk cafe. Let me tell you, they showed us a real good time. Some of the French don't like us Yanks too much, but these girls sure didn't let it get in the way."

Back to women again. Well, at least he's off the subject of Lee, Clare thought.

"And Belgium. Right there on the Avenue Louise, eating one of those waffles you can buy at little stands all over..."

When they left Morgan's, Lee and Marion were still eating. Clare managed a casual wave in their direction, wondering if she should have dragged George over and introduced him. See, this is my boyfriend. Isn't he handsome?

Now, sitting in his folks' car, Clare allowed George to kiss her and fondle her, returning the kisses with enthusiasm. The thought of Lee with Marion seemed somehow to act as a spur for her with George, although the new, more sophisticated George was a little frightening in his ardor.

When he suggested he come in with her that night she refused. "I only have a single bed," she said. "It wouldn't be very comfortable."

"Heck, we can take care of that," he said, starting the car and turning it quickly in her driveway. "Let's go back to town and find a motel."

Clare did not protest. She was not quite sure why. Maybe it was because she was twenty-four years old and had never been to bed with anyone. Certainly most of her girlfriends seemed to feel that was a real liability. Much of their talk centered on who had and who hadn't "done it," all of which had left Clare feeling young and naive.

George picked the newer motel on the east end of town. He had made a stop at a bar on the way, and now he was pulling a bottle of Scotch from a paper bag.

"See if they've got some glasses in the bathroom. I'll get some ice."

Clare was glad of something to do. The motel room smelled stale. It was clean, she guessed, but cluttered with a large double bed, two big chairs, a dresser and luggage stand.

"Here." He handed her a glass filled with liquor and ice. "I know the British would be appalled at the ice in this," he said grinning, "but I like it that way."

"You went to England, too?" Clare felt the unfamiliar burn of the whiskey as she swallowed a good gulp of it.

"Sure did." He was shedding his uniform jacket now, untying his shoes. "Boy, those pubs are great. And no matter what people say about British reserve and all that, the girls I met sure weren't reserved at all."

"You sure talk a lot about the women over there. Why are you bothering with me?"

"It didn't mean anything. I just wanted you to know I'd had some experience. I learned a lot over there."

"I guess you must have. I've never done this before."

"There wasn't anybody while I was gone?"

"No. George, I'm not sure I want to do this now."

"Hey." Suddenly the old familiar George was back in this man's body. "Look, you don't have to. I mean, it's been a long time since we've seen each other, but I knew as soon as I saw you again that you were still special."

"Do you think we could just hold each other for awhile?"

"Sure. Hey, this is kind of nice. Okay if we kiss?"

"Yeah. Your mustache tickles."

"Oh. Not too much, I hope."

"No, it feels kind of nice." George was a gentle and considerate lover, concerned by her initial pain. But the pain was secondary to pleasure.

"I think maybe I wouldn't mind taking off some clothes," Clare said. It was okay suddenly, very okay.

Later, they cuddled together under the sheet and George reached for his cigarettes. "Want one? They're Dunhill's. British."

"I'll try one." Clare inhaled and coughed. "Geez. Those things are strong. Maybe I'll skip the cigarette part here. All the novels say that's what you do after..."

George chuckled. "What you're probably gonna do is leap up and tell me to take you home, because you have to milk the cows..."

"Well, I do. But I'd just like to stay here all warm and cozy for awhile." Clare yawned.

George covered her with the sheet and blanket. "I'll get you home in plenty of time," he said.

She was actually a little late getting home the next morning.

"I'm sorry," George said. "I know you like to be on time with the milking, but I didn't wake up like I thought I would. It was nice sharing a bed with you." He grinned.

Clare smiled back at him. "Yeah, I slept really well myself. The girls can manage for once."

"Hope so. I'd come in and help, but I promised Nathan I'd be out there in the barn at home to help him. He's gonna be mad that I'm late."

They kissed good-bye, and Clare found herself floating through her chores. So that's what it's like, she thought. It's okay. Especially the closeness. I wonder what it's like for Lee...?

Clare's late return home was observed from across the road by Marion who was just getting up. "Your neighbor got home from her date pretty late," she said to Lee when Lee came in from her morning barn chores.

"Oh?" Lee shed her boots and barn jacket.

"Yes. She and her boyfriend George rolled in about 6:30 a.m. this morning."

"Must have been a good night," Lee said as casually as she could. "What were you doing up so early?"

"Bathroom," Marion said. "All the wine last night. Her boyfriend is a handsome fellow."

"I suppose he is." Lee started to fry bacon."Air Force blues help, too."

"Oh, sure. I'll bet they spent the night together in some motel."

Lee dropped an egg on the floor. "Shit," she said, using a towel to clean up the mess.

"Shit, indeed," Marion murmured softly to herself. She had started out planning to tease Lee about her neighbor, but there was something about Lee's reaction that kept her from it.

⁊≱

George left for Vietnam in January, and Clare saw him off with a pang of regret. She knew from news reports that it was no small thing to be sent there. In February President Johnson ordered continuous bombing of North Vietnam. George was assigned to an air base as part of the ground service personnel for the aircraft used in the bombing. He and 184,299 other young Americans were in Southeast Asia by the end of 1965.

And that was the year Lee made her last payment to the bank. Les' house was no longer needed as collateral. She felt relief when she made the last payment and invited Les and Wade to dinner to celebrate.

"Congratulations!" Wade said immediately on arrival. He hugged her and then presented a bottle. "The best champagne they have in town. Dom Perignon."

"Wow. I am honored."

"You did good, Lee," Les said sincerely. He threw an awkward arm around her. "I knew you would."

"That's sure more than the banker thought I'd do. Remember?"

"I'll say. Stuffy little guy, wasn't he? With a fancy name."

"J. Humphrey Porter. The third," Lee said, smiling.

"Ah, the Porter dynasty," Wade said.

"They must artificially produce those banker types somewhere," Les said.

"He thought you and I were married," Lee said to Les.

"To each other?" Wade pretended shock. "Heavens."

"Yeah, he got quite a constipated look when he realized we weren't, and you were the farmer. Took him a long time to get that loan approved. I'll bet you're glad to be done dealing with him."

"Oh, he hasn't turned out to be so bad," Lee said. "Told me somewhere back a year or so to call him Jack. That's better than J. Humphrey."

"Yeah. I'll bet he'd even lend you money now that you don't need it." Wade poured champagne into the three tulip glasses he had bought specially for this occasion.

"You're right. When I paid them off, he came out of his office specially to tell me that." Actually, Lee was pleased. Women did not have their own credit in their small town and now she did.

"Well, let's drink a toast to the paid-for farm," Wade urged, handing around glasses bubbling with champagne.

"And a toast to our new project," Les added, raising his glass.

"What project? I hope your house being tied up as collateral hasn't meant you've been unable to do something?"

"Not at all," Les assured her with a quiet smile. "This is something we've been thinking about for quite awhile. The time might be right for us to do it."

"We're going to open a new restaurant and bar to compete with Morgan's," Wade said. "There's nothing else here. The cafes all close at six and the bars don't serve food. Morgan's is just so...dead."

"A lot of people go there," Lee pointed out.

"Sure they do, because there isn't anywhere else close by. There's more than enough people around here to support two nightclubs."

"That's what we're betting on," Les added. "We've already talked with the bank. They're interested."

"Not J. Humphrey?" Lee asked dryly.

"Of course not," Wade said. "He's in agricultural loans. Although, I'd certainly hope there might be some beefcake in the bar once it's going."

"Where will your new restaurant be?"

"In the Old Mercury," Wade said excitedly. "Can't you just see it?"

Lee could. The Mercury was in a solid turn-of-the-century brick building. Its owner had aged and so had the bar. They had both died in 1963 and the building had been vacant ever since. It was large enough to make a good-sized restaurant and had good old-fashioned bar fixtures as well.

"Who's going to cook?" Lee asked.

"I am," Wade said casually. "I used to be a chef at a place in Minnesota before I met Les and came to live here."

"I didn't know that. You never cook at home."

"That's different. I'm a chef. Les cooks at home."

"I'll be the bartender," Les said. "I've done that, too. And Wade is already getting back into practice with the cooking.

"When is this going to happen?"

"Late in the summer, probably. If we can get the loan going and the building purchase out of the way, we can get workmen in to start remodeling right after Memorial Day."

"It sounds great. I hope it works."

"You'll be our first customer, our guest," Wade said.

"I'll be your first paying guest," Lee corrected.

Small ads announcing that the New Mercury was coming started appearing in the local weekly paper right after Memorial Day. Les quit his job at the wood products factory to oversee the remodeling and order restaurant materials. Wade chafed at having to stay on at the factory.

"I want to quit, too," he said. "I'm sick of cue sticks and golf clubs. I want to get ready."

"Not until we start up," Les insisted. He was having second thoughts about the whole thing. He was forty years old and Wade was thirty-five. They could lose everything: the house, all their savings. It was all riding on this one gamble. Maybe they were too old.

But he had only to look at the enthused Wade planning menus and figuring food costs like a true professional to realize that they probably should have done it long ago. Wade's need to go to the Minneapolis bars had disappeared. With the excitement of the restaurant, he was content to stay at home, planning and practicing his cooking. Les had been worried about what Wade would want to serve, but Wade knew the local appetites.

"Nothing too spicy or with a lot of sauces," he decided. "Maybe one or two specials like that so people can be adventurous if they want to. I know the deep-fried fish will sell the best. That and the steaks. Plus chicken for those who can't afford steak."

Their grand opening came in August of 1965. It was the first opening of a new night spot since Morgan's opened twenty years before. People crowded in to the New Mercury and filled all the tables, spilling over into the bar as well. Les began to lose his harried look as the first week slid into the second and business stayed brisk.

Lee brought Marion to the new restaurant during the second week. It was a Saturday night and busy, but not so crowded as it had been at first. Marion's critical look turned approving as she took in the snowy white starched tablecloths with purple cloth napkins at each setting. Crystal-style water glasses clinked with ice as the waitress set them down, serving properly from the left. The menus were printed on heavy stock in gold and black. Both the waitresses and Les at the bar were dressed in white tops and deep purple vests, with lavender skirts for the women. Purples and lavenders had been carried out in the walls and hangings. It was different by local standards but tasteful, restful, and very charming.

"I sure didn't expect anything like this," Marion said. "I'm impressed. This is great."

"I think so, too," Lee agreed, proud of Les and Wade's efforts. Often Marion's down-putting remarks were a sore spot with Lee. Too many times she'd felt the need to close ranks and defend her territory against what she saw as unfair and inaccurate criticism. Marion, in turn, was amused by Lee's defensive response and often deliberately aroused it.

But not on her first visit to the New Mercury. She complimented Les and Wade until they both glowed. "I love it," she said. "I know it's going to be a big success for you."

"I sure hope so," Les responded. "We've got a big debt to pay off first, though." Les knew practically to the penny what they had to make each night to meet payments and operating costs. If there was a slow night, he worried about it.

"We'll make it," Wade said. He took a more carefree approach to the whole business, just as he did in his private life.

Clare was one of the few local folk who did not check out the new restaurant. She knew Lee went often. Her folks had even been there, which had surprised her.

"Kind of tarted up," her dad said about it.

"Well, I thought it was lovely. Such pretty colors," Eve countered. "And such good food. Marsh introduced us to the owners, and they were not at all what I expected them to be."

"Couple of queers," Ed muttered.

"They were charming," Eve protested. "Marsh works in the bar on weekends when it's very busy, you know."

Clare knew. She also knew he spent a lot of his free time with Les and Wade. And with Lee. He seemed to like the men and had continued his easygoing friendship with Lee.

Clare felt left out when she would see Marsh over at Lee's. She supposed she could walk over and be a part of the laughter she knew was going on, but somehow she couldn't bring herself to do it.

Marsh never talked of girl friends. He was close-mouthed to Clare about his life at college. He had graduated in 1964 with honors and was now in graduate school partly because of a real interest in further education and partly because he did not want to be drafted and sent to fight in an Asian war. In some ways he was still the same old likeable Marsh, but in subtle ways he had changed.

He still helped her with haying when he could, but he helped Lee, too. And Clare thought he seemed closer and more open with Lee than he was with her. They seemed to talk a separate language sometimes, with hidden meanings Clare could not decipher. Sometimes the sight of him with Lee in her yard left Clare jealous and very lonely.

CHAPTER ELEVEN

Shortly into 1966, Lee began to notice that Marion was not as eager to have her come to the city. "The weather's just too bad for this weekend," Marion told her in a phone call. "I don't want you on the road."

"It's such a tiring bus trip after a long work week," she said on another occasion in February. "It's been hectic here, Lee. I'm just too tired to come to the farm or have you come in."

"Okay. We'll try again another weekend," Lee agreed. She was disappointed in not being able to see Marion but the weather really had been miserable. And she could understand that Marion might sometimes be too tired from work. Lord knew she was often tired from her own hard farm work.

In late March it occurred to her that she had not actually seen Marion since shortly after Christmas. That was a long stretch for the two of them to go without getting together. Too long, Lee decided. I wonder what's wrong?

A phone call to Marion would have been the quick way, but Lee reasoned it might be better to just go and see her and find out in person what was going on. She drove into the city the last weekend in March, without announcing she was coming. It was almost noon by the time she arrived on Saturday.

She parked her pickup and walked back a block to Marion's apartment building. She rang the bell and waited on the steps. The snow was melting in warm sunshine, birds were singing, and Lee should have been feeling as springlike as the weather, but instead a hard ball of nervous worried energy kept bouncing around in her stomach.

She rang the doorbell again, and this time heard sounds of feet coming down the stairs to the front door. Marion opened the door. She was wearing the chenille bathrobe Lee had given her two Christmases ago. Its blueness was faded now from washings. Lee could see she wasn't wearing anything underneath.

"Lee. My God," Marion said, dismay on her face.

"Well. Can I come in?"

"I guess you might as well," Marion said resignedly. "I don't know how to say this, but…"

"You're seeing someone else," Lee finished for her, as matter-of-factly as she could, around the lump in her throat and the lead in her stomach.

"I'm sorry. I never meant for you to be hurt."

"Who is she?" Lee wasn't sure why she asked it. What difference did it make who she was?

"She's someone I met at work, believe it or not. She's my age, just about. In her fifties, too. I was too old for you, Lee."

"I didn't think you were. Funny, you kept saying it would be me who found somebody else." Lee wasn't laughing. She and Marion had never talked about loving each other. She knew Marion had been very fond of her. Marion had never said she loved her and yet Lee had thought she did. She assumed their relationship would go on for a long time yet, had wanted it to because she believed she loved Marion. She didn't know what she felt now except that a huge gaping hole had opened inside her, and she was free-falling into it. She hadn't hit bottom yet, but she would soon, she knew.

"You'd better come in," Marion said. "We can't just stand here talking like this. Come up and meet Nila."

That was the last thing Lee wanted to do. But her feet automatically climbed the stairs they had eagerly climbed so many times before. They followed Marion's slipper-clad feet across the hall to the apartment door and through the doorway into the living room. Lee stood as awkwardly in that room as she had years before when she and Marion had picked each other up at the Trocadero.

"Sit down," Marion said nervously. "I'll put on some coffee. We, that is…Nila and I were just getting up."

A jab of pain hit Lee at the words. She pictured herself and Marion sleeping late so many mornings in this apartment, rising in the afternoon to have coffee and toast, then leisurely going back to bed for some more lovemaking. Now Marion was doing it all with someone else.

The last thing Lee wanted right then was coffee or to meet Nila. But here she was. Marion was out in the kitchen running water, and there were stirrings from the bedroom.

The door opened and a small dark-haired woman came out hesitantly. She was very slender, and her face was beautiful with a piquantness that touched Lee. Graying hair framed her face. She was wearing a yellow bathrobe.

"Hi," she said uncertainly. "I didn't know Marion had brought anybody up."

"Just me. I'm Lee." Lee said it with a dry mouth.

"Lee! Oh my God." Nila's face changed from puzzled friendliness to horrified dismay. "Lee," she repeated.

"This is embarrassing," Lee said with a faint sardonic smile that hid her pain. The woman looked, well, nice. She was clearly mortified to be caught like this by Marion's ex-lover. Ex-lover... Lee guessed that's what she was now.

"It sure is," Nila said. "Marion said she was going to talk to you about us."

"Yeah, I wish she had," Lee said. It was no good. She couldn't hide the pain. It was there in her face, plain to see and in her eyes which she could not keep lowered.

Nila saw it all. "I'm so sorry," she said. "I wish you hadn't found out like this."

"What does it matter? I'd have had to find out some way, and this is probably as good as any. It makes it pretty clear where I stand now."

"I suppose it does. And it's not quite as bad as you think. Marion and I, well, we... This is the first time..." Nila broke off, embarrassed. "We wanted to, I think, before, but I'm married and I couldn't..."

"Messy," Lee commented. Somehow it made it worse, to know she had come almost as if by radar on the very weekend the two women had thrown caution, or whatever restrained them, to the winds.

"Very messy," Nila agreed eagerly. She was talking to fill air space, cover her embarrassment. "Frank, my husband, I don't know what I'm going to tell him. He's away this weekend. Otherwise I couldn't have come here. We see each other at work and have lunch together and then I go home to Frank. I've never been with a woman before. I never imagined I would want to. But with Marion..." Her voice trailed off, and Lee could see anxiety and confusion mingling on Nila's face.

Marion came hesitantly into her own living room. "Well, at least you're not throwing things at each other," she said, trying for humor. The attempt fell flat, and she sat down in an armchair with a sigh. "Maybe you should both throw things at me. I feel crummy about this."

"Good," Lee said with a malice she seldom displayed. "Why didn't you tell me? You always said I'd be the one to leave you. If I had, I'd have told you before it got to...to this point."

"Would you really? I wonder." Marion regarded Lee with a twisted smile. "It's not that simple. I kept putting it off. I know I should have told you what was happening. It crept up on us, but we knew. I knew. I didn't want to hurt you."

"Really?" Lee's sarcasm was cutting. "I suppose it hurts less this way, coming in and finding you in bed with someone."

"We weren't..." Marion protested.

"But you had been. What difference does it make?" Lee's initial hurt had given way to an anger she had seldom experienced and never voiced. "Why didn't you tell me what was happening?"

"I'm sorry." Marion suddenly looked old and defeated. Lee saw the difference in their ages etched on Marion's face and felt a moment of remorse.

The feeling faded with a refueling of her anger. "Dammit! I was worried about you. So I come in to see what's going on and this is what I find."

"I know," Marion agreed. "You have to understand neither of us meant for this to happen. Nila's married, for God's sake."

Even in the midst of her anger, Lee was horrified at herself. She didn't do this sort of thing. Sometimes when she was frustrated with work on the farm, when a repair did not go well, she might throw something or swear a little, but it wasn't like her to show it in front of others. As she examined it, the anger dissolved, and tears came. Lee tried to keep them inside by tensing her facial muscles, which only resulted in hastening their flow. She felt Marion reach out to her.

"Oh honey, I'm so sorry." Marion pulled Lee against her into the soft material of her robe and stroked Lee's back as Lee fought the tears.

Nila left the room because she didn't know what else to do. In the bedroom she quickly put on her clothes which had been scattered here and there, dropped in haste the previous night. She was almost out the door when Marion stopped her. "You're not leaving," Marion said softly.

"I really think it would be best if I did."

"No, it wouldn't. This isn't easy for any of us, but it won't help if you leave."

"I shouldn't have come," Nila said. "I'm married. You have a girlfriend. This is too complicated."

But Marion was shaking her head. "It's my fault Lee didn't know. I've known how I felt about you for a long time, and I should have told Lee."

Lee was recovering on the sofa, watching this exchange with resignation. She was honest enough to admit that what she saw now on Marion's face was very different from the way Marion looked at her. She got up and walked quietly around the two women, who were gazing at each other, resolving something without words. Marion called her back, but Lee kept going. She wished for more poise and wit, but all she could think to say was, "Good luck."

As Lee walked to her truck, part of her felt very calm and detached from the scene at Marion's apartment. Her emotions had been numbed as thoroughly as novocaine deadened one's mouth at the dentist. She knew the numbness would soon wear off, and the pain would still be there, throbbing away. But for the moment she was able to get into her pickup and drive away.

She considered what she should do. She had the weekend off and it seemed a pity to waste it. She could do some shopping at the new malls, but she didn't need anything. She could check into a motel and go to the bars tonight. But she had not been to the bars at all since she and Marion had met. The bars had moved. That whole area near Washington Avenue, Wade had said, had been leveled for urban renewal. Lee had no idea where the new bars were.

What was she going to do, walk up to someone and ask where the gay bars were? Maybe some women could carry that off, but Lee didn't think she could. Besides, she didn't want to go to a bar. She wanted what she no longer had. For a moment the pain came back, but she shoved it aside. She found herself driving out of the city. She didn't really want to go back home, but she didn't want to do anything else, either.

When she reached town, she turned the truck down the street where Les and Wade lived. It was an instinctive seeking out of the only two people she knew who would listen and perhaps understand what she was feeling.

Les answered the door, dressed in his purple work vest.

"You're getting ready to leave for work," Lee said. "I shouldn't have come."

"Of course you should have come. What's wrong?" Les knew something was wrong. Lee looked crushed and bereft. He took her arm and propelled her into the house.

"Hi!" Wade said, coming lightly down the stairs, fastening his white shirt as he came. "What's wrong?" he asked too.

"It's... Marion has... somebody else."

"Oh, no," Les said, his face showing his concern. "Is it... serious?"

"Very." Lee felt the numbness wearing off now. The pain was there sharp and new.

Les awkwardly put his arms around Lee and hugged her wordlessly. Wade patted her shoulder. "You'll find somebody else," he said meaning to comfort. But his point of reference was different than Lee's. He thought in terms of new sexual encounters in bars, and Lee thought of cozy warmth in bed.

Les watched the pain surface in Lee, and said nothing. He had felt it a little himself every time Wade got the itch to visit the bars. "Why don't you come with us down to the New Mercury?" he suggested.

"Yeah, we'll treat you to the best meal you've ever had," Wade offered. "A fine wine and some cocktails, too. You'll be our special guest."

Lee went to the New Mercury with them and let herself be installed at a small table next to the bar, close to Les and near the kitchen door so Wade could dash out now and then to bring her special treats. She ate and drank and drank some more. And when the evening was over she allowed Les and Wade to take her back to their house and tuck her into their spare bed.

Their warmth and caring helped, but it didn't remove the knowledge that what she and Marion had was over. Even now Marion and Nila were probably in bed together, Marion's face eagerly turned toward Nila.

Once she was back home on Sunday afternoon, Lee began to plan activities to keep her occupied and leave her tired at night. She welcomed the spring field work, the fence fixing, the summer haying, corn cultivating, oat harvest. All the work would hopefully have a restorative effect. Work went on even when other things ended.

CHAPTER TWELVE

It was Marsh who clued Clare in to what had happened to Lee. He heard about it from Les and Wade.

"I knew there was something wrong with her, but I could not quite figure out how to ask her about it," Marsh said when Les told him. They were sitting with Wade at the New Mercury bar late on a Saturday night after the place had closed.

"Yeah, Lee can be pretty close-mouthed sometimes," Les said. "This thing ending with Marion has really hit her hard. I wish there was something we could do."

"I think we're the wrong sex to do it," Marsh said with a grin. At twenty-four, he was a tall, lean young man with a pleasant, seemingly open face that hid a lot. His association with Les and Wade had been deliberate because he had sensed early on, even in high school, that he was like them.

"Women sure seem to get more emotionally involved," Wade said.

Marsh nodded. He thought his own response to something like that happening would be to go to a bar and find somebody else, but he was sure that would not appeal to Lee.

He watched her closely that June as he helped her with the haying. She seemed so remote and detached. *Like she's turned off her emotions*, he thought. His attempts at humor and teasing were not successful. Lee would just deliver an automatic smile that didn't reach inside.

"When do you finish graduate school?" she asked, ignoring his jests.

"Next spring," he said. "I hope this damned war ends before then. I'm not a chicken. I'd fight if I had to, but this whole thing in Vietnam just doesn't seem worth losing lives over."

"Well, you'd probably go in as an officer anyway," Lee said soberly.

"Maybe. Boy, wouldn't that be a sight?" He tried humor again. "Lieutenant Marshall Lewis. I wonder if they allow officers to carry swagger sticks? I'd be quite dashing in a uniform, anyway."

"Only lieutenant?" Lee attempted a retort. "I'd think you'd want to start as a general, at least."

"Well, General Lewis has a nice ring to it. And those little stars they put on your uniform and cap would be quite nice. Do you think they'd mind if I got some little star earrings to go with them?"

"I'm sure they'd understand," Lee said dryly, with a faint smile that wasn't up to her usual standard.

"Hey," he finally said. "I know about Marion. Les and Wade told me."

"Tattle-tales," Lee said.

"Worried about you is more like it. So am I. We clumsy males do love you, you know, in our own shy ways."

"You're all such strong, silent types."

"Well, tongue-tied sometimes, anyway." Marsh touched her arm gently. "We all want you to be happy again."

"I know. You guys are...good friends."

Later that same day Marsh helped his sister bale some hay. An idea began to form in his mind and he grinned to himself as it took shape. Here are two independent females, each farming alone, he thought. My sister is writing to George in Vietnam but I can't see how that can come to much. She's too independent to get into a marriage.

He watched Clare as she handed bales off the wagon to him to put on the elevator next to the barn. "You're getting to be a good-looking broad," he said to her. It was true. She was filling out in the right places, if you liked women. She carried her height proudly, not stooping as some tall women did. Her short brown hair curled a little around her face and, really, now that he looked at her, her face was appealing, with its short straight nose and pleasant open expression.

"Thanks, I think. Compliments from you? What do you want?" Clare asked with mock suspicion.

"Oh, nothing much. Just your life savings and your pickup for tonight," Marsh said.

"I knew there was a catch. Okay. The pickup you can have. As far as the savings, well, lots of luck. I ain't got none."

"A rich farmer like you?" Marsh reeled toward the hay elevator in surprise. "My illusions are shattered, to say nothing of my dreams for instant wealth."

"My heart bleeds for you."

"I knew it would." Speaking of bleeding hearts, he thought. Now how do I insert this tactfully into the conversation?

"I see you've been helping Lee, too."

Aha. Perfect opportunity. He nodded. "She's kind of down these days."

"Oh?" They had finished unloading the hay. Clare sat down next to her brother on the hay wagon and wiped the sweat from her face with a red bandanna handkerchief.

"Here. Let me have that, too." He wiped his face before replying. "You know she had this woman, Marion? Well, Marion is seeing someone else."

"Oh." Clare digested that information slowly. Some unidentifiable weight shifted off her and she didn't know why that should be.

"I think she could stand some cheering up," Marsh said. "I know she was really good to you when you first moved here…"

Clare nodded. "I might have fallen flat on my face without Lee's help. She was great. Maybe I'll go pay her a visit when the hay's done."

Later in June, when Clare had finished not only the hay but a trip through her corn with the cultivator, she turned her thoughts and her feet toward her neighbor. It was a warm day, but early enough in summer for the air to still be fresh.

She found Lee out back of the barn, repairing a board in the fence. "Hi. Beautiful day, isn't it?"

"It is a nice day," Lee agreed, although she hadn't noticed it until now.

"Too nice to work, I think. I'm seriously considering playing hooky." Clare smiled cheerfully at Lee, thinking, she does look different. Depressed and older somehow. She must have cared about Marion a lot.

"Are you?" Lee managed a smile. Clare sounded so eager and enthused it made her feel old in comparison.

"Want to come along with me, maybe go on a picnic?"

At first Lee was going to refuse, unable to shake off the gloom that had been with her all spring. Clare's eager cheerfulness was almost grating. But it really was a nice day, and spending it with Clare wouldn't be hard to take. "Sure," she finally said, amazed that some of the depression she'd been fighting had just lifted.

"Great." Clare seemed all energy. "Meet you out by the road in half an hour. I'll throw together some things and we can buy whatever else we want at the grocery store."

Lee watched her stride away. The athletic grace and energy of Clare's body made Lee smile.

In thirty-five minutes they were in Clare's pickup heading to town for food. They bought ham and rolls, apples and pears, got beer and a bakery treat and headed east of town.

They spread out an old blanket underneath a shady elm near a small lake. The sight of the blanket took Lee back years to their first picnic together. With a jolt she remembered her attraction to Clare and realized that Marion had been an interlude. She almost smiled as she thought of what Marion would have to say about that if she knew.

With the food, beer and idle talk, Lee felt herself relaxing in the warm sun. She closed her eyes, feeling sleepy and almost content. She realized she was healing from Marion and Nila, the wound no longer so fresh and sore. It was possible to think of them together without as much pain. It was even possible to wonder how they were. Lee realized she wished them well.

Watching Lee doze in the sun, one arm over her eyes, Clare was glad she had thought of the picnic. Lee had looked so morose that at first Clare had not been sure she should bother her. Clare knew she'd probably sounded too bouncy and cheerful, but she hadn't known how else to react. I couldn't just go up to her and say: I'm sorry it didn't work out with Marion and gee, it's funny we never discussed her. Well, at least Lee looks more relaxed now, Clare thought, settling down next to her on the blanket.

"You're getting some gray," she said involuntarily.

Lee opened her eyes and smiled. "Well, I am thirty-four."

"Getting to be an old lady," Clare said, teasingly.

"Yeah, just about over the hill."

"The gray hair suits you. It's kind of distinguished."

"Well, thanks. I think." Lee was surprised to find an interest in Clare stirring again. "If it was your brother saying that I'd be ready to duck for an insult."

"Marsh does have a pretty ready wit," Clare agreed. "But I'm not my brother."

"No. Even I can tell the difference. You're much better looking."

"Good thing he's not here. He'd be crushed."

"I doubt it somehow," Lee said dryly.

૨ઙ

The picnic was the first of many things Lee found herself doing with Clare that summer and fall of 1966. It was pleasant to take in a movie, go to an auction, shop together in Eau Claire. Lee was struck by how attractive Clare had grown. At twenty she had been tall and gawky, endearingly so, Lee thought with a smile. Now she was tall, filled-out, more assured and definitely beautiful to Lee, with her short brown hair still making her look younger than her mid-twenties. Her eyes sparkled with wit and humor. Her face was still open and revealing, but its gentle expression was part of a beauty that went much deeper.

All of Lee's old feelings were being rekindled, although Lee knew she shouldn't allow that to happen. She's still writing to George Hansen in Vietnam, she reminded herself. That's his class ring she wears around her neck. But it was easy to forget about George and dismiss his importance to Clare.

"Boy, am I glad that's done," Clare was saying to Lee and to Orrin Grimes. "It was so muddy in the fields this fall, I thought you'd never be able to chop the corn for me."

"Well, I got you both done," Orrin said, pleased himself to be through with their corn. "It's been a hard fall to get work done, let me tell you. I still have 150 acres of corn to chop for other people."

"Helps when you have good equipment," Lee said, unable to keep her eyes off Clare, unable to stop at this most inopportune moment the feelings of pride and attraction from surfacing. I'm in a bad way, she thought.

"You sure have that," Clare said. "A new John Deere tractor with a cab and a new Gehl chopper. Boy, you guys must be doing okay."

"It's the custom work that makes it possible," Orrin said. "Here comes the school bus. What do you want to bet it's going to stop here, if Butch sees the John Deere in your yard?"

"No bets." She knew ten-year-old Butch was already driving the tractor and helping in the barn. A chance to ride home with his dad on their newest purchase would not be missed if Butch could help it.

The bus stopped at the end of Clare's driveway and soon a short red-haired boy dashed around in front of it.

"Hi," Butch said shyly, his freckled-face turned already to the John Deere. "Can I drive it home, Dad?"

"Well, just ignore us all," Orrin said good-humoredly. "You can ride with me. I might let you drive a little."

"Great." Butch smiled shyly at the women and ran off to climb up on the large green tractor.

"I think you might have a farmer there," Lee said.

"Could be. He's eager now. Trouble is, when they get big enough to really help, then they aren't interested anymore," Orrin said. "But I hope he'll want to farm."

"I think he might," Clare said. She handed Orrin a check for his work in her fields.

"Thanks, both of you," Orrin said. He pocketed Clare's check along with the one Lee had brought over. "See you both when it's time to pick cob corn."

"I can't believe it's fall already," Clare said, watching as Orrin Grimes and his son drove out of her yard.

"I know. Seems like the summer went really fast." For Lee it had gone too fast, every moment she spent with Clare precious.

≥≈

Clare was writing frequently to George. She had not mentioned Lee in her letters. Somehow she knew George would not like to hear about the time she spent with her neighbor.

He had signed on for a second tour of duty in Vietnam but was regretting it, even though he'd been promoted to Master Sergeant. He was going to get out of the Air Force as soon as he could, maybe because from where he sat NCO stood for no-chance-outside.

It's a dead-end thing, he said in a letter. *I'll be back home next year by Christmas. Then we need to settle things between us. What I would really like is for us to get married. Would you be willing to take a partner in your farm? I'll have some money saved that I could put in it. I think about you a lot over here and I miss you. Think about it and I hope you'll say yes.*

Clare put off replying to George about his proposal. It was flattering in a way to know there was a handsome guy in the service who wanted to marry her, but she didn't think she was ready for marriage yet. There was plenty of time yet before she needed to give him a firm reply.

≥≈

That time evaporated though, in days of work. The letters from George now demanded an answer. Clare felt confused, and she took her bewilderment to Lee.

"You're my closest friend," Clare said. "I don't know what to do. I can't decide whether I should marry George when he gets out of the Air Force."

Lee sighed. Decision time was here for her, too. "I can't tell you what to do about that. That has to be your decision."

"I guess it's time I got married and settled down," Clare mused. "I'm not getting any younger, and I think I'd like to have children."

Lee listened with hidden pain. During the last year she had been feeling optimistic, buoyed by the regularity of Clare's company, and the frequent little touches Clare gave her. Now she felt pushed into making a declaration she wasn't sure Clare would want to hear.

"I don't think George is right for you," she began.

"Why?" Clare was watching her closely. They were standing in Lee's kitchen, at the sink, where Clare had been helping Lee peel potatoes and carrots for a stew.

Lee gestured with her knife. "He just isn't. I can't explain it..." Yes, you can, she thought. Tell her what you feel. Tell her that ordinary girlfriends aren't as close as we've become.

What Lee felt was in her eyes and on her face. She put down the paring knife and tentatively put her hand on Clare's shoulder, ready to remove it if Clare flinched away.

For an instant Clare felt the hand of love touch her and she covered Lee's hand with her own, in an impulsive expression of a feeling she had never fully acknowledged. She felt Lee's hand tighten, heard her sigh, felt rather than saw Lee lean closer.

And then all of the neighborhood, the church parishoners, her high school girlfriends, and the entire local community seemed to rise up in Clare's mind and condemn her. She could see her mother sighing and shaking her head, her dad gruffly disapproving. Panic and fear made her wrench away from Lee.

"I can't. I'm not like that, Lee." In a haze of pain and fear she could see Lee's stricken open face. In slow motion she saw Lee's hand fall to her side and then reach out again toward her.

"Clare, look, I'm sorry, but that's how I feel. I care about you. I thought..."

"No. Not like that. I think I'd better go." Clare could not bear to see Lee so nakedly open, so vulnerable to hurt.

"Can't we talk about this? "

Clare shook her head. "There's nothing to say."

"There's everything," Lee said. "Don't turn away from me. I know you feel something for me. I've felt it."

"We were friends. That's all. Friends."

"And now we're not? Because I touched you."

"I can't deal with this. I really can't." Clare walked to the door. She knew she was hurting Lee but she couldn't help it. Her whole self image was at stake here. She couldn't be like Lee, not for all the tea in China.

❧

Shortly after the New Year in 1968, the local paper carried the announcement of the forthcoming marriage of Clare Lewis to George Hansen. Lee read it without surprise. She had made no attempt to contact Clare since the scene in her kitchen, nor had Clare come across the road to see her.

It's over, she thought bleakly. Whatever we had is gone and I'm back where I was before. Alone. Damn. It hurts, even if Clare and I were never... That part of it may be important, but it's not all there is. The sharing was so nice.

Throughout the spring Lee buried herself in the farm work, just as she had after the breakup with Marion. This was worse, though, she thought, because she could see Clare from across the road, at work on her own farm. Or the time she'd run into Clare in the grocery store, pushing her cart down the canned goods aisle. Lee's heart was beating faster and her breathing tightened, as she waited for Clare to look up from her grocery list.

"Hi," Clare managed to say, ducking her head away from Lee.

"Hi, yourself." Lee stared at her, willing Clare to make eye contact, but Clare was off down the aisle, pushing her cart fast.

Lee had not failed to notice the diamond engagement ring on Clare's finger. I can't believe she'll go through with it, she thought.

Marsh came home for the wedding in July. His first stop after unpacking his suitcase was at Lee's. She greeted him with a hug. "You're getting taller, if that's possible."

"No, just broader. There aren't any hay bales to tote in New York. Manage okay without me this year?"

"It was tough, let me tell you," Lee informed him. "I found a high school boy, one of the Nelson kids, to help out. He helped over at Clare's too."

"Ah, yes. My sister, the bride-to-be. Do you see anything of her?"

"No." Lee's answer was a flat statement.

"I haven't stopped there yet. But my folks are so delighted that their little girl is settling down and marrying, it's almost disgusting. Mom's fluttering around, talking on the phone about dresses and shoes and bouquets. Dad holds up George as the ultimate example of the red-blooded American male, complete with military service record."

"Where is George? I haven't seen him yet."

"The groom is still en route, I understand. He got his very honorable discharge from the Air Force back in May, but he's been seeing the good old USA before settling down. Sort of a last fling or something."

"Isn't that nice?" Lee said sarcastically. "You men always have to have your last flings. While the women stay home and try on their wedding dresses."

"Hey, don't stick me in the same category with George," Marsh protested. "I'm having flings but not like that. And I doubt if my sister has been spending much time trying on her outfit."

To her mother's dismay, Clare had indeed not been spending time worrying about her clothes for the wedding. "I wish you'd show more interest," Eve complained. "That nice Marsha Henderson Parker is home and wants to give a shower for you. All your old girlfriends will be there."

"I know. It's nice of her. But I'm busy, Mom. There's so much to do if I'm going to be gone for a week after the wedding."

Clare went to the bridal shower and endured the endless fittings for her dress.

She did these things in a mist of unreality. It was hard to realize these preparations were for her own wedding. Perhaps it will seem less unreal when George gets here, she reasoned. She had spoken with George on the phone several times since his discharge in May. He was in Spokane, then Los Angeles and Las Vegas, Denver, and New Orleans when he called. The calls were brief and unsatisfying. Now that she had decided on the marriage, she wanted George home. He finally arrived a week before the wedding, driving unannounced into her yard right after morning chores. He found her in the milk house, sanitizing her milking equipment.

"How's the farmer?" he asked, grinning at her in the doorway.

"George!" She gave him a spontaneous hug.

The changes that had begun when he'd left had, if any-thing, deepened. Physically he was broader, and there were new lines on his face. His smile was humorless, far from the innocent, shy grins she remembered.

And he was cynical, bitter about Vietnam and the growing war protests in the United States. "I spent the best years of my life over there, doing what I thought I should do, and I come home and find I'm practically a criminal."

He was rough and more demanding in bed. Their first innocent explorations of each other seemed a long time ago. Clare lay beside him in her new double bed and listened to him snore, feeling confused. This new George was not the man she had expected to marry.

It must be Vietnam, she decided. He'll be okay once he's been home for awhile. Her misgivings grew in the week before the wedding. They were out in her yard, regarding the exterior of the farm house one day.

"It needs paint," George decided.

"I know. I haven't had money or time, though, to do it."

"I'll get some paint. I want it to look good. A nice yellow will do," he said.

"I don't like yellow," Clare protested.

"Well, I do," George said. "And I'm the one who's going to paint it yellow."

It was a small thing, she knew, but it left Clare upset.

George's attention was now on the house across the road. "She keeps it neat, I'll give her that," he said, a strange tight look on his face.

"Yes, she does," Clare agreed, remembering too vividly the last time she was in Lee's house.

"You spent a lot of time with her, I heard."

"For awhile I did, yes."

"I don't like queers. Saw enough of them in the service." His face reflected his dislike. "She try anything with you?"

"Not really," Clare said casually, as casually as she could, thinking with pain of the destroyed friendship. I miss her, she thought. I miss not being able to share things with her. But I couldn't be what she wanted. I just couldn't.

ૐ

Marsh stopped back in at Lee's the day before his sister's wedding. "The big rehearsal is tonight," he said.

"That's exciting."

"Yeah, I can tell you're thrilled to bits. I'm just an usher so my part isn't too much in need of rehearsing."

"I thought you'd be asked to be an attendant."

"Nope, George has too many brothers. I guess there was a big debate over which three should get the honor as it was." Marsh shrugged. "I was just as happy to stay out of that."

"How's Clare?" Lee asked the question casually, but Marsh answered it with deliberate detail.

"Looking harrassed and frazzled, if you ask me. She hardly had time today to do more than hug me and say hi. Too busy with some last-minute fitting with Mom and trying to tie up loose ends on her farm."

"I can imagine."

"Maybe too busy to let herself think about what she's getting into."

"I suppose George isn't so bad..."

"Not if you like them big and handsome and sort of mean-looking. He's changed, Lee. Not for the better, if you ask me. I don't know what Vietnam does to guys, but I don't think it did anything good for George. I've seen him a couple of times and well..." Marsh shrugged. "I wish my sister wasn't marrying him."

"So do I," Lee said, and the pain of knowing Clare really was marrying George was plain for Marsh to see.

"Hey. That bad, huh?"

"Yeah. That bad. I'm a silly old fool, I suppose, thinking maybe it could have been different..."

"I thought it, too," Marsh admitted. "I don't suppose Clare would suddenly change her mind?"

"I doubt it. Seems unlikely. I'm not on her list of popular people right now. I've hardly seen her, but she avoids looking directly at me when we meet."

"I guess you didn't get a wedding invite, huh?" Marsh tried to inject some humor into the conversation.

"Not likely. I wouldn't go anyway, if I had."

"I wish you would go. At least I could wink at you now and then when handling all those Hansens gets too painful. There must be hundreds of them. Besides, my sister is going to need you someday. Maybe not right away, but someday she's going to wake up."

"What's that got to do with going to her wedding?"

"Probably not much, but come anyway. I'll invite you. And what would people think if you didn't come?" Marsh's voice cleverly mimicked his mother. "And George won't turn down a gift. He's greedy. Gets more excited than Clare about the loot she brings home from those awful showers."

"If you think I'm giving George a present, you can think again."

"Not even a little roach poisoning to sprinkle on his cereal?" Marsh teased.

"Well, maybe some rat poison," Lee said. "Arsenic for the asshole."

"Razor blades in his favorite candy."

Lee was grateful for Marsh's company. He had a sense of humor that verged on the bizarre, but it helped to be able to joke like this.

"My poor sister," Marsh said. "I pity her. I really do. Marriage has always been preached to her. I heard it so many times at home. And she caved in."

"Probably because I scared her."

"Well, don't go blaming yourself. There aren't many who can stand up to the pressures society puts on people."

"Why do I have the hunch you're getting political?"

"I do hang out with some radical characters these days. Must be rubbing off."

"I wish a little would rub off on me. Maybe I could accept this better."

"You're doing fine. Put on a happy face tomorrow and come to her wedding."

"I don't think I can do that." Lee's face was bleak.

"Sure you can. People around here do talk, you know. If you don't come, what will they say?"

"She's suffering from a broken heart?"

"Spurned lesbian stays home. Makes a great newspaper headline, doesn't it?"

Lee smiled weakly. "That's kind of how I feel. Spurned."

"She'll see the error of her ways someday," Marsh said in a reassuring voice.

"Maybe," Lee said, thinking there was no way she was going to spend her life waiting around for a married woman to leave her husband. Without her being able to prevent them, tears burned out of her eyes and down her cheeks. If it had been anyone but Marsh there, she would have been mortified.

"Oh, gee," Marsh said. He put his arms around her and felt Lee relax into them. He could feel her body shake with sobs, hear them muffled against his shoulder. He held her silently until her crying quieted.

II

INTERLUDE

September 1982

The funeral for George Hansen will be held at 2:00 p.m. at St. Paul's. The local radio station carried the announcement of the funeral and described the accident that killed him for three solid days. Clare heard the announcement again and again as she did chores. It was as though she had to hear about the accident from an official source to make herself believe that it had happened. She could have turned off the radio anytime, but instead she let it tell her what she already knew so vividly.

On that Friday afternoon in late September she and George had fought, and he had stormed out of the barn and climbed the chute of a recently filled silo. She had been too angry at him and his stubbornness to warn him to be careful. She had thought only of her rage at George for insisting on spending money they did not have on a new tractor they did not need.

Then he had come falling back down the chute. There had been a horrible dull echoing clatter as his body descended sixty feet, bumping ladder rungs all the way down. The enclosed chute had expelled his body, dumping it onto the hard ground. Even then, she had not thought about odorless, colorless silo gas.

For an instant Clare had stood in mute horror. Then she had run to him, feeling for a pulse and then, running as fast as she could into the barn where there was a phone, somehow she had dialed the right numbers. An ambulance had appeared quickly, but it had already been too late.

Silo gas is a sneaky silent enemy on farms. It lurks just above the surface of the silage or haylage in a newly filled silo. Sometimes it stays around for weeks and can overpower its victims with every breath they take, rendering them unconscious. They then either slump to the surface of the silage and lie there until discovered or they fall, as George did, back down long silo chutes.

Leaving the top door open above the filled level of the silo is often enough to keep silo gas at bay, a simple life-saving precaution. George had not done it because George was one of those farmers who ridicule the idea that a silo can be a deadly place.

Shocked, with the sound of his falling still echoing in her ears, Clare felt the world around her shift and wobble. The next days would be endured on reserves of adrenaline. In addition to the shock of the death, there was the ritual of the funeral to go through. In rural Wisconsin that ritual is very prescribed.

It starts with the undertaker who, if he knows his business, will quickly become a sturdy figure to guide the survivors through the maze of proper etiquette. Clare knew the local funeral director through her own attendance at dozens of funerals over the years. He had a sense of humor and what seemed like genuine compassion.

The ambulance took George's body directly to his mortuary and Clare followed, literally stunned, driving automatically. She knew she was in what was called shock, knew she still did not believe the accident had happened. She felt relieved to have an actual concrete thing she needed to do.

The demands on her that first afternoon were light. She entered the mortuary uncertainly, standing forlorn in the large foyer, hypnotized by the small desk stand where soon, she thought, people would be entering their names in a guest book for George.

James Ludgate came quickly to greet her. He took both her hands in his and said, meeting her eyes: "I'm sorry." It felt to Clare like he was sorry.

She allowed herself to be gently led off to the right to his office where comfortable rose-upholstered chairs formed an intimate area in front of his desk. He poured her some coffee in a good china cup, saw her settled with it in one of the chairs. She watched his lean wiry body in its somber well-cut suit, watched the capable hands that would soon be handling George's dead body and felt somehow reassured.

"Well, this is very unexpected," he said as he sat down with his own cup of coffee. He leaned forward toward her as he spoke. "There was nothing the emergency crew could do?"

Clare shook her head. "He was just...dead."

"Excuse me. Of course they did what they could. It's just that this has shaken me, too. I've seen you and George for so many years, coming here for other people. You're young yet. I find something like this much harder to deal with than the older people who die."

His words set the right tone for Clare. To know that it was not easy sometimes to do what he did was oddly comforting to her.

They went over George's obituary that first afternoon. James Ludgate took down the facts quietly and accurately, as though they had all the time in the world. He arranged for the funeral to be held on Monday at St. Paul's. He set up the visitation for Sunday afternoon and evening.

"That means I need you to come in early as you can tomorrow morning and decide on the casket," he said matter-of-factly. "Do you have someone you would want to come with you?"

Clare shook her head. She supposed she could ask her parents but they would be so upset she knew they would upset her more. And she did not want George's brothers or, God forbid, his mother. If Marsh were here, she thought... But he's not. Then from somewhere inside, deep buried, came the thought of who she wanted.

She nodded at last. "Yes. I'll bring someone with me." If she'll come, she thought.

They went on to discuss flowers, the organist and soloist, the minister and the clothes George would be buried in. Clare would bring them in the morning. She went to her car feeling as though she were sleepwalking, dimly aware of so many things to do. People needed to be called, and there was all the regular farm work.

She did the calling first. She hoped she would get George's dad, but it was his mother who answered. It was not easy to break the news.

Mabel had to have it repeated several times before she could realize that one of her sons had died. Then she said, as though it explained his sudden and premature death, "I told George over and over he shouldn't have married you." With that, she burst into tears and slammed down the phone.

Clare ignored the sharp hurt she felt from her mother-in-law's words and dialed another number. Lee answered on the second ring. Told of George's sudden death, she simply said: "I saw the ambulance."

In the old days before Clare had married George, Lee would have gone across the road to find out, but the marriage had ended that simple solution. She had learned early that she was not welcome.

"Of course I'll come with you," she said promptly when Clare made her request. She didn't hesitate at all, although it was even longer than the fourteen years of Clare's marriage since they had been close. Lee could still hear Marion saying, "When she needs you, you'll come running." Lee guessed Marion had been right about that.

"Do you need some help over there with chores and things?"

"Would you? I haven't thought... There seems to be so much to do...and I haven't told Chad. He's not back from school yet."

"I'll come over right away." Lee had her own chores, but the work connected with her thirty cows was much less than that involved with Clare and George's eighty-cow milking herd. And Chad was going to be a shocked young boy. Lee knew he and his dad had been close.

By the time Lee got over there, Chad was home, and it was obvious that his mother had just told him.

"You mean Dad is dead?" He was almost shouting. "He fell out of the silo? Dad wouldn't do that. He's strong. He wouldn't fall." His face revealed his anguish. "You...somebody...pushed him!" With that thirteen-year-old Chad ran out of the house.

Lee thought the boy was a lot like his mother must have been at his age. Tall already and gawky, he had an open face that would stay young long after others his age had matured.

Clare watched her son run away. The words he had spoken simply bounced off her. Shock was useful, she told herself. "That's twice I've been accused of being responsible for George's death." She said it aloud, unthinkingly.

"Who was the other? His mother?"

Clare nodded. She brushed a weary hand through her short brown hair. At forty-two, she had no gray yet and her face was unlined. Lee was aware that she was starting to show her own age. Her fifty years had brought definition to her face and more gray to her dark brown hair.

"I'm sorry," she said, meaning it. She was sorry.

"We fought over a stupid tractor he wanted to buy just before he went up the silo."

"That's not a very pleasant last memory," Lee said.

"No, but it's fairly typical of my life with George. We had some good times, but there were bad ones too."

"I know," Lee said and she did. It wasn't possible to live next to the Hansens' farm without being aware of their ups and downs. Voices carry in the country.

"It's funny," Clare said. "James Ludgate asked me if I had anyone I wanted to help me tomorrow and I couldn't think of anyone but you, and yet it's been a long time since we've even talked together for this long."

"Over fourteen years," Lee said. She spoke matter-of-factly, as though the years had not been of much consequence.

"Since I decided to marry George," Clare said. "But you came. Thank you."

⁊➧

Word spread quickly. Many farm people had CB scanners which picked up police and ambulance calls. When the calls were of interest, the listeners often picked up their own phones to spread the word. By the time Lee and Clare had fed the Hansen herd of cattle, the first dishes of sympathy food began to arrive.

Stella Grimes brought over a hotdish and date bars and a huge sympathetic hug for Clare. Lee's sister-in-law, Linda Collins, brought in a loaf of homemade bread, a big cabbage salad, and sugar cookies. A steady stream of neighbors and family members brought food all through the evening. Lee had to take some of it home because Clare's refrigerator was overflowing.

The outpouring was a generous, nonverbal show of support and sympathy. It was also practical because Clare would have no time over the next three days to worry about cooking. Eating would be secondary, her hunger gone, but she would eat because so many kind people had brought her food.

Chad was a worry to Clare. He did not show up again until she was milking. Then he scuffled aimlessly through the barn, staring accusingly at her. His lost hurt look made her want to hug him to her but she knew any attempt to do so would be rebuffed.

-113-

"You need to eat something," she told him after chores.

"I'm not hungry." He picked at Stella's lasagna.

"I don't suppose you are." Clare hadn't been able to force much food into her own mouth. She reached a hand out to touch his shoulder. He jerked away. "Hey, I know it's awful, Chad. But it happened."

"Yeah. I'm going to bed." His averted face told Clare he must be crying.

In the morning when she needed to go to the funeral home she took Chad to her brother's place, hoping Harry or Diane could provide the comfort Chad would not accept from her.

James Ludgate greeted Clare and Lee with warm hand-shakes and soothing words, then he led them through the financial aspects of the funeral. After outlining the costs, he led them out of his office and down to a section of the basement that he had set up as a display room for caskets.

This was the part Clare had been dreading. Her dread was visible, and Lee gave her hand a reassuring squeeze. She'd been through this before and knew it was off-putting to suddenly enter an entire room full of empty open caskets with price tags on them.

"Good heavens," Clare said softly as she walked into the room. Then, something strange happened. She began to price-shop, almost as though it was just another purchase.

"Most people settle in that range," Ludgate said helpfully as Clare returned to the medium-priced caskets. And it was a help. It was important somehow to do the right thing: to be neither too cheap nor too ostentatious in selecting George's coffin. She settled at last on a bronze-colored steel casket.

James Ludgate approved the choice. Clare and Lee left soon after meeting the minister who would officiate at the funeral. The morning had been almost therapeutic, Clare decided. In an understated, easy way both Ludgate and the minister had led them through a discussion of death and dying. They had matter-of-factly accepted what she told them of Chad's reaction and offered help and support.

At the viewing the next afternoon, Clare began the long process of receiving handshakes and sympathy. She responded politely to each and every person, including George's mother, Mabel. In public Mabel tended to gush artificially over this daughter-in-law she detested. Now she gushed and wept in equal parts, and Clare bore it stoically.

George looked, well, dead. People came by the open casket and commented on how much he looked like he was sleeping. This was almost an expected remark and it covered up an awkward spot. What else do you say when viewing a dead body? Others said a variation of it: he looks so natural. Clare had said it herself many times at funerals. Now she heard it again and again.

Harry and his wife, Diane, brought Chad with them in midafternoon. The boy stood and stared down at his father in the bronze casket. There was a spray of flowers on the casket over the closed part that hid George's legs. The flowers had a ribbon around them that said DAD in big gold letters. Clare had bought the spray for Chad. Now he eyed it, and his face screwed up as if he might cry. Instead he said, "It looks crummy."

He shook off his mother's comforting hand and went back to Harry and Diane. Diane shrugged at Clare. Chad allowed his aunt to place both her hands on him in comfort. That hurt, but Clare had to acknowledge that her son had always been closer to his dad than to her.

All afternoon and through the evening friends and neighbors and relatives came to view George's body and offer their condolences to Clare and to George's parents and brothers. And to Chad. The Hansen brothers and their wives, like many other rural families, brought their children to funeral visitations at a young age. They were exposed to death young and maybe that was a good thing, Clare thought. Not that Chad's attendance at other visitations seemed to be helping him to deal with this one. Maybe there was nothing that could help.

When the last of the visitors had trickled out, James Ludgate came quietly over to Clare. "I'm going to close the casket now for the night," he said, making Clare think of someone announcing he was going to cover the bird cage or put the cat out. She choked back an hysterical giggle. Ludgate misread the giggle as a sob and patted her arm.

Mabel Hansen moved as if on cue to stand in front of the casket. Her huge sobs filled the quiet room while her husband and sons shifted uncomfortably. Clare knew she should go to the woman and put an arm around her shoulders in comfort, but she couldn't make herself do it.

Instead she stood dry-eyed. Chad looked at her with disgust. "At least Grandma cares," he said. Aghast, Clare stared at her son. In her shock, she was holding herself together to endure the funeral ritual. I care, she wanted to say, but to say it would be to unleash a tidal wave of emotions: loss, hurt, fear, and pain.

Ludgate smoothly inserted himself into the heavy silence following Chad's remark. Brushing past Chad, he went to comfort Mabel Hansen with soft words and a hand on her arm. He folded the soft fabric of the casket liner over George's upper body and shut the lid, making a small ceremony.

"Well," Mabel sighed. "I guess we better go."

"Yes." Clare looked toward her son. "Coming home with me tonight?"

Chad eyed her, Ludgate's whispered words fresh in his mind: "Be kind to your mother. This isn't easy for her, either." Too full of angry pain to head the words yet, he shook his head. "I wanna go with Harry and Diane."

"All right." Clare was tired, drained from the hours of being on public display, and she knew arguing would accomplish nothing. She would try to talk with Chad after the funeral.

Wearily she drove herself home. There had been no time to worry that the chores were going well in Lee's capable hands and those of the neighbors and Hansen brothers who had come by to help. Now she was relieved to see the barn lights were off but surprised to find her house lights on.

Lee was sitting at the big kitchen table, drinking coffee with Marsh. Clare felt suddenly weak with relief. She had wanted Marsh to be here and here he was. "I couldn't get you on the phone. How did you know to come?" she asked, clinging to him.

"I didn't. I just happened to come, that's all. I'm sorry, Clare. It must have been horrible."

"Oh, God." Clare closed her eyes seeing again the scene at the silo. She held on to her brother tightly.

෨

The day of George's funeral was warm and bright. Clare and Marsh came early and gathered with the other chief mourners in the church basement. They sat numbly as they waited to be herded up to the pews at the front of the church.

George's flower-bedecked, flag-draped coffin stood in the center of the aisle. Off to the right was gathered the entire Hansen family. Cousins, brothers, nieces, nephews, aunts, and uncles of George squeezed in the pews.

Clare took in little of the service. She felt detached and unable to cry. As she listened to the muffled sobs of Mabel and the other Hansen women, she realized that Chad expected her to cry. He sat watching her in stony silence.

She rose automatically from the pew at the right time and followed George's casket out of the church. Chad and Marsh came after her. Then came Mabel and George's father and the brothers and their wives, all filing silently out behind the casket. All waited as the pall bearers placed it in the hearse. At the grave a group of VFW members raised rifles and fired a salute to a fallen comrade, and the minister said a few words. People filed back to their cars, fallen leaves crunching under their feet.

Back at the church basement, the mourners felt released to talk and laugh while they ate a lunch. After all, funerals were social occasions. They provided a chance to see people one probably did not see any other time, except maybe at weddings. It was an opportunity to visit, to generate a feeling of warmth and goodwill that inspired many folks to say, "It's such a pity we only get together at weddings and funerals," not realizing those occasions were the only times they had anything in common to get together for.

Folks finally drifted home. The church ladies rattled dishes in the kitchen as they cleaned up. Clare made her own exit, clutching a neat zipped plastic pouch full of sympathy cards.

Chad came with her this time. He came reluctantly, but she had insisted. She felt helpless and futile around him, knowing the loss of his father was severe and realizing that somehow she would have to make it up to him.

Marsh had hugged her and gone home to their folks, promising to come back the next day. "I'll help however I can," he told her.

She had seen Lee, just a glimpse of her in the church during the service. Now as she drove into her farmyard, Clare heard one of the silo unloaders running and a faint smile lit her face. Lee was here helping.

PART TWO

1968-1982

CHAPTER THIRTEEN

She had felt him start. "George?" Clare said sleepily. She reached out and turned on the light on the bedside table and shut off the alarm clock. "George, what are you doing on the floor?"

"What the hell kind of alarm clock is that? I thought..." Clare knew what he thought. He'd been having these dreams ever since he'd come back from Vietnam. Now he shook his head as if to clear it, and as he got up off the floor Clare could see that his body was shining with sweat. His teeth rattled as he got back into bed beside her.

She pulled the covers back up over him. He snuggled under them next to her and she pulled him against her, feeling his body shake. His eyes were shut tightly, but moisture leaked from under the lids.

"Would it help to talk about it?"

"I don't know. I don't think I can yet. I never wanted anybody to see me like this..."

"It's okay."

"Who but a dairy farmer would bring an alarm clock along on their honeymoon?" George attempted to make light of the terror the clock had brought back for him.

"It was your idea, remember? You were the one who wanted to get up at dawn and go fishing."

"Oh, yeah. That's right. It seemed like a good idea at the time..." He burrowed in closer to her.

By the end of their week-long stay on a Canadian lake, Clare knew that she would not be ending her marriage abruptly, as she had wanted to do on her wedding day. More of the old George had appeared the longer they were together, and his nightmares about Vietnam had formed a bond between them.

"You're the only one who knows I have these damned dreams," he told her. "Maybe I came back to normal life too quick. I keep expecting somebody to take a shot at me."

"Maybe if you can talk about it, they'll go away."

"Yeah. I wish there were some other vets around home I could talk to." But he sounded hopeless, and she doubted he'd try to contact anyone.

"Well, maybe work will help. The second crop hay will be ready as soon as we get back."

George chuckled. "Spoken like a true farmer. Well, I guess I get to find out what farming is like again. It's been awhile. You married me to get cheap labor, I knew it."

"What other reason could there be?"

"You know, sometimes I can't really think of any. I'm kind of a liability. Likely to throw you to the floor in the middle of the night thinking there's an attack going on." He made a deprecating gesture.

It was difficult for Clare, when they returned to her farm, to reconcile this private image of George with the public one he displayed to other people. He almost strutted around the farm when the milk hauler was there. He bragged about how "my" cows were doing. He did not consult Clare when machinery salesmen came and wanted to talk to the "boss man."

In the eyes of the local community he was the farmer now and she was the wife, even though the farm was hers. Clare could not believe it, but magically, with the appearance of a male on the scene, the farm had ceased to be hers.

The ironic part, Clare thought, was that George knew so little. He could talk farming by the hour, but his practical knowledge was limited. He seemed to believe farming involved driving powerful equipment.

Cleaning pens and planning the breeding and feeding of the animals, balancing the cows' rations to make the best use of home-grown feeds wasn't farming in George's eyes.

But as Clare knew only too well, these things were more important to the financial health of a dairy farm than any piece of equipment. Shiny new equipment was nice, but crops could be planted and harvested with what they owned already.

George couldn't see it that way, and hardly anything could make them so furious at each other.

"Even the queer has a new Allis Chalmers D-15," George shouted.

"She earned it," Clare countered. "The 'M' is good enough."

"It's old and it's gonna wear out someday. What then?"

"It'll last a lot longer if you don't treat it like it's a stock car down at the local speed pit," Clare flashed.

"For God's sake, you don't know anything. I saw a nice new International 656 down at the dealer's today."

"We can't afford it."

"I wish you'd wise up. You don't save to buy a tractor. You buy it and let the tractor pay for itself by being used."

"We still can't afford it..."

"Look, if the queer can afford a new tractor..."

"Let's get one thing straight," Clare said between clenched teeth. "Don't call Lee Collins 'the queer.' I'm sick of it. She's a good person. She's our neighbor. Don't call her a queer."

Startled at her own vehemence on the issue, Clare waited for George's response. Where did that come from? she wondered. I didn't know I felt so strongly.

He was silent a moment. When he spoke his voice was not angry. "Okay," he said. "Now about that tractor..."

"You're impossible. Talk about a one-track mind..."

Clare found she could stand firm on money matters, even though she knew it irritated George that she held the purse strings. Both their names now appeared on the milk check, but Clare was the one who paid the routine bills and kept the farm accounts.

George did not mind her doing those things because most farm wives did them. It hurt, though, to have to admit he couldn't deal on equipment because he had to ask his wife if it was okay. Most guys used that as an excuse when they did not want to make a decision, and the machinery salesman was pressing them. "I got to ask the wife," they would say, but with them everybody knew it was just an excuse. George felt everybody knew when he said it that it was true.

When Clare informed him she was pregnant, shortly before Christmas of 1968, George practically danced. You're sure? That's great. That's really great." George hugged her in delight.

"Clare had been a little worried. "I didn't know how you'd feel," she told him. "We never discussed kids."

"I guess I just assumed we'd have them someday."

"I think I'm scared," Clare admitted.

"I helped deliver a baby once. In Vietnam. It was scary because we were under a mortar attack."

"Well, at least one of us is experienced," Clare said wryly. "Although I guess I've assisted at enough cow births to have some idea how to go about it."

"It'll be fine. You'll be fine," George said. "What a great Christmas present."

As Clare's pregnancy progressed, she finally gave in to George's pleas for some new machinery.

"I think this really is the right time," George insisted. "I'm going to need it if I'm going to handle both the barn chores and the crops. A bigger tractor to start with, and some better tillage equipment too."

"We'll have to get a loan," Clare said.

"Yeah. PCA probably has the best rates."

Production Credit Association was a government-backed loan agency that provided short-term and intermediate-term credit to farmers and was cheaper than commercial banks.

"We can give you credit, George," the PCA loan officer said. "You've done a good job there. No real estate debt. That's outstanding."

Clare listened as the loan officer talked on, addressing his remarks to George, praising George for a debt-free farm. She waited for George to set the man straight, to say how it had been Clare who'd paid off the loan, but he said nothing.

"We'll take a security interest in your machinery and cattle and set the loan at $10,000," the loan officer said. "I see no problems at all with this."

When they were out of the PCA office, Clare exploded. "Why did you just sit there and let him praise you for a debt-free farm? Why didn't you say something? How could you just let him assume it was you?"

"You could have said something yourself," George hedged. "Hey, it doesn't mean anything. We'll both be signing the papers."

"Darned right we will. And it does mean something. It means a lot to me. I worked hard to pay my debt. I don't like it when people assume it was done by somebody else."

"Hey, that's just how people are. Most women aren't farmers, you know."

"So that excuses it? God, that makes me mad."

"We can set him straight when we go sign the papers," George told her.

"Oh, skip it. Just skip it." Clare slammed the car door and sat in silence on the way home with angry tears filling her eyes.

They spent the ten thousand dollars in about ten minutes at the machinery dealer's, though George had spent considerably more time there earlier, examining equipment and enjoying the feel of being a buyer. He chose a used tractor in the end, but it was a late model International capable of pulling a four-bottom plow. The plow he picked was new, as was the disk. In the end they kept the old "M" as a second tractor but traded off the old three-bottom trailer plow and disk. It amazed Clare to discover that the plow she had paid $50 for at an auction was now worth $350 in trade.

The salesman wrote up the bill of sale and passed it across his desk for their inspection. Clare looked at it and passed it back.

"My name should be on this, too," she said, her voice shaking. It felt as though she had ceased to exist as anything but a pregnant wife.

The salesman's eyebrows rose, and he looked to George for confirmation.

"Yeah, her name should be there, too. She was the farmer before I came on the scene."

"Oh? That's unusual. I bet she was relieved to hand it over to you." The salesman tried for a little humor.

"She hasn't handed it to me. We're partners now, and I'm still working my way into it."

Clare looked gratefully at George.

"Well, I'm sure you'll be a big success. Really make something of the operation. This machinery you're getting will upgrade you considerably."

Later in the car going home George said, "I begin to see why you got angry at PCA. Everybody really does assume it's the man who farms."

Clare felt relief at his words. Some of her anger dissolved in knowing that George understood.

❧

In 1969 milk prices rose slowly to almost $5.00 per hundred pounds. The increase was welcome to Clare because with the note for $10,000 she worried about money more than ever. She always carefully figured monthly finances, estimated feed costs, and projected income ahead for several months. It would be tight, but she thought they could swing their payments.

It was amazing to her to think that they were paying $250 per month to PCA for machinery purchases when that amount was more than her monthly payment for the whole farm had been. But Clare also knew that it would not have been possible to buy the farm in 1969 for what she paid in 1960.

At PCA the loan officer had worked out a schedule of their assets and liabilties. The assets had increased dramatically. The farm alone was now worth $30,000, double what she had paid for it. With the machinery and cattle she and George had assets worth $50,000. Looked at in that light, a debt of $10,000 was not so bad, but it still had to be paid off.

Gradually, Clare had to turn more of the farm work over to George. She kept on milking into June, but she finally had to turn that chore over, too, because by then she was simply too big to be able to manage milking cows with any degree of comfort or safety.

She went into labor right in the middle of first crop haying. George was out in the field raking hay.

"You sure?" he said. "I'll get Nathan to help me finish this."

"I need to go in. Now."

"Oh. Right. Oops. I'd better shut off the tractor first." He fumbled nervously for the switch. "There. I'll get the car. Oh. You've got the car out."

"I thought you said you'd had experience with this."

"Not that much experience." He slammed the car door and turned the ignition key. "Oh. I guess it's already running."

In spite of the labor pains, Clare giggled. "Do you want me to drive?"

"I'll manage. I hope." George grinned sheepishly at her. "You'd think I was having the baby."

Their son was born shortly after Clare reached the hospital. It was not an easy delivery, and when it was over Clare slept exhaustedly. She woke to find George hovering over her.

"Did you get the hay in?" she asked sleepily.

"You bet. It's raining now, so it was a close thing," George said. "I saw him. He's big and kind of red-faced and ugly, but I guess most babies are at first."

Clare yawned. "Boy, I sure do understand why those heifers make such a fuss about calving."

They named the baby Chad Edward, Edward for Clare's dad and Chad because George wanted it. "I knew a guy named Chad once," he said. "I... he was killed in Vietnam."

"Oh?" Clare said inquiringly, but George didn't seem to want to tell her more, so she didn't push it.

His nightmares continued intermittently. He would thrash himself awake, drenched with sweat. Clare felt helpless, able only to offer the comfort of her arms.

"Got yourself two babies, I guess," George said after one of his bouts. "I'm sorry. I wish these damn things would go away."

"Well, at least you don't need to be burped and changed," Clare said lightly. "I wish you'd talk about it. Maybe that would help."

George just shook his head. "I can't yet."

Chad Edward was baptized at St. Paul's in July. With the entire Hansen clan present, the church was packed.

"Gee, the Hansens are multiplying like rabbits," Marsh said to Lee the next day. He had come home from New York to be one of Chad's godparents. "I felt like a sardine, packed into St. Paul's with all those Hansen grandchildren."

"Talk about a fish out of water," Lee said with a wry smile.

"Yeah. Horse of a different color or something. At least Clare seems pretty happy with the baby. And George, believe it or not, is a doting father. Feeds Chad his bottle. Changes the diapers. Goos and coos at that kid like you wouldn't believe."

George had eyed his brother-in-law with disfavor. Marsh's trim mustache and trendy clothes somehow struck a sour note with him. And Marsh's views on Vietnam did not help.

"Your brother is pretty condescending," George said to Clare. "He acts like I must be simple-minded to have gone to Vietnam, while he got out of it by going to college forever. I went because I thought it was the right thing to do, and now I'm dumb for not staying out of it."

"I'm sure he didn't mean that."

"Damned right he meant it. A lot of good guys didn't come back from there. Maybe it was a stupid war, but just because we were in it doesn't mean we're stupid, too."

"I know."

"Oh, don't humor me," George said. "And another thing. Your brother spends a lot of his time with our dear neighbor and with her que...gay male friends, doesn't he?"

"Well, sure. He and Lee go back a long way. What are you saying? Are you saying my brother is gay?"

"I wouldn't doubt it. In fact, I'd bet on it."

"I don't believe it," Clare said, but without much conviction. By the end of July, when Marsh left, she was pretty sure George was right. It explained his close relationship with Lee and with Les and Wade.

It was Marsh who told Lee in a letter about what he had missed in New York by going home for Chad's baptism. "There was a riot, believe it or not. On July 28, just before I got back, the patrons at this bar on Christopher Street, the Stonewall Inn, rioted when police did their usual harassment number. The whole thing went on for several days. You know how I hate to be left out of things. I'm sorry I missed it. All those drag queens right out there with the lesbians beating up the police. It's started a movement here for gay rights. I've joined one of the groups. I think you'll see some fireworks. It might even make mention in the papers someday."

Lee appreciated Marsh's letters and wrote her own witty replies. Through him she learned of a lesbian group called The Daughters of Bilitis which had been on the scene since 1955. She looked forward to their bimonthly magazine with its upbeat and positive view of lesbians.

Through the book reviews in the *The Ladder*, Lee learned of books with lesbian characters. Marsh was pressed into service in New York to hunt them down. The bulky packages she received from him were great sources of delight to her.

They helped to take her mind off her across-the-road neighbors. Clare's marriage seemed to be lasting, and Clare made no effort to seek Lee out. Lee felt regret for the lost friendship but knew there was no point in dwelling on it.

Her own farming operation was running smoothly. Her Jerseys milked well, and she had been slowly replacing and upgrading her machinery. The agricultural magazines Lee read talked about ensiling hay for cow feed instead of baling it. Lee began to think that might be a good idea. She knew as she got older that she was going to find it harder to handle the volume of baled hay she needed for her small herd of twenty-five milk cows.

To get the milk cows and the young stock through the winter when pasturing was impossible, she needed to cut, rake, bale, and handle between 8,000 and 10,000 bales of hay. Each bale weighed about fity pounds. That meant she had to carry and stack a total weight of 200 to 250 tons of hay. Once it was harvested and stored, it all had to be thrown down from the haymow, bale by bale, and fed to the cattle, which meant lugging the same tonnage again.

In 1970 Lee looked at the cost of building another silo for haylage. By the time she had added on the cost of harvesting equipment and another silo unloader, the total outlay was approaching $20,000.

It was twice what she'd paid for her whole farm. She knew her Jerseys couldn't support that kind of expense. Scratch that idea, she decided. I'll develop tough old muscles and hire high school kids to help. I'm not going to get bigger and add more cows just to pay for it.

Instead of the haylage idea, she looked at another option: that of buying the kind of hay baler that threw the bales into a high-sided wagon. It eliminated the need for an extra person to stack bales on the wagon as they came out.

A new baler equipped with the thrower would cost about twenty-five hundred dollars. Lee decided her present flat racks could be adapted into thrower wagons. She would do the work of building the sides herself. To make the system complete, there was a haymow conveyor system that allowed one person to unload the hay onto an elevator which carried the bales into the haymow. Lee reasoned that her herd could easily support the total cost of thirty-seven-hundred dollars and she added the new baling system in the summer of 1970.

George Hansen stood in his farmyard and watched her use it. "I see the quee... Lee got herself a new baler with a thrower," he told Clare at the noon meal that day. It was a scorching hot June day, dry enough to be out baling by eleven.

"Did she? Good for her." Clare was attempting to convince their year-old son that the spinach on his plate was actually edible.

"We should get one too. It would save a lot of time and money. We could get the hay in sooner and we wouldn't have to hire any help."

"We can't afford it," Clare said automatically.

"It wouldn't cost too much. I priced one when I was in town last week. The dealer had three brand-new basket thrower wagons he'd give me a good deal on, too." George took the spoon from Clare's hand. "Here. I'll try him for awhile. You need to clean the spinach off your face."

"How much money?" Clare wiped her face on a towel.

"Five thousand dollars for the whole package including a haymow conveyor. Hey, this stuff isn't that bad, kiddo. See.

Yum. Good stuff. If I eat it, so can you. Down the hatch, right? Ooops. Anyway, I think I can get the dealer down to forty-five-hundred dollars."

"It's too much."

"You always say that. If Lee can afford it, so can we." George gave up on the spinach and let Chad push it around his plate.

"Not this year. There's the PCA loan still to pay off. We're barely making the payments on that, and the cows just aren't doing well enough."

"I knew you were going to bring that up," George said defensively. "Just because I didn't get all of them bred back as quick as you thought they should be."

Clare shrugged. "Well, you didn't. And I still don't understand how you let so many of them get mastitis. We've got too many cows milking on three teats."

"Okay, so maybe I didn't do the best job in the barn while you were taking care of Chad. What's that got to do with upgrading the equipment?"

"The milk income is what pays for it all. Until the cows are doing better again, we can't afford new equipment." Clare wiped spinach off the table and off Chad's head.

"Okay. You're right. You do a better job than I do in the barn. You've got more patience."

"You do fine with the field work," Clare told him.

"Yeah, maybe I'm not cut out for this farming thing." George looked discouraged. "I wish we had a pipeline milking system. At least that would make the milking easier."

"We can't afford that, either."

"Yeah, I know." He pushed back his chair. "Well, back to the salt mines."

Clare watched him trudge slowly out of the kitchen. She stacked their plates and ran water to wash them. Maybe George is right, she thought. Maybe he isn't cut out for farming. Swell. We're up to thirty cows now and it's a lot of work, especially with Chad to look after too. I can't do it all alone.

CHAPTER FOURTEEN

The 1970s were an optimistic decade for agriculture. Farmers were being urged to plant more and more acres to meet the demands of the world market. A growing population in the United States with money to spend meant more demand for meat and dairy products and thus good prices to the farmer. In 1970 the price of milk was $5.12 per hundred pounds. By 1976 it had risen to a new high of $9.16. While the cost of production rose too, it did not outpace the rising income of dairy farmers. Optimism was in the air.

A new crop of university-educated agricultural experts began to be heard from. Their message to farmers was to take advantage of the market by getting bigger—expanding the herd, buying more land and bigger machinery.

The sky was the limit, these experts said. Anyone who stayed the same size was a fool. A farmer with thirty cows and one-hundred acres of land was underemployed. Double the herd size. Farming is a business.

Some of their advice was good. They advocated the use of milk testing to cull low-producing cows. They urged better sanitation to help control mastitis. But the experts did not have crystal balls, nor were they blessed with great insights into what the future might bring.

Some farmers tried to take all of the advice with a grain of salt, but many got caught up in the push for expansion. "Bigger is better" was preached so often that it was hard to ignore.

By 1976 world grain prices had fallen, but dairy prices stayed up and then went even higher. By 1978 farmers were getting $10 for a hundred pounds of milk. By 1980 the price was up to $12.67. The lower grain prices meant that dairy farmers could purchase cattle feed cheaply. Grain farmers were feeling tougher times, but the dairy sector was still riding high. While a few people urged caution, that advice got lost in the continued push for larger farms, bigger herds, and more equipment.

Lee deliberately stayed small. "I'm only one person. I can't become a giant operation," she explained when expanding farmers wondered why she didn't join them. Her cow numbers rose during the 1970s but only to thirty head. She financed a small addition to her barn, increasing the number of stalls and expanding her pen space. She put in a stainless steel pipeline to update her milking methods thus eliminating the need to handle the milk.

While Lee was staying small, Orrin and Stella Grimes, along with their son Butch, expanded heavily. Their 250 acres grew to over 600 by 1980. They put up additional silos, added on to their barn, and built a milking parlor, all with borrowed money.

Clare and George went through the early '70s struggling to stay afloat, with George slowly learning to accept the demands of dairy farming. In 1971 Clare gave in to George's pleas and they bought a thrower baler, three wagons, and the same conveyor system Lee had. They had to borrow again from PCA to do it, and Clare worried because their loan never seemed to get smaller. But by 1972 their herd was producing well again.

Their loan officer at PCA recommended they begin using milk testing to improve their herd. Through this management tool George finally began to see how each animal's production affected their income. Part of the appeal of testing for George was that because they were on official test their results were compared with the test results from other farms. The highest test results were published monthly in the local paper.

Of course, in 1972, it was customary to print only the name of the male farmer when recognition for high production was given. George gloried in the number of times his name appeared.

"We're in again," he said to Clare as he pored over the latest edition of the weekly paper. "Orrin Grimes is doing good too, but we're not far behind him."

"Is Stella's name in there?"

"Nope. Hey, everybody knows Stella works too. It's just how it's done."

"Well, I don't know how Stella feels about it, but it makes me mad. Maybe I should write a letter to the paper."

"You want people to think you're into that women's lib stuff? Bunch of bra-burning queers."

"Somehow I doubt they're all burning their bras," Clare said, wishing she could talk to Lee about the women's liberation movement she was reading about in the papers.

"Yeah, some of them probably never needed them in the first place. They're just a bunch of frustrated women who can't get men."

"I'm sure that's not it at all. Did you read that series in this week's St. Paul paper? Every day they had an article on what women's lib is actually about, like better pay. Equal pay for equal work..."

"Nope. I didn't bother with it. Hey, look at this. Butch Grimes is on the basketball team."

Clare bleakly listened to George read from the sports section of the local paper. She supposed it was expecting too much to wish her husband was interested in something besides farming, sports, and watching TV.

But she couldn't fault him in his role as a father. He shared the responsibility for Chad to a much greater degree than most men did.

That behavior was unusual in the Hansen family.

"Such a shame you can't spend more time caring for little Chad," her mother-in-law Mabel told her at one of the Hansen family get-togethers. "Now Gloria here is so good with her boys. She just spends hours playing with them."

"She isn't milking cows either," Clare pointed out, carefully keeping her temper in check. Her mother-in-law did not like her, and she had to admit the feeling was more than mutual.

"Of course she isn't. Nathan does that. There are just certain jobs I think should be left to the men," Mabel said to the room at large. "Why, I just saw on TV today some awful thing about the Senate approving some amendment to outlaw sex discrimination. Equal rights amendment, I think it was called. Now, isn't that the most ridiculous thing?"

"It certainly is," Gloria said eagerly. "I don't see why those women think they need equal rights."

Nathan nodded. "Yeah, you'd think they thought women were as good as men."

Everybody laughed, except Clare. "Well, we all know women are better," she said, unable to help herself.

"Better at getting their own way, you mean," Nathan said, chuckling at his own wit. "Now Gloria, she can whine and complain and get me to do what she wants. But she's a good housekeeper and mother, I'll sure have to say that."

"Some women certainly seem to think they're better," Mabel said, eyeing Clare but smiling sweetly. "But we all know we couldn't manage without the men."

Clare couldn't seem to get away from talk of women's lib. It surfaced at the meeting of the church ladies' group she had joined when she got married. The Circle met at the members' homes monthly and this month she was hosting it. Stella Grimes arrived early.

"I made it," Stella said. "Had to rush through the milking , but I'm leading the Bible Study tonight and it could get nasty."

"Oh? You planning to deny the divinity of Christ or something?" Clare asked as she set out plates and napkins on the dining room table.

"Nope. Worse than that. I'm gonna discuss women's lib." Stella sat down at the table with a relieved sigh. "Feels good to get off my feet. I wish they made comfortable women's work shoes."

"I wear men's boots," Clare said. "They work pretty well. You're not seriously planning a discussion of women's lib with my mother and Gloria and Mabel Hansen, are you?"

"Well, that's what tonight's lesson takes up. I must have done something very wrong to be the one who gets to lead it."

"Yeah, well, it's probably just because you farm with Orrin like you do."

"Men's work boots, eh?" Stella wriggled a nylon-clad foot. "Boy, maybe I'll give them a try."

"Don't let Mabel know you're thinking of that."

"Heck, she doesn't scare me. Much."

Clare laughed. "I'm glad you got here early. I never get to see you, except when you come with Orrin to do our corn."

"I know. Awful isn't it, how busy we all get. I thought with Butch old enough to help, it would be better, but I guess we've just got more work."

"Don't we all? Sometimes I almost envy somebody like Gloria who only has her housework and her boys to look after."

"Don't you let her hear you say that!" Stella admonished. "And don't you go leaving me out on a limb tonight when I get going on this study lesson."

"Hey, I'll do my best, but I can just see my mother looking at me reproachfully if I say anything."

"To say nothing of your mother-in-law. Well, we'll get through it somehow," Stella said. "I hope."

Later when the other women had arrived and settled themselves around Clare's table, Stella began her Bible lesson.

"We're doing Ephesians tonight," she said, rustling papers nervously. "This is the book that has that passage in it about women, wives, being subject to their husbands because their husbands are the head of the house. Do you think these words apply today?"

"Of course they do," Gloria said. Other women nodded. "All this talk about women's lib is anti-Biblical."

"That's right," Eleanor Perkins said. "The libbers want to ruin the family. I, for one, don't want to go out to work. I like being a housewife."

"But what about the women who have no husbands and need to support themselves? " Stella asked. "Don't they deserve equal pay for equal work?"

"I don't see why," Gloria said stubbornly. "If they wanted to they could get married like the rest of us."

"Maybe they don't want to or maybe their husbands died or left them with a lot of kids to support," Clare pointed out. "Shouldn't they be able to earn a decent living?"

"I suppose so," Gloria said grudgingly. "But what do they need to go and take men's jobs for? If those women were satisfied with women's work, maybe their husbands wouldn't leave them."

"Somehow I doubt that's why they left," Clare said.

"Well, I don't. This women's lib stuff just turns men off," Gloria insisted.

"I don't blame them at all," Mabel said. "I certainly don't need a constitutional amendment to protect me."

"That's for sure," Stella muttered under her breath to Clare. More loudly she said, "Well, what about all the women who don't have nice husbands? Don't they need some protection?"

"I still come right back to the Bible." Gloria tapped her black-bound book. "It says it all right here. We have to listen to the Bible and not to a bunch of women who're angry because they can't get men."

"Well, read on in Ephesians, then," Stella urged her. "Paul tells slaves to be obedient to their masters, but we don't have slavery anymore. Maybe we don't need to take everything in the Bible and apply it today."

"Yeah," Clare said. "These are different times from then."

"They sure are," Gloria said. "I don't know they're better either. All this women's lib and queers wanting rights. Plus the niggers out there rioting all over the place. Maybe slavery was wrong, but I sure think niggers have gotten too many rights."

Clare opened her mouth to protest, but she was beaten to it by a supporter of Gloria's words.

"I'll say they have," Eleanor Perkins put in eagerly. "Do you know they can get into schools where whites can't anymore? My sister's son found that out, I'll tell you."

"Your sister is married to Donnie Peterson, isn't she?" Mabel asked.

"That's my other sister. Delia is married to Don's cousin Larry Peterson."

"That would be Emil and Edna Peterson's son?"

"That's right. She was a Severson."

"Of course. Isn't she a cousin to Lois Hines? Who did Lois marry?"

"She married Dan Ludwigson, you know, Marie and Herman's son."

Clare exchanged an exasperated look with Stella. Stella raised her eyebrows and rolled her eyes. "They're good for twenty minutes when they get going on geneology," she murmured to Clare.

"Don't you dare ever quit the Circle," Stella told Clare later when the rest of the women had left. "If you quit I'll have to quit, too. I couldn't take it alone."

"I wonder why either of us is going."

"That's a thought. Why are we?"

"I don't know exactly, but probably because we want to fit in."

"Yeah. I wonder why that's so important."

"I'm beginning to think it isn't so important anymore."

"You going to quit the Circle?" Stella asked.

"Probably not. At least I do get to see you when I go."

"Well, thanks." Stella grinned. "Maybe we should arrange some other way to get together."

"Yeah, maybe we could go burn our bras in front of the post office or something."

"Hey, wouldn't that make Mabel's eyes bulge out?"

"They already bulge pretty good whenever she looks my way."

Later, as Clare made her way to the bedroom where George lay snoring, she realized that her mother hadn't said a word tonight against "women's lib."

CHAPTER FIFTEEN

While Clare was busy hearing about women's lib, Lee was busy reading about it. "All those books you sent were great," she wrote to Marsh in New York. "But they do make me mad that women have been so passive and so stupid for so long. And that book, *Lesbian/Woman* by Martin and Lyon was very good. It's so nice to read something so positive about lesbians for once!

"I'm going into Minneapolis more often now. I even saw Marion and her lover Nila at the Gay '90s bar. Let me tell you, that gave me a shock or two, but I recovered pretty decently when I saw how happy they are. Nila got a divorce and they live together. I'm glad for them."

"Now don't you go getting uppity ideas from all those women's lib books," Marsh admonished in one of his letters back. "First thing I know, you'll be telling me to take a hike because I'm a guy. I can see why some of the hubbies get nervous when their wives start spouting equal rights. But I'm not in their class, I hope."

Lee agreed with that. Her anger at men in general was tempered by her long friendships with Les, Wade, and Marsh. Many of the women she met through the gay bars and the Women's Coffeehouse in Minneapolis didn't feel any men were redeemable. Their lesbian identities had come about through feminism. It sometimes seemed to Lee that they had become lesbians not so much from a love of women as from a hatred of men and male privilege.

"It's hard to realize that I'm an 'older' lesbian to the women I meet at the Coffeehouse," she wrote Marsh. "Many of them are still in their twenties, and somehow I almost resent how women's lib has given them permission to do and be what I struggled to do and be on my own for longer than many of them have been alive. They're fine women, except I think some of them look down on me because I still have men friends. They just dismiss all men but I can't do that. You and Les and Wade have been and are too important to me."

Lee often found herself sitting on her opinions when she went to Minneapolis' women's community. She wanted to be part of it in at least a small way even if it didn't seem likely she'd find anyone to be involved with. Many of the women she met seemed too prickly to get close to, but then appearances could be deceiving, as she'd learned when she met Marion.

Still, it didn't seem likely that she would find what she had with Marion. And closer to home, it looked like the Hansen marriage was lasting. Lee saw so little of her neighbors that they might as well not have been there. But that they were she was very aware, especially when suddenly she would see Clare striding across her yard, tall and slender and busy.

Then all the feelings would come flooding back, and an empty aching loneliness would threaten to overcome her usual pleasure at being by herself on her farm. It was at times like this that she made herself go to Minneapolis, made herself seek out other women to at least be friends with. Life was too short, Lee knew, to waste too much of it regretting what could not be.

In the late 1970s there was more than ever to go to Minneapolis for. There were frequent live performances of what was known as "women's music." Cris Williamson, Meg Christian, Holly Near, Margie Adam, and Alix Dobkin seemed to pass through town at least once a year, and Lee saw most of their performances. She went often to Amazon Books over on Hennepin, where the selection of lesbian reading material was better than ever.

A weekend visit to the city might include a visit to Amazon, dinner out somewhere nice, then some time at the Saturday night dance at the Women's Coffeehouse on Groveland and finally a drink or two at Foxy's or the Townhouse, where Lee finished the night by doing what Marion used to do: sit and watch the women.

In 1978 Lee was forty-six years old. She didn't know how you were supposed to look at forty-six, but she didn't think she looked too bad. Women who watched Lee watch them saw a short woman in tailored slacks and tailored shirt, with the shirtsleeves rolled up to reveal strong forearms. Her dark brown hair had streaks of gray in it and her face had lines and wrinkles, but the wrinkles gave her face an interesting rugged look. Her green eyes were bright and filled with humor.

Every now and then as Lee sat with her back to the bar at Foxy's or the Townhouse and watched the women dancing, someone would stare back at her. Because Lee did not look as menacing as Marion had in her day, a few approached her and struck up a conversation. Sometimes that was as far as it went. But once in awhile Lee had a girlfriend for awhile.

Tremayne was the girlfriend in 1978. She was tall and thin and wore her hair clipped aggressively short. Tremayne was a lesbian separatist with no patience for men. She had no time for straight women and boy children, either. Or for people who smoked or who were fat. According to Tremayne the only true lesbian was one just like herself. At first Lee was acceptable to her because Lee was an older lesbian who had come out long before it was a political issue.

She lived with Lee on the farm for about four months, helping with crop work and the cattle. Tremayne had never so much as seen a cow or a bale of hay before she came.

Lee and Tremayne found old Daisy and her calf late one afternoon when they went walking out to round up the herd for evening milking. Daisy was placidly nibbling on grass and the tiny Jersey calf lay curled up nearby. With their reddish coat and dainty hooves, Jersey calves look like fawns. This one seemed very delicate.

"Oooh, look at her," Tremayne cooed. Daisy, an old hand at calvings, stood nearby as this tall human approached her calf. "Can I touch her? Will I hurt the calf if I touch her?"

Lee was amused. Who would have thought Tremayne-the-tough would fall to pieces over a calf? "I don't think you could hurt her. Go ahead and touch her."

"Oooh, she's so sweet. Little calfy, aren't you sweet?" Tremayne carefully reached out and stroked the soft red coat. The calf uncurled itself and sat up. "She likes it! Don't you, sweetie?"

Daisy went back to eating grass.

"Want to help me bring the calf in?" Lee asked.

"Sure. How do you do that? She's so fragile."

Lee didn't tell Tremayne that little calves may look fragile, but they're anything but helpless. This one looked to be about twelve hours old. Probably born right after we turned cows out to graze this morning, Lee thought. Its coat had been licked clean and dry by Daisy.

Lee approached the calf and felt between its rear legs to determine its sex. "It's a heifer," she said. "Well, let's get the calf to her feet. Then we'll see if it'd like to walk home."

"Walk? You expect that dainty little thing to walk home on her own?" Tremayne was horrified.

"I'm sure she's capable of it," Lee said dryly. Tremayne was looking at her as though she had suggested vivisection.

To prove Lee's point the heifer calf chose at that moment to stand up. She did so quickly and easily and with such speed that Tremayne stepped back in surprise. The calf took a good look at the human who had been gently stroking her, let out a disgusted blat and ran agilely around to hide behind her mother.

"I scared her," Tremayne said. "I'm sorry, little calfy."

Daisy, alerted by her calf's approach, decided this human might be a threat after all. With a quick reassuring lick to her calf, Daisy turned and headed toward the woods at the back of the pasture. Her calf galloped rapidly after her.

"Oh, shit," Lee said. "Now we can spend the next hour trying to catch them."

Twenty minutes later they had Daisy and her calf cornered against the back fence of the pasture. Daisy eyed them both warily, and the calf poked her head around her mother's brisket to get a peep at the panting humans.

"You cover that area right there," Lee ordered. "Don't let the calf get by. Grab her and sit on her if need be."

"I couldn't do that!" Tremayne was horrified. While she was busy being shocked at the idea, Daisy and her calf slipped right by her. Tremayne reached out a hesitant hand to stop them. Daisy looked with disdain at the hand and loped easily around Tremayne, with her calf loping right beside her.

Thirty minutes later, they had the cow and calf cornered again against a side fence of the pasture. The half hour had been spent climbing up and down the woody hillside, slipping in mud and cowpies and dodging brush. It was now late enough in the day so the mosquito population was out in force, buzzing and stinging. Tremayne swatted at them constantly.

"This time don't let that damned calf get by," Lee commanded.

Tremayne nodded. Now her face was determined. Lee approached the cow and calf, moving them slightly toward

Tremayne. She reached out to grab the calf, but the little Jersey eluded her hands and skipped after her mother toward Tremayne, who stood resolutely, her legs apart, feet braced, ready.

Daisy went handily by her, but as the tiny calf attempted to do the same, Tremayne reached out and grabbed for it. Her hands slid over the fine coat of hair, slid down the tail. Tremayne, aware of Lee's eyes on her, grabbed the tail and managed to hang on. The calf let out a terrified and indignant blat. Her tiny rear feet kicked out and connected sharply with Tremayne's knee.

"Ouch! You little bitch," Tremayne said. "Effing little brat."

Lee chuckled as she quickly came to help subdue the calf. "Still think she's a little sweetie?"

Tremayne stuck out her tongue.

She stayed around for another couple of months after that, and Lee thought she liked the farm. But, in the end, Tremayne was bored, both with Lee and with the farm.

"Nothing ever happens here," she complained. "All we ever do is work and if we don't work we go see your friends Les and Wade. Isn't there anything more to your life than that?"

"Not too much," Lee had to admit. Tremayne had left out all the reading Lee did, and the letter-writing to Marsh and now to other lesbians whose names she had gotten from "The Wishing Well," a lesbian contact service.

Tremayne had no time for reading and certainly none for the Wishing Well, dismissing the writers as lonely and closeted. "I don't see why you bother with those gay men, either."

"They've been good friends to me," Lee defended.

"But they're still men." For Tremayne that was condemnation enough. Her eyes narrowed, and her mouth set when men were present. She did not like the inseminator or the milk hauler or the Surge soap routeman or the co-op feedman.

"You sure have to deal with a lot of jerks," she said to Lee. "I wouldn't bother."

"Well, there don't seem to be too many women doing these jobs," Lee said.

"I'll bet the women around here never get a chance at those kind of jobs."

"I'm not sure the women want them," Lee pointed out, knowing it would do no good to mention to Tremayne that much of the work was hard and unglamorous. Just as when Marion had criticized rural ways, Lee felt herself closing ranks with rural men and women, feeling protective of them. She could criticize rural people herself, because she felt much more a part of them than she ever would of city lesbians. But she sure didn't want outsiders like Tremayne picking them to pieces.

There were others before and after Tremayne, other women who filled a need for Lee for awhile and then moved on. With most of them she parted friends and kept in touch on an irregular basis. None of them came close to touching her as deeply as she had been touched by Clare.

They did, however, help to keep the pangs of loneliness at bay. It was just that sometimes those feelings surfaced and would not be denied, and Lee could only smile ruefully at herself for her foolishness in thinking that Clare would be interested in her and yet there had been a time when it had seemed possible.

Through the entire decade of the 70s, Clare was only on Lee's property one time, and that was to use her phone. Her unexpected knock had caught Lee in the house preparing her solitary noon meal. Lee could feel her eyes widen with the surprise she felt at seeing Clare once more. She felt, too, a vague little stir of hope as she opened her door to Clare.

"Well, hi," Lee managed to say, knowing she sounded awkward, and very aware of the strange extra beat her heart was doing.

"Hi," Clare said back. "How have you been?"

"Pretty good. You?" Lee backed out of the doorway and Clare followed her into the house.

"Okay. Could I use your phone? Ours is out of order and I need to call the inseminator for a cow."

"Sure. Help yourself." Lee tried to sound casual, but she felt anything but casual. She wanted to reach out to Clare and somehow break through the barrier that separated them.

Lee watched her as she made the phone call. Clare looked tired, but that was to be expected. There was a lot of work over there. She also seemed wary and on guard.

That both amused and irritated Lee. What on earth does she think I'll do, attack her as she dials my phone?

"Well, thanks," Clare said. "The call was long distance but it shouldn't be very much. I think this will cover it." She held out a quarter to Lee.

"Forget it," Lee said. She tried smiling at Clare, hoping for Clare's old smile in return.

"I'd rather pay." Clare didn't smile and Lee wanted to shake her.

"And I'd prefer you didn't," Lee said. She knew she was sounding stubborn about it. "You never know, I might need to use your phone sometime."

"That's true. Well, thanks again." Clare was walking toward the door. Lee sought for a way to stop her.

"I certainly haven't seen much of you and George," she said weakly.

"We stay busy." Clare was still moving toward the door.

"I imagine so, what with all the work and a son to care for too." Lee felt like she was babbling nonsense, but she couldn't seem to stop.

At the door Clare turned toward her and just for a moment something passed between them, Lee was sure of it. A spark of old feelings, a recognition of each other, flared briefly and then was gone.

"Well, good-bye," Clare said and Lee was left alone in her house again, to finish preparing a meal she had no appetite for.

As Clare walked swiftly back across the road, she was aware of so many emotions stirring within. To be in Lee's house again even so briefly had touched off memories she thought she had thrown off.

I never meant to hurt her, Clare thought. I shouldn't have gone across to use her phone. It just...I thought I'd put all that behind me when I got married and I *am* married and I have a kid. And yet...

She never finished the thought and there was no time later to dwell on it.

"You call the inseminator?" George asked as they ate lunch.

"Yeah. I used Lee's phone. Ours should be fixed by tonight..."

"Why did you go over there?" George demanded.

"I thought it would be quicker to just go to Lee's."

"I never did push you about her. People talked about the two of you before we got married, you know."

"I suppose they did," Clare said, not wanting to talk about it, not wanting George to disturb her own troubled thoughts.

"You pay her for the call?"

"She wouldn't let me."

"I don't want us owing her anything." George's face was grim as he pushed back his chair. "I'm going over there and pay her."

"For heaven's sake, it was just a few cents," Clare pointed out to him.

"Makes no difference to me how much it was. I don't want us owing her at all."

"Why?" Clare heard herself ask.

"You know damned well why. I don't know what her appeal was to you, but I know it was there. And I don't like it one bit." He slammed the door behind him and Clare sat down at the table with a sigh. Okay, she admitted to herself, you know George is jealous of what he senses you felt for Lee. What you *felt*? she asked herself. Be honest for once, at least to yourself. What you feel is more accurate, isn't it? The knowledge caused her to close her eyes in pain and then to cover them with her hands, as though the darkness would erase both her agony and the belatedly acknowledged understanding.

George strode across the road and knocked sharply on Lee's door. She opened it and regarded him with a faint smile.

"Getting more social over there these days?" she asked.

"Not likely," George said. "Here." He held out a dollar bill. "Payment for the phone call."

"I don't want your money."

"Take it."

"Don't be silly. The call was brief. I don't need to be paid for it."

"You're going to be paid." George let the dollar bill flutter to rest at her feet.

"Well, I can certainly see what it was that attracted your wife to you. You display such charm," Lee said sarcastically.

"And I can't see what it was she saw in you," George said, meeting Lee's stare with a hostile one of his own.

"I can assure you, you have nothing to be jealous about," Lee heard herself say to him.

"Jealous? Of a...queer? Not likely."

"What then? Do you know what shrinks say about people who display such open homophobia? They say those people are just reacting to what they fear in themselves."

"What a bunch of crap." But George's face took on such an odd expression that Lee suddenly wondered if she hadn't struck a nerve.

"Maybe. Maybe not," she said as casually as she could. "If you ever want to talk about it, I might be able to help."

"Sure. You've got a degree in psychiatry, I suppose?"

"No. Just a few years of living is all." Lee found herself actually smiling at George, which was something she would certainly not have expected she would ever do. "Look, George. I...don't exactly think we'll ever like each other, but...no, don't snort in disgust or whatever. I'm not sure what I'm trying to say, except that I think we both care about Clare. In our own ways. Why don't we just let it be?"

"She married me…"

"You don't have to remind me," Lee said with a rueful smile.

George watched her for a moment and then said, "Rumor has it you conduct orgies here."

"Don't I wish," Lee said straightfaced, and then, to both of their surprise, they burst out laughing.

"Well, I guess people like to think the worst," George said.

"I'm so glad I've provided the town with conversation."

"Tell me, am I right in thinking that Clare's brother Marsh is a que…is gay?"

"I think Marsh would not object to my saying you're right," Lee said carefully.

"I wondered is all." George looked thoughtful. He seemed about to say more and then thought better of it. "I should get back to work. Keep the money." He picked up the dollar bill and handed it to her, then cleared his throat. "I apologize for coming here and throwing it at you."

Lee smiled. "Forget it." She took the dollar. "Thanks. You can use my phone anytime. And…"

George nodded. He turned and walked back across the road, waving over his shoulder at her as he went.

She mentioned the two visitors to Les and Wade that night over an after-milking meal at the New Mercury. "It was the most unexpected conversation I've ever had with anyone. I don't believe it, but I'm on better terms with Clare's husband than I am with Clare."

"Well…Isn't that interesting. George Hansen, huh?" Wade said. "I don't believe the man has ever even been in here."

"Nope," Les agreed. "I suppose if you're that scared inside, as he may be, you don't go anywhere near what he would call queers."

"Poor guy," Wade mused. "I must say, it all sounds like a mess out your way. Soap opera stuff. You lust after the wife. The husband is jealous and scared of that because he's scared deep-down. And what about the wife?"

Lee shrugged. "That's the sixty-four thousand dollar question. I'd swear she feels something for me. Maybe it's disgust. Maybe it's something nicer. I don't know."

"Well, I bet you'll find out someday," Wade said bracingly. He sat down next to her at the bar and removed his chef's hat.

"It's funny. I'm sure a lot of people mouth words of disgust about us, but that sure doesn't stop them from coming here. The good people of the area seem to have an unnatural need to check out the queers. And since they have to spend money to do it, we do okay."

"Business must be good then."

"You bet. People may come out of curiosity the first time, but after that they come back for the good food," Les said. "At least I think they do."

"Most come back for that, but some of the young guys come back for something else." Wade winked at Lee. "We won't mention what that is, but it's sure cut down on the need to go to the bars in Minneapolis."

"Running your own little gay bar on the side, are you?"

"Sort of." Wade almost smirked. "There's some good stock here. I've sampled some of the finest farm boys around. You wouldn't believe who if I told you..."

"Please don't. I wouldn't want my innocence ruined by knowing." Lee grinned at Wade. She didn't approve of Wade and his need to have sex so casually, but in view of her own sexual activities, which often began as bar pickups, she didn't think she should judge. It was just that his encounters seemed so barren of anything besides sexual satisfaction. She supposed he got the rest of whatever he needed from Les.

"Wade's been quite the popular lad with the local boys," Les said. He shrugged as though to cast away any hurt he might feel. "Long as they're of legal age, that's fine. Once in awhile we get one or two in here who aren't. I hate to turn them away, but it would be our necks and the bar and restaurant license if we got caught with the young ones here."

"And that's just for letting them drink," Wade quipped.

"Well, anyway, I'm glad this place is doing so well for you." Lee looked around at the nearly empty restaurant. It was late and the diners had been fed and sent home replete. A few late drinkers lingered at the other end of the bar and at some of the tables. It was a cozy, intimate place, she decided.

"We're going to close up for a couple of weeks next winter," Les said. "We haven't taken a break together since we opened. We decided we could afford to get completely away from it for awhile."

"Yeah, but I hope the diners don't go permanently back to Morgan's while we're closed," Wade said half-seriously.

"They won't. Morgan's gets their group and we get ours. Sometimes they're the same people actually," Les pointed out.

"Where are you going on your two weeks off?"

"You'll never guess." Wade leaned in closer. "A few years ago this would never have even been thought of, but we found out about this all-gay cruise going around the Caribbean. Sandy beaches. Lots of sunshine. Lots of men. Paradise."

"Anita Bryant would be so distressed," Lee said.

"Yeah, well I guess we won't have to worry about Anita being on board as the entertainment."

"And you'll love every minute of it," Lee said to Wade. She raised questioning eyebrows to Les.

He shrugged. "It was Wade's idea, naturally. I guess it will be okay."

"Of course it will. You'll have fun," Wade told him. "We'll get to do lots of things together. It'll be good for you to relax and get away for awhile."

"Yeah, I guess," Les said. "If it's what you want to do, we'll do it." His expression as he answered Wade was both indulgent and resigned.

CHAPTER SIXTEEN

By the mid '70s, George was pushing for them to expand. "We could sure use some extra acres," he told Clare. "We're buying way too much feed. I think we should talk to Harry about selling us your home place."

Although Clare trotted out her standard "We can't afford it," this time her feelings were mixed. "Harry's let the place go," she admitted. "Now that Dad is so crippled with arthritis, he's not out there much to help."

"Yeah, it shows. Sorry to say it, but your brother just shouldn't have been a farmer."

"I know. It's funny. Everybody, especially Dad, pushed Harry into it when he was young. I wonder what he would have done if there had been a choice?"

George shrugged. "Maybe he can find out. He's not that old. I'll bet we could get financing from Federal Land Bank with no trouble. I talked to Orrin Grimes yesterday and he said he'd gotten financing to buy that eighty back of his place. FLB is eager to lend."

"Well, I'm not eager to see us borrow. We still owe to PCA and that never seems to get any smaller," Clare pointed out. They kept renewing the PCA loan year after year, paying the interest and almost paying it off sometimes. But then they would need to borrow again to finance some piece of machinery or to put a pipeline in the barn. Their thirty-six stalls were in full use for milk cows and the herd average rose each year. Clare supposed they were doing well enough, really, but all of this talk about borrowing made her nervous.

"We could use Harry's barn for young stock," George said eagerly. "Maybe he and Diane would want to keep the house. Now that Diane's got her own beauty shop in town, Harry can take his time figuring out what he wants to do."

"You really think he wants to sell?"

"I know he does. He wants to get out."

"Maybe it makes sense," Clare said.

Her reluctance to borrow more money was being overcome by a sense of pride at making something of her farm.

After some hedging around, Harry decided it would be a good idea to sell. He and Diane kept the house. When Clare and George made an offer of forty thousand dollars for the rest of the farm, he accepted it with secret relief.

They went to Federal Land Bank to finance the purchase. The land they would use as collateral was still in Clare's name, but the loan would be in both their names, since George was going to be an equal owner in the newly purchased land.

A loan officer sat down with them and figured their net worth. It was customary for the loan officer to do the figuring. The farmer sat and watched, contributing necessary information—often just a guess. "How much is your equipment worth?" the loan officer asked.

George shrugged, and before Clare could run figures through her head, the loan officer said, "I'd guess it in at about thirty thousand dollars. Sound right?"

"I guess so," Clare said. She watched him write in thirty thousand dollars.

"And you've got thirty-six cows on official test with a production of..."

"Sixteen thousand pounds per cow," George said with pride.

"That's good. The state average is down there around eleven thousand. So, your cows should be worth, oh, about twenty thousand dollars," he decided.

"And your own farm is worth sixty thousand dollars. That gives you a total worth of one hundred ten thousand dollars. And all you owe is fifteen thousand dollars to PCA. With your assets we can definitely go the whole forty thousand dollars."

"Great," George said.

Clare was not so sure it was great, but she went along with it.

"We require that the loan be backed by life insurance to cover it in the event of the farmer's death," the loan officer informed them. "It's not too costly, but it is mandatory."

The application covered only George, of course. Clare supposed it didn't matter, really, but it made her angry. It sure was a man's world.

She had a son who was likely to claim his full share of this man's world someday, she thought. By then, Chad was seven. "I want" was Chad's favorite expression. When Clare said no, he could always get what he wanted from his father. Whether it was a pair of cowboy boots or a pony, a cheap water pistol or an expensive BB gun, if Chad wanted it, he got it.

The current want was an expensive fishing rod. "Dad has one," Chad insisted to his mother.

"Your dad knows how to use it too. Wait until you've practiced casting with his old rod."

"You never let me get nothing," Chad pouted, scuffing around with his shoe at a piece of kitchen linoleum that was coming loose.

"Don't do that, Chad. And stop pouting. You just got a new tackle box."

"Yeah, but...You're mean. I'll go ask Dad. He'll let me."

He probably will, Clare thought. She thought that perhaps they should have had more kids, but she, at least, hadn't wanted more.

She and George did not have sex that often anyway. Both of them worked hard and at night the last thing either of them wanted was sex. George fell asleep in front of the TV and Clare wanted a chance to read, although she seldom made time for it.

With the purchase of Clare's family farm, their acreage doubled to 240 acres, and they needed bigger machinery again. In 1978 George argued for switching from baled hay to haylage, so they put up another silo. The new silo meant they needed a forage chopper, a blower, a bigger tractor, and two self-unloading boxes.

George assured Clare they could make the payments easily. "The price of milk is up over ten dollars," he said. "The PCA says another forty thousand dollars won't be any problem. We've always made our payments on time and you know land values are up, cows are worth more too, so our net worth is higher than ever."

"I know, but..."

"Come on, Clare," George said impatiently. "You always drag your feet about this stuff. Makes me mad. If we're gonna farm, let's do a good job."

"I thought we were."

"Not good enough. Look at Orrin Grimes. He's really expanding, and even Nathan is getting bigger than we are. We can't just sit here and spin our wheels."

"I wouldn't exactly say we're idle."

"Of course not, but thirty-six cows isn't very big. The PCA says we've got to get bigger."

"Oh?"

"Yeah, you'll hear all about it when we sign the papers. I agreed when I went down to see about the loan that we should do that. It's a condition of the loan."

"What? Don't I have any say in this anymore?"

"Of course. But you don't understand how this works. Guy Smith down at PCA says they're really encouraging their borrowers to expand."

"I get the feeling you haven't told me everything yet, have you?"

George looked defensive. "Hey, you haven't given me time."

"Well, I'm giving it now."

"Just wait until we get to PCA. Guy will tell you about it."

"Somehow I get the feeling I'm about to be railroaded into doing something I won't like."

"You always act this way when we borrow money. I wish you'd relax with it. It's just part of farming."

"It sure isn't a part I like." Clare knew that most of their arguments circled around borrowing money, but she couldn't help it. She had never become comfortable with going into debt as casually as George would like.

Guy Smith at PCA had indeed made it a condition of their silo loan that they expand their herd. He and George talked convincingly of the benefits of getting bigger, and in the end Clare agreed.

But it was costly to build onto their barn. They added a low-roofed steel structure to the existing building, an addition that had room for forty-four more cows.

The total project rose from the forty thousand dollars needed for switching to haylage to a ninety thousand dollar debt. Added up with their existing PCA loan of twelve thousand dollars and the FLB loan of thirty-seven thousand dollars, the new loan brought their total indebtedness to one hundred thirty-nine thousand dollars.

"That's no problem," Guy Smith at PCA assured them. "You've got plenty of net worth to cover it. A debt of this size against your total assets of $260,000 is just no problem at all."

"We do have to pay it back," Clare pointed out.

"Heck, I'm not worried," George said, his earlier anger at her gone now that the papers were signed. "Interest rates at PCA and FLB are low. Besides, I don't think most farmers worry about paying it all off like they used to. You have to have a debt to get ahead. Everybody knows that. Maybe you won't ever get it all paid off until you sell, but it doesn't matter."

Even Clare had to concede it looked like George was right. Milk prices kept right on rising. In 1979 they were up to $11.75. By 1981, they reached an all-time high of $13.62. Land values rose as well. In 1979 an acre of Wisconsin farmland was worth $850. By 1981 that acre was worth $1100.

But by 1980 Clare was beginning to be seriously worried by their large farm debt. The 1978 expansion loan had been the beginning, not the end, of their borrowing. They were making the payments, but the payments kept getting larger as they borrowed more money. The PCA loan of 1978 had been consolidated in 1979 with the FLB loan so that all their borrowing was backed by the farmland they owned, which meant that as far as Clare was concerned, the FLB owned their land.

She knew the trend was not to worry about repayment. You were supposed to keep turning the debt by using it to finance more expansion. In 1979, when they had consolidated the loans, they had also borrowed more money.

By then they had a herd of eighty milk cows and needed another larger silo. George had his heart set on a big blue bottom unloading Harvestore. It cost sixty thousand dollars.

As usual they argued about it loudly and angrily, and in the end, George got his way. A blue monster was added to the row of silos on their farm. Their debt climbed again, but the FLB loan officer assured them it was okay. After all, they had assets worth over four hundred thousand dollars now. Adding a silo just increased their assets. It also brought their debt up to one hundred eighty thousand dollars.

Later that year, when Clare was already worrying about meeting their payments, George decided they needed a manure storage facility. There was the usual routine with the loan officer at FLB. This time he had another piece of advice.

"I see you have 240 acres. You must have to rent extra cropland, don't you?"

"We sure do," George said. "We rent all over hell. Let me tell you, it's no fun dragging equipment up and down the highway. Some of the drivers never even slow down when they pass..."

"Isn't there any land nearby you could purchase? With your herd size, you could use more land, and of course it would be a good investment."

George shook his head. "Orrin Grimes has bought up most all the land close by. There just isn't much left."

"Isn't there an eighty across the road, owned by some woman?"

"You mean Lee Collins' place?" George said, looking thoughtful.

"Yeah. That's the one. Sort of a hobby farmer, isn't she?"

"Well, she sure hasn't expanded much. She has some Jerseys and still bales her hay."

"Maybe you should feel her out on selling. The land would be handy to your farm and I think we could go fairly high on it."

Clare was rolling her eyes while George was nodding and pondering out loud. "Yeah, you know, I hadn't thought about that land as being available, but now that you mention it, it would be great. I wonder if we could get it for seventy-five thousand dollars?"

"You might have to go a little higher than that. I think you could go up to eighty-five thousand and come out fine. We'd go along with that amount."

"Great," George said.

They finished the paperwork on the addition to their debt, which brought the amount up to two hundred thirty thousand dollars. "This is well within your limit," the loan officer said. "Your assets are over five hundred thousand dollars now."

Clare shook her head. "I just can't believe we have that much in assets."

The two men laughed indulgently. "These larger figures take a little getting used to, I suppose," the loan officer said patronizingly, as though the little woman could not comprehend anything bigger than the amount needed to buy groceries or pay for a new outfit. Clare burned with anger.

Later in their car George went on about Lee's land. "We wouldn't really need the barn, but maybe we could put a hired hand in the house. Or later when Chad marries and takes over the farm, we could fix up that house and retire there."

"That's a long way off. He may not want to farm."

"He will. She's done a pretty good job of keeping the land up to fertility. Wouldn't be much we'd have to do there."

"You're not serious." Clare was horrified at the thought of their pushing Lee off her farm. "Lee worked hard for that farm.

I don't want her just swept aside as though her efforts haven't been worth anything. Forget that idea," she said angrily.

"Hey, it was just a thought," George protested.

"Well, make sure it stays that way. I won't have her bothered by us, as though her farm is so small it's just there to be gobbled up." Clare's voice shook angrily.

"You don't have to get so upset about it. Like I said, it was just an idea."

"And it stinks." Her anger was mixed with fear over the endlessly spiraling debt, the endlessly increasing work, and the hopeless feeling she sometimes had. Where will it end, she wondered. How much bigger can we possibly get?

Later that week, when Clare had gone into town to buy groceries and run farm errands, George stopped work and walked across the road to Lee's. It was late summer, with just a touch of fall's sharpness in the air. Lee was out back of her house splitting wood. He watched her for awhile unnoticed, as she swung her splitting mall, effortlessly and accurately whacking the right spot in piece after piece of wood.

"You make that look easy," he finally said.

Lee turned at the sound of his voice and wiped sweat from her forehead. "Years of practice. And you know the old saying, wood warms you twice."

"Once when you cut it and again when you burn it," George finished for her. "Farming going okay?"

"It seems to be. You're sure expanding over there. I saw the Harvestore people over again yesterday."

"Yeah. We're getting a Slurrystore."

"That's what I thought. I can appreciate the need. My thirty Jerseys put out enough manure. Handling that stuff is probably my least favorite farm chore."

"I'm with you there," George said. He knew this was the moment when he should ask Lee if she'd be interested in selling. He didn't say anything.

"So, what brings you over today?" Lee asked, wondering why he was here.

George shrugged. "Clare's off to town and I...just got restless. Didn't feel like working."

"Well, you both do enough of it over there," Lee said, upending an unsplit chunk of wood and sitting down on it. "It's a nice day. Had to force myself out here to do this."

George hestitated a moment and then found himself a chunk of wood to sit on. "I'm glad we burn fuel oil. I don't think I'd have enough energy left these days to split wood."

Lee smiled slightly, cautiously. "I'll bet. Well, that's one advantage of being small."

"I guess it is. You know, when you were splitting wood there you kind of reminded me of a guy I knew in Vietnam. He had that same easy way of doing things."

"Oh?"

"Yeah. Chad was a medic. All hell could be busting loose around him and he just went on doing what he had to do."

"I thought you were in the Air Force."

"I was. But you can't figure out the brass sometimes. I was trained to service jets. At first that's what I did but on my last tour they, somebody anyway, got the bright idea I should service helicopters, Army ones, yet. I didn't know beans about them, but I learned." He leaned forward on his chunk of wood.

Something in his face as he spoke told Lee to squash her anti-Vietnam views and listen. "It was bad, right?"

"Very bad. I was at a base in the Highlands, where there were lots of Cong around. The helicopters were medvac units, bringing in wounded from platoons fighting out on hill this or hill that. We used smaller copters to bring in the wounded to our base and then either patch them up right there or transfer them to bigger copters for a flight to bigger medical facilities."

"I know so little about Vietnam," Lee murmured.

"Doesn't everyone?" George said ironically "You know, nobody really gave a shit about us and what we went through, doing what we thought was the right thing. I sometimes felt the government and the military didn't give a goddamn either. We'd get a shipment of medical supplies and by the time it got to the base, it was just plain stripped down to nothing. Half the time the medics had no drugs. Sometimes no bandages. It all got ripped off before it got there." There was a long silence as George sat on the chunk of wood.

"You mentioned somebody named Chad. Did you name your son for him?" she asked cautiously.

George nodded. "Yeah. Chad was...Chad died."

"I'm sorry. He meant something to you, didn't he?" Her question was an impulsive response to George's tone of voice.

George sat on his chunk of wood with his eyes closed, and Lee was shocked to see tears leaking beneath his lids. He opened his eyes and stared at her. "You're gonna laugh. The irony of it..."

"I don't think I'll laugh," Lee said.

"No? Maybe not. We got a lot of mortar attacks on the base. Usually when we were busy transferring wounded. But just any old time, to take us by surprise. One day we, Chad and I, were just sitting kind of like this, talking like we did a lot. I could talk to that guy about anything. Anyway, they attacked and nobody was expecting it. A round of mortar went off practically at our feet, and Chad was hit. I dragged him to shelter, and by the time another medic could get to us, it was too late. He...died in my arms."

George's voice broke and Lee, without thinking about who this was, reached out a comforting hand. She could think of no adequate words.

Finally George spoke again. "Now comes the part where you're gonna laugh, at least inside. I had some of Chad's belongings. His letters from somebody back home in Iowa. Somebody named D. Larkin. I didn't snoop and read those letters, I just thought when I came home I should return them to the person who sent them. I thought the person was some girl he was writing to. So I went to Waverly, Iowa, before I came back here and I looked up D. Larkin."

"And?"

"And D. stood for Dan. Chad was...gay. And Dan was this great big tall guy, older than Chad was. He just went to pieces when I handed him the letters. I didn't know what to do."

"What did you do?"

"I've never told anyone this. I put my arms around him and just held him. Then he asked if Chad and I had...had been lovers. It floored me. I never even thought of Chad that way."

"But you still named your son Chad."

George nodded. "He was such a...an alive person. He was just a real special guy."

"And you loved him," Lee said.

"I guess maybe I did, but not like..."

"Not like a queer? I've never understood just where the dividing line is between acceptable and unacceptable loves. What difference does it make?"

"I don't know. Sometimes I wish...I wish I'd at least have told him. I've had nightmares for years about him dying like he did."

"And you've never told anybody? Until now?"

"Yeah." George grinned sheepishly at her. "Until now. I saw you splitting wood, and I wasn't prepared for how much you reminded me of him. Just little things like that trigger the memories."

"Well, it's not the first time I've been mistaken for a guy," Lee said lightly.

"Well, you do kind of dress like one," George said carefully.

"And you and lots of other people don't approve?"

"As far as I'm concerned you can wear anything you damn well please."

"So glad I have your permission."

"Somehow I doubt you really needed it."

"You're right, but it's nice to know at least somebody around here isn't going to tell me to stop buying workshirts in the men's department."

George chuckled. "I begin to see why Clare likes you so much."

Lee shrugged. "I didn't know she did anymore."

"Oh, she does. I used to call you 'the queer' when we were first married. One of our first arguments got really going when I opened my mouth and let those words out. I never knew she could get so mad." He paused, shaking his head. "Of all the people I might have told, I never thought it would be you."

Lee shrugged and grinned at him. "Just goes to show you, anything might happen."

"Speaking of that, here comes my wife and she does not look happy."

Clare strode quickly around the corner of Lee's house, anger and anxiety driving her feet. She had come home from town to find George nowhere in sight. It took very little guesswork on her part to figure where he might be.

"If you've been bothering Lee about this land purchase thing, I..." She began talking before she had quite reached where the other two were sitting.

"What land purchase thing?" Lee asked. "You didn't tell me about that."

George looked embarrassed.

Clare had reached them. "I'm not going to be responsible for what I do to you, George Hansen, if you've been bugging her about selling her farm."

"I didn't..."

"He never mentioned it," Lee assured Clare. "So that was in your mind when you came. What made you not bring it up?"

"I found I couldn't. I don't want your land anymore. It was a dumb idea, you were right, Clare."

"That's a relief," Lee said. "I think. This is sort of puzzling to me."

"It was nothing," George assured her. "Just a dumb idea the FLB loan officer had that you might want to sell."

"I don't," Lee said mildly but firmly.

"Well, good. I didn't bring it up, honestly, Clare."

Clare was looking from George to Lee, puzzled. Her bewilderment was visible to the two of them sitting there companionably on chunks of wood.

≥●

"I hear you bought the Harmon place," Orrin Grimes said to George that fall. Clare and George were attending the wedding of Butch Grimes to Sally Peterson.

"Yeah, we did," George said good-naturedly. "You got all the close-in places so we had to go a little farther off."

"Well, it should be a good farm. About 200 acres, isn't it?" Orrin asked.

"Two-hundred-ten, actually," George said. "All good crop land." They had paid $185,000 for it, more than either Clare or George had expected. Their debt with FLB was now nearly $400,000, against assets of $750,000.

"Whoever thought any of us would get so big," Stella said to Clare, giving her a hug as the Hansens worked their way through the reception line. "Thank God we've got Butch and Sally both interested in farming."

"I just hope Chad is interested in it someday," Clare replied, aware suddenly that Lee was right behind her in the line. She was still puzzled over the change in George's attitude toward Lee. Her husband had maintained an almost embarrassed silence about what had gone on between him and Lee. Clare's curiosity was high, but she couldn't pry anything out of George. She watched now as Lee greeted Stella.

They exchanged a friendly hug and Lee said, "Gee, Stella, but you look good today. Young enough to be the bride's sister."

Stella blushed with pleasure and shook her head, pointing to her deep auburn hair. "Silver threads among the gold, kiddo. I feel more like the bride's grandmother some days."

"Not today, I hope."

"Nope, today I feel just like the mother of the groom. I was probably more nervous than he was."

"It was a nice wedding," Lee said. "And Sally sure seems like a good person."

"She is. She's a farm girl, too." Stella chuckled. "It's probably too bad one of us isn't interested in housework."

There were people waiting in the line so Lee moved on, joining Clare and George as they stood nearby.

"Hi, neighbor," George said.

"I hear you found some land," Lee said to him. She smiled at Clare, who managed to smile back. Her heart was pounding, which brought a flush to her face. Lee looked so fit and trim and so unbelievably dear that Clare could think of nothing to say. She watched disbelievingly as Lee and George talked, watched Lee's easy smile and the fine wrinkles that crinkled upward from her eyes.

Clare lost track of their conversation, absorbed in her emotions. There was something about the almost conspiratorial way they talked to each other that made her feel left out. What's going on here anyway, she wondered. My husband hated Lee. Now he spends an afternoon in her company, and the hatred is gone. I should be pleased, I suppose, but somehow I'm not.

Her confusion was not lessened as Lee turned to include her, placing a friendly hand on Clare's arm. It was all so unreal that Clare had trouble responding.

"Uh, yeah. That's right. Chad's eleven. His dad spoils him too much sometimes," Clare managed to babble out. She was very aware of Lee's touch. For some reason George didn't seem to find that threatening anymore.

"I'll bet he does," Lee said with a look to George that again left Clare feeling as though she was missing something.

"Look you guys, what's going on?" she blurted out. They were walking slowly now away from the church across the crowded parking lot. "I'm missing some link here."

Lee and George exchanged a look. "Up to you," Lee murmured.

George shrugged. "I don't know what to say."

"Come on, you two," Clare said. "If I didn't think it was so unlikely, I'd say you were having an affair."

Lee burst out laughing. "Sorry, George," she said.

"Hey, I'm not that bad, am I?" George said with mostly pretend hurt.

"Not at all. Just the… ah…wrong sex," Lee said, thinking to herself that Clare looked very attractive in her puzzlement.

"Well, I guess I can rule out the affair," Clare said wryly. "But you've got me puzzled."

"I can see where you might be," Lee agreed. "We sort of came to an understanding, I think."

"Yeah. I guess we did," George said.

"Well, that's nice," Clare said uncertainly, looking back and forth at the two of them, her husband who was familiar and dear to her, and Lee who she knew with certainty was also dear.

CHAPTER SEVENTEEN

Lee could not help but contrast the light-hearted Grimes wedding with the heavy, very sad funeral she attended just a week later. Wade had been buried out at the cemetery on the edge of town.

His death had happened so quickly. He had gone swimming on Labor Day with a group of younger men he'd been hanging around with. They were the local gay contingent, the closeted, sometimes married, group that gravitated to the New Mercury.

They had gone up to a lake for a picnic, and even though it had been cold and rainy, the whole group had gone swimming. Wade had been right in there with the rest of them, clowning and mugging in his brief bathing suit, swimming and then toweling off, shivering in the rain. It had all been a lot of fun, Wade had assured Les who had stayed home to mind the bar.

By the next Wednesday, Wade had a bad cold and a cough that wouldn't quit. He went to their doctor, and the doctor prescribed an antibiotic.

"Should fix me up in no time," Wade told Les, even as the cough continued to worsen. "You just have to give these drugs a little time to work. I can cook tonight. No problem."

Les became frightened as the cough did not improve. It rattled deep in Wade's chest and shook his whole body. The coughing fits left him weak. By the next weekend the cough still was not better, and Wade seemed to have the flu as well. His weakness increased with bouts of diarrhea.

"I'm calling the doctor," Les said finally on Sunday. Wade protested but he was too sick to move from his bed. The doctor, a man Les had gone to for years, diagnosed pneumonia. "Better get him to the hospital," the doctor decided. He did not like Wade, but he told himself he was doing his job impartially.

"He'll be fine," he did say to a very worried Les. "Just needs a little hospital care, is all." These fussy gays, he thought, worried over a little illness. As bad as women.

By Tuesday Les was frantic. He paced out of Wade's room to the nurses' station down the hall. "Isn't there something more to do for him? He's so sick."

The nurse on duty shook her head. In truth, she was worried too. "The doctor's off duty today. He'll be in tomorrow," she said to Les, trying to be reassuring.

On Wednesday the doctor was busy and only had time for a cursory glance at Wade and his chart.

"I'm worried about this one," the nurse said. "He's not responding well to the antibiotics you have him on."

"Give it a little more time." The nurse made a note on Wade's chart and they moved on.

Les and Lee were with Wade all of Wednesday afternoon. "He's not getting better," Les said. His eyes were sunken and circled from lack of sleep. "I'm staying with him tonight."

"You need sleep yourself." Lee was equally concerned.

"I want to be with him," Les said. "I don't give a damn about sleep right now."

Wade died early on Thursday morning, with Les at his side. His death was sudden and unexpected, and Les reeled with the shock. He called Lee, who rushed to the hospital.

She found Les in the patient lounge. "Wade is dead? Just like that?" She pulled Les close.

"He was only fifty. I can't believe it. They shooed me out of the room. I just wanted to sit there, just for a little longer. But they said I had to leave so the body could go to the undertakers. And they wanted to know his next-of-kin. I'm his next-of-kin, but they wanted somebody 'real.' A blood relative, like I'm nothing to him."

Lee held him close and felt anger well up equal to her grief.

"They said they'd call his sister in Edina to handle the funeral arrangements. His sister! She hasn't spoken to him in years and now she gets called. What about me?"

"They're just following the law," Lee said as soothingly as she could.

"Damn the law!"

"I know. Do you want me to call Ludgate's and see what's happening?" Les nodded and Lee found a phone in the hospital lobby and with a shaking hand dialed the funeral home's number.

"Ludgate's," a pleasant male voice answered.

"I'm calling in regard to funeral arrangements for Wade Carlton," she said. "I'm calling for Mr. Carlton's friend and partner, Les Jones."

"I've been trying to reach Mr. Jones," Ludgate said. "As his partner, perhaps he would be willing to make the arrangements. It seems Mr. Carlton's sister hasn't the...time to do it."

"Yes, Mr. Jones would be willing." More than willing, Lee thought.

"Thank God!" Les said when she told him. "She never gave a damn about Wade. Will you come with me? I want to do it, but I don't think I can do it alone, knowing it's for Wade."

"Of course," Lee said.

They went to the funeral home that afternoon and were mistaken by Ludgate for husband and wife. Lee thought how typical it was of people's thinking. She wanted to blow the bland expression off Ludgate's face by telling him that Les was the surviving spouse or widower or whatever, but she didn't do it. Les was suffering enough, hardly able to function.

"I understand Wade's sister didn't want to make the arrangements?" Lee said to James Ludgate after he had graciously seated them in his office.

"No. She did not," he said briefly, thinking of the woman's actual words: you can pickle him in alcohol and bury him in a cardboard box for all I care.

Of course he had heard rumors about the two men who ran the New Mercury. Les, the other man, seemed to be married anyway, so who knew what was behind the sister's actions?

"I'm sure this must be a loss for you," he said now.

Les sighed and nodded, wiping his eyes again on a handkerchief.

"It's good of you to be willing to make the arrangements for your partner. I'm sure you'll miss him. As will many of us. He was a wonderful cook."

Les nodded again.

"It's about the matter of payment," Ludgate said delicately. "At such a time I know it is difficult to worry about mundane details..."

"I'll pay," Les said.

"That's very generous of you, Mr. Jones. There are, of course, some things we need to go into today." He asked for details of Wade's life. "There is only the one survivor? How sad," he said.

"He's survived by me," Les said, his voice breaking. "I was his partner for years. That ought to be worth some mention, shouldn't it?"

"Yes, of course. We'll put: survived by his sister Helen Lawton of Edina and by his partner Les Jones."

"Put it the other way around," Les ordered. "I was closer to Wade than his sister ever dreamed of being."

"But it's customary to put the blood relatives first..."

"I'm paying for the funeral, aren't I?"

Ludgate nodded. He changed the funeral notice.

Since Wade had no church, the ceremony would be held at the funeral parlor. A nearby church basement would be the site of the lunch, since Ludgate felt they might have a crowd. "Mr. Carlton was a well-known local figure for his restaurant work," he said.

Ludgate suggested a minister. "The Reverend Lyal Miller is always willing to come in on these occasions where there isn't a regular minister. I'll call him now and set it up. He'll want to talk with you today, offer some comfort, I'm sure."

"All right," Les agreed. "When?"

Ludgate made the call. "He'll come when we've completed the arrangements. In about an hour."

They went on to pick the solo hymns. Neither Lee nor Les had been inside churches much in recent years, but they remembered old favorites.

"I think 'Crossing the Bar' would be good," Lee suggested. "It's based on a poem by Tennyson. Somehow I think it would suit Wade."

"And I want 'Beautiful Isle of Somewhere,'" Les said. "They sang that at my mother's funeral." He wiped his eyes again. "My God, we're actually planning Wade's funeral. Wade is lying here somewhere dead. I can't believe it." He put his hand over his eyes. "I just can't believe it."

Ludgate murmured comforting phrases until Les had control of himself. "Now we need to decide on a casket," he said. Les and Lee followed Ludgate down some stairs to an area in the basement. Lee touched Les' arm in reassurance as they entered the room full of caskets. She had expected Les to have a hard time here, but he quickly made the decision.

"I want the oak one," he said firmly. It was an expensive casket, but it seemed just right for Wade. He did not care what it cost.

Ludgate stroked the polished wood of the casket. "This is a fine choice," he said, much as a furniture salesman might lend his approval to one's selection of a bed.

There were other details, fees to be discussed, a cemetery plot to arrange. Ludgate would take care of that, too.

"Make it large enough for two bodies," Les said. "In the old part of the cemetery, if possible."

Ludgate looked at him strangely but wrote down the request. By the time the final details had been discussed, the Rev. Miller arrived and came into the office to join them. He shook hands with Les and then with Lee.

"I'm sorry for your loss, Mrs. Jones," he said to Lee. Lee meant to correct the mistake, but let it go.

The Rev. Miller was at least in his sixties. He looked older, but Lee thought he would be retired if he were much older than that. He had gray lackluster hair that was thinning on top and had probably never been very thick. His eyes were a faded blue, his shoulders slumped with too much stooping over a desk. His handshake was firm, though, and he greeted them with what seemed like genuine sympathy.

"I never met Mr. Carlton, so I'd like to know something about him to make the funeral less impersonal for those who survive him." His voice was dry and emotionless. Lee decided his church couldn't be one of those Holy Roller ones. She could not imagine the Rev. Miller working himself up to an emotional fervor.

He sat and listened as Les talked brokenly of Wade, unaware that Les was deliberately, automatically as a matter of course, censoring what he said. He talked only of the Wade known to the public. The kind, gentle man, the generous man, the talkative joking Wade. He did not talk about the Wade who went to gay bars and on gay cruises.

"He was a wonderful friend and partner," Les said.

"I'm sure he was," the Rev. Miller nodded kindly. "I understand there is a sister?"

"She won't be here," Les said. "Wade wasn't close to her."

"I see," the Rev. Miller said, but he did not see. Later when he went back to the parsonage next to the small white church, he spoke to his wife about the funeral.

"I thought those two who ran the New Mercury were homosexuals," she said. His wife was younger and in some ways both sharper and blunter than Lyal. He had an easygoing acceptance of people's differences that she did not seem to have. At sixty-two he could have retired if there had been enough of a pension to retire on, but his pension would be slim.

His wife was only fifty, but living with him seemed to have aged her prematurely. Her thick black hair had a considerable portion of gray in it, and her green eyes sat hooded by their lids much of the time, their attractive brightness hidden and suppressed by the dowdy pale-colored shirtwaist dresses she wore.

Lyal shrugged in answer to her question. "I would have thought so myself, but the surviving one seems to be married. They are, of course, unchurched."

"Of course," Frances Miller said with a touch of cynicism. That was why they needed her husband's services, she knew. But since the fee was never less than thirty-five dollars she didn't complain. The extra was always welcome.

"Oh, and Mr. Ludgate suggested you as the soloist for two songs. I told them you would sing. He's arranged for an accompanist."

She nodded. "What songs?"

"I've got it written down here." Lyal consulted a worn engagement book.

"I'd better go over them tomorrow then. I haven't sung 'Crossing the Bar' in a long time." Frances liked that song. It pleased her to be asked to sing, which she genuinely liked.

"Are you going to the visitation?" she asked.

Lyal nodded. "I think I will. It sounds as though the deceased had few survivors. There may not be many people there. The Joneses are paying for it, even though there's a sister somewhere. She wasn't interested in coming."

"Strange," Frances said. "Perhaps I'll come with you, if you think it would be appropriate." She was curious about this one, having heard rumors about the men who ran the New Mercury. She and Lyal had never been in there, not even for a meal. They did not drink and there was never extra money for eating out.

At the visitation, Lee felt Les tremble as he took his first look at the dressed-up dead body of his lover and friend. She felt like trembling and crying herself to see Wade lying there looking almost natty in his best blue suit and soft blue shirt. It brought back memories of a much younger Wade in Minneapolis, excited over some clothes he had just bought.

"His hair is wrong," Les said in a whisper.

"What?"

"Somebody combed his hair wrong," Les repeated. "It never looked like that."

"You're right," Lee agreed. Wade's hair had always fallen to one side. Ludgate had combed it in the other direction.

With a well-developed ability to sense when something was wrong, Ludgate was at their side. "How should it go?" He brought a comb out of his pocket. "I'm so sorry. I couldn't remember how it had been." He combed Wade's hair carefully back into its normal position. "Is that all right, now?"

Les nodded. "That's much better. Don't you think so, Lee?"

Lee agreed and suddenly experienced an unreasonable need to giggle. It seemed so prosaic a thing to worry about, but she could see it was important to Les that Wade look 'normal,' if such a thing is possible for a corpse.

"He looks so much like he's asleep," Les sighed. "I wish I could just wake him up and it would be all right again."

"I know." Lee patted Les' arm. His eyes were full of tears and she felt her own eyes prickling. Ludgate had discreetly stepped away. She put her arm around Les.

Lee had been worried that the two of them might need to sit in the visitation room alone for six hours, but her fears proved false. Those first few minutes alone by the casket were the last.

A steady stream of people came to view Wade. They also seemed quite willing to express their sympathy to Les. The local gay men, the closeted ones, came out in force, one by one, to shake hands with or hug Les, murmuring a few words of sympathy. What neither Lee nor Les had anticipated was that there would be so many others.

It seemed as though anyone who had ever had contact with Wade came to express their sympathy to Les. Little old ladies who had enjoyed being jollied along by Wade came in force. Couples with children came. Other merchants. The owners of Morgan's. The people Les and Wade and Lee had worked with at the wood products factory. There were hugs and gentle words from the strangest and most unlikely sources.

Lee was touched to see these people put aside prejudice and express their sympathy with Les' grief. It was very heartening and helpful for Les to have all these people come.

The Rev. Miller and his wife were among the visitors later in the evening. Lyal Miller liked to time his attendance toward the end. If a few words of prayer were wanted, he would deliver them. He and his wife came into a still-crowded room, the visitors having stayed to chat with each other. A comforting murmur of voices filled the room and the Rev. Miller was relieved to see that Les Jones looked more in control of himself tonight, not so broken and stunned as he had been just yesterday afternoon.

When there was a break in the line of people coming up to Les, Frances and Lyal went over to him. Miller shook Les' hand and introduced his wife.

"And this is Mrs. Jones," he said, indicating Lee to Frances.

Lee shook her head. "No, I'm not Les' wife. I'm Lee Collins, a good friend of Les and Wade."

"I see," Lyal Miller said. His wife shook Lee's hand and felt her own grasped in a firm handshake.

There was an uncomfortable silence. "It was very kind of you both to come tonight," Lee said.

"We were pleased to come," Frances said, in her pleasant musical voice. As usual for her, her green eyes did not quite meet those of the person she addressed. They slid over Lee quickly and were shuttered halfway by downcast lids.

"Yes, of course," her husband added. "I see you've been busy receiving people."

"Yeah," Les said. He was still moved by the display of support. "I never thought so many people would come."

"Why shouldn't they?" Lee asked, although she too had worried no one would. "You and Wade knew a lot of people. Everybody liked Wade."

"I guess they did." Les' eyes filled again. He wiped his handkerchief across his face.

"We'll see you at the service tomorrow," the Rev. Miller said. He shook hands with them both again, his handshake firm and supportive. He had decided against offering a prayer.

His wife followed him back out of the funeral home. In the car on the way home she spoke. "I thought you said he was married."

"I was wrong, it appears."

"Should you be doing a funeral for a homosexual? I'm quite sure that's what those people are. The woman too, probably."

"I don't see why not," Lyal said mildly. He knew the Biblical prohibitions but was not as upset by them as his wife seemed.

"I'm sure the church members would not want us to condone that type of behavior."

"I hardly think my officiating at the man's funeral suggests any such thing."

"It might to some people. Perhaps I shouldn't sing either." Frances couldn't explain to Lyal why she was so concerned about not antagonizing church members. But Lyal was getting old and where would they go if some issue like this caused the members to decide to find another minister?

"I see no reason to change our plans."

"All right," she agreed. "But it might be misinterpreted bu some people."

"The man is dead," Lyal pointed out. "I'm simply helping to bury him."

The service for Wade Carlton was well-attended. Ludgate had to have his assistant bring in more folding chairs. The room overflowed with people, including Wade's sister, who had called Ludgate early that morning and demanded details of the service.

Ludgate had been observing Mrs. Helen Lawton since her arrival. She had stared into the casket but made no pretense of mourning Wade. There had been no basket or spray of flowers from her. The casket area was thick with floral tributes, from Les, from Lee, and mostly from men, Ludgate had noticed while placing them.

The woman was seated in the chief mourner's row down a seat from Les and Lee. She was elegantly clothed, and her hair was carefully styled. She crossed and uncrossed her legs impatiently. Her lips were set in a thin line, and she did not acknowledge that she knew Les.

The service began. Lee took little notice of the reverend's dry words, but she did sit up when his wife sang. The woman had a beautiful clear voice, high and yet with depth to it. Lee watched Les daub at his eyes during the solos.

She and Les rode to the cemetery in Les' car. Lee drove because Les could not see through his tears. The plot the undertaker had obtained was in the old section under huge evergreens. On this bright fall day the artificial green of the carpet around the grave seemed garish. Wade would have laughed at it, she thought, and made some remark about fairy green.

The dry-as-dust minister was reciting the familiar words, the final words.

...From dust we came, to dust we return...

When it was over, Ludgate extracted a knife from his pocket and sliced off a flower from the casket spray Lee had bought. He handed the flower uncertainly to Wade's sister. "Perhaps you would like a remembrance," he said.

The woman brushed his outstretched hand out of the way. "Give it to the queer," she said, moving away to leave Ludgate standing with the flower in his hand.

"I'll take it," Lee said. She took the bloom and handed it to Les, knowing that Les would want it.

Ludgate watched this with a perplexed expression.

"Come on," Lee said to Les. "We need to go to the lunch."

"I suppose we do." Les stared blankly at the grave. He was holding the flower as though it were something very special and precious.

He followed Lee back to the car, and they drove to the church where the lunch was being held. With the burial over, the release of tension brought talk and laughter to the tables. Les listened to it morosely, sipping Ladies' Aid coffee and nibbling now and then at the food on his plate. Helen sat off by herself, drinking coffee only.

Later when most of the people had eaten and left, she came over to Les. Ignoring Lee, she said, "My brother is dead."

Les nodded.

"Did he leave a will?"

"No, I don't think he ever made one," Les said, not really registering.

"I see. I'll consult a lawyer locally then. I want to be sure I get my brother's estate. I'm legally entitled, I'm sure." With that she turned and left them.

Lee felt a chill pass over her. With no will, the woman was probably right.

In the weeks that followed the funeral, the aftershocks of Wade's death still rippled for Les. The loneliness and emptiness of the house the two of them had shared was hard to take. Even harder to bear was the knowledge that because Wade had made no will, his sister inherited everything Wade owned.

When Les and Wade had gone into partnership with the New Mercury, they had done so under a legal arrangement known as "tenants in common," which meant they had undivided half interests in the property of the restaurant and bar. Because they were unmarried, their lawyer had suggested this arrangement, not proposing a joint tenancy, which would have allowed the property to legally pass to the survivor, even overriding a will or lack of one.

Now Wade's sister was entitled to half of the New Mercury. Les could thank his lucky stars he had never offered Wade a half interest in the house, which had been Les' family home. Helen Lawton's attorney had checked that out very carefully, and had almost reluctantly concluded that Wade and therefore his client had no claim on it.

"What will you do?" Lee asked him when he told her of the situation.

"I don't know. I think the New Mercury is through anyway. I don't want to run it without Wade."

"So you'll put it up for sale?"

"Yeah. What's the point of anything else? She gets half the proceeds. All our years of work and half of it goes to that...that bitch. Do you know she's been through my house trying to pick out anything of value that Wade had? She even took the gold chains and ring I bought him. I should've buried them with him," Les said with a vehemence that was uncharacteristic of him.

Lee sympathized, but it surprised her that the two men had been so careless in their financial dealings. Lee had read enough horror stories to be very aware of the lack of legal protection offered gay people by the law.

"Well, that woman is in for a surprise," Les said. "My attorney says I can bill Wade's estate for the funeral costs I paid. She won't get half if I can find a way to reduce it."

"Good for you," Lee said. "But I wish you didn't have to sell the restaurant."

"Yeah, I know, but I closed it up when Wade died and I can't bring myself to open it again. I talked to a realtor yesterday. It may take awhile, but it will sell, I think." He shrugged. "I'm fifty-five. Feel like a hundred some days. I've got some savings. I'll be okay. Wade spent a lot of his share of the profits, thank God, or his sister would get that, too. I'll be okay."

He spoke so bleakly, though, that Lee hoped he would not start dipping into the alcohol he had for the most part resisted drinking even as he dispensed it to others.

CHAPTER EIGHTEEN

Ronald Reagan came into the White House in 1981. Supply-side economics with a trickle-down effect sounded pretty much like business as usual to Lee. If you read history, as Lee did, you knew that it sounded a lot like the old laissez-faire capitalism of the last century when there had been no labor laws, no minimum wages, and whatever the little people got certainly was what trickled down from the rich.

For dairy farmers 1981 was a deceptive year. Milk prices rose again to level out at $13.62. But interest rates were also in a steep climb. Property taxes were going up too. Farms in Wisconsin made up just 1.5% of the taxable units but paid 10% of the property taxes.

And 1981 was the year George decided they needed another Harvestore for the storage of high-moisture shelled corn, which was becoming a popular livestock feed.

"It'll pay for itself," George insisted. "Our herd is up to almost twenty thousand pounds per cow now. With the corn in their ration, they'll go a lot higher."

"But look what's happening to our interest rates," Clare argued. "They used to be down around 8.5% with FLB. They're up to 10% this year and FLB can raise them anytime they want to."

"Interest is just another tax deduction," George said impatiently. And it was true. With the interest they paid out, their taxes were almost nothing. But they had to have some actual income to live on. Each month there was less of it.

"You'll see. This interest thing will turn around," George said. "Reagan won't hurt the farmers. He believes in us."

"Maybe so," Clare said doubtfully. She was halfway glad he'd even bothered to ask. He seemed to feel no compunction these days about buying pieces of machinery on credit without telling Clare, a bad habit that ignited some of their worst arguments. George would hand her a sales contract and say, "I bought a new cultivator (or wagon or disk or tractor). Here's the payment schedule." In exasperation, Clare would attempt to reason with him about the need to plan the purchases. "We can't keep on doing this," Clare told him. "We owe too much already."

"Oh, come on. We're big farmers now. This is a business like any other. It makes good sense to buy when you need it, before the price goes up again."

"I know that's what the experts say," Clare said. "But somehow in their talk about assets and equity, they never seem to discuss simple arithmetic."

George snorted. "That's just for accounting and taxes. We're talking management here."

"I'm talking paying the bills. Sit down and look at the bills with me. Maybe then you'll see what I'm talking about."

George was not aware, as Clare was, that it took half of each month's income just to pay their creditors. That left only half the monthly income to settle regular bills and live on. It wasn't enough.

In 1982 the price of milk went up for the last time, rising just a dime, to $13.72. The small rise was more than offset by increases in property taxes, interest, and basic expenses. Interest rates rose to 13% on Clare and George's FLB loan.

Other costs were up as well. Machinery spare parts cost more. So did fertilizer and seed. Breeding fees, milk testing, tractor fuel, insurance, all were up. Clare had to shuffle basic bills around to get them paid on time. She became an expert at paying a bill just before interest was charged on it.

By shuffling the money around, she managed to make it through into April without missing any payments. But in April they needed to buy fertilizer, seed, lime, and chemicals to plant their crops.

She couldn't work the bills for those items into her budget, so she had to let them slide beyond the thirty days interest-free period the local Farmers' Union Co-op offered.

George was too busy in the fields to allow her to show him the figures. "You can deal with it," he said. "I've got to go work up those fields on the old Harmon place if we're gonna get any corn crop."

"But we don't even have the money to pay for the seed," Clare told him.

"We'll manage. We always do."

Lee was feeling the squeeze, too. With her thirty Jersey cows she had more than enough work, even if the farm magazines told everyone they were under-employed with that number of animals. She'd just like to see one of those desk jockeys putting in her hours and still say she was under-employed.

Whoever had decided that small farms such as hers were unprofitable was not familiar with a paid-for operation. Lee might need to borrow some money when she wanted to replace machinery, but her needs were much simpler than the Hansens'.

In the spring of 1982 the local chapter of the Jaycees named Butch Grimes as its outstanding young farmer. His picture with Sally and their year-old daughter Angie appeared on the front page of the local paper.

George rustled the paper with a jealous rage. "It burns me up," he said. "They pick Butch Grimes and who is it that made that farm? Not Butch."

"Butch is okay. He's always worked over there. You know that."

"Sure, but outstanding? Come on. What about us? Haven't we been pretty outstanding? No one ever recognized us."

"It's just a local award," Clare said. "It doesn't mean a thing."

"It does to me. I'd like some recognition, too. When we got married, you had a small farm. Just look at what we've built."

"I know," Clare said. To herself, she thought, we've built lots of debts.

What neither Clare nor George could know was that while Orrin Grimes was certainly proud of his son for getting the award, he did not feel quite right about it, either. Not that Butch wasn't a good farmer. It was just that Grimes' Farms, Inc. was twelve full months behind in its payments to the local Farmers' Union Co-op. He did not feel anyone should be passing out awards to folks on farms where that was the case. But the Jaycees were not using financial solvency as a measurement of what it took to be outstanding. Not yet.

The spring of 1982 also saw the sale of the New Mercury. The building was sold to a developer from St. Paul, and the fittings were going piecemeal to the highest bidder at auction.

Lee attended the sale with Les and wondered how he could bear to watch.

Les did not seem too upset. "I never thought that would sell so well," he said as someone paid top price for the old back bar.

"I think most of it is going okay."

"Part of me hopes it won't sell at all well. Did you notice who's here to make sure she gets all her money?"

"Wade's sister," Lee said.

"In person. She'll get a tidy piece of change out of this. I just wish we'd had the sense to set it up legally for each other. But who knew Wade would die so young?" Les sighed, remembering.

Lee thought she could smell alcohol on Les' breath. If he was drinking again, he was handling it well. She hoped he had only felt the need of a few drinks to get through the sale. "What will you do when this is settled?"

"Oh, I don't know," Les sighed again. "The sale and this whole thing with Helen did at least fill my time. I don't know what's next. With my savings I can live okay. Won't be grand, but I'll have enough. Maybe I'll travel a little, see some of the country."

"Buy yourself a van and take your bed with you," Lee encouraged.

Les grinned. "Yeah, I could do that. If it was Wade, he'd have a huge bed filling the whole back end. Just in case opportunity knocked."

"Yeah," Lee agreed, remembering Wade.

"I think I'll just get a single bed and hang out a 'do not disturb' sign," Les said. Lee could smell the alcohol stronger this time.

❧

The Rev. Lyal Miller, aged sixty-four, died in the spring of 1982, leaving his wife Frances, their son Richard and his wife Patricia, and two grandchildren. He had been collecting a small pension for two years when he died. The amount he received was not enough to live on, but with the continued salary his Good Hope congregation paid him, he and Frances had managed.

Now, with Lyal dead, the widow's portion of Lyal's pension was going to be small, about $250 a month. Frances would have to do something. She was accustomed to having a man in her life to take care of things. So, it was with a sigh of relief that she welcomed home her son Richard and watched him take charge, make the funeral arrangements, and handle the finances, if only briefly.

Richard was an assistant pastor at a large Assemblies of God church near Chicago. The salary was a good one, and the church vigorous, but Richard wanted his own turf. When the board of Good Hope approached him about stepping into the pulpit his father had just vacated, he was agreeable.

Frances was delighted. Richard had a take-charge attitude she appreciated. He was at once aware of her financial precariousness.

"You'll live with us," he said. "In the parsonage, of course. I'm going to reinvigorate this church. Dad let it slide too far. I guess he was old and tired. I want to attract a younger element. It's out there," he assured his mother. "Statistics suggest that younger people are fed up with hedonistical liberal lifestyles. They want a faith. I'm going to provide that for them."

Frances was skeptical but pleased to have her son and his family back home. It meant she did not have to leave her safe haven. She had to move out of the big bedroom, of course. That was for Richard and Patricia. And the two smaller rooms on the second floor needed to be for the children. Frances moved up to the large open room on the top floor.

It had been her storage area, but she cleared the accumulated junk out and held a garage sale. With the mess gone, it was a cozy enough place, and the junk sold well to a variety of buyers who eagerly pawed through Frances' cast-offs. She was looking forward to a little spending money from the proceeds.

As she counted out what she had made, Richard stopped by the dining room table. He fingered the dollar bills and checks and change. "I see you did well on that old stuff, eh?"

"Yes. I was surprised. I took in almost $100. $97.53, to be exact. I don't know where the spare three cents came from."

"Pretty good," Richard said with his easy smile and pleasant voice. He picked up the cash. "Why don't you endorse the checks and I'll take care of them? We can use the extra money until I can get this church going again."

It seemed churlish to suggest she had been looking forward to using the money for herself, maybe to buy something in the way of clothes. She endorsed the checks. Richard pocketed the money, except for $7.53.

"You'd better keep a little for yourself," he said with his charming smile.

Frances almost said thank you.

❧

By the end of August 1982 Clare could breathe a sigh of relief. She had managed at last to bring the Farmers' Union account for fertilizer, chemicals and seed up-to-date. Somehow she had actually gotten it across to George that they did not have spare cash for extra expenses.

"No more meals at Morgan's for quite awhile."

"I can live with that. Your cooking is bearable," he joked.

"It'll have to be. Chad isn't to have any special things, either. He has plenty of toys."

"I hate to see us skimping on our kid, but if it's just for awhile…"

"It may be for a long time," Clare said. "The way the economy is going…"

When she had finished paying the August bills and could look ahead and plan into September, she told George the news.

"We're even again at the Farmer's Union."

"Hey, that's great. See, I knew there was nothing to worry about. Just a short-term problem."

"Don't go getting ideas," she cautioned quickly. "We still need to go easy. I'm afraid Federal Land Bank may raise their interest rates another half percent this September."

"What's half a percent," George said dismissively. "That doesn't sound like much to me."

"It is when you're talking over four hundred thousand dollars in debt. That's two thousand dollars a year in extra interest."

A further breather came in September when Clare wrote a check for the last payment on a tractor. That had been the 100-horse John Deere George had bought in 1978. Clare made the mistake of telling George that the tractor was paid for. His ears perked up.

"That's great," he said. "See? We're doing fine. I think I'll go down and look at the new John Deeres. They've got a great-looking 110-horse with cab down on the lot."

"No, please don't." Clare felt exasperated. What had she been preaching to him all summer? "We cannot afford to buy a new tractor."

"But we need a bigger tractor again. If we can make payments for four years, we can do it again, right? Besides, John Deere has a low-interest program to finance it."

"I don't give a damn how low the interest is. We can't afford the principal, never mind the interest. Haven't you been paying any attention to what I've told you? We just don't have the money to do it." Clare felt near tears with frustration.

"And I don't want to see us sit here and stagnate because you're scared we can't pay the bills. That's what's gonna happen if we don't keep upgrading and improving. We'll get left behind and suddenly we'll be stuck with a bunch of out-dated junk."

"That seems unlikely at the rate you've been replacing things," Clare said sarcastically. "Surely all this shiny stuff you buy has some useful life to it."

Her pleas fell on deaf ears. On Friday morning after chores the John Deere salesman came out to talk with George. He said hello to Clare who was in the milkhouse.

"Bossman around?" he asked.

"If you mean George, yes," she said. She hated that expression.

He waited to begin his sales pitch until he and George had shot the breeze a little. "Looks like you had a good crop year."

"We sure did," George said. He leaned casually against the open milkhouse door, so that Clare, working inside, could not help but overhear the conversation.

"Been a good year for a lot of farmers," the salesman said.

"Yeah. I had good hay yields and the corn looks like it's going to be better than last year. I may try some soybeans next year."

Clare, listening, was aware that the "we" in George's talk had become "I," a switch he made when he was talking with salesmen and loan officers and other farmers.

The salesman moved into his sales pitch. "Now that 110-horse you been looking at. Want you to know I got another farmer looking at it. Just thought I should stop out and see if you want it. I told the other guy you were looking and that you had first chance to buy it. I just don't want any hard feelings around these things, you know?"

Clare listened in disgust. George was eating it up.

"Well, I offered you forty-eight thousand dollars on her," George said.

"I know, I know, but I got to make a buck too. And those 110-horses are popular sizes." The salesman paused briefly. "I've sold a lot of them this summer. This is the last one on the lot. Emil Mason, over on the other side of town, you know him? He got one. Thinks it's just great. Good fuel economy. Great lugging power. Got the best cab in the business." The salesman droned on, giving George time to think.

Clare finished the milkhouse cleanup and came out to stand next to George. George looked guiltily at her, aware of her disapproval. "The wife doesn't think we should buy another tractor."

The wife. Clare snorted.

"Well, 'the wife' manages the finances here," she said. "And we just can't afford another tractor right now. It won't do you much good to make a sale if we can't make the payments, will it?"

"Oh, now I'm sure that's unlikely," the salesman said with a smile and a wink for George. "I know you folks always pay your bills. Not like some I know. Your credit is always good with us."

"And I'd like to keep it that way," Clare said. "Okay?"

"Well, sure. Now, I just can't quite meet that $48,000 offer, George. But here's what I'll do. I'll split the difference with you. Sell you it for $49,000."

"All right," George said. "I can live with that."

"Well, I can't," Clare said. "We can't afford that tractor at any price. I don't care if you're giving it away with Green Stamps."

"Oh, once you get that smooth-running machine out here, you'll change your mind," the salesman said, uncertain now if he had just made a deal or not.

"It's a great performer," George said to Clare, placatingly. "You'll see, it'll pay for itself in no time at all."

"Right. It mints money while it plows." Clare noticed with anger that the salesman was drawing up a sales agreement. Did no one listen?

George laughed nervously. "Well, maybe not quite, but we need the bigger horsepower." He signed the sales agreement.

After the salesman left, Clare turned angrily to George. "I can't believe you went ahead and bought it. I just can't believe it."

"And I can't believe how much you embarrassed me in front of that guy. Made me feel about two inches tall."

"I embarrassed you? What did you two do to me? You ignored me. It was like I wasn't in on this at all. This was something between the men."

"Look..." His voice rose shrilly. "I was just trying to buy a piece of equipment to keep this farm running smoothly. And you go and humiliate me."

"I suppose it wasn't humiliating for me to be ignored?"

"I don't give a damn if it was or wasn't! 'We can't afford this. We can't afford that.' If it was up to you we'd still be sitting here with about thirty cows and some old beat-up equipment."

"And who's to say we wouldn't be better off? All the debts, and now you want to make more. Where are you going?"

"Up the goddamned silo. We were going to open it after chores, remember? Maybe I should just throw haylage down with a fork so we don't use money for electricity to run the silo unloader."

"Don't be ridiculous. I'm trying to keep this farm afloat. You want to sink it."

"Just get off my back about this crap, will you?"

George stalked angrily toward the silo. Those were the last words they exchanged.

III

INTERLUDE

June 1983

The day was warm and sunny with the gentle yet intense warmth of early summer. Green was the predominant color of the landscape. There was the green of new corn growing toward knee-high before the Fourth of July, the deep green of oat fields almost in the boot stage, and the green of recovering hayfields already showing bright young shoots of second crop alfalfa. Occasionally there was also the ranker green of first crop hay yet to be cut.

As Clare drove farther east of town into the sudden rise of hills, a trace of spring still showed in new leaves on trees and bushes. Lee had her right arm out the open pickup window, warm sun tempering the rush of wind across her skin.

The good blacktop road gave way to a gravel washboard, and Clare slowed her speed. Lee could hear snatches of birdsong from the trees that crowded up to the edges of the road. The trees were so close that in some spots their crowns formed a sheltering canopy over the pickup. The sun's warmth was not quite able to penetrate the denseness of leaves, but occasionally a shaft of light shone through with all the intensity of a spotlight.

It was an ideal day for a picnic. Clare was watching for the perfect spot to stop and spread out the old blanket. She and George had never taken time for picnics.

Clare stopped the pickup by the edge of a trout stream. There was a grassy expanse of open space with a large old oak tree near the bank to provide some shade if the sun got too hot.

The silence was broken by gentle noises: the trout stream rippling over rocks, birds singing, small animals rustling off into the underbrush away from the human intruders.

Lee stood beside the truck enjoying the feel of warm sun on her bare arms, liking the tranquil spot Clare had chosen. It had been a long time since she and Clare had done anything like this together, yet it seemed so natural and easy.

She didn't know what had prompted Clare to invite her on this picnic, but she knew what had made her accept. Funny how the passing years hadn't changed that. Here she was at fifty-one, looking older and grayer each passing year, and yet she was feeling today like she was twenty-one and the whole of her life lay before her.

Clare took a deep breath of fresh woodland air and felt herself shed some of her burdens, casting them out into the woods and stream. She was not going to even think of Chad and the farm and...

She thought instead about herself and Lee. Now that's something I haven't handled very well over the years, she told herself wryly. I sure couldn't deal with my feelings around her. Such total panic! Such panic that I married George, when instead I should have... But at least the marriage got me Chad. She'd said she wasn't going to worry about Chad today, and here she was already dragging him into her thoughts. But her problems with Chad were hard to shed, even for a few hours.

She smiled across the truck bed at Lee, who was digging around for the blanket. For a moment Clare panicked. I hope I can handle this, she thought. I hope I'm able to.

Lee smiled back when she looked up. She had the blanket in one hand, and the picnic basket in the other. Clare thought she'd never seen anyone she liked the looks of better than Lee. Her gentle face was crisscrossed with lines and wrinkles that deepened when she smiled. Her short compact body radiated strength and capability and yet suggested gentleness and comfort. Her eyes sparkled with a deep brown that looked at Clare directly, taking her into their depths. Lee's chin was strong, her ears small, her lips full and firm but soft and so gentle-looking.

No, maybe I'm not quite ready to deal with her lips, Clare thought with a nervous inner chuckle.

She walked around the back of the truck. "Can I take the picnic basket?"

"I've got it. Grab the cooler, why don't you?" Lee walked off to survey the area for the perfect picnic spot. "How about right here?" She gestured around her at a grassy level spot near the oak tree, just above the sloping stream bank.

"Looks perfect." Clare put down the cooler and grabbed an end of the blanket to spread it flat on the ground. It was an old plaid blanket, one she'd kept for all the years since that last picnic with Lee.

"Want to eat right away?" Clare asked. She waited for Lee's nod and then began to unpack the lunch she had put together after chores that morning. There were pieces of fried chicken, a potato salad, cheese and fruit, and chocolate chip cookies for dessert.

Lee opened the cooler and brought out her contribution to the meal: orange-flavored mineral water and a bottle of California wine. She watched Clare spread out the food and wondered how being together like this again could seem so natural, so unforced. It had been nearly twenty years since they first met. Clare's tall angular frame had filled out nicely, Lee thought. Her short hair was showing some gray, hard to see among the light brown. Her face was unwrinkled yet, but had lines around the eyes.

Such clear green eyes. And the mouth. Full, with lips that curved upward in a slight smile as Clare became aware of Lee watching her.

Her eyes met Lee's and Lee withdrew, blushing. For God's sake.

Fifty-one years old and you're blushing. She felt herself blush harder.

"I probably shouldn't ask you what caused that," Clare surprised herself by saying.

"No, you probably shouldn't," Lee said back. "I'm not sure I'd be able to tell you, anyway." She felt suddenly shy and busied herself opening the bottle of wine, working the cork out with practiced skill.

"What kind of wine did you bring?"

Lee held up the bottle.

"Ah! An Inglenook Blush wine. That was an appropriate choice." She said it straight-faced, watching Lee turn red again. Then she chuckled and Lee had to join her, laughing at herself. Laughing, too, because she had never known that Clare could joke like this. She poured wine into the glasses Clare held.

"I wish I could think of an appropriate toast."

"And I think I hope you don't somehow," Lee said ruefully. She raised her glass. "To a perfect day."

"I can drink to that." Clare clinked her glass against Lee's. She sipped some of the wine and watched Lee over the rim of her glass. *Now why was I afraid of* her? *Why did I run when she looked at me that way back in the '60s? And why did I stay with George for fourteen years in a marriage that was, well, less than perfect?*

"You look deep in thought," Lee said.

"I was. I was thinking that I...should never have married George."

"Well, that's a deep thought. I certainly wouldn't argue with you on it."

"No. I don't suppose you would. It's a nice day and I don't want to ruin it with morbid thoughts. Let's eat, shall we?" Clare felt herself backing off, afraid to go further.

"Sure," Lee said easily. She took the offered piece of crispy chicken. A nice new glimmer of hope began to glow inside her, and she ate with an appetite that had little to do with hunger.

The wine was relaxing Clare. She had a second glass. So did Lee. Their third glass emptied the bottle.

"This is a very nice wine." Clare paused and then spoke again before she could stop and think not to. "And that was also a very nice blush." She studied Lee. "Hey! you're doing it again. You look nice when you do that."

"Thanks, I think. I never realized you were into teasing."

"I never have been, much," Clare admitted. "It must be the wine. Or the blush." She chuckled, feeling daring and carefree.

Lee was watching her closely. There was a puzzled, hopeful expression on her face. "Do you know what you're doing?" she asked.

"Yes. No."

"Well, I'd say you were flirting with me. And the question I have is, if I respond, will you run away?"

"Like I did before?"

"Yes. Like that." Lee found her heart was beating rapidly as she waited for a reply.

Clare looked away and then back. "Well, my folks have been hinting I should get married again."

"I think they meant to a guy."

"Yeah, I'm sure they did. Maybe I'm just playing around with you to scare myself into another marriage. George has a single brother just a year older, you know."

"No, I didn't know," Lee said. Her mouth felt dry.

"Hey, I'm teasing you again. I went too far, didn't I?" Clare reached out and touched Lee's arm lightly. "I'm sorry. I'm not doing this very well and you're not helping all that much."

"I'm not the one who ran away last time, either," Lee said with a sharpness that caused Clare to remove her hand from Lee's arm.

"No. You're right. I'm the one who did that. And I've spent a lot of years regretting it."

"Well, why did you stay married to him? I got the impression you knew at your wedding it had been a mistake."

"I did," Clare shrugged helplessly. "But I'd married him. He wasn't a bad man. I felt I had to give it a chance and then Chad came along and we had all those debts. I did care about George too, Lee. I didn't love him, but..."

"You cared about him, I know," Lee said resignedly, thinking how often women have said those words. To justify staying in marriages, to excuse male behavior, to deny themselves happiness.

"And now I'm supposed to just step back in time with you to where we were fifteen years ago?" Lee felt vague anger stirring. "Is that it?"

"Sort of...I don't know..." This was not going as Clare hoped it might on this summer day warm with sunshine and promise. A cloud passed over the sun and Clare shivered.

"Look," Lee was saying, intently watching Clare, who made herself watch Lee back, "I don't know what you expect from me. I'm fifty-one years old and you're...what, forty-three? We're not kids. And when you ran from me before, it hurt."

"I'm sorry. I know I wasn't very brave then."

"And maybe I wasn't brave enough either. But now you're flirting with me, and I don't know where you expect it to go. I'm not interested in a nice sterile little friendship with you. I wasn't then and I'm not now."

"I know. I mean, I think I know, but back then when you looked at me and touched me, the idea of being involved with a woman scared the hell out of me."

Lee's long-ago hurt still felt fresh and newly raw. It put anger into her voice. "So what *do* you want from me?"

"I don't know. I mean, I'm not sure."

"She's not sure! Swell. Wonderful. She's not sure," Lee said to the trout stream.

A startled bird flew up behind them at the loudness of her voice.

"No. I'm not," Clare said steadily. "But I do know I want you to stop treating me like I'm still a naive twenty-year-old moving in across the road. I'm forty-three. A widow for God's sake. Yes, I got scared into a marriage. And I have a kid I don't even get along with sometimes. My folks want me to remarry. My mother-in-law thinks I'm an unfit mother. Nobody seems to think I should want or need anything for myself. You don't think I can figure anything out for myself anymore than the rest of them do. I'm trying, believe me. Who was it invited you on this picnic anyway? Me. I did. Because I…suddenly, no not so suddenly…I wanted to…"

Her voice trailed off because she could not find words for what she wanted.

Lee watched her closely, the anger softening.

When Clare spoke again, her voice was quieter. From somewhere some humor had crept back into it. "I'm not sure of a lot of things. I don't know a lot of things, but do you know what I want right now?"

"No." Lee kept her eyes on Clare's eyes.

"What I want right now is…to kiss you."

"Well. Why don't you, then?" It was a challenge and an invitation.

"Hey," Clare said later. "That was nice." It was a moment of discovery. So that's what it's like to kiss her, Clare thought. It's wonderful.

"So glad you liked it," Lee said. "Going to get up and run away?"

"Nope. Think I'll just stay right here. Maybe I'll move over a little closer. My neck doesn't like this position."

"Anything to accommodate your neck."

"So kind of you… Do you think we could do that again?"

"I don't see why not. Many times, probably."

"Yeah, I don't suppose lips ever wear out."

"Not so I've…noticed."

"You've done this a lot."

"Well, I've had some practice."

"More than I have, I think."

"You're not doing badly at it."

"It seems to come naturally. Feels right. In fact, you feel right to me," Clare said.

"I was hoping I might."

"I won't run this time."

"It might be hard to. I've got you pinned down here pretty tight."

-184-

The afternoon sun warmed them outside and another kind of warmth rose from within. They lay curled together on the old plaid blanket. They might have stayed that way all afternoon, talking and caressing, but the loud sound of a trailbike churning up gravel and coming closer forced them apart and made them sit up. A helmeted rider roared by on the gravel road, kicking up dust and pebbles in his wake.

"Well," Clare said.

"Well, indeed."

"I wish he hadn't come by."

"Me, too, but the wider world does have a way of intruding, especially when you pick such a public spot."

"Yeah, I guess it does. Next time I'll park us under a bush."

"Is that how it's going to be? Nice picnics from time to time?"

"No, I just meant..."

"Every sixteen years or so you'll decide, gee, I'd like to go on a picnic again with Lee and neck in the woods."

"Don't be so prickly. I don't want to wait another sixteen years for it."

"No? How long? Ten years, maybe?"

"How about ten seconds?"

"That long?"

"No..."

"We could go home," Lee suggested.

"My house is occupied," Clare pointed out.

"I know, but mine isn't."

"That's true..."

They refolded the old blanket and packed up the picnic gear. Clare drove them back out of the hills. They rode in silence. Somewhere during the journey Lee reached out a hand to Clare. They finished the ride holding hands.

Clare shut off the engine. They sat in the silent truck in Lee's yard.

"Are you sure?" Lee asked.

"As sure as I can be."

"I don't want just an afternoon."

"I know that. Neither do I. Look, I wasted almost sixteen years because I was too damned scared of us and because I worried about what everybody else would think. Now I'm tired of worrying about other people's opinions."

"How about the scared part?"

Clare's smile was rueful. "I'm still scared, but not enough to run away again."

"That's good, because this time I think I would come after you, which is what I probably should have done before."

"I don't know what would have happened if you had done that."

"Probably nothing different than what did happen, but I've often thought I should have tried."

"Why didn't you?"

"I guess I was scared, too."

"Aren't we a fine pair of frightened females, though?"

"I like the sound of 'fine pair,'" Lee said. "Are you going to come in my house with me?"

Clare paused before answering. The question had significance. "Yes, I am," she said.

PART THREE

September, 1982-June, 1983

CHAPTER NINETEEN

In the months after George's death, when the shock of the accident began to wear off and the reality of day-to-day life settled in, Clare had to assess her financial situation. As she shuffled papers and examined file folders of mortage agreements and insurance policies, she came upon the latest life insurance policy their loan officer at FLB had written up on George. I forgot about this, she thought. Can it really be true? George's life was insured to the full value of the FLB loan.

"God," she said aloud. "It pays off the whole thing. My God." She regarded the simple piece of paper in her hand. "This thing pays off over $400,000 in debt. Just like that. My God."

How ironic, she thought. I burned with anger when that first male chauvinistic loan officer insisted that the insurance should be in the "chief farmer's" name. And now because of it I'm out of debt to FLB. My God, she repeated to herself, awed and amazed and sharply aware of how guilty she felt to be so relieved.

"I can't believe it," she said aloud, glad there was no one in the house to hear her. "I can't believe it. I'm sorry, George."

Here I am, talking to someone who is dead. I'm not debt-free but close, very close, and all because of an insurance policy I resented being issued in the first place.

There were still obligations for farm machinery payments, car and truck payments, and a small note at the local bank. Once Clare had cancelled out on George's most recent tractor purchase made the day of his death, what was left was a very manageable debt.

"I still don't believe it," she repeated to herself. If Clare was having trouble believing her new status of nearly debt-free farmer, the Grimeses down the road were wishing the same was true of them. Like many farmers in the early '80s, they had borrowed heavily.

In 1980 Congress passed a bill called the Farm Credit Act Amendment. This gave Federal Land Banks the power to lend money up to 95% of the appraised real estate value of a farmer's land.

As long as land values continued to rise, the balance sheets looked healthy. But partway into the 1980s, land values began to fall. Suddenly there were no longer enough assets to cover the liabilities and, at least on paper, farms like Grimes Farms, Inc., no longer looked financially healthy.

Farmers like the Grimeses had been urged to borrow money. They had been urged to do so by every farm magazine they read, every farm expert they heard, every loan officer they dealt with. Suddenly, when the situation changed, the experts, the farm seminar leaders, and above all the loan officers were no longer there to support them.

"Imagine that," Stella said to Sally and Butch. "Today we were told by our loan officer at FLB that we weren't 'financially alert' enough. Whatever that means. Supposedly we haven't been watching our assets and liabilties close enough. He demanded a detailed balance sheet from us before he would even consider looking at our loan payment problems."

"That's a switch, isn't it?" Sally asked. "I remember the last few times when all he wanted was an estimate of what everything was worth. I thought it was kind of strange."

"It may have been strange, but that's how they've always done it. Until now," Stella said. "I got so mad, and maybe I shouldn't have, but here was this...this pompous man being all righteous and telling us we had to be better financial managers. As though it's all our fault prices are way up for what we buy and interest rates are high. What we had to do with that is beyond me."

She and Orrin were sitting with Sally and Butch at the younger couple's kitchen table. Sally poured them all more coffee and sat down next to Butch.

"So we can get them their precious balance sheet, can't we?" she asked.

"Of course," Stella said.

"What good will a balance sheet do anyway?" Orrin asked. He was feeling depressed and ashamed. He had always prided himself on their ability to pay their bills. To have to admit there were problems was humiliating.

"It's a magic piece of paper," Stella said sarcastically. "Makes everything all right as long as you've got one. Only it doesn't. Lord knows, I've spent enough time lately pushing numbers around on paper, trying to figure some way to just stay even and pay the bills. There just isn't enough money to live on when we pay all the bills. I don't know about the rest of you, but I do like to eat. I get weak and cranky when I don't."

Orrin smiled slightly. His ability to banter back at Stella seemed to have disappeared lately. He wished he could stand up as spunkily around their money quandaries as Stella seemed to be doing.

"I'll get a job," Sally offered. "I've been thinking about it for awhile and I know I could get my old secretarial job back at the wood products factory."

"I thought you hated that place," Stella said. "Besides you do so much work here we'd be lost without you. I don't know how we managed before Butch had the good sense to marry you, really I don't." She looked across the table at her daughter-in-law with genuine affection.

Sally returned the look with a grateful smile. She had been accepted into this family in a way her own family had never accepted her. At home she had worked, been expected to, but it had been taken for granted as something a girl child did before she left home to get married. Here she was an equal partner with Butch and Stella and Orrin.

"It wouldn't be forever. I hope," Sally said. "You're right about me hating the work, but I'm good at it even so. The biggest problem is what to do with Angie."

"Yeah, I'm sure they wouldn't welcome a two-year-old crawling among the filing cabinets," Stella said. "I can just see how much trouble she could get herself into there."

She paused to watch her grandchild scuttling around the floor, pushing a toy tractor ahead of her and making tractor noises. "Doesn't she have any dolls?"

"She doesn't like dolls," Butch said fondly. "I bought her a big soft cuddly one, but she'd rather play with that tractor of mine."

"That figures," Stella said. "She'll be out on a real tractor by the time she's seven."

"Not if we can't pay the bills. We could lose this place," Orrin said, his voice morose.

Stella patted his arm. "I know," she said. "I know."

"We're not going to lose it. Damn this economy anyway." Sally spoke strongly. "I'll go to work and that will bring in food money for all of us. Do you think you could keep Angie somehow, Stella? If I have to find somebody to keep her, it'll eat up what I'd make."

"I guess that might be the best solution, if you're determined to kill yourself working," Stella said, visibly touched that Sally was so willing. "She'll slow me down some, won't you, Pumpkin? But at least I won't be able to say I never see my grandchild."

Butch had been silent during most of the talk. "If Sally's gonna get a job, I am, too. The milkhauler says they always have trouble keeping people on the night shift down at the creamery."

"You're crazy," Stella said. "You're not seriously considering working nights there and days here?"

Butch shrugged. "I've been thinking about it for awhile. The pay's good, ten dollars an hour and there are benefits. I can get insurance for me and Sally and Angie."

Stella shook her head. "You're both nuts. Crazy. There has to be some other way..."

"What other way?" Butch asked. "We all know what we owe, and what we make on this farm isn't enough to cover it."

Stella looked at her son and shook her head. "Yeah, I know. But there's so much work here. Your dad and I can't do it all anymore. There's the custom work too."

"We'll manage," Sally assured her. "Really we will, Stella. We'll both still be working here."

"I wish I had your optimism, but I don't. I just see more and more of this as the years go on. Damn, maybe we'd be smarter to just sell out and get out."

"No way," Butch said. "I don't care what I have to do, but I'm not going to quit."

"Oh, I'm just talking," Stella assured him. "Can't I be depressed and discouraged once in awhile? Lord knows there is reason enough."

Stella mostly kept her discouragement to herself as both Sally and Butch went out to work. Sally got her old job back at $6.50 per hour. Butch went to work at the creamery on the night sanitation crew. His pay was $10 per hour, with paid holidays, sick leave, a pension plan, and insurance.

His hours were from 10:00 p.m. to 4:00 a.m. Sally worked days.

Rushing home at 4:30 p.m., she'd pick up Angie at Stella's, get some supper for Butch and send him to bed for some sleep. Then she'd join Orrin and Stella in the barn, taking Angie with her. She was back in the house by 8:30 p.m., putting Angie to bed, washing clothes, and catching up on housework until Butch left shortly before 10:00 p.m. She'd then go to bed and try to sleep until Butch came home.

They both started the day by going to the barn at 5:00 a.m. Sally left the barn chores early to get Angie up and dressed and over to Stella's by 8:30 p.m. Then she would leave for work again while Butch made himself some breakfast and caught a nap before going out to continue the farm work for the day.

It was a grueling schedule. Sally and Butch were both thankful for weekends, when there were just chores and crop work. Weekends were almost like having time off. They were both young enough to have good reserves of energy. That and the knowledge that the bills were being paid kept them going.

Orrin frequently thanked whatever powers there were for the good fortune to have a son and daughter-in-law like Butch and Sally. He was aware that the extra money was making a difference. Even the delinquent Farmers' Union Co-op bill was being whittled down.

They were paying right on time, though, for new purchases, plus managing to pay off some of the delinquent amount. So the Co-op's announcement in the spring of 1983 that it would no longer extend credit for spring planting needs came as a severe blow.

Stella read the letter announcing the new policy. "It says here they won't sell on credit if your account has been delinquent in the past twelve months. No credit at all. Just straight cash."

"How are we gonna pay cash for everything we need to put in the crops?" Butch asked, as the four of them once again held a family conclave.

"I don't see how we can do it," Orrin said.

"Well, we'll have to," Stella said firmly. "There must be a way."

"Damn. I feel like we've been knifed in the back." Butch crumpled up the Co-op letter announcing the credit changes. "We've been good customers there."

"But we haven't been paying customers," Stella pointed out.

"We've been trying our best. This just really burns me. This is our Co-op." Butch's indignation seemed registered in every freckle on his face. "You'd think they'd make exceptions. I mean, we intend to pay."

"So does everybody else, I imagine," Stella said dryly. She was almost amused by how hurt the men were. She could see it made sense. The Co-op could not let some of its patrons pull the whole operation down.

Sally had unfolded the crumpled letter and was rereading it. "It says here that those who have made arrangements to pay off their past-due accounts should stop in and talk to the manager about planting needs and how to handle paying for them. It sounds to me like there might be some leeway after all."

"Yeah? I thought they said no exceptions." Butch took the letter from Sally.

"Maybe that's more to scare everybody a little," Sally suggested.

"Well, it sure scared me. I may be totally gray by the end of the spring work," Stella said. She took the letter from Butch. "If we could even get them to agree to a one-month charge on the planting needs instead of cash on delivery, I think we could do it."

"So do I," Sally said.

Orrin and Butch both shook their heads. "We can't ask them to do that," Orrin said. "It would look like we're begging."

"So? Then we'll beg," Stella said.

Stella went to the local Co-op and came back with a one-month credit extension for Grimes Farms on their planting needs. It still would not be easy, but the extension helped.

"It wasn't so bad," Stella told the rest of them. "It was easy once I got there. You just have to go and do it, that's all." Looking around at her family, she knew she wanted their farm to survive and damned if she wouldn't get out there and fight for it.

CHAPTER TWENTY

Over the fence line at the Hansen farm, Clare and Chad faced a bleak fall and winter of 1982-83. She and George had needed to work long hours to manage their expanded farm. Eighty cows waited each day to be fed, milked, cleaned up after, their health seen to, their breeding kept up to date. It had been a big job for Clare and George together, and often in busy times they'd hired an extra hand.

Now there was mainly Clare. The extra help that had appeared at the time of the funeral had melted away and here she was with all the cows to care for, fall plowing to do, and she was exhausted.

I'm not sure I can do all this, she thought wearily as she pulled off her barn boots one late September evening. The chores were finally done and Chad had retreated to the television set again.

It's too much. I miss George, she thought. I miss him a lot. We did work well together, and there was someone to share the problems with. How will I ever get the corn combined and in the silo before winter? I'll have to find somebody to help, that's all there is to it.

She hired back the young boy they had used the previous summer. Mike was eighteen now, out of high school, and not planning any further schooling. She took him on full-time with some qualms. George had always given him orders. Mike tended to ignore Clare, acting as though she were a piece of the landscape. But at least for awhile the extra workload was off Clare, and she could devote some of her time to other problems.

Those problems included her brother Marsh, whose surprise visit at the time of George's death had been such a comfort to her. But it had been anything but comforting to learn why he was home again.

"I need to talk to you," Marsh had said a few days after the funeral. "I know this isn't the best time, but maybe there isn't any really good time."

Something in his voice warned Clare. "You sound very serious," she said, turning to look directly at him.

"Well, it seems I'm dying," he said.

"You're kidding. Marsh, tell me you're kidding." Clare felt her heart turn leaden.

"I've got this new thing they call AIDS. Or rather the virus that's behind it."

"AIDS? Oh, my God." Clare's mouth felt dry and her mind seemed barely able to register on his words.

"I'm not sick with it yet. The guy I lived with died from it."

"The guy you lived with..." Clare repeated.

"Clare, I'm gay. I thought you probably knew."

Clare shook her head. "No, I mean, maybe I sort of knew, but you never said..."

"I know. I couldn't. You seemed upset enough about Lee being gay."

"Lee..." Memories, unwelcome ones, came flooding back to Clare. She shook her head. "You're dying. How...how soon?"

"I don't really know. I'm not sick yet."

"Have you told Mom and Dad?"

Marsh shook his head. "That's next. I wanted to tell you first. Because I hoped maybe you'd be...understanding."

"What am I supposed to understand? That you came home to die?"

Marsh looked helplessly at her. "I'm sorry. I wish it hadn't been like this, just after George's death. But you need to know."

"Isn't this...thing very contagious?" Clare was trying to remember the little she had heard about AIDS. The disease had seemed almost exotic, nothing that would ever concern her.

"It's not spread by casual contact," he said as though he had used the words many times before. "It's spread through the exchange of bodily fluids and in blood. I won't contaminate you if I hug you."

There was something in the way he said the last words that reached beyond the numbness in Clare. For that moment, at least, she saw his fear in the lines on his face and experienced his hurt. Before she could think, she put her arms around him and pulled him close. He clung to her and cried.

In the days after Marsh's announcement, Clare felt as though another piece of her world had fallen apart. It wasn't any too solid before, she thought. But Marsh being at risk for AIDS had really shattered it.

My brother is probably going to die. She tried the words out to herself and shrank from their meaning. I can't face this, she thought. Not on top of everything else. Then she felt selfish. Marsh was having to face it, and she knew he wasn't getting any support from their folks.

The dejected set of his shoulders, and the grimness on his face had told her that immediately when he'd come back from breaking the news.

"They didn't take it well?" she asked.

Marsh sat down wearily at the kitchen table. "You could say that. Dad just walked away. Mom...cried, of course. I could understand her tears, but the accusations..."

"Hard to take."

"Yeah. Very hard. But I guess she had to say them."

"I don't think Chad should be told," Clare said.

Marsh stared at her. "You're kidding. If I'm staying here, doesn't he need to know?"

"I thought it would be better if he didn't." Even to herself her words sounded weak. But how, she thought, could she tell her brother she was ashamed to have her son know? And more than that, ashamed to have other people know.

"I don't think that's very realistic, Clare. I mean, at some point I'm going to be sick and I'm going to die. Surely Chad will wonder why."

"I don't even want to think about it," Clare said tightly. "I mean, I just faced one death."

"I know." Marsh roused himself to remember what his sister had just gone through. He saw with surprise that she didn't look so young anymore. Her face was drawn, her eyes tired. What a mess, he thought.

"Do you really think Chad needs to know?"

Marsh nodded. "I'll tell him, if you like."

"Okay." Clare agreed reluctantly, knowing that to tell Chad was to tell the entire Hansen family and thus the whole community. A shiver of fear and shame went through her at the thought of everyone knowing her brother had come home to face the AIDS virus.

At thirteen, Chad was growing taller and more gangly by the day, his feet and legs sometimes clumsy with the quick growth. He had greeted his uncle eagerly at first, pleased to have him staying at the house.

The news of Marsh's AIDS changed his attitude totally. Now Chad avoided Marsh when he could and when he did speak to him, it was with disdain.

"How come you're staying here?" Chad demanded one night at supper.

"Because your mom said I could."

"Why don't you go stay somewhere else?"

"Chad, that's rude," Clare said weakly.

"Everybody says he shouldn't be here," Chad said.

"Who is 'everybody'?" Clare asked with a sinking feeling.

"Oh, lots of people. Grandma Hansen..."

"You told your grandmother?"

"Sure. She listens to me."

Clare caught the implication. "And I don't?"

Chad shrugged. "Not much. She says Marsh deserves to die."

"Your grandmother is wrong," Clare said. But she did not say it with conviction. She was aware of Marsh looking at her with a hurt expression on his face.

"Dad sure didn't deserve to die," Chad said. "It's not fair."

"I know," Clare agreed, wishing none of this was happening. It felt overwhelming, and she was certain she wasn't handling any of it very well.

❧

Clare had been reluctant to deal with the mountain of thank-you notes that needed to be sent to all the people who had shown their sympathy when George died. Finally it could not be put off any longer. She accepted the offer of help from Mabel and Gloria.

Now, the finished notes were stacked on her kitchen table in neat piles ready to be mailed. Gloria and Mabel had left, and Clare sat alone at her table. She felt raw and confused from the conversation that had accompanied the work.

"I see they've left," Marsh said, coming into the kitchen.

"Yeah, it's safe to come back, you rat, leaving me to deal with them alone."

"Hey, I just thought it might be easier if I wasn't around." He sat down next to his sister.

Clare stared at him, trying to fit the picture Mabel and Gloria had of Marsh with her own image.

"What's wrong?" Marsh asked.

"Nothing. Everything," Clare said. She did not know what to say to him. She could still hear Mabel, her face so righteous looking, saying, "A man like that should not be around a young boy."

"Something sure isn't right. Mabel and her daughter-in-law have anything to say about me?"

"Yeah, plenty." Clare closed her eyes, as though there might be some help for her in the darkness. Gloria's words about Marsh were fresh and vivid: "You know what they say about that sort of man. And with this AIDS, you can't be too careful."

"I guess they weren't exactly singing my praises, huh?"

"Not exactly." Clare opened her eyes again and looked with pain and confusion at Marsh. She saw her dearly loved brother, but she also heard Mabel. "I've lost George, and I don't want my grandson exposed to AIDS. I couldn't bear to lose him, too," Mabel had said.

Marsh was silent, staring thoughtfully at Clare. With a twisted smile he said, "They don't want me around Chad, do they?"

Clare started to deny it and then nodded. "They want me to ask you to leave."

"Poor Clare," Marsh said. He meant it. He could see in his sister's face the conflict she was experiencing. "You halfway think they're right about me, don't you?"

"I don't know what to think. You're my brother, but this disease is so scary..."

"Hey, you don't have to tell me scary. I know. I'm the one that's got it, dammit."

Clare put a trembling hand over her eyes. "I don't think I can take this, Marsh. I'm sorry. It's just that there's been too much..."

Marsh inhaled deeply and exhaled with a sigh that was sad and resigned. "Okay. I won't make it harder for you. You've got enough on your hands right now without having me to deal with, too. I think Lee will let me stay with her. I'll go there tomorrow."

Clare started to protest, but it was a feeble effort. "It might be better if you did."

"Yeah. Better." Marsh stood up. "Think I'll go for a walk. Don't wait supper for me. I'm not very hungry right now."

"Oh, damn," Clare said aloud when Marsh had left the house.

❧

Clare saw Marsh from a distance out in the yard at Lee's, but she did not, in the next weeks, attempt to talk to him. I've hurt him, she thought and yet I didn't know what else to do. I'd been worrying about some of the same things Gloria and Mabel had.

Now as she prepared for her turn to host the monthly church ladies' circle, she felt dread at encountering Mabel and Gloria again. I don't know if I can stand their triumph, she thought.

Her mother was the first to arrive. "Do you need some help?" Eve asked, putting her purse on the kitchen counter. "I thought I'd come early just in case. I know how busy you are."

"Thanks, Mom. Put out these plates, will you?"

"How is Chad?" Eve asked.

"Missing his dad and none too pleased to have me for a mother these days."

"I know he was close with George. He's taken it hard, hasn't he?"

"Yeah."

"And how is Marsh?"

"I haven't seen him lately. He's staying with Lee. Lee Collins."

"I see." Eve did not see, really, but she didn't know how to ask why. "Your dad is taking this very badly."

"I know. What about you, Mom?"

Eve turned toward Clare, her eyes suddenly teary. "I just want to cry every time I think of it. I didn't know my son was…gay. I wish…" She wiped her eyes. "I want to see him."

"Well, why don't you?"

"You know your father when he gets stubborn."

"Yeah, I seem to remember a time or two." Clare smiled.

"I should be more independent, I know," Eve said. "I guess I'm not. But, I do want to see Marsh. I don't care about whether he's gay or what he is. I just know that he's going to die, and I want to see him."

"Mom…" Clare didn't know what to say. She was suddenly ashamed of how easily she had allowed Marsh to leave.

Eve picked her purse up off the counter. "If he's just across the road… I'm going to see him."

"Now?"

"Yes, now." Eve moved resolutely toward the door. "I'll be back later. Start the group without me."

"Well," Clare said aloud, silently wondering if her mother had considered what the women of the church circle would have to say when she returned.

Clare was not able to concentrate on the Bible study Gloria was leading. Her mind was across the road. The Bible study was just over when Eve walked into the room.

"You're late tonight," Mabel Hansen said, her tone of voice inviting some explanation.

"I've been to see my son," Eve said simply.

The silence was strained. Finally Stella Grimes broke it. "How is Marsh?" she asked, her voice concerned.

Eve shook her head. "I'm sorry," she said her voice breaking. "He's...much the same as he always was. But he's going to die..."

Stella put her arm around Eve. Other women murmured in sympathy. Gloria and Mabel sat watching, their eyes bright and busy. Suddenly Clare wanted to shake the two women. Instead she sat quietly as Stella spoke comforting words to Eve.

Mabel suddenly spoke. "I've just lost a son, Eve. I know how you feel."

Eve nodded. "Thank you."

Both Clare and Gloria stared at their mother-in-law in surprise.

CHAPTER TWENTY-ONE

Since George's death Clare had been experiencing recurring nightmares in which his fall from the silo was replayed again and again. She would wake from them shaking, her heart pounding. And she would think, I should have warned him. I should have said "Wait and we'll hook up the blower, run some air in first." I shouldn't have let him go up that chute. It's my fault. We were arguing.

When she passed by the silo that had killed him she averted her eyes from it, from the area below the chute, as though George's body might still be lying there. And she could not make herself climb that silo. It remained untouched. She knew the upper door still stood open.

There were so many conflicting feelings running through her, she couldn't seem to get a grip on any of them. Just when she thought she had one in hand it would slide away. She needed to talk to someone who would let her think out loud. She needed someone to offer some solid words.

It seemed such a natural thing to go across the road to Lee. Who else was there? Not Marsh right now. Not her mother who was having her own problems dealing with Marsh. Certainly not any of George's relatives.

She put on her barn jacket and boots and stepped outside. Mike's car was down by the barn where he was doing the evening feeding.

It felt strange to be walking into Lee's yard. She had done it so seldom in the last fourteen years. Lee was in her barn feeding. Of course. She should have known that. She stood just inside the door watching Lee measure out cow feed carefully, add soda and extra minerals, pour on some cottonseed for top dressing. Lee's cows were contentedly eating, which had a soothing effect on Clare, but some of her agitation must still have been visible.

"What's the matter?" Lee asked when she came up to her. "You look white. Are you all right?"

"Yes...no..." Clare floundered.

"No, you're not. Sit over there on that bale of hay and pet a cat or something for a minute. I'm almost through feeding."

"I don't want to bother you..."

"No bother. Here. Hold the cat." Lee thrust a large red purring object into her hands. Automatically she began to stroke it, the purring a comforting sound as the cat curled up in her lap. Some of the tension began to lift, the fog to clear.

"Feeling better?" Lee sat down next to Clare on the bale. In her denim barn jacket, a short-brimmed cap on her head, she looked both capable and gentle.

Clare nodded. "I think I am. Who's this?"

"Oh, that's Mort, the resident tom. He has it all figured out. Hang around the barn for milk and scraps. Let the females go off hunting." Lee reached down and stroked Mort's head. He opened one eye in acknowledgement and then settled in more snugly against Clare.

"George didn't like cats, so we never had any. After Caesar died we didn't get another dog either. I think I'll get a dog again. Maybe Chad would like that."

"How's Chad?"

"Surly, sullen, and away for the weekend with Harry and Diane."

"Things not going well with him, I take it?"

"Not at all. He and I weren't very close before George died. Now we're even farther apart. He blames me."

"You weren't to blame, were you?"

"Sometimes I think I was. We fought, and then I let him go up the silo without running the blower. I should have stopped him."

"But could you? Could you have stopped him?"

"I don't know. I should have tried."

"But you didn't do it and now you can't change it, right?"

"Lee, it's haunting me. I see George's body fall in my dreams. I can't go up that silo. I can still hear how he sounded falling down the chute, hitting against the rungs." Clare shook involuntarily.

"Not a nice image," Lee said matter-of-factly.

"And I feel guilty because I don't feel worse about him dying. I do feel bad, but..." She retreated from that thought and rushed ahead down a more acceptable path. "And I miss him in lots of ways. It's so lonely in the house. It's lonely in bed. There's so much work to do. Mike is working for me, but he's just a kid really. I've had so much other stuff to do. I'm starting to settle the estate, get things back in my name. There's all the corn to combine. I'll need to run the combine. I can't trust Mike and Chad isn't helping at all. He watches TV when he's home. I—"

Lee's hand on her shoulder stopped Clare in mid-sentence. "Slow down. Take it easy. You're working yourself back up to the state you were in when you came into the barn. You're scaring Mort too."

"Oh, yeah." Clare smiled a little as Mort looked up, puzzled and offended. "I must have been digging my hand in too hard, I guess."

"You know you can ask me for any help I can give. I haven't been back since the day of the funeral because I knew you got Mike to come full-time. But I can help. What do you want me to do?"

"Just listen," Clare said in a whisper that had some tears in it. She had not cried at all, not at the visitation, not at the funeral or the grave, and certainly not in the time since then. Now tears stung her eyes as she fought them.

"Let them fall." Lee stroked Clare's arm briefly.

"I guess they're going to whether I want them to or not."

"Good." Lee was a silent but comforting presence, not intruding too closely on Clare, but there, strong and calming.

Later Clare wiped her eyes. "I think Mort's a little wet."

"He doesn't seem to mind." Lee stroked Mort's soft fur and the sound of his purring sounded loud in the silence between them.

"How's Marsh?" Clare asked finally.

"Depressed and trying to hide it. What happened to make him leave your place?"

"Mabel and Gloria said some things about Marsh, a few of which I'd been thinking too, I guess."

"Such as?"

"Oh, like how Marsh might molest Chad. We might all get AIDS. That he sort of deserves it for being a homosexual. I'd been thinking those things too."

"Do you still think them?"

"No. I don't know. Not that he'd molest Chad, but the rest..."

"They're common enough thoughts. Lots of people have them."

"But you don't, do you?"

"No," Lee admitted.

They were silent for awhile, the purring cat a bridge between them.

"What did you and George talk about that day he came over here?"

"He never told you?"

"No." Clare smiled faintly. "I...it left me very curious."

"I imagine it did. We talked, or rather George told me something about his time in Vietnam."

"He told you? Just like that?" For some reason, that knowledge hurt Clare.

"Not quite just like that, but I think he felt I would understand. He had a good friend over there. A medic named Chad." Lee nodded at Clare's expression. "Yes, he named your son for him. Chad died in an attack on their base. He died in George's arms. George never forgot it. He also discovered on visiting Chad's hometown that Chad was gay. He met Chad's lover, and it shook him badly."

Clare shook her head. "I don't know what to say."

"It's too bad he didn't tell you."

"I wish he had. I wish..." Clare shook her head, tears starting again. "Oh, George, I'm so sorry..."

Lee sat silently beside her.

"Do you know I'm almost debt-free?" Clare laughed bitterly. "I spent my whole marriage in debt, hating it. Now I'm out of debt because of the life insurance and I feel so damned guilty because I'm so glad, so relieved..."

"Not the best way to clear a debt," Lee said. "But it happened."

"Yeah, it did and I feel so terrible..."

"So what's wrong with that? Feel guilty for awhile. Wallow in it. You'll get tired and quit it someday."

That advice was not what Clare had expected, but in a way it made sense. "All right," she said. By giving in to it she seemed to feel less guilty already.

"About Marsh," Lee said. "He can stay here with me as long as he wants to, but I know he wants to see you and be on good terms with you. He was so glad when your mom came to see him the other night."

"How did that go?"

"It went fine. It was awkward at first. I don't think your mother knew quite what to expect of me. I think she was surprised to find I was so ordinary."

"I've never thought you were at all ordinary," Clare said. "You're...anything but that."

"Well, thanks. Anyway, Marsh can stay here as long as he likes and that will keep the Hansen clan happy, I hope."

"We're right back to you giving me advice and help, aren't we?" Clare said ruefully. "Fourteen years of marriage and when it ends, I'm right back over here. Holy cow, I must be nuts."

"If you don't want it, don't come," Lee said abruptly.

"I do want it. I'm ashamed, that's all. I come back the very day George dies. It's safe because I'm a widow."

"I don't think you thought about that at all."

"Maybe not, but I'm thinking about it now. I married George to avoid you."

"I thought you probably did."

"And that hurt you."

"It didn't make me feel real good."

"I'm sorry. I'm a mess, aren't I?"

"Oh, absolutely. A real mess."

"Now you're humoring me."

"Well, what should I do?"

"I...I don't know." Clare shrugged and suddenly smiled a tiny smile. "I'd better get back. There are the cows to milk..."

Clare stood and Lee stood, too. Mort protested, but soon settled in on the vacated bale.

"Will you be all right?"

"I think so. Talking to you helped." She did feel better. Not quite so confused. A little less hurt and upset and scared.

CHAPTER TWENTY-TWO

Marsh's life had started to disintegrate the day he and his partner Gene learned they were both HIV positive. Almost as soon as he got the news, Gene just seemed to give up. Miserably and helplessly, Marsh watched his lover's health deteriorate. He saw good friends melt away when they learned the two of them had the virus, the fear visible in their faces.

Not much was known about AIDS then, and not much help was available to them medically or emotionally. Even living in New York, support was hard to find. Rumors abounded about how AIDS was spread and why it happened. Marsh felt helpless to deal with it, and especially the effect it was having on Gene.

"I'd be better off dead," Gene told him.

"No," Marsh protested. "What about me? If you die, I'll be alone."

"We'd both be better off dead than practically pariahs." Gene had become bitter, and that anger rubbed off on Marsh. At first he had felt guilty and ashamed, an attitude the larger population seemed to suggest he should hold. He blamed himself and his lover for the virus. The hysteria of the religious right fueled his anguish, with their pronouncements that the virus was a gay disease, brought on by sinfulness.

But gradually the guilt and shame gave way to anger because so little was being done to learn the cause of AIDS and because he and Gene were too young to die. By the time Gene developed the first lesions on his arms, Marsh felt resignation. It chimed together to produce a bitter attitude he'd never held before. The good-humored, smiling Marsh was now often silent and grim.

Gene died of Kaposi's sarcoma, horribly disfigured at the end. After nursing Gene for months, Marsh found himself pushed aside by Gene's family who came to claim the body and ship it back home for burial.

He was furious with these parents who had so little compassion for Gene when he was alive. They pawed through the apartment he and Gene shared, removing Marsh's belongings as well as Gene's. Since so much of what the two of them owned had been bought jointly, Marsh could not bring himself to protest; he felt beyond caring.

"Take anything you damned well want," he said, turning away as Gene's brother sorted through their record and cassette collection. It felt like a desecration to Marsh to have this stranger violate their home. But nothing mattered anymore. Gene was dead.

Shortly after his death, Marsh sat down in the stripped apartment and faced facts. He had just lost his job. Too much missed time while he was nursing Gene, so they said. The landlord did not seem eager to renew the lease, which had been in Gene's name. His insurance company sent a letter that very day, cancelling coverage. There seemed to be nothing left in New York for him, no friends, no job, nothing.

Marsh took his remaining meager possessions and drove home to Wisconsin. He thought he was arriving with no expectations, but it felt to him like more bad luck to reach town just in time for George's funeral, and find Clare, who he had hoped might be supportive, in shock.

Now, staying with Lee, he still felt depressed most of the time. Oh, he could sometimes bring up some humor from somewhere, but it felt forced.

Lee was a stable rock. He didn't know what he'd do without her. Clare's attitude hurt, but Lee was so accepting he only wished everyone could be like her.

"Did you have a good report at the clinic?" Lee asked him.

"Yeah, I'm healthy enough. Now." He had been into Minneapolis for a checkup. While the virus had not progressed into AIDS, the fear of how quickly that could change was always with him.

"I saw Clare today."

"Oh? How was she?" He kept his tone carefully neutral.

"Scared. Upset. Feeling guilty. George's death put her almost out of debt."

Marsh felt some remorse. "I keep forgetting she just lost her husband, jerk though I thought he was."

"George wasn't such a bad guy. And Clare misses him. Even I miss him a little," Lee said.

"You're kidding."

"Nope."

"Now that's something I find hard to believe." Marsh was truly distracted from his own misery now, and curious.

"Believe it," Lee said. "I don't think George would mind your knowing this..." Lee proceeded to tell a very interested Marsh about George's friend Chad.

"I'll be darned," Marsh said. "Well, well. Somehow I like you better for knowing it, George, and since I may be seeing you soon, that's probably a good thing."

It made Lee uncomfortable when Marsh referred to his death. Call me a coward, she thought to herself, but I don't want to face this loss.

ਪ੍ਰ

Christmas 1982 didn't seem very merry, Clare thought, as she wrote cards to friends and relatives. She was very aware of how empty the house seemed without George. He'd always been an eager participant in Christmas festivities, enjoying buying gifts for Chad and herself. Now Clare was finding it hard to be enthusiastic, and she and Chad had just had another fight.

"But I want to go to Harry and Diane's on Christmas Eve," he had insisted.

"You'll see them the next day at Grandma and Grandpa's."

"I don't care. I don't wanna stay here with you."

Clare winced. "Well, perhaps we should just forget about Christmas entirely then."

He said nothing for a long moment. "Oh, all right, I'll stay home."

"Good. Your uncle Marsh is coming and so is Lee Collins. I want you to be polite to them."

"Yeah? Why?"

"It *is* Christmas, Chad. Let's try to get along, all right?"

"I'm only staying 'cause I ought to," he told her.

"Merry Christmas to you, too," Clare said to his retreating back.

Inviting Lee and Marsh had been spontaneous, and now Clare was regretting it as the four of them sat down to eat her

Christmas Eve meal of oyster stew. Chad sat sneering silently at the three adults, who were having a hard enough time as it was. Although Clare and Lee tried, Marsh was no help at all.

"Well," Clare said, when the dessert had been finished, "Let's go open some presents, okay?"

The sight of the colorfully wrapped presents seemed to cheer Chad, at least. He willingly took on the duty of passing them out, obviously pleased that so many of them were for him. Clare knew she had been more liberal in her spending this year than she usually would have been. Buy my kid with gifts, she thought ruefully.

"These are neat," Chad said as he examined the cross-country skis his mother had bought him. He was soon surrounded by mashed-up wrapping paper and heaps of gifts. After another few minutes of enforced politeness, he announced he had to make a phone call and bounced away. Comparing presents, Clare thought.

Meanwhile the adults were opening their own gifts more sedately. Lee was politely grateful for the book Marsh had given her and the box of stationery from Chad via Clare. Lee had brought small gifts for everyone, nothing much, just tokens.

Clare's gift to Lee however was not a token. "This is too much," Lee said when she had unwrapped the handsome and very expensive soft leather jacket.

"I thought it would suit you," Clare said. "Try it on." She had debated about buying it, not because of the price, but because it seemed almost too personal a gift.

Lee slipped her arms into the jacket and turned to model it. "It's beautiful. I've always wanted one like this, but you shouldn't have gotten it."

"But I wanted to. It fits nicely, doesn't it?" Clare found herself blushing.

Marsh was watching the two of them with the first sign of interest he had shown all evening. A look of amusement was on his face. Well, what do you know, he thought. My sister and Lee after all these years…

"You look great," he said to Lee. "Dykey as hell. You need a little beret or something to make the outfit complete. Plus high leather boots and maybe a whip. I should have compared notes with you, Clare, and gotten her something."

"The whip probably," Clare said. "Well, we haven't been talking much lately."

"No. I know. Maybe we can change that?"

Clare nodded, smiling at him. "I'm sorry, Marsh. I should have been braver around..."

"Forget it. I doubt if I'd've been any braver. It's hard with this thing and so little being known."

"It still doesn't excuse me," Clare insisted. "I missed you."

"Well, well, absence does make the heart grow fonder," Marsh quipped, to cover his pleasure. "I wonder if it's worked with Dad?"

"You could come along with us tomorrow and find out," Clare suggested. "Harry and Diane will be there, too."

Clare and Chad picked up Marsh at noon the next day. Lee was busy preparing a turkey dinner. The good smells and the bright Christmas music on her stereo briefly lifted Clare's spirits as she waited for Marsh to put his jacket on.

"Say hi to Les for me," Marsh said. "Sorry I'm missing him, but I'll be in touch soon."

"I know he'd like that," Lee said. "I hope your visit goes well."

"Yeah, me too." Marsh appeared nervous, rubbing his hands together and fidgeting. "If not, I may be back for some of that turkey."

Clare's mother opened the door at their ring. Eve had been all set to wish her grandson a cheery "Merry Christmas," but her words never made it out. She saw Marsh standing there and walked straight into his arms.

"Merry Christmas, Mom," he said.

Eve wiped tears off her face. "I hoped you might come. I don't know what your father will say, though. We don't discuss you at all."

"He's in the living room?" When his mother nodded to him, Marsh said, "I'll go on ahead then."

His dad was sprawled in his recliner just staring at the tree. Marsh thought how much older he looked, older and not so healthy as when he'd been busy farming. Not enough for him to do, he thought.

"Hi, Dad," he said.

Ed looked up at him. He grimaced. "I see you're still alive."

"Yeah. Pretty healthy still. Merry Christmas."

Ed grunted. "Thought you'd be dead by now."

"Did you hope it, too?"

"Damned right I did. What father wouldn't? A son like that." There was silence. "Your mother's been pretty upset about you. I suppose she's glad to see you?"

Marsh nodded.

"Figured she would be. You hurt her a lot, you know."

"I know. I didn't ask to get AIDS. I didn't ask to be gay."

"Maybe not. Might as well sit down."

Marsh sat, thinking how hard it must be for Ed to maintain the expected toughness. The invitation to sit down was an opening, however small.

"I been reading about this AIDS," Ed said. "I guess you can't get it just being around someone with it."

"That's right."

"A lot of people think you can. The Hansens down the street sure do."

"I know."

"You still staying out there with that Lee Collins?"

"Yeah. It seemed better that way. The Hansens..."

"I heard," Ed said. "Made me mad."

"It did?" Marsh was surprised.

"Bunch of hysterical females, the whole damned family."

Marsh grinned. This sounded more like his dad. "The men too, huh?"

"Worse than any queer," his dad said gruffly.

CHAPTER TWENTY-THREE

Stella Grimes put down the latest copy of *Hoard's Dairyman* with an angry thump. "Doesn't that beat all?" she turned to Orrin. "They're talking about cutting the support price for milk again. Got to get it down so we US farmers can compete in the world open market. Open market! That's a joke. Europe pays Its dairy farmers heavy subsidies and then dumps its extra milk on this world market at lower prices than their farmers get. And we're supposed to be able to compete with that?"

Orrin shook his head. Stella sure did get worked up about the political end of things. He just knew they were struggling to pay the bills. And now the government had set up something called a Dairy Diversion program which paid farmers to reduce their milk production. Didn't pay them much, but it was being touted as a big handout to dairy farmers.

"And this Diversion thing. Another joke. Nobody mentions that we're all being assessed fifty cents on each hundred pounds of milk to pay for it." Stella was still steaming.

"I know," Sally said. She and Butch were eating with Orrin and Stella. Their small daughter, Angie, dressed in tiny bib overalls, played on the floor by their feet. "Nobody asked us if we wanted a Diversion. Nobody asked us if we wanted to fund it, either."

"Nobody asked if we could afford to fund it. In fact, to look at the newspapers, you'd think it was a welfare payment to dairy farmers," Stella said, her anger still very high. The sudden loss of over eight thousand dollars in income had hurt.

They weren't in the Diversion program but they had to help pay for it whether they were or not.

"Yeah, funny how the media never seems to mention that most of the Diversion is being funded by farmers," Sally said. "You get the impression that they don't know much about farming. Or care."

"Well, we may not exist anymore at all if this economy doesn't change soon," Stella said grimly. "We better face facts. We could lose this place."

"I know," Butch said. "It scares me." He reached down to gather up Angie, as though holding her would bring him some comfort.

"We better hope Angie isn't interested in farming," Orrin said gloomily. "I just don't think I want to see her struggling like we're having to do."

"Well, she's a little young yet to worry about it," Sally pointed out. "But I bet your own folks probably said the same thing, didn't they?"

"But that was the Depression, then," Orrin said.

"I wonder what this is?" Stella said. "Sure feels like something pretty similar to me."

Orrin and the rest of his family lost some of their gloominess as winter gave way to the warmer days of spring. In spite of their financial morass, the Grimeses felt their usual spark of excitement. Springtime on the farm is full of hope.

After the long winter it was good to be out in the fields preparing them for new crops, to see the greens coming slowly back to the landscape, to know that on this bare field in a few weeks delicate plants would be emerging and growing. Those tiny plants, with a little luck and some sun and rain, would become oats or corn, soybeans or alfalfa, and maybe, just maybe the prices would be better by fall.

Orrin thought it was likely that farmers had a little soil in their blood. Otherwise why would they gamble like they do, betting enormous sums on the haphazard whims of Mother Nature?

He knew he could be discouraged sometimes, but he didn't think he or other farmers gave up easily. They could watch crops wither and die one year and come back and gamble again the next year that the same thing wouldn't happen. No, they didn't give up easily, Orrin thought, not when the soil was in their blood.

Marsh found spring to be more hopeful, too. He helped out at Lee's and over at Clare's, driving a tractor to work the fields. It felt good to him to be out in the fresh air, contributing to the work of preparing for new crops.

Later, when the planting was done, he surprised himself by moving to town to stay with his folks for awhile. His mother had been hinting she would like that and something told him this was the time to do it. At least Ed didn't protest his presence. He and Eve talked together more normally now, on every subject except AIDS, which they avoided altogether.

Marsh helped Ed turn the earth in the garden. It seemed a very small plot compared with the large fields he had helped make ready for planting, but it was satisfying as he and Ed worked side by side, turning the earth with spaded shovels, loosening each clump and turning it over, fresh and full of earthworms.

The garden was next to the fence line of the small lot, and on the other side of the fence Marsh could see that someone had been making a similar attempt. The two gardens were right next to each other across a low picket fence that had seen better days.

One day, as he was out working alone, he noticed that someone was working over in the neighboring yard: an older woman, spading up the soil. Once Marsh had finished setting in his tomato plants, he picked up his spade and stepped across the fence. "Want some help?" he asked.

Startled, Frances Miller looked up, casting a quick glance his way. "That would be nice of you," she said uncertainly. She seemed about to say more, but went back to spading instead. Marsh joined her and together they silently turned over the rest of her garden. Halfway through the task Marsh decided he needed a break. The sun and the work on this late May day were making him sweat. He felt weak, too, and didn't know if it was because he was doing more physical work than he was used to, or if it was because of the disease. The trouble with the damn disease was that you never did know.

He sat down in the grass by the edge of the garden and Frances, after a moment of hesitation, joined him. He hadn't looked closely at her until now. She appeared to be older than he was, maybe in her fifties, tall and dark-haired, with graying tendrils that had become messed up by her garden labors. Marsh knew this property was connected to some sort of church but he hadn't any reason to know more than that.

"Warm today, isn't it?" he said. She nodded. Her eyes swept over him and then back down, and Marsh caught a flash of their bright green color.

"What are you going to plant?"

"Oh. I hadn't decided. I never used to have time to do much gardening, but this year I thought I would try it again." She did not say she had the time because her son and his wife and children were in the parsonage now. Or that she had been gradually shunted aside from both the housework and the church.

She was called on to babysit evenings when her son and his wife wanted to be in attendance at church functions, but her daughter-in-law was really taking over the house. She felt like an intruder in what had been her own home for so many years. The gardening was an attempt to reclaim some area of it for herself, some area besides the third floor room where she slept.

From that beginning they went on to chat about the weather, the chances for good crops, introducing themselves somewhere in the proceedings.

Frances knew who this kind man was, of course. The whole neighborhood knew that Ed Lewis' homosexual son with AIDS was staying with them. Marsh looked very tired now, she thought, and she wondered if it was because of the AIDS. Her own son had ordered her and his family to have nothing to do with the Lewises while their son was here.

"They say it isn't catching," Richard admitted. "But we'll take no chances. We don't want that kind of person around the kids anyway. If he was interested in repenting his sins, it would be fine to minister to him, but I doubt he wants to."

Frances thought the younger man didn't look as though he believed he had any sins. Marsh leaned back on his elbows, relaxed, tanned, and quite healthy. There was a weariness about his face, true, but he certainly did not look ill.

"I'm not sick with it yet," Marsh said, correctly guessing at her thoughts. "But it could happen anytime."

"Oh," Frances said, disconcerted that he had picked up what she was thinking so easily. "That must be awful"

"It's not the greatest," Marsh admitted.

Frances supposed she should be using this time to sound out whether Marsh would be interested in being ministered to, helped to change his ways. Her son would expect it of her. Somehow that did not seem what she wanted to do. It felt nice to just sit relaxed on the grass and chat about gardening and whatever else came to mind. Her son and his wife were so busy these days with their plans for the church that they had no time for anything else.

"Well, Frances," Marsh said. "We'd better finish this spading. I bet you've got plenty of other things to do."

"Oh, I keep busy," she said, thinking it was mostly makework. Sorting clothes for her daughter-in-law. Doing some mending. Visiting the hospital patients she thought would want her company.

"I'll help you plant, too, if you like."

"That would be nice," Frances said, deciding it would be.

"I had help from the Lewis' son, spading the garden," Frances said at dinner that night when there was a pause in her son's talk.

Richard looked up and over at her. "The one with AIDS?"

Frances nodded.

"I'm not sure that's a good idea," he said.

"Why? He seems very nice. It was kind of him to help me." Frances was surprised to find herself defending Marsh.

"Perhaps so, but we don't want you getting his disease."

"I doubt that will happen. I'm sure it's not spread so easily."

"These people are sick in more ways than the physical," her son reminded her. "Surely you can find something else to do instead of garden right next door to him? I don't feel we need a garden very badly anyway. The seed will cost some money, won't it?"

"Not very much. And fresh garden produce is delicious," Frances pointed out. "It's much better than what we buy. Besides, I believe Marsh said they had some extra seed he'd be happy to give me. I would hardly need to buy anything, perhaps just some cabbage and tomato plants."

"If she's enjoying it, why not let her?" Patricia intervened. She was just as happy to have her mother-in-law occupied outside the house.

"Well, make certain the man wears gloves in our garden," Richard said. "I'm not sure this is a good idea at all."

"Why?" his mother couldn't resist asking.

"Well, as you know, we're trying to put some life into the old church here. We're trying to attract the solid young couples of the community. If it's known we seem to approve of someone like that, what will people think?"

"You could always say I'm ministering to him," Frances said, half in jest. She knew she was not going to minister to Marsh, and she could not have told herself why.

Richard took her words seriously. "That's true. It might look good if it's known we're attempting to save that sort."

"As long as they don't start coming to church," Patricia pointed out.

"True. We don't want that. Collections were up nicely last month. We'll be able to paint the church soon. I need a new suit, too."

Frances had noticed new faces in the pews these last Sundays. She knew her son was working hard to attract more people, paying people, as he put it.

With the advent of Reagan as president, fundamentalist right-wing groups had claimed a political victory and now, a few years into his presidency, the religious right seemed to be gathering strength. Jerry Falwell's Moral Majority was frequently in the media. Pat Robertson and Jim and Tammy Faye Bakker were popular on television shows of their own. It was a hopeful time for fundamentalists.

It was not surprising that Frances' son wanted some of this success to rub off on himself. There were fundamentalist churches popping up everywhere. One large one down by Chicago had a Sunday attendance of thirty-five hundred people. Richard did not expect that up here where the main-line churches still had a pretty good following, but he did hope to draw a lot of their members away. Richard was offering a firm moral way of living where there was black and white but no gray. All the answers were in the Bible. The main-line churches offered too many choices, left too much leeway in people's lives. Richard's church gave hard and fast rules for life.

But he wanted a happy church. He liked that phrase. It was one he'd heard from the wife of one of the young couples who had come over from the Presbyterians. A happy church, yes. With lots of spirited hymns and toe-tapping rhythms. There would be guitar music and skits and all sorts of cheery things going on.

Frances was both amused and irritated by her son's plans. She contrasted them with the way her husband had ministered, accepting little pay, being there for anyone who needed a minister. Including homosexuals. It might have been nice to have lived more comfortably, she thought, but mostly she preferred her husband's gentler ministry to the aggressive way Richard was setting up a profit-making enterprise.

In the meantime Richard was using her widow's check to supplement his own coffers. He was waiting on the third of the month for her to endorse it over to him. Lately, she'd been keeping back fifty dollars for herself. Though Richard didn't like it, he didn't protest.

Frances began to look forward to her gardening stints with Marsh. On the days when he did not come, she didn't linger long over the gardening, but when he did, she worked till dusk. It was good to have someone to talk to.

At fifty-three, Frances didn't feel like she was quite done with life, but she had no idea what she should be doing, either. She found herself telling Marsh all about her husband's death, the arrival of her son and his family, the lack of money.

"I can relate to that for sure," Marsh said with a grin. Some of his old good-humor and wit was slowly coming back. "I don't have much money, either. But who would hire me around here, knowing about the AIDS?"

"And who would hire me? I suppose I could clerk or waitress, but where? The bad farm economy seems to be affecting the town too."

"I read somewhere that when one farmer goes under, it hurts three people in non-farm jobs," Marsh said. "At least I can go out and help my sister and my friend Lee. Their farms always need an extra hand. Trouble is, they don't pay much. They can't really afford to." He shook his head. "Sure wish I'd been able to stay in New York."

"Is that where you lived?"

"Yeah. I liked it there, but then Gene got sick and died. I lost my job and my apartment and came back here. I was pretty bitter about it all."

"You're not feeling so bitter now?"

"No. Not so much." He didn't say it, but he thought that his friendship with Frances had helped. Here was someone who was not a family member or old friend to whom he could talk. Mostly Clare and Lee and Les, too, looked uncomfortable and tried to change the subject when he brought up AIDS and what that most likely would mean for him. He knew they found it too upsetting to talk about. Frances listened calmly and usually said something that was comforting or suggested that she understood.

CHAPTER TWENTY-FOUR

Clare felt overburdened with work that spring. She knew the farm was too big for her. Mike worked well, mostly, but he lacked the experience to be really efficient as George had been. She missed George for that, and somehow knowing more about him had let her stop feeling so guilty about his death. And as she began to look ahead rather than behind, she was able to look at Lee with new eyes.

Maybe it was just an old view she had not let herself see before, blinded as she had been by the need to conform and marry. But now just the sight of her neighbor in the grocery store, at the feed mill, or even out in her yard was enough to cause a little extra fluttering heartbeat.

She felt such warmth and comfort and, yes, love, in Lee's company. Not that there was time to do much together. All this work, Clare thought. It's too much. But just the same, it was nice to indulge in a daydream or two about Lee. Probably nothing would come of it. And probably nothing should.

She had noticed how people in town treated Marsh. She had overheard the nasty cracks, and she knew there had been some threatening phone calls at Lee's. Nothing had come of it, but did she really want that kind of hate directed at her?

And then there were her parents, struggling already with Marsh's AIDS and his homosexuality. Could she burden them further? Certainly her caring for Lee shouldn't be viewed as a burden, but Clare knew that was how her folks would see it. It was hard, this whole thing, all mixed up with responsibility and where her own happiness fit in.

Of course there was Chad to consider, too; he was still as rude as ever. He was just squeaking by in school, his grades barely good enough to allow him to be passed on into high school next fall. He was minimally polite to Lee and he ignored Marsh altogether. And it seemed to Clare as though he barely tolerated her. She felt helpless to know what to do with Chad, so unable was she to communicate with him. It was a relief sometimes to let him go over to Harry and Diane's, or Nathan and Gloria's, or even to Mabel's. Never mind if the Hansen women acted triumphant. Clare didn't care.

Now, as she geared up and moved into harvesting the first crop of hay, she felt concerned about getting it all done. There were so many fields, so many acres, to cut and chop. So much work to do herself, so much organizing of Mike and Chad.

Mike took her orders with a patronizing smile that said he knew better. Clare knew he didn't. But she let many things slide by just to keep it peaceful. There was enough to worry about without needing to find a new hired man.

Luckily they were nearly through with the first crop of hay when her patience broke. Mike had been sent out to use the hay fluffer, a machine that gently ruffled up the windrow of mown hay, making it dry down to ensiling quality more quickly. She had sent Chad out to the machine shed to grease the forage chopper and fuel up the tractor. Clare herself was busy greasing the blower, putting air into a tire on one of the self-unloading boxes, and making a hotdish for the evening meal.

At noon Chad and Mike came straggling in for what was supposed to be a quick lunch of sandwiches, so they could get back out working on the last of the hay as soon as possible. Mealtimes were not good for the digestion, Clare felt, since they were often silent and full of tension between herself and Chad. Mike was an onlooker, his face suggesting he thought Clare incompetent, both as a farmer and as a mother. Today she tried to make a little conversation.

"How did the fluffing go?" she asked Mike.

He shrugged. "I didn't do it. Didn't think the hay needed it."

"It certainly did when I looked at it."

"Well, I didn't think it did," Mike said.

"I see." Clare let it go. Maybe the wind had come up and dried it more since she had been out.

"Get the chopper greased?"

"Nope. Couldn't find the grease cartridges," Chad said.

"Why didn't you come and ask me where they were?"

Chad shrugged. "There also wasn't enough fuel in the tank to fill the tractor."

"It didn't occur to you to come and tell me?"

"You didn't tell me to do that," Chad said defensively.

Clare held her temper. "No. That's true. It didn't occur to me." Clare called the local Co-op service station and ordered diesel fuel only to find that the regular delivery man was on vacation and the substitute might not be able to get there today. She sighed and hung up. "How much fuel did you get in the tractor?"

"I dunno. Maybe a little."

"Swell," Clare said. "Just swell." She pushed aside her paper plate with the half-eaten sandwich on it.

Before she could rise, Chad said, "I want to go to Harry and Diane's this afternoon. Can I?"

"No. You're staying home. We may be running late with chores if we're going to finish the last of the hay. We'll need you to help."

"I don't want to." Chad's voice was stubborn.

"I don't care whether you want to or not."

"Yeah, I know. You don't give a shit about me," Chad said in a sulky voice.

"That's not true." Clare was aware of Mike watching this exchange with his usual supercilious smile. "Don't you have something to do?" she asked him.

"Not really," he said.

"Well, go find something," she snapped.

Mike left the table with his second sandwich in his hand. "Maybe I'll go look for another job," he said.

"Swell, that's just what I need. Not that you're all that reliable anyway."

"Like I said, think I'll go find me something else."

"Fine. Good. Just don't expect me to have time to write you your weekly check today then. I'll mail it to you, minus the time you didn't put in today."

"Okay with me." Mike sauntered out of the house.

Great, Clare thought. Wonderful. Fine and dandy. The hired man has quit. My kid needs to be talked to, but there's all that hay to chop. And no fuel in the damned tractor.

Chad moved away from the table.

"You come back here," Clare said sharply.

He came and sat down.

"Maybe it's time we talked. It's not the best time for it, but maybe it's as good as any. So you think I don't care about you?"

-220-

"Yeah. You're always shipping me off to be with some-body. Grandma Hansen says she thinks you hate me because I remind you of Dad."

"What?" Clare said.

"I think you do, too. You hated Dad, didn't you?"

"No, I did not hate your father," Clare said carefully. "Sometimes we fought, mostly about spending money I didn't think we should spend, but I did not hate your father. You miss your dad, don't you?"

"Yeah. A lot. It was a shitty thing to happen. Grandma Hansen says you were glad when it did."

"I wasn't glad. I certainly did not want your dad to die. Did it ever occur to you that I might miss him, too?"

"You really didn't want him to die?"

"No, never that."

"Grandma Hansen says Marsh is bad. He's going to die, too, isn't he?"

Clare wanted to strangle Mabel. "Your grandma doesn't know everything. Marsh is not bad, but yeah, he's going to...to die." She hated having to say those words.

"The kids at school say he's a queer. That's what people call Lee Collins, too."

"I know. People use it when they're ignorant."

"Grandma isn't ignorant," Chad protested.

That's a debatable point, Clare thought. "On that subject she is. But so are a lot of other people. Look, Marsh is my favorite brother. Not that I don't love your Uncle Harry, but Marsh and I were closer in age and were together a lot when we were growing up."

"He's okay, I guess, but the kids at school say I must be like him. They call me Little Queer."

"I had no idea. Why didn't you tell me?"

Chad shrugged. "I didn't think you'd care."

"Of course I care! Listen, Chad, kids can be cruel when they don't understand something."

"Yeah. I hate school."

"I begin to see why." Clare thought she should have talked to Chad long ago. No wonder he was sullen and sulky, hard to handle. She didn't blame him. Maybe Mabel was partly right, she thought. Maybe I've let my ambivalence about George get tangled up with my feelings about Chad.

"I guess I could stay home this afternoon," Chad offered.

"That would be good. It looks like I'll need you to handle the loads. Do you think you could do that?"

"Sure. I can do it just as good as Mike."

"Well, that's great. Let's go see if we can siphon some fuel out of one of the other tractors." For the first time in a long time Clare did not see a scowling expression on her son's face.

Mike's car was gone from the yard, so Clare and Chad did the last of the chopping. She came in with Chad on the first load to make sure he understood how to start up the blower and get the load positioned correctly by it. She was surprised to find Chad must have been paying attention while he was lounging around. He handled the tractor and other equipment carefully and well. Remembering that much of the problem with her son seemed to come from not talking enough with him, she was careful to compliment him on his part of the work.

"We don't need Mike, do we? I can do his work. School's dumb anyway."

"You can't quit school even if it is bad."

Chad's face turned petulant again. "I don't want to go back this fall."

"You have to," Clare said. She felt her habitual impatience with her son returning.

"I won't," he said and walked away.

"Come back here."

Chad ignored her and kept walking.

"Swell. Just grand. Chad, we're going to get this hashed out even if we're late with chores," she called after him.

A car drove in. It was her parents out for one of their drives to the country. "I see you got the haying done," Ed said.

They showed every sign of staying and chatting. Clare found her patience going again. "I do need to get the chores done," she said. She had no idea where Chad was either. He had taken his bike from the garage and ridden down the driveway.

"It's too much for you," Eve said. "All this land and the cattle. You should get married again. You need a man around to take up the burden."

Clare wanted to tell her mother that it had been a man who had created the extra burden in the first place, but she was already late starting the chores. There would be no time to eat before milking tonight. Instead she sent them over to Harry's. "If you see Chad, tell him to come home," she called after them.

She had barely begun feeding when Mabel and Merlin Hansen drove in. She concealed her irritation as best she could and walked across the yard to their car.

"See you got your haying done," Merlin said in a conversational tone. Clare was struck by the similarity to her father's words. Two old farmers, retired, but wanting to stay in touch. Farming in their blood, she guessed.

Mabel broke her tolerant reverie. "Nathan puts his machinery away as soon as he's done using it," she said, indicating Clare's equipment still sitting out where they had left it. "It looks so much tidier and more efficient that way."

"I haven't had time to put mine away yet," Clare said, concealing an urge to grit her teeth.

"No? I hear your hired man's left," Mabel went on. "It didn't surprise me. Young men shouldn't have to take orders from a woman."

It amazed Clare how quickly news could travel in the country. Chad must have gone to Nathan's, she decided.

"We saw Chad at Nathan's." Mabel confirmed Clare's thought. "He's looking thin, poor boy. He's going with Nathan's boys to a softball game tomorrow afternoon."

"Just so he's home in time for supper." Clare eased the Hansens out of the yard. She managed to complete the feeding and was just starting to move in the milker units when a stranger walked right into the barn.

"I need some gas," he said. "Ran out down by the corner. Gauge wasn't working, I guess."

"I'm sorry. No gas. We run diesel tractors."

"Oh?" The man did not believe her. "No gas?"

"Nope," Clare said.

"Well, could you take me to someone who has it? I've really got to be in town by eight."

"I'm sorry, but I couldn't," Clare said in a firm tone, amazed that he would expect her to stop milking and ferry him somewhere.

"But it wouldn't take long," the man insisted.

"Try the farm just across the road," she suggested, hoping Lee would never know she had sent her a gas case.

That was the final interruption. The chores were done at last. Chad came strolling in as she finished up cleaning the milkhouse.

"I ate at Nathan's," he said.

"So I imagine. I could've used some help."

"I didn't feel like it."

"Maybe I didn't feel like doing the chores either. But they have to be done. That's the way it is."

"I want to go to a ball game tomorrow."

"So your grandmother told me. Be home for supper."
Clare was too tired to face any more discussions.

The phone rang. "You send me the gas man?" Lee asked.

"I'm sorry. I did."

"He didn't offer to pay."

"I thought he'd be one of those."

"Nice of you to send him my way," Lee said dryly.

"I'm sorry. I really didn't have any gas, though. Tell you what, I'll make amends for it," Clare found herself saying. "How about a picnic tomorrow? We're done haying, and I know you are. Want to go with me?"

There was a pause before Lee answered. "Sure." As though they went on picnics every other day or so. As though it hadn't been sixteen years since the last one.

IV

INTERLUDE

October, 1984

Lee was the only one present when Marsh died. No one had expected his death that particular October night. He had been ill for months, wasting away, covered with the purple lesions of Kaposi's sarcoma. For awhile they had expected each day to be his last. Then he had seemed briefly better.

Just that afternoon he had reminisced with Lee and Les about going to Minneapolis with Wade for the first time. It had been a bittersweet look into a past they had all shared. Perhaps it was only the disease that made that time seem happier.

Lee had chosen that night to stay with him. The four of them took shifts to always be nearby. When the virus had begun its deliberate destruction of Marsh's T-cells, the white blood cells that fight infection, he had come to live in Lee's house. The local hospital had not wanted him. There was one doctor who would examine him, but in 1984 few life-prolonging treatments were available. Living in Lee's house gave him some freedom and, until late in September, he had been able to enjoy it.

Then the illness accelerated, and Marsh went rapidly downhill. A high fever, a cough that would not quit, and diarrhea were added to his list of ailments. There were also the growing number of purple lesions disfiguring his body.

Eve, and sometimes Ed, came to see him as frequently as they could stand, but the pain of each visit was obvious to everyone. They came out of love, but neither of them was sorry he had moved out to Lee's, or that he had arranged for other people to look after him.

His older brother Harry came to see him once. The sight of his younger brother disfigured by purple splotches and suffering from other ailments so unnerved him, he did not come again.

Before his death, Marsh planned his own funeral, making the arrangements for the disposal of his body. Maybe it would not matter to him once he was dead, but he wanted to tidy things up, leave in good order.

He died shortly before Lee was ready to settle in on her sofa for some sleep. She went in to check on him first. He appeared to be sleeping, only when she went closer it was evident that this sleep was one from which he would not awake. Finding his body so still in death shook her badly.

Her hands trembled as she went to the phone to set in motion the arrangements Marsh had made. Call the doctor first, so Marsh had ordered. Her call reached the man at home and he agreed to come right away.

Next she called Clare. Then Frances and Les. And next Ludgate the undertaker, who had been clearly relieved to know Marsh did not want embalming. Instead his body would be taken to a crematorium in Minneapolis. The ashes would be returned, and a memorial service held then. There would be no need for Ludgate to risk the disapproval of the community for handling the body of an AIDS victim. Ludgate told Lee he'd be out early in the morning for the body.

That left the night. Marsh's body would lie in the hospital bed in Lee's house 'til morning.

Marsh had made no special provision for dying at ten in the evening. He had, perhaps, imagined dying during the night, his cold body being discovered in the morning. Or perhaps dying during the day. But not when James Ludgate, with two other deaths to handle that day, could not come for the body.

First die, first served, Lee thought. She could hear Marsh chuckling about that. Take a number for better service, he might have said.

Clare came in then, breathless from her quick dash across the road. "Is it true?"

"I think he just went in his sleep," Lee told her, tears suddenly in her eyes. They hugged tightly and walked together into the bedroom. Clare went to the bed, stroking Marsh's still face.

"Oh, God, I'm glad it's over for him, but..." she said.

"I know. I miss him already." Lee put her arm around Clare and they stood holding each other, glad of the comfort.

The doctor arrived next. He examined Marsh's body. Lee and Clare watched him as he impersonally checked to make certain

"He's dead," he said finally, as though there had been some doubt. "Have you made arrangements?"

"Ludgate's coming in the morning," Lee said.

"I'll leave the death certificate here then." At the bedside table he wrote it out. Turning towards the bed, he touched Marsh's face. He stood for a moment as though to say good-bye and rearranged the covers gently around the body. Not so impersonal now.

They saw him to the door. "Send me any bills that haven't been paid," Clare said.

The doctor shook his head. "Marsh made arrangements. Nothing is owed."

"I don't believe it," Clare told Lee when the doctor was on his way out of the yard. "Marsh didn't have the money."

"Even doctors can be generous sometimes," Lee pointed out.

Two cars turned quickly into Lee's driveway. Les came first, followed closely by Frances. They walked to the house together. Les was looking old. This death reminded him too vividly of Wade going. It seemed so pointless, these younger men dying. Here he was, still alive and pretty healthy, too, except for the aftereffects of his occasional drinking bouts. He thought he might like a drink tonight when he got home.

Frances' son had protested when he found out where she was going and why. "He's dead. What's the point?" he'd asked.

"There will be arrangements. I promised Marsh I'd help," she told him, brushing a tear away. Besides, she wanted to come, to be part for a little longer of the group around Marsh. She brought her Bible along. At the sight of it her son nodded approvingly.

They stood in the bedroom with Marsh's body. The four of them, three women and one man. Marsh's caregivers. Only Marsh no longer needed them. There were hugs and sighs and tears. Then they met each other's eyes.

"I don't suppose there's any point in our staying," Clare said reluctantly.

"No, but it seems wrong somehow to leave him here all alone," Frances told her.

"People used to stay with the body. Before undertakers," Les said.

"Let's stay." Lee was the one who said it, but they all nodded.

"I'll put on some coffee," Clare said.

"And I'll make some more calls. Your folks and brother need to be told. Do you want me to?" Lee asked, aware of Clare's pain.

"Would you?" Clare touched Lee's arm in a gesture that was grateful and loving.

Lee called Ed and Eve, murmuring sympathetically to Eve, who she was much closer to than she had ever expected to feel. She called Harry and spoke with Diane.

Then she called Stella Grimes. Stella said she would let the neighbors know. She asked about arrangements. Lee explained about the memorial service after the cremation. She mentioned that the four of them were going to stay the night with Marsh's body. She was talking just to fill the time because, quite frankly, she thought it was going to be a long night.

"Coffee's ready," Clare called.

"Good," Lee said. She joined the other three at the kitchen table. There was silence for awhile. Death's impact was taking hold, drawing them together.

"I'm glad he didn't suffer any more than he did," Clare said.

"Yeah. I remember Wade and that awful pneumonia. Nobody knew anything about it then," Les said.

"Marsh hated the purple splotches," Frances spoke. "He joked about them, but he hated them."

"Well, my brother was vain about his appearance," Clare said, smiling at Frances.

"I'll say. Almost as bad as Wade." Les smiled, remembering them both.

They drank more coffee and the memories flowed until they were laughing, wiping away tears, laughing again.

A knock at the kitchen door made them all turn. Stella Grimes walked into the room with a cake pan. "I just thought since you were all here you might want some food," she said.

"Oh, Stella, thanks," Clare said, hugging her and crying again.

"I hope he didn't suffer too much." She went in to view Marsh alone and came out wiping away tears, remembering other deaths.

Clare got her a cup of coffee. Les found her a chair. She sat with them and they ate her cake, giving her the usual compliments with genuine pleasure. Lee found some ice cream in the freezer to go with the cake.

"Marsh liked ice cream a lot toward the last. Said it was one thing that still tasted good," Lee told Stella.

Stella smiled. "He was a kind man. I wish I'd had time to come see him more often. I always went back home feeling cheered up after I'd been with Marsh. His sense of humor was so good."

"He lost it for awhile," Clare said. "When he first came back from New York. I'm just glad he had so many good friends around him when he died."

"This is almost like a wake," Stella commented. "I suppose I should go home, but I don't want to. Maybe I shouldn't say this, but I'm having a good time."

"Me, too," Les said.

"Well, that seems right," Clare decided. "Marsh certainly wouldn't have wanted us to sit around moaning and keening."

"No. Not him. I'm glad we decided to stay." Lee said it for all of them. And Stella thought how good it was to sit with these people, how warm and friendly the atmosphere was in this house of death.

At some point during the night they lit candles in the bedroom, turning off the lights. It seemed the right thing to do. Frances said a silent prayer for Marsh while the others were out of the room. She wanted to. She knew Marsh had not held traditonal Christian views, but she felt he would not have minded her prayer.

Toward morning, when the five of them were beginning to yawn, a knock at the door revived them. Clare went to open it, noticing that the sun was just starting to show some redness in the east. Dawn had brought Ludgate.

He came in looking tired. "I've been up all night too," he said. "I somehow thought you might be here, so I came now." He looked uncertainly at them. "I hope that was all right?"

"Of course. There's some coffee and cake," Lee offered.

"I'm hungry," Les said. "Maybe we could have some bacon and eggs?"

"Good idea." Clare started cooking bacon.

Ludgate sat down at the kitchen table with a cup of coffee. He hadn't expected to be offered food, but it was very easy to settle in to the warmth of this group of mourners. He felt his tiredness leaving him.

They all ate hungrily, the good taste of bacon and eggs and buttered toast with fresh coffee refreshing them. Then it was time for Ludgate to remove the body. Clare felt a terrible pang at the thought. It had seemed comforting to have her brother's body in the bedroom, to watch over. But now the night was done and it was time to place his body in the box he had ordered. A simple cheap box to be burned with the body in it. Before Ludgate began, the five mourners gathered once again by the bed.

Without hesitation Frances opened her Bible. She read:
For everything there is a season and a time for every
matter under heaven,
A time to be born and a time to die;
A time to plant, and a time to pluck up what is planted...
The Lord is my shepherd, I shall not want;
He makes me lie down in green pastures.
He leads me beside still waters;
He restores my soul...
When she had finished Les helped Ludgate move Marsh's body to a gurney. Together they wheeled it out of the house. Marsh had not wanted to be buried in special funeral clothing. Give my clothes to Goodwill, he had directed. Don't change what I have on when I die. And they hadn't. He left in his pajamas.

The sun was up now, the day beginning. A new day with no Marsh in it. No Marsh needing them. All four of the caregivers felt the emptiness. Stella sensed it, and gave each of them a warm hug.

There would be the obituary notice in the local paper and on the radio. It would state clearly that Marsh Lewis had died of AIDS. Eve would cringe when she read it and yet would feel a sort of pride in her son's honesty. Mabel Hansen would shake her head at the bold effrontery. "Like he was proud of it," she would say disapprovingly.

There would be the formal memorial service at St. Paul's. It would provide some comfort for Ed and Eve and Harry, which was why Marsh had wanted it held.

But for the five people reluctantly ending their night together the memorial service had already been held.

PART FOUR

June, 1983-October, 1984

CHAPTER TWENTY-FIVE

Clare knew, in the summer of 1983, that there were problems to be reckoned with in her own life, Chad being a major one. The farm economy was miserable, with many unhappy farmers forced into holding auctions because they had too much debt and could not continue. Clare knew the price of milk was dropping again and expenses were continuing to rise.

She knew that she and Lee were very fortunate to both be nearly debt-free. There were even horror stories circulating in the farm community about farmers who became so depressed that they literally could not get out of bed and go to the barn to care for their cattle. Sometimes the cattle would wait for their owner for days, manure building behind them, the mangers empty of food. Finally someone from off the farm would find them, usually the milk hauler, but there would be dead cattle among the crying, starving animals.

But all these things seemed almost unreal to Clare as she and Lee spent the summer of 1983 in a glowing world of their own, where outside annoyances and problems could not penetrate.

"I think we must be making up for lost time," Lee said one summer evening when the farm chores on both their farms had been rushed through. She wiped sweat from her face with a towel and gently wiped Clare's sweaty face too. "I think I'm getting too old for all this rushing around."

"Don't be silly, you're not old. It's just that we've been rather busy these evenings."

"Busy? Is that what we've been? Here. Let me get you a washcloth. You've got what looks like cow manure on your cheek."

"Heavens," Clare said. "Wonder where that could have come from?"

"A cow?"

"Well, I do see enough of them in the course of a day." Clare let Lee wash the offending spot. "It's so nice being over here," Clare said with a sigh of contentment. "I could get used to all this attention."

"Well, good. I was sort of hoping maybe you could."

"Were you? Did you have something more in mind than cleaning me up?"

"Maybe. Could be. Definitely, I'd say."

"That probably explains why you're removing my shirt?"

"It might have something to do with it."

"Or were you planning to throw me in your bathtub and get me really clean?"

"Not unless you throw me in too."

"It could be arranged. Here. Wait a minute. That's not fair. You've still got all your clothes on."

"So?" Lee's hands moved slowly on Clare's body.

"So it's not fair. Let me equalize things here a little. Hey. That tickles!"

"Good. Serves you right. You thought it was just fine last night to tickle my feet, remember?"

"That was different." Clare was making some progress in clothing removal herself.

"Oh, sure. Different how?"

"Just different. There. That's much better. All that clothing was a nuisance."

"It sure was." Lee entwined her arms around Clare, pulling her close, enjoying the feel of Clare's naked body against her own.

The external world could not compete. Farm work, Chad, Marsh, Mabel, and Gloria all seemed distant and unimportant in comparison to the sheer joy of spending time with Lee, building a relationship with Lee.

By September, however, Clare found she had to descend from Cloud Nine occasionally as many other concerns began pressing in. Fortunately Mike had returned to work the Monday after the day he had quit.

"I thought you quit," she said to him when she came out to find him in the barn.

"I came back." Mike kept on cleaning a calf pen.

"Why?"

"Because I kind of like it here." He grinned sheepishly at her. "You're a pretty good boss. I could do a lot worse. I shoulda told ya I didn't think the hay needed fluffing."

"I guess you were right. We got it in without it being fluffed," Clare conceded.

She and Mike managed to work together a little more harmoniously after that; he was even improving at the work he did. In September she raised his salary. He seemed set on staying.

When school began, Chad seemed set on staying away. "I don't want to listen to the kids calling me queer."

Clare supposed she was a "queer" now too. Probably people were talking. Something in the way her son spoke told her he knew, although she and Lee had said nothing to him. She figured he'd have to be blind, deaf, and dumb not to have noticed how much time his mother spent with Lee.

"All right," she said. "Sit down and let's talk. You're fourteen and starting high school. You know as well as I do that you have to go. Besides, it's a new school."

"Yeah, but the same old kids will be going there with me. I won't go," he said stubbornly.

"You have to go. It's the law. You can't quit school until you're sixteen and even then it would be a lot better if you finished."

"I don't need it to farm."

"Yes, you do. Farming is a complex business these days. You need to have good reading and math skills. You need the science, and for sure you need the agriculture courses."

"I don't care." Chad's face was set. "I just won't go."

"Try it, please. I know you don't like it and I don't blame you. Would it help if I talked to the principal or the teachers?"

"That would make it worse."

"I suppose it would," Clare agreed.

Chad still protested going, but Clare was firm. She felt exhausted from the struggle, though, when he finally slouched onto the bus the first morning. She held her breath when he got off it again that night.

"How was it?" She was anticipating the worst.

"Okay, I guess. Nobody said anything to me. But they may," he added.

"And maybe they won't. Will you keep on going?"

"I guess so."

"Look, if it gets too bad, I've been thinking. There are private schools. If you can get your grades up where you used to have them, I think we could manage to send you to one. You could go without anybody knowing about Marsh."

"Or about you?" he shot out at her, closely watching her response.

"Me?" Clare said, buying time.

"Yeah. You and Lee."

For a moment Clare was silent, uncertain what to say. "Lee is very important to me," she said finally. "I care about her. A lot. And...and that isn't going to change. I don't know what people say, but I want you to know that Lee is a good person. And I'm still your mother, you know. I care about you too."

"Yeah? Well, I don't want to go to a private school."

"Why not?"

"Because I'd have to leave my friends."

"I thought you said you didn't have any friends."

"Of course I've got friends." He gathered up his new high school textbooks and marched out of the kitchen.

"Kids. Who can figure them?" Clare said later that evening when she had rushed through her milking and gone across to Lee's for a brief visit.

"Other kids maybe," Lee said, watching Clare. "So he knows about us?"

"Yeah, he does."

"Well, nobody ever said your kid was dumb." Lee smiled faintly. "Doesn't surprise me at all. We've practically worn a trail in the blacktop between here and your place."

"I guess we have. I don't think I handled it very well with him. Maybe I should have said more..."

"He'll be okay," Lee said encouragingly. She hoped it was true. She still went from day to day wondering whether Clare would get scared and run again.

"I hope so. I just hope he doesn't decide to tell all of George's relatives." Clare brushed a weary hand through her hair.

"Do you think he would?"

"He might. If he decides it would serve him. He hates school and I'm forcing him to go."

"Well, I hope he doesn't. Maybe he won't."

"Maybe." Clare sounded uncertain. "You know what I'd like? Just once in awhile to be able to actually sleep with you. It seems a small thing to be able to spend the entire night with the person I love, but it's important to me."

"I hope it won't always be this way." Lee felt a rush of pleasure at Clare's words. She reached over and stroked Clare's arm.

"You must think I'm nuts to worry like I do." Clare leaned closer to Lee.

"Nope. Just practical."

"Well, I'm sick of being practical. Enough of practical for one day." Her eyes met Lee's and Lee grinned.

"Okay. If you can't have the pleasure of listening to me snore all night, how about we go sit on my sofa and neck?"

"Me? Neck with a queer? Heavens," Clare said grinning back.

~

Marsh continued to stay with his folks through the fall and winter of 1983. He saw Frances off and on, over the side fence as she worked gathering the last of her garden produce. With the dying plants and falling leaves, Marsh was depressed again, certain he would not see another spring. Let his dad take the garden back again. Ed had abdicated early in the season, leaving the bulk of the garden work to Marsh.

He kicked fallen leaves around and watched as Frances dug and cleaned off her carrots. From his somber silence she knew he was out of sorts with the world.

"What's the matter?" she asked. "What's bothering you?"

"Dying," he replied. He knew she would take the bluntness and not shrink back.

She nodded. "It bothers me, too. I think of it more in the fall, when everything is dying for the winter. My belief says there is a resurrection. Sometimes that helps me. Sometimes it really doesn't."

"I don't think I share your beliefs exactly, but it would be nice to think there was something beyond this life," Marsh said, coming over to sit on her lawn, crunching dead leaves.

This was the moment when she was supposed to gently lead him to Christianity, to some sort of repentence, and to her son's church. Instead Frances said, "I think that's what all the churches, all the religions have in common. None of us wants to think there's nothing after we die."

"Yeah. It's comforting to think there's some power bigger than we are making the decisions. Mostly it's comforting, except when people decide that power has already excluded people like me. My mother is convinced I'm going straight to hell."

"My son would share that belief," Frances said quietly.

"What about you? Do you think I'm going to hell?"

"I don't know."

"No hotline to God? No special inside knowledge?"

Frances smiled at his words. She shook her head. "Nothing like that. Not even a hotline to my own son these days. He's very busy making a successful church. I always thought it was successful when my husband and I were in charge. It wasn't very big. The people didn't give a lot of money. But it was a loving place to worship. Nobody was excluded."

"Not even gays?" Marsh couldn't help asking.

"I don't know about gays. I don't think it ever came up. Not directly. But I do know my husband was the one to do the funeral for the fellow who ran the restaurant..."

"Wade? He did Wade's funeral?" Marsh was interested.

"Yes. I sang. Two songs, as I remember..."

"Well, I'm sorry I missed all that. I didn't know you could sing."

"Can't every minister's wife?" Frances said self-mockingly. "Actually, Richard's wife doesn't."

"And she wouldn't have done it at Wade's funeral in any case."

"Probably not."

"I guess your son and his wife are aiming for something different than the church you and your husband ran. Financially successful, maybe?"

"That's part of it, but not all." Frances frowned. "Lyal and I always thought it wasn't our right to judge people. Even gays," she said before Marsh could ask. "I'm not saying we were perfect at it. I'm sure we did judge sometimes. But Richard and Patricia see it as their right, maybe even their duty, to judge and exclude people. People like you. People on welfare. My son says they're just lazy and should not be encouraged."

"Letting them come to church would encourage them?"

"I don't see how, either. Maybe he doesn't think they would give enough," Frances said.

"Could be. Does he plan to check people's bank accounts before letting them in the door?" Marsh asked. "I'm surprised he hasn't objected to me being in the yard."

"Oh, he has. But he thinks I'm out here converting you," Frances smiled.

"Well, that explains why you always come gardening with your Bible and tray of religious tracts," Marsh grinned back.

"I've never!"

"I know. How come?"

"It's none of my business," Frances said.

"Well, if it will keep you in good with your son, feel free to bring on the tracts."

"I don't like tracts."

"Don't like...Frances, how can you say that?" Marsh pretended to be shocked.

"Richard would hand you several, I'm sure. But I'm not Richard."

"For which I am duly thankful," Marsh said.

Frances supposed she should be feeling some guilt for talking like this about her son. But she was glad for someone like Marsh who could make light of the situation.

Later Marsh insisted on carrying a basket of carrots for her to the parsonage door. He set them down quietly, pantomiming stealth, tiptoeing back to the side fence. She had to laugh at the ridiculous sight he made.

CHAPTER TWENTY-SIX

In October Chad came home from school with a black eye and bruises on his face.

"A fight?" Clare asked, alarmed.

"Yeah. I tried to ask this girl, Stephanie Johnson, to go to the homecoming game with me and she turned me down because she said I was a queer and then kids started laughing and making cracks. I got mad and hit somebody. I got suspended for two days for starting the fight." He handed his mother a note from the principal.

"It must have been quite a fight," she said inadequately, feeling stunned and angry.

"Yeah." He said it with a kind of pride. "I gave Gordy a bloody nose."

"You gave your cousin Gordy Hansen a bloody nose?"

"He and the others call me queer. They say you and Lee are queers and snicker about it."

"Gordy and his brothers do?"

Chad nodded. "Yeah, and some other kids. Everybody knows."

Oh swell, Clare thought. Her anger over his suspension blurred into confusion and fear.

"At least I don't have to go back until Monday. I hate it."

"I suppose you do. I would, too."

"Yeah, well, it's your fault. You and Lee and Marsh. If you weren't all such dumb...queers."

"Don't use that word," Clare said sharply. "It's an ignorant word. I don't want to hear it come out of your mouth again."

Chad stared at his mother, surprised by her vehemence. "That's what you are, isn't it?" he said.

"There are other words to use. I'm tired of hearing that one. We have done nothing to be ashamed of or for you to feel ashamed of."

"I wish...I wish I was somebody else's kid," he muttered and then turned abruptly away, leaving his mother standing in the yard, helpless and hurt.

Before she could follow him into the house a familiar car came speeding into her driveway, stopping with an angry screech of brakes. Clare watched as her sister-in-law got out of it and slammed the door after her.

"All right, this is the last straw." Gloria's face was red with anger. "Your son gave Gordy a bloody nose and bruised his face. I won't have it!"

"I just heard about the fight," Clare said. "It looks like Gordy landed a few punches too."

"Good!"

"I wouldn't put it that way. Did Gordy tell you what the fight was about?"

"No," Gloria admitted.

"It seems your sons have been calling Chad a queer. I wonder where they get that from?"

"My sons are just normal boys," Gloria defended.

"And so is mine. Are you suggesting that he isn't?"

"It's a wonder if he is, given who he lives with. You and that Lee Collins." Gloria glared at Clare, daring her to dispute it.

With a sinking feeling she kept hidden, Clare stared back at George's brother Nathan's wife. She had never liked Gloria much. It didn't appear Gloria liked her either.

"Well?" Gloria pressed.

"Well, what?" Clare evaded.

"Are you going to deny it?"

"No. It's none of your business, Gloria, who I live with."

"And I say it is, when kids are involved. Mabel and Merlin don't want their grandson raised by a queer."

"Are you speaking for them too?" Clare managed to keep her voice level, not revealing the fear inside.

Gloria nodded. "Of course. Mabel and I have discussed this."

"I'll bet you have," Clare could not keep from murmuring.

"And this fight is the final straw. It says to me that Chad should be raised by somebody else."

"He's my son and he'll be raised by me." Clare said it firmly, she hoped.

Chad came out the back door, dressed in his old chore clothes. He saw Gloria and Clare and swerved to avoid them.

"Not so fast, young man," Gloria ordered. "You owe my Gordy an apology."

"What for? Gordy got what he had coming," Chad said, staring defiantly at his aunt. "Anyhow, you told him about Mom and Lee, didn't you? I thought you were my friend."

"Well, of course I am..."

"That's what I thought." He looked at her with teenage scorn. "I'll sure never trust you again." Chad turned abruptly away and walked across the lawn toward the garage.

Both women watched him go. Clare turned to Gloria, who was now looking less angry, deflated by Chad's obvious disdain.

"Let's go inside," Clare suggested. "I'll make some coffee and maybe we can talk about this more calmly."

It was a peace offering. For a moment Gloria hesitated and Clare thought she was going to refuse. "Okay," Gloria sighed. "I guess I could use a cup."

Clare served some cookies with the coffee. Gloria ate a couple. "These are good," she said, reluctantly. "I should get the recipe."

"Lee made them," Clare had to inform her. "You'll have to ask her."

"Oh," Gloria said.

"Yeah. Well, that brings us back to the subject, doesn't it? Me being an unfit mother because of my...ah...involvement with Lee." The subject was scaring Clare badly. She realized with a shock that this was the first time she had admitted aloud to anyone that she was involved with Lee. How ironic, she thought, that it should be to Gloria, one of my least favorite people.

"It's just not natural, what you're doing with her and I've never liked her. She's so..."

"Do you even know her? Lee is both strong and gentle." Clare's hackles rose in defense of Lee. "And, it really isn't any of your business what we are to each other," Clare said firmly.

"You and Lee Collins just sort of frighten me," Gloria said in a low voice. "You are both so darned...capable. Somehow I just feel like I'm a nobody."

Clare stared at her sister-in-law. "That isn't true," she said. "I've never thought you were anything but capable yourself.

You're a good cook and you help Nathan too." How odd it seemed to be reassuring this woman who had always seemed so self-confident.

"Yeah, but you and Lee run farms on your own. And do all the stuff I do, besides."

"Well, we try, but you'd better not look under the beds because we don't have time to dust," Clare said with a grin.

Gloria chuckled reluctantly. "I hate dusting myself."

"Join the crowd. And you're raising three boys," Clare added.

"Sometimes I feel like I'm raising a mother-in-law, too. Mabel comes over so much," Gloria admitted.

"You always got on with her better than I did. Do."

"I wish I hadn't told her about you and Lee."

"You do? Why?"

Gloria shrugged. "Merlin said it was your own business and I guess he was right, but I...sometimes I think I've been jealous of you. You seemed to have it all, you and George."

"And George died," Clare reminded her. "It's been very hard on Chad. It hasn't been easy for me either. And my brother has AIDS. If that's having it all, well, please, spare me."

"I know. I...look, I shouldn't have gotten so upset about Gordy's bloody nose. I'm not sure why I did."

"Forget it," Clare said. "Kids take what they hear and use it on each other, but I think it will all blow over." I hope it will, she thought.

"It's just that sometimes...at home...we've got so many bills and Mabel is around so much. I don't mind Merlin nearly as much as I mind Mabel. And the debts..." Gloria's voice trailed off, and Clare realized with amazement that her sister-in-law was confiding in her.

"Farming is hard these days, but I'm sure you and Nathan are doing a good job," Clare said reassuringly.

"I guess. Nathan works so hard, but the boys just don't seem very interested. Sometimes it's more work trying to get them to do a chore than if I did it myself."

"I know just what you mean. The TV set seems to be Chad's favorite thing. I just don't remember my brothers and I sitting around so much."

"Our boys just don't want to work." Gloria took a sip of coffee and stared at Clare. "I didn't think I'd be telling you all this."

"To be truthful, neither did I, but I'm glad you are. I'd guess Mabel doesn't quite fill the bill for someone to talk to."

Gloria smiled sheepishly. "I shouldn't say it, but no, she sure doesn't."

Clare escorted Gloria to the back door. "This was a much nicer visit than I thought it was going to be," she said. "For a moment there, I thought maybe we were going to have to fight each other, like the kids did."

"Well...of course if it had come to blows, you can be sure I would have won," Gloria said.

"No bets on that one." Clare chuckled. "Come again, if you feel the need to talk."

"I may do that."

Clare watched Gloria's car drive out of the yard, thinking talking sure beat trying to scratch each other's eyes out.

"Is she very mad because I beat Gordy up?" Chad asked as he came out of the garage toward her.

"She started out mad, but it's okay now."

"Good," Chad said with relief. "I mean, I was mad at him, but he's my cousin and we were friends."

"You will be again."

"Yeah. Maybe." Chad sounded doubtful. "Wish I didn't have to go back to school."

"I think you'll find Monday that you'll be treated with more respect." Clare hoped that was true. She hated to think you had to beat people up to get respect, but that really seemed to be the way the world worked.

And on Monday afternoon when Chad got off the school bus, he announced, "It was okay. I heard somebody yell out 'queer' down the hall once, but I just ignored it. Pretended I didn't care."

"Good," Clare said.

Chad shuffled from foot to foot. "I didn't really mean what I said about wishing I was somebody else's kid," he mumbled.

"Well, good. I wouldn't want to trade you off either."

"It's just hard is all. Lee gonna move over here with us?"

His question took Clare by surprise. "I don't know. Would you mind if she did?"

He shrugged. "I guess not. You're always over there or she's over here anyway. It would probably make sense. Everybody knows about you anyway."

Clare almost laughed in relief.

&

It was not until after Christmas that Lee moved in with Clare. It wasn't really convenient for Lee with her own chores and farm work, but she said she didn't mind. It was so pleasant to actually live together.

Marsh came to live in Lee's house. He had by then discovered a suspicious purple lesion and knew without being told that it was KS, Kaposi's Sarcoma, the same cancer that had killed Gene.

In January after he had moved in, he went into Minneapolis to an AIDS clinic. Frances drove in with him. He'd felt foolish asking her, sure she would say she couldn't go.

Instead she had agreed immediately. "It will make a nice trip for me," she had said. But Marsh knew she was going because she did not want him to go alone. He wondered if she had told her son.

They went for a walk in Loring Park after his appointment. It was a cold day and few other people were out. Squirrels darted out at them, opportunists seeking food. Marsh stared blindly at them.

"I have it," he said.

"I thought you did, just from the way you came out," Frances said. "I'm sorry." She put a comforting hand on his arm.

He glanced down at it. "Sure you want to do that? Your son would be shocked. Probably send you in for a test at the Red Door Clinic."

"My son doesn't enter into it," she said.

"How about your religion?"

"My religion is more flexible than my son's, I'm finding. He doesn't know I came with you today. If he had known, he...I don't know what he would have done."

"Locked you in your room, maybe?" Marsh asked, his spirit returning. "Swallowed the key? And then taken Ex-Lax when he wanted it out."

"You're impossible," Frances said.

"I'm hungry. Must be all those squirrels begging for handouts. Let's go eat."

They sat in Annie's Parlor over thick hamburgers, homemade french fries, and rich hot fudge sundaes.

"It's hitting me about now," Marsh said, putting down his hamburger. "I really do have it. It's not reversible. There's no magic cure. Now if somebody important like Reagan had it, maybe they'd find a cure. But not in time for me."

"How long do you have?"

"I don't really even know that. It seems to vary from person to person. I'm scared," he said.

"I know. I would be, too."

"You? With your firm religious beliefs? Why?"

"Because I wouldn't want to die. Not yet. When my husband died, I thought about it a lot. He wasn't so old. Just in his sixties. It could happen anytime. To me as well as to you."

"It's a little more unlikely that it will happen so soon for you."

"True. I hope I'll be ready when it does."

"I'm not ready," Marsh pounded his fist on the table. "Damn it, I'm not ready! I want to stay alive."

"Maybe we're never ready," Frances said. Her bright green eyes, once so hooded, now were able to meet and hold Marsh's eyes, offering support and calm comfort.

"How can I be hungry?" Marsh asked. "I'm going to die and I'm hungry."

"I guess because you're not dead yet," Frances smiled back at him.

CHAPTER TWENTY-SEVEN

Butch returned home one Monday morning early in June from his night job at the creamery. As usual he helped with the milking and then tried to take a short nap. Stella had an early dental appointment and had left Angie with him that morning.

At least this way he had some time with her, Butch reasoned, as he lay awake with his daughter on the bed next to him. It wasn't often these days that either he or Sally had the leisure to enjoy Angie. Their extra jobs had put them on a terrible treadmill, and the worst of it was that there seemed to be no end in sight.

He watched Angie playing in the sunlight, so cute with her bright red hair. Maybe she'd be spared his freckles. He hoped so. There was so little time with her these days. He felt a sharp pang of regret, but what could they do?

At least Butch and his folks had worked out a good system to handle the hay chopping and ensiling. When Stella got home from the dentist, they put it into action. Orrin drove tractor on the chopper, chopping huge loads of haylage. Stella hauled each load to the silo, where she unhooked and turned it over to Butch, who pulled the load to the blower where it was unloaded. Stella took an empty box back to Orrin, who, if he was on time, would have a third box chopped full to be hauled back to Butch.

With Sally at work during the weekdays and Stella handling a tractor to pull the loads, Butch had to watch out for

Angie, who was just three and was walking well enough to get into trouble wherever she went.

Butch and Stella had worked out a play area for her in a spot of June sunshine. They had set up a temporary pen for her of mesh fencing stretched between posts. It wasn't the fanciest arrangement, but it seemed to be holding Angie, who was happily tossing a large blue ball up and down.

The bright sunshine was putting Butch to sleep as he oversaw the unloading of each box of haylage into the blower. He yawned and stretched frequently to stay alert, wishing for an end in sight to their outside jobs. Sally seemed to be holding up better than he was. He was so bone tired these days he could hardly concentrate.

He finished unloading and carefully backed the huge box away from the blower. From the corner of his eye he saw that Angie's ball had gone over the top of her fence. She was dozing on a blanket in the sun, so he left the ball where it was while he unloaded the next box Stella had brought in.

God, he was tired. Must be, because he usually didn't mess up coming into the blower like this. He had brought the load in too far out. The haylage would hit the ground coming out of the box. Nothing to do but back up and try again.

He hated delays because of such stupidity on his part. He ground his tractor into reverse and backed away from the blower faster than he usually did, backing the eighteen-foot-long, ten-ton load to a point where he could remaneuver and come in correctly.

It was only after he had shifted out of reverse and into low that he looked down to his right and saw the bright yellow of Angie's blouse. She lay still just behind the rear tractor wheel.

"Oh my God." He shut off the tractor and jumped down. His mind registered on the blue ball lying beside Angie. She got out to get the ball and I didn't see her. *I didn't see her. I didn't see her.*

He felt sick. Don't touch her. Could be broken bones. Call an ambulance. Call from the barn, it's closer. He was incoherent on the phone but within minutes the ambulance was there, medics bending over his daughter.

Stella arrived back with another load just as the ambulance pulled in. She left the tractor running, jumped off it, ran to where the medics were. She saw Butch. "Oh, no. Not Angie," she said. "Is she all right? How bad is she?"

"I'm afraid she's not all right," one of the emergency people said gently.

"She's...dead?" Stella felt like she'd been kicked in the stomach. She couldn't seem to breathe.

The ambulance took the body away. Butch stood by his tractor. There were small bloodstains on the ground. Angie's blood.

Stella went to him, saw the white face stark behind his freckles. "What happened?"

"I ran over her, backing up. I didn't see her. I didn't see her, I didn't see her."

"Oh my God," Stella said. "Oh, no. Oh, Butch." Her face mirrored the anguish on her son's.

"Mom, I didn't see her, I just didn't see her." He shook with sobs and Stella put her arms around him.

"Of course you didn't. It wasn't anybody's fault." She soothed him as best she could, though nothing was in focus yet. Their world had just fallen apart.

"Sally," Butch said. "Somebody's got to tell Sally. Oh, God..."

"Will you be all right if I go call Sally?"

Butch nodded, tears rolling down his face. "Tell her...I didn't see her."

Stella went into the milking parlor to call Sally. It took awhile. First the line was busy. Then she was put on hold.

"It's important," Stella said. "Tell her it's urgent." And then she wondered why. Angie was dead. There was nothing Sally could do for Angie. But maybe for Butch. Maybe for each other. They could comfort each other, she hoped. Oh, God, and Orrin had to be told...

"Hello. Sally? I've got some very bad news..."

Sally was on her way. She had carpooled with a neighbor that morning, but somebody was bringing her home. Sally would not be fit to drive anyway.

Oh, God, why? Stella asked the empty milking parlor. The place they spent so much of their time seemed cold and unfriendly with no cows in the herringbone stalls.

She was coming out of the barn when she heard the noise. A sound she heard often enough in November when hunters were circling the woods in pursuit of deer. Stella began to run.

"No!" she said aloud, as though that word would stop what was already done. As though it could put back in place the bits of bone and brain and blood spattered all over the kitchen. From Butch, his body slumped sideways in the chair.

"Oh my dear God," she murmured backng out of the room, unable to take her eyes off the sight of her son.

Call the ambulance. From the barn. God, not from in there. I can't go back in there, Stella thought. And Sally. Sally should not see...Oh my God.

For the second time that day an ambulance came speeding past Clare's. A county police car sped right after it. Both had lights flashing and sirens blaring. Clare could hear the sirens even over the noise of her forage chopper. She saw the vehicles turn into the Grimeses' driveway.

She came into her yard and stopped the tractor, waving to Lee who was at the blower. They jumped into Clare's truck and followed after the ambulance, arriving just in time to see Butch Grimes' covered body removed on a stretcher from the house. A sheriff's deputy came out carefully carrying a shotgun.

"Oh, God..." Stella's face seemed to Clare to have shrunken and twisted with grief. Clare's arms reached out of their own accord to encircle Stella and she could feel the tight tenseness, the controlled tremors that showed how she was holding herself upright by sheer will.

A car turned in the driveway and stopped. Sally got out and saw the ambulance and the police car and Stella. She began to run toward Stella.

"Butch? Where's Butch?" Sally said.

"In the ambulance. You don't want to see him, honey," Stella said. "After Angie was taken away, while I was calling you, he went into the house...He blew off his face with the shotgun. Oh God, Sally. You don't want to see...The kitchen..."

"Not Butch too. Not Butch." Sally's voice rose in anguish.

"Orrin doesn't know yet," Stella said. "He's waiting in the far field for another wagon...Oh, God." Her face and voice lost their rigid control.

Sally felt numb. She heard all the words. On some level she knew what they meant. Angie and Butch. But it was unreal to her. Static filled her ears. Yet from a great distance she heard her voice say calmly, "Would you two tell Orrin? I don't think I should leave Stella right now..." She had her arms around her mother-in-law.

"Of course," Clare said instantly, glad there was some way to help even if it was not a task she wanted. She and Lee drove out through the Grimeses' fields to the one Orrin was working in.

Clare told Orrin directly, Lee standing by. She watched him shake his head as though to clear it. He left the tractor and chopper in the field, the tractor still running. It was Lee who went back and switched off the key. He got into the truck cab with Clare and Lee and sat looking blindly at the fields as they drove him home.

One look at Stella and Sally told him it was all true. They formed a tight threesome, knotted together with grief. They spoke disconnected words. Lee and Clare stood helplessly by.

Stella straightened up at last. "There are things we need to do. Funeral arrangements. Ludgate will need to be told."

"I'll call him," Lee volunteered.

"Use the barn phone," Stella said quickly. "You don't want to see..."

"I'll come right out," Ludgate said. "In a case like this..." With his calm professional manner, Ludgate shepherded the three survivors across the road to Orrin and Stella's house. He set Stella to making them some coffee and he talked openly and calmly about what had happened.

Other neighbors joined Clare and Lee in the yard, pulled as though by magnets to the scene of the tragedy, the news spreading fast on the police radio scanners. Nathan and Gloria Hansen came. Clare's brother Harry. Lee's brother Dan and his wife Linda. Other neighbors. They formed a tight little knot of concern and sorrow in the Grimeses' yard.

"We'll do all their hay," Harry said.

"Milk the cows."

"Clean up the kitchen," Lee offered.

Within an hour a mammoth neighborhood effort was underway. People who had not seen each other in months were now working side by side in the field. At one point that afternoon three tractor and chopper rigs gobbled up the Grimeses' hay. Eight self-unloading boxes waited at the blower to be unloaded. Four haybines moved in precision through the hayfields, laying out neat swathes of hay for chopping the next day.

Clare and Lee and Linda and Gloria took on the grisly task of cleaning up the kitchen. Another sheriff's deputy put in an appearance, took one look at the bloody scene and left, telling them they could go ahead and clean it up.

The women cleaned and scrubbed and used a strong-smelling disinfectant, as though they could wipe away what had happened.

Harry volunteered to milk the cows for as long as they needed help. Linda Collins said she'd help him. And the next day the entire neighborhood was back, working side by side. In the cleaned-up kitchen Gloria, Mabel, and Eve worked with other neighbors to prepare huge meals for everyone. Marsh came over in a long-sleeved shirt and tackled the garden, weeding with a vengeance.

As the Grimeses moved in shock through the funeral preparations, the sight of all their neighbors working for them was overwhelming. So many people with such good intentions created an atmosphere of powerful harmony, energy, and love.

Marsh was still working in the garden when Stella passed by on her way across the road to her own home. His face was half-hidden by a broad-brimmed hat, and at first Stella did not recognize him.

"Marsh Lewis? Is that you? Should you be out here doing this sort of thing?" Marsh was aware of the genuineness of her concern.

"Won't hurt me at all," he assured her. "I'm so sorry about what happened. Believe me, we all are."

"I know," Stella said. "I know. I don't know what we would have done without all of you."

"I wish we could do more," Marsh said.

"You're doing as much as anyone could, all of you," she told him. Marsh was struck by how at this time of tragedy, Stella could still transmit such warmth.

He heard her greet Nathan Hansen warmly too, saying, "It's just amazing what you people are doing. Marsh Lewis is even weeding our garden."

Nathan said, "Well, that's one big weed we could all do without around here."

It took Stella a moment to register on what he meant, and when she did her response was automatic. She raised a powerful farm woman's arm and slapped him. "If I ever catch you saying rubbish like that again, so help me I'll spank you," she said fiercely.

Nathan backed away, holding a hand to his reddening cheek. "Hey, I didn't mean anything."

"We've had enough death around here," she said. "Don't go wishing for any more."

"I'm sorry you had to hear that," Stella said to Marsh when Nathan had gone from view.

"I'm not," Marsh replied. "That slap was one of the nicest things I've heard in years."

Still muttering about that "Hansen insect," she went on her way, leaving Marsh smiling.

The funeral for Butch and Angie Grimes was the largest ever held at St. Paul's. The tragedy briefly brought all the neighbors together. It was a shame, someone said, that it took something like that to get together nowadays. But that's the way it was with the bigger farms and no rural schools anymore.

When the funeral was over, Orrin plunged headlong into work. Sally went automatically to her job at the wood products factory and automatically to the barn, morning and night. Stella did her own work in the house and on the farm, bleakly aware that for her the purpose in saving the farm was gone.

CHAPTER TWENTY-EIGHT

Frances said to Marsh, "it must have been horrible for them."

"I imagine it still is. For Stella, especially. She was the one who found him."

"Stella. She's the one who slapped Nathan Hansen?" Frances was learning all about the neighborhood and its residents as she visited Marsh in the country.

Marsh nodded. "She sure took him by surprise. Me too. In all her grief she could still do something like that."

"My son would agree with Nathan, you know."

"Of course. It goes without saying. How is the bigger and better church coming? Is it really bigger and better?"

"Well, it's certainly bigger. More people are coming all the time. Richard's talking about building another church."

"So it can expand even more?"

"Of course. I spend my evenings watching the kids so Richard and Patricia can be free to organize all sorts of church groups. I have to admit they've stirred up lots of activity."

"Well, people are probably ripe for it. You hear a lot about how we have to get back to decency. I have to wonder, was it really more moral years ago?"

"I don't know," Frances said. "Maybe we just didn't hear everything like we do now. The media is all over."

"I'll say." They were sitting in Lee's living room surrounded on three sides by her walls of books. Marsh indicated them. "If you ever lack for anything to read…"

"I'm a little scared of your friend Lee," Frances said. "She seems so intimidating. I don't think she'd like me borrowing her books."

"That's just her way. She's had to be strong. It wasn't easy for her setting up farming in the '50s. She's just had to be tough. But she's mellowing out nicely now."

"Why is that?"

"Well, I suspect it has something to do with my sister," Marsh said with a mischievous twinkle.

"Your sister Clare? The one whose husband died in an accident?"

"The one and only. Lee and Clare are lovers, you know."

"I didn't know." Frances did not think she wanted to know either. Marsh said it so casually. Usually with Marsh she could forget the sexual part of his homosexuality. From his teasing expression, she suspected the reminder was deliberate.

"You don't approve?" Marsh was too good at reading her face.

"No, I don't think I do. It still seems an unnatural thing to me."

"Well, I did a lot of unnatural things in my day then," Marsh mused. He didn't seem upset by her calling it that. "I stopped when I found I had the virus. If it's sexually transmitted, I didn't want to infect anybody else. Condoms and safe sex aside, there's still some risk. Besides, for some reason, it just doesn't seem all that important to me anymore." He looked closely at Frances. "Hey. You're blushing. Hasn't anyone ever talked about sex with you before?"

"It's not discussed much in my circle," she said, knowing she sounded stiff and stuffy. "I see no reason why it should be."

"No? Might be better if it was." Marsh was chuckling. "You must have done it once or twice, Frances. You did have a son. Or was he an immaculate conception?"

"Hardly," Frances's face tightened into a frown.

"Well then. You must have enjoyed it a little bit, didn't you?" Marsh pressed.

"I don't see that it's any of your business whether I enjoyed it or not," Frances said stiffly.

"Aha! Keep my nose out of your bedroom, right? That's what gays have been asking people like your son to do."

"It's not the same at all," she objected.

"Why not?"

"Well, because...because what you do is wrong. God never intended it that way. It's a perversion."

"How would you know? Have you tried it?"

"Of course not. But there's so much promiscuity among homosexuals."

"I suppose you're going to tell me all heterosexuals are monogamous?"

"Not all of them, of course, but most of them settle into marriage with one partner."

"And then divorce and go on to another partner. Come on, Frances. For gays, there hasn't been any encouragement to marry and stay together as a couple. And yet a lot of us do, on our own. No official ceremony. No gifts for the new couple. No family support when things are hard. And if you think Lee and my sister are promiscuous, you're nuts. For one thing, they wouldn't have time!" He was laughing now.

"But it's still unnatural. No church could approve it."

"Where have you been? There are gay ministers around. And churches that accept gay people without trying to change them. The Unitarians do. The United Church of Christ and the Reform Jews. So, it's not as though everybody takes the same attitude as your son's church."

"My son maintains that homosexuals don't have to be that way. That they can change anytime they want."

"Go straight? Why would we want to?" Marsh asked. "I probably spent more time being promiscuous than I should have. So did a lot of straight guys my age, if locker room talk is anything to go by. The bragging some of those guys did. I finally did meet Gene. We lived together for six years. I think we would have stayed together a lot longer if he had lived. I never wanted to go straight. And I doubt that I could have. My sister tried for fourteen years of marriage to George. She got scared into it and I really don't know if she was ever very happy. I can't imagine that George was happy with her either. Life's too short to spend it living up to somebody else's idea of what's right for you."

"But the sexual part of it is clearly wrong," Frances said. She had never talked or heard so much about sex before.

"Is it really? It's always felt just right to me. And you heterosexuals are really hung up on the sexual stuff, aren't you? It seems strange to me that any power who created us would have provided us with so many ways to have pleasure through sex if he or she didn't intend us to use it that way. Think about that, Frances. If sex was just for routine reproduction of the species, then why does it provide so much pleasure in such a variety of ways?"

"I wouldn't know about that." Frances could feel herself blushing in embarrassment.

"No? Well, I'm an expert, or used to be. At least with men. I couldn't give you any firsthand information about women. You'd have to go to see Lee and Clare for that." He was teasing her now.

"I can just see me doing that," Frances retorted to cover the embarrassment she felt. "Your sister and her...ah...Lee frighten me. They seem so independent."

"And you're not?"

"Not really."

"Maybe you've just never had the chance to prove it to yourself. You could do anything you wanted to do. Drive a cab. Fly a plane, get involved with a woman..."

"You're impossible!"

"And you're blushing again. I'll bet you're just a latent lesbian at heart," Marsh teased.

"I am no such thing. I'm a widowed grandmother. That's all. I wish you'd get off this subject. If you don't, I'm going to leave." Her green eyes were angry and indignant.

"Hey, I've upset you. I didn't mean to, but you know us gays. We just can't resist a chance to recruit." Marsh was still smiling.

"Well, that's certainly what my son thinks," Frances said with diminishing anger. She found it hard to stay angry at Marsh, even if he was outrageous at times.

"I'll bet he does. Probably wishes we'd recruit him."

"If my son knew what we were saying, he'd...I don't know what he'd do."

"Nothing very pleasant, I'm sure. I'm sorry to have to say it, Frances, but I don't think your son and I would hit it off very well. I wonder why the two of us do?" He regarded her with fondness.

"I don't know." Frances found herself smiling back at him, her green eyes tender. She could never have explained how much she cherished this odd friendship.

ช

Clare and Lee were aware of how much time Marsh spent with his widowed friend Frances, but they too had trouble understanding it.

"I met her at Wade's funeral," Lee said. "She sang. She had a lovely voice, very clear and true."

"And beyond that?"

"She seemed shocked when she realized Les and I weren't a happy couple."

"She seems shy to me," Clare said. "But Marsh likes her, so there must be more to her than we think."

"Maybe," Lee said but she found it hard to imagine.

"We should go over and see Marsh more than we do," Clare said. "But it's so hard seeing him and knowing he's going to die."

"I know." Lee's expression turned somber at the thought. She was awkward around Marsh these days, too aware of the purple marks and uneasy about mentioning his death. She could lend him her house and she knew Clare gave him money, but she wished they could give him more of themselves.

She knew they weren't the only ones. Harry and Diane had visited once and hadn't been back. Eve was a faithful visitor, but her husband did not come often.

On Eve's last visit she had encountered Lee again, working in the yard. By then, Eve knew that Lee was living with Clare. "It's very nice of you to let Marsh stay in your house," Eve said as she passed by on the way to her car. "I wanted him to stay at home, but it was so difficult for Ed."

Lee brushed her graying hair back off her forehead and regarded Eve. Clare's mother was looking her age. She walked as though each step brought her pain. Lee thought of all the years of hard work Eve had put in on the Lewis farm. "I'm glad I could help out," she said. "Marsh and I have been friends for years."

Eve nodded. "I know. At least I do now. When Clare bought her farm..." Eve gestured across the road. "I didn't like it that she'd be living across the road from you."

"Really?" Lee was surprised that Eve was bringing this up.

"Yes. And now you're living with her over there."

Lee nodded, sensing that Eve was finding this difficult.

"I don't understand it, any of it. Marsh and this horrible AIDS. And now my daughter and you." Eve shook her head, confusion in her eyes.

"I care about Clare very much."

"Do you? I used to worry about what people would say, and maybe I still do, but it all seems so pointless really. Ed would be so angry and upset if he knew you were...not just staying at Clare's."

"And what about you? Are you angry and upset too?" Lee asked, watching Eve's face.

For a moment Eve stared unseeingly at the nearby fields. Then her faded blue eyes met Lee's. She smiled faintly. "No. All these years I thought I would be and that I should be, but I'm not, at least not much. I don't understand it, but...I can accept it."

"I'm glad. I'd never do anything to hurt Clare. I hope you know that."

Eve regarded Lee with a penetrating look. "I think I believe you."

The sound of boots crunching on the gravel driveway broke their brief rapport. Clare walked over to them.

"Hi, Mom. Been to see Marsh?"

"Yes. The lesions are getting worse." Eve's eyes filled with tears. "At least he doesn't seem to be in pain."

"I hope he won't be," Lee said.

"Well, Ed will be wondering where I've been."

"Same old Dad," Clare said with fondness.

"Some things don't change. Sometimes it's almost nice to know that. There are so many changes these days." Eve moved slowly toward her car. Then she turned back to the two younger women. "I hope you'll be...happier than you were with George," she said to Clare.

"Mom..."

"Your dad will be wondering where I am." Eve turned again and painfully walked to the car.

"Let her go," Lee said. "She said more to me than I ever thought I'd hear. More than my own mother ever said."

≈

Marsh felt like he was under quarantine. Besides Frances and his mother, few people came to visit. He seldom went anywhere. It was hard to see the uneasiness, the fear, and sometimes the disgust on people's faces. When he could, he had Frances do his errands in town.

In August the bottom fell out. He was ill enough to need a local doctor, who recommended hospitalization.

"I'm not sure that would work," Marsh said. "The hospital is small. Where would they put me? I can't imagine, given the AIDS hysteria, that they would want to put me in a room with somebody else. Or take me at all."

"The law says they have to take you," his doctor pointed out. He was the same man who had mismanaged Wade's illness. He had learned a few things since then about the HIV virus and the range of diseases that came with it. He had most importantly learned some compassion as his own nephew had the disease. It was hard to ignore when it hit close to home.

"I'd like to stay here if I can," Marsh insisted.

"You'll need care. Who will help you if you're not in the hospital?"

"I'll figure something out."

He discussed it with Frances when she came to visit. "I can come part of the time," she said willingly. "But my son demands me for babysitting most evenings now."

"The unpaid mother's help," Marsh chided.

"Well, I'll be an unpaid nurse if I help care for you," she retorted.

"You're right. I'm sorry. I'd also like to get my sister and Lee and Les, if they'll come."

"Ask them," Frances said.

"I can't. They might say no."

"All right. I'll ask them. You're a chicken."

Frances went across the road with trepidation. She hadn't been fooling when she'd admitted to Marsh that the two women frightened her. Clare was so tall and powerful-looking and Lee, though shorter and more compact, was often somber and almost forbidding. Frances remembered Lee from the funeral, but neither of them had acknowledged they had met before.

Now she came into the kitchen and watched Lee sit down across from her, eyeing her soberly. "How's Marsh?" Lee asked.

"He's deteriorating rapidly. That's why I'm here."

"I didn't think it was purely a social call," Lee said with some sarcasm.

Frances was getting irritated. "It might be nice if you and your...Marsh's sister would pay a few more social calls across the road."

Lee looked at her in surprise. She started to respond defensively and caught herself. "You're right," she said. "We haven't gone to see Marsh as much as we should."

"He's missed you both."

"And we miss him, but neither of us seems to know what to talk about when we go. So we just sit there and it's very awkward."

"Well," Frances said, "he may be dying, but he still has his sense of humor."

"We haven't seen much of it."

"Or of him," Frances asserted.

Clare came in. She nodded at Frances. "What's up?"

Frances looked her over, the green eyes managing to boldly take in this sister she hadn't seen much of but had heard so much about. Clare's open face appealed to her more than Lee's shuttered, defensive look.

"We were talking about Marsh. He's getting worse," Lee said.

"Oh."

"And Frances here says we've been negligent about going to see him."

"I'd go more," Clare said, "but I can't seem to talk to him anymore. I guess I don't know what to say about his illness."

"Or about his death," Frances pointed out.

"I can't just come right out and say to him: Marsh, you're dying and I wish you weren't. I wish you hadn't been so dumb that you went and got AIDS."

"Is that how you feel?" Lee asked.

"I guess it is," Clare said in surprise.

"Tell Marsh," Frances said.

"I couldn't do that."

"Why not? Your brother doesn't pull his punches."

"But he's dying."

"Yes, he is. But he's not dead yet. Don't treat him like he is," Frances said with a forcefulness that almost shocked her.

"You must care a lot about my brother," Clare said.

"I do." Frances couldn't have explained to anyone just why, but it was true. When she'd been a wife and mother she had assumed that those would be her primary relationships. There would be grandchildren to love, but her husband and son would be the main people she cared about. Now she was discovering that there were other relationships. This one with Marsh was completely outside her experience.

"Frances is right," Lee said to Clare. "He isn't dead yet, but we probably started mourning him right about the time he told us he had the AIDS virus."

Frances was surprised to see a softer expression on her face. For the first time, Frances could understand a little of her appeal.

"What do you want us to do?" Lee asked.

"He's going to need care. Probably around the clock."

"And he wants us to help," Lee said.

Frances nodded. "He was afraid you might refuse, so he sent me to ask."

"The big chicken," Clare said.

"That's what I called him too," Frances said. "He just clucked in response."

※

Frances went right from Clare's to see Les Jones. She was certain if she left it until the next day she would not do it at all.

Les did not remember her. He wouldn't even let her in the door until she had explained she was a friend of Marsh's.

"Thought you might be another Jehovah's Witness," he said. "I made the mistake of letting one in last week. She didn't want to leave." He grinned at her and his face became boyish. "I finally had to make a pass at her and, believe me, that was as painful for me as it was for her."

In spite of herself, Frances smiled.

"Ah, well," Les sighed. "I don't get a lot of company so I suppose I can't be too fussy. How is Marsh?"

"Not so good." She watched as his face fell. She supposed he was probably close to sixty, but it was hard to tell. Les had grown a large bushy mustache and his hair was still thick and wavy. A gold chain glinted at his throat. Les caught her eyes on it.

"It was from my partner Wade," he said. "I never wore it while he was alive. Didn't, don't like jewelry much, but..."

"It looks good on you," Frances found herself saying. "About Marsh..."

"It's not going to be long, is it?"

"I don't know. Probably not. He's going to need care. He wants to stay in Lee's house. Would you be willing..."

"To help? Of course. I've wanted to do more, but I didn't think anyone would want me to. When you start to get older, you're seen as incapable of doing anything."

"I suppose that's true."

"You just wait. You're young yet. It comes to us all."

"Not that young," Frances said. "My husband was older. He died awhile back."

"I'm sorry. It's never easy to lose a spouse." Les sighed. "Somehow I thought you might be one of Lee's city friends. But I guess they don't come so much anymore."

It took Frances a moment to realize that Les had been thinking she was gay. Her face started to redden.

"Now I know why you look familiar," Les said suddenly. "You sang at Wade's funeral. Your husband preached..." He broke off. "Marsh hasn't gotten all religious or anything, has he? I don't think I..."

"No, he hasn't changed in that way," Frances assured him.

"Good. I mean... I guess I don't understand how he's come to be friends with you."

"Neither does my son. Richard is pastor of the church my husband and I ministered to. He isn't very tolerant of difference."

"Doesn't like queers, huh? I think I may have read some of his letters in the local paper. Didn't he write suggesting we all be rounded up and quarantined?"

"It sounds like something he might say," Frances admitted.

"He won't be visiting Marsh, will he? I don't think I'd be able to be polite anymore. As I've gotten older, I find I have much less patience for bigotry."

Frances assured him that Richard would not be putting in an appearance. It struck her as funny and she laughed aloud.

Les joined her laughter. "Must be a trial for you, having a son like that."

CHAPTER TWENTY-NINE

The Grimeses slogged along through the rest of the summer with Sally maintaining her sanity through her work in town and Stella gardening furiously every spare moment she had. Orrin resisted any attempts to talk about what had happened.

"But we need to make some plans," Stella said to him one August morning. It was a Sunday and she had toyed with going to church, but she knew she would have to go alone. Orrin had not gone since the funeral.

"I don't want to talk about it," he said, scraping back his chair. "I'm going out and check the pasture fences today. Be back in time for supper."

"Don't you want lunch? I'll pack you a sandwich."

He shook his head. "Had enough at breakfast."

"But, Orrin, you have to eat. And we can't go on avoiding the whole issue."

"I'm going now," he said, placing a feed cap on his head.

The door slammed after him and Stella shook her head. Damn, but it was hard to talk to him anymore. There were plans that needed to be made, financial matters that needed attending to, and Stella just could not get him to sit down and talk. She knew he was trying to shut out the memories and deny the deaths.

Well, they happened. Stella knew that only too well. Her nights were miserable with dreams of Butch and Angie. She automatically washed the breakfast dishes and a few minutes later was seated at the same kitchen table where she had found

Butch. It took some effort for her to sit there calmly as Sally brought her coffee.

"I need to talk," Stella said. "And I sure can't do it with Orrin these days."

Sally sat down with her mother-in-law. "I've noticed that," she said. "Orrin keeps to himself since it happened."

"You didn't see this kitchen the way I did," Stella said suddenly, words spilling out. "I can't get it out of my mind."

"I still can't believe Butch did that. I've asked myself why so many times," Sally said. "If only I'd been home, if I could have gotten here sooner. Maybe I..."

"Now don't start blaming yourself. God knows, I do that enough for all of us. If only I'd stayed with him. I should've sent Angie to a babysitter..."

"I tell myself it happened and there's no use saying 'what if' and 'if only' but I still do."

"Me too. All the time," Stella admitted.

"And the loneliness. Stell, I hate coming into this house at night. It's so dead in here now, so quiet."

"Oh, honey, I know. It's awful. Do you think it will ever get better?"

This conversation opened the door to many more. The two women drew strength and support from each other and watched in sadness as Orrin went his silent way. The family conclaves did not happen anymore. Now it was Stella and Sally who sat down together to figure finances.

"I got word from Butch's insurance company today," Sally said. "He took out his life insurance policy eighteen months ago. The company has a rider saying they don't pay benefits if a suicide occurs within the first two years. They did send back the cash value of the policy and they had the nerve to ask me if I might want to invest it in one of their policies for myself."

"Damn," Stella said softly.

"And that life insurance policy you and Orrin took out on Angie? Well, that pays us double for accidental death." Sally swallowed with difficulty before she spoke again. "Twenty thousand dollars for Angie."

"My God," Stella said. "What I wouldn't give to have both of them back. Isn't it awful to be calculating on the dead like this?"

❧

Through August and most of September Marsh was better again. The disease seemed to be playing with him, gripping hard for awhile, then letting up, igniting hope. The four care-givers weren't needed again until late September when he suddenly became worse. They became adept at mopping up vomit, changing sheets and pajamas, and at cooking up tempting bits of food to lure Marsh into eating.

His weight dropped radically, and when Stella came to see him a few days before the end of the month, she was shocked by the change from just two weeks earlier.

"Still think we shouldn't get rid of this big weed?" he quipped at her.

"I'd like it if you were a whole lot bigger one."

"Yeah, so would I," Marsh admitted. "I've often wondered how Butch had the guts to actually pull the trigger."

There was a shocked silence.

"I'm sorry," Marsh said contritely. "I'm getting too care-less with what I say. I shouldn't have said that, but I've thought about doing it and I can't."

"Don't worry about it," Stella said. "You took me by sur-prise, is all. You know, you're the first person besides Sally who has ever referred to what Butch did. Most people avoid it."

"Most people avoid talking about death, period," Marsh said. "I hope I didn't hurt you."

"No, you didn't hurt me. Have you really thought about doing it to yourself?"

"It's crossed my mind. It might be easier on everyone if I did. We're all waiting around for it to happen."

"Don't ever think it would be easier." Stella was vehement. "I don't think there is any 'easy' way for the people left behind. Suicide is such a violent act. At least Butch's seemed like that."

"Yeah, well, don't worry. I'm too big a chicken to do it. Besides, I guess I want to keep on living as long as I can."

"I wish Butch had felt that way. I get angry sometimes that he didn't trust us enough to face what happened. We knew it was an accident. We knew he wouldn't ever deliberately hurt Angie."

"Poor Butch," Marsh said. "And poor you folks, without him." He reached out a comforting hand to Stella, who held it with tears in her eyes.

Marsh was learning to trust the four people who cared for him day and night. He hadn't realized at first what that would involve for them, how dependent he would become. At times he thought it would have been better if he had gone to a hospital or a nursing home and been cared for by more impersonal help.

He marveled that all four kept coming through for him day after day. Frances' participation was the hardest to understand. Marsh was pretty sure she hadn't shared the whole story of what she was going through at home.

In August when Marsh had asked her to be one of the four, Frances had not hesitated to agree. What she had hesitated about was telling her son. She put off telling him through the rest of August and into September, past the arrival of her widow's check. This time she gave Richard just seventy-five dollars and kept the rest for herself.

His eyebrows rose questioningly when she gave him the reduced amount of money. "What's this? Have they suddenly cut your benefits?"

"No. I'm keeping most of it this month."

"You're keeping it," he repeated. "Why?"

"I may have a need for it. I have to keep the car running. I'm helping to look after Marsh Lewis through what may be his last illness."

"Marsh? I didn't know you still saw him."

"Frequently," she said.

"I suppose it didn't occur to you that Patricia and I might object? We've taken a firm stand against unrepentant homosexuals in our church. What will the congregation think if they find out you're actually caring for one?"

"Perhaps they might think I'm doing my compassionate Christian duty of helping the sick."

"I suppose you see yourself as Mother Theresa?"

"Not at all. Marsh is a dear friend."

"Is he? Doesn't it occur to you that there might be some danger of acquiring the disease yourself?"

"Not really," she said. "I wasn't planning to sleep with the man, just help care for him."

"Mother!" Richard was genuinely shocked.

"There is some risk, I suppose," she admitted. "But Marsh has insisted we all take precautions when handling any of his bodily fluids."

"You're handling his... Who are these other people?" he asked.

"Friends of Marsh, his sister..."

"Homosexuals, all of them, I don't doubt."

"Yes," Frances admitted reluctantly.

"I thought so. I don't even want to know how you fit into this...this perverted arrangement."

He could not persuade her to give it up. He tried threats and cajoling. Neither worked. An uneasy atmosphere descended on the parsonage. Frances far preferred being with Marsh and his other caregivers to being at home.

The reprieve in September was pleasant. Marsh was in top form and able to get around with some help. On one of his best days the four took him on a picnic in the hills east of town.

It was a warm day, with clear blue skies and mild summer-like temperatures, ideal for a picnic.

Clare had brought chicken and wine. Lee had prepared potato salad. Frances made a cake in the parsonage kitchen under the disapproving eye of her daughter-in-law who seemed to begrudge her even the use of the oven. Les brought blankets and folding chairs and fussed about getting Marsh settled in the car and then out of it at the picnic site.

Frances watched his fussing with amusement at first, but the amusement changed as she realized what she was seeing was loving care. Would my own son treat me this well she asked herself. The answer was not reassuring.

Clare and Lee had finally gotten over their discomfort with Marsh. Frances watched them, struck by the warmth they generated in each other's company. When the four of them got going on memories, Frances felt vaguely left out.

Clare noticed her expression. She moved her lawn chair over next to Frances. "They can go on for hours, those three. I didn't share their experiences back then. I was busy being a wife and mother, probably not a very good one," she admitted with a rueful smile.

"Your husband died, didn't he?"

"He was killed falling from a silo," Clare said bluntly. "It was very hard on our son to have that happen. He's still having a bad time."

"I can imagine." Frances felt on safer ground here, talking to Clare. She at least had been married. Sometimes the gay jokes and jibes the others indulged in seemed too much. "How old is your son?"

"He was fifteen last June. Eager for the next year to fly by so he can get his driver's license. I dread that day." Clare's face shifted expression, and Frances could see the resemblance to Marsh very strongly.

"Marsh mentioned your son was having a bad time around the AIDS and..."

"Yeah, the AIDS and me," Clare said. "He's put up with a lot at school and from my husband's relatives because of it."

"The other kids were calling him names?"

Clare nodded. "At least it was better this last year. Kids get tired of it after awhile, thankfully, but Chad's still an outsider in many ways. He's a loner because of it, I think. At least he reads a lot."

"My grandchildren are too busy with social activities to read or be read to. Either that or they watch TV."

"Chad used to watch a lot of TV. Finally I had to stop it."

"What did you do?"

"I got rid of the it. That was last winter. George had bought this huge color set. When Marsh moved in across the road, Lee and I took it over there."

"So that's where it came from! Marsh seldom has it on," Frances admitted. "Was your son upset?"

"Very, but he recovered," Clare said with a smile. "We brought a lot of Lee's books back. We put them in the space where the TV had been and Chad took the hint."

As they talked, Frances found herself relaxing with Clare, enjoying the conversation. In fact, she found all these people who cared for Marsh to be kind and loving. Even though sometimes their talk seemed exotic, Frances felt so warmed in their presence that she dreaded returning to the cold formality of the parsonage.

The contrast seemed so great now. She wondered why she had never noticed before how sterile and rigid her son and his wife seemed. Their children were still young enough to be spontaneous, but already Frances could see Richard was working on changing that. Had she and Lyal done the same to Richard when he was young?

Lee moved over to sit on the ground by Clare. "You two look absorbed in talk. Am I missing something?"

"We've just been deciding kids watch too much TV," Clare said.

"That's new? I got left behind over there when Les and Marsh got going on their experiences from here to the West Coast. Les must have had quite some travels those two years right after Wade died."

"I wish I'd known Wade," Clare said. "I remember seeing him around in the '70s, but of course I wasn't seeing anything of you then."

"That's for sure. She was too busy farming with George," Lee said to Frances.

"And you were busy with all those women who came out from the Twin Cities. I used to see them over there…"

"You did? I didn't think you'd noticed."

"How could I not? There were so many of them. A steady stream of women," Clare said with a good-natured smile that suggested she might be exaggerating.

"Oh, sure. Make Frances think I was totally awful."

"Well, you were."

"You're just jealous because they didn't turn in at your driveway."

"Jealous? Me? Certainly not," Clare said with mock indignation. "More like unconscious during that time, I think. My marriage was not the greatest," she said to Frances.

"So I gather," Frances said dryly. This was alien talk to her, and somewhat uncomfortable. But the good-humored teasing and affectionate glances suggested that these women cared deeply about each other. Frances could not remember in her marriage that there had ever been such rich moments of gentle teasing.

"What a great day," Marsh said later when he was back home and in bed. "I'm exhausted, but it was worth it. All those nice memories…"

"You have some wonderful friends," Frances found herself saying. It was her turn to spend the night. "I like them. And your sister, too."

"Well, well," Marsh said, fighting sleep to snipe at her. "The good minister's wife likes the gays. Who would have thought it?"

"The good minister's widow may throw something at you if you act too smart about it," Frances retorted.

"Hey, I wouldn't dream of doing that. I'm very glad you like them, Frances. But I'll bet you didn't really think you would, did you?"

"Oh, go to sleep. Trust you to make me sorry I admitted I do."

"I think I will. I'm going to sleep well tonight," Marsh yawned. His eyes closed and he was immediately snoring.

Frances moved quietly out of the bedroom. She settled in on the sofa and tried to sleep, but she wasn't tired enough yet. The shelves of books around the room felt like a cozy shield to her. She thought she'd read for awhile, sure now that Lee would not mind if she dipped into the library.

She let her eyes wander over the titles, some of which she shunned because of one word: lesbian. Such a charged word.

It had conjured up all sorts of depravity. But that was before she met Lee and Clare. Now she wasn't sure what it suggested. Strong women, maybe. Shared emotions. Love?

She chose instead *The Works of Anne Bradstreet.* A poet. An early American poet, it seemed. Frances had never heard of her. The book fell open at a poem and her eyes read part of it:

By nature, Trees do rot when they are grown,
And Plums and Apples thoroughly ripe do fall,
And corn and grass are in their season mown,
And time brings down what is both strong and tall.

It certainly does, she thought. Time and disease. AIDS. Marsh. The simple statement in the poem's lines touched her, bringing tears. Damn, she thought, although she wasn't much given to swearing. I miss him already.

PART FIVE

Late October 1984

Frances put away her groceries in the refrigerator and cupboards. She unpacked her own dishes and silverware, items that had been stored away up on the third floor of the parsonage when her son and daughter-in-law had moved in. There were more boxes of her possessions in the car. She had carried them out of the parsonage alone. Her son had refused to help in what he considered a foolish undertaking.

He had not realized she was serious about moving out until Frances had begun lugging her boxes down the long series of stairs from the third floor. Richard had stood in the small front hallway of the parsonage looking stern but puzzled.

"Mother, I can hardly believe you're doing this to us. I thought we had a good arrangement."

"Perhaps you should ask Patricia how good she thought it was," Frances suggested.

She knew her daughter-in-law was relieved to have her leaving. Frances could understand that living with a mother-in-law might not be easy, especially when that mother-in-law insisted on hanging around with "undesirables."

"I'm sure she's as shocked as I am," Richard said. "Why did that...that woman offer you her house?"

"Because she's a good and generous person. A good friend," Frances said.

"She's a homosexual, Mother. What am I going to tell the church people?"

"I'm sure you'll think of something." After some hesitation she reached up and gave her son a kiss on the cheek.

He stiffened and drew back. "Good-bye," she said.

On the way out to Lee's house, Frances thought about why indeed Lee had offered her the house. After Marsh's death Frances had come back to Lee's house to gather up the items that had migrated out there while Frances was being a caregiver. She had packed up reluctantly, thinking how bleak it was going to seem now. Living at the parsonage had little appeal for her and what was she going to do with her time?

"Hi," Lee's voice broke in on her thoughts. "I thought you'd be back soon for your things. How's it going for you?"

Frances shrugged, feeling tears near. "Okay, I guess. I miss Marsh. It seems so strange not to need to plan our days and nights around him."

"Yes, it does." Lee perched on the edge of the empty hospital bed and watched Frances search around the room for missing belongings. "What are your plans?"

"I don't really have any," Frances admitted. "I guess I'll go back to the parsonage and see what happens."

"You don't sound exactly thrilled by the prospect of being back there all the time."

"I guess I'm not," Frances said honestly. "It's not a good arrangement, but with my small income there doesn't seem to be much choice."

Lee was silent for awhile. "Why don't you stay here?" she offered. "The house should be used. I'm very well settled across the road with Clare. I don't need it."

"That's kind of you, but I couldn't afford the rent."

"Who said anything about rent? Pay for the utilities and we'll help you find wood to burn."

"But I couldn't possibly accept..."

"Why not? You got anything better to do?"

"No..." Frances admitted. "But I wouldn't feel right not paying you something."

"So help us with some of the cooking and farm work once in awhile," Lee said.

She smiled appealingly at Frances. "You're staying, aren't you?"

So Frances had moved in. She did not know how long she would stay, but for the present it was a wonderful offer. Maybe someday she would decide to move, to do something else. For now she had a home again instead of a third floor room in someone else's home.

She heard the back door open and close. "Sorry we're late," Clare said. "I had a cow calving and Lee had to fix a waterbowl in her barn. I brought over a hotdish for noon. Didn't figure you'd want to cook while you're getting settled."

The two women began to lug in boxes for her, helping her rearrange Lee's furniture to make room for her own possessions. She had left the larger items of furniture for her son to keep or for a garage sale some day. Frances knew Richard was almost as distressed over the loss of her income as he was over her.

"Anybody in here?" Les called out from the front door. "I came to take the hospital bed back to the rental place," he said as the three women came to greet him. "I see you're getting settled?"

"Yes." Frances smiled at Les, liking him for his ability to mingle well with them.

"You're just in time for lunch," Lee said. She gave Les a hug. Frances wished she had the easy ability these people had, to hug and give hugs in return. She still hung back when she greeted them or said good-bye, wanting to exchange a hug but not quite daring to. She thought they probably felt the same way about hugging her.

"Brought you a housewarming gift," Les said casually. He handed over a bouquet of cut flowers.

Frances had never received flowers before. Not from her husband or from her son or anyone else. She was very touched. "They're beautiful," she said. "I'll put them on the table to brighten our meal. Thanks, Les." Before she could hesitate and think better of it, she gave him a hug which he returned strongly.

"Do you think if we brought her flowers she'd hug us?" Lee asked Clare.

"Don't embarrass the woman." Clare smiled at Frances.

"Why not? She blushes nicely when she's embarrassed."

"You two are almost as impossible as Marsh," Frances said with a smile.

"Sure seems strange without him around, doesn't it?" Les sighed.

"I miss him," Frances said simply. The others nodded.

"Well, let's eat," Clare suggested. "I think my hotdish isn't too bad, if I do say so myself. It's just an old calico bean thing I can toss together quickly." She uncovered the casserole dish and set it on the table.

They found their usual places. Frances brought out her own silver and dishes, thinking, these are my first guests. How appropriate. With Les' flowers in the center of the round table and the four of them eating companionably together, Frances felt a warm bond. It seemed to her as though in giving care to Marsh they had also been discovering each other.

"I'm so glad I'm here," she said spontaneously.

Lee grinned at her. "See. Told you it was the right thing to do."

A knock on the back door saved her from needing to make a reply. Frances, because this was becoming her house, rose and went to open the door.

"Can I come in?" Stella Grimes asked. "I was just coming back from town and I saw the cars..." She came to sit at the table, protesting that she hadn't stopped to steal their food.

Soon she too was eating. "I just thought I'd stop and see how you all are." It had angered Stella greatly to discover that most of the neighbors had not even bothered to send a card or bring any food to show their support. These were the same people who had given so generously at the time when Butch and Angie died. It was as though Marsh's death was unimportant.

"How are things going for you?" Clare asked.

"Oh, well, about the same. We're struggling along. I get so mad sometimes when I read the papers and the farm magazines," Stella said. "The experts are now saying we were all poor managers to get ourselves so far in debt. Never mind that they were the ones who advised us to do it."

"The experts have short memories," Lee agreed. "I can't stand their pious remarks. As though they're the only ones who know how to farm."

"I'd like to see them do it half as well," Stella said. "Get a little dirt under their fingernails instead of sitting all neat and tidy at their desks. Did you hear the latest? The government is planning to lower milk support prices and keep lowering them until we get the message. They say the lower prices should be a clear signal to us dairy people that we're producing too much milk. I don't notice anybody talking about lowering the prices we have to pay for stuff, though."

"Nope," Clare agreed. "Things we buy just keep getting more expensive. You can only tighten up your management so far. Then it means milk more cows and hope the extra milk will balance out the higher costs."

"I'd just like to get my hands on those idiots," Stella declared. "They say they want to keep the family farm but everything the government does suggests they don't give a damn. The big one thousand-plus herds can probably handle the lower prices but I'm not sure how long those of us with one hundred cows or less can stand it."

"I know," Clare agreed. "I'm just glad we don't have the huge debts we had when George was alive. But what happens if Chad wants to farm? How can I sell it to him without crippling him with a huge debt?"

"It's sickening. You know," Stella said, "sometimes I'd just like to say to all those people in the cities, grow your own damned food if you don't like the way we do it for you. People eat cheap in this country, by God! They want the picture-perfect fruit but not the chemicals that make it possible. They want the convenience items in the freezer case and then they wonder why their grocery bills seem high. It costs money when somebody cooks the food and packages it up all nice and fancy. Next thing you know they're gonna want somebody to pre-chew their damned food."

Les laughed at her vehemence. "I hope you'll still let me have some milk, Stella, when you all stop producing it for us."

"Oh, you. Yeah, I'll let you eat. Sorry, but I just get so mad sometimes." Stella paused and looked around at her friends. "You know, sometimes I wonder why we're doing it. The long hours. The financial headaches. And I have to think both Angie and Butch might still be alive if it hadn't been for all the financial pressure we've been under."

The other four were silent, considering. Clare thought, what is there about us that makes us keep working long hours when so many people in this country don't anymore? We work hard and we do our best and then we're told it's either too good a job because there's a surplus, or it's not good enough because we can't pay our debts.

"How are Orrin and Sally?" Lee asked finally.

"Oh, well, Sally's doing all right. It's hard for her, coming home to that big empty house. But she and I...We've gotten so much closer since the accident. We talk about everything. I listen when she needs to talk about her anger and pain and she does the same for me. I suppose it's kind of like having a daughter. No." Stella thought a bit. "No, I'd say Sally's become the best friend I ever had. She could have left Orrin and me after the accident. I wouldn't have blamed her if she'd walked right out. But she says she married Butch for better or for worse and this sure is the worse. She's not gonna leave, she says."

Frances thought of the biblical story of Naomi and Ruth. "Entreat me not to leave you..." Mother-in-law and daughter-in-law; in the Bible story, the daughter-in-law was worth more to Naomi than seven sons. In those days, given the male slant to everything, that was really saying something. Frances felt tears form behind her eyelids as she heard Stella talk of Sally. Such strong women, just going on when many might have quit.

There seemed to be so many ways of women being close to each other. She had never thought about lesbian relationships and yet here were Lee and Clare, their caring so heartening to see. And now there was a mother-in-law and a daughter-in-law being each other's best friends. Frances tried to imagine herself being friends with Patricia and failed utterly.

"How's Orrin?" Clare was asking.

Stella shrugged. "He goes along, keeping busy. I wish he'd talk about what happened but he won't. He just plunges into the work. Works until he's too tired to hardly see. Then he does it all over again the next day. I'm afraid for him sometimes. I wish I could understand men. Excuse me, Les," she said.

"That's all right," Les assured her. "Some of us don't communicate as well as you women do. I was like that after Wade died. I kind of ran. Went traveling all over. Never spoke to anyone. Never really saw where I'd been. At some point I guess I realized I couldn't just keep running. But I still miss Wade."

"I'm sure you do," Stella said. "I sure miss Butch and Angie." She had come to like Les.

"Maybe I could help with Orrin." Les' voice was hesitant. "I don't know him, but I do know what he's going through. If you think I could help, I'd be glad to try." He made the offer expecting to be turned down but hoping he wouldn't be. Marsh in his illness had been someone to focus on, but Marsh was dead now and Les was lonely.

He shrugged and smiled into the silence that followed his offer. "I may be an old queen," he said jokingly, "but I am still a man and maybe I could reach something you can't."

"Well, just so you don't come in drag," Stella quipped. "I don't think Orrin's ready for that."

"Might shock him right out of his funk," Lee said.

Stella hesitated about taking Les up on his offer, feeling pretty sure Orrin wouldn't respond. But then she thought, what can it hurt? I like Les and I want to see him once in awhile.

"How about coming out for dinner next Sunday noon?" she asked. She was glad when she saw the pleased smile on Les' face.

"I'd love to," he said.

It amused Frances to try to imagine her own son faced with Les across his dinner table. She hoped Stella's husband would respond more easily. Les was lonely, she realized suddenly. I'll invite him out often when I'm settled.

The five of them lingered at the table, reluctant to break up the gathering. Finally Stella rose. "Time for me to get on home. There's always so much work these days."

"Since I'm going to be living out here, perhaps there are things I could help you with?" Frances offered. "I'd be glad to help if you think I wouldn't just be in the way."

"I'm sure you wouldn't be in the way, but I can't ask you to do that. We couldn't afford to pay you anything," Stella said.

"Who said anything about pay? I'd like to help if I could."

"Well, then I'll say yes. Never turn down free help," Stella said jokingly to the rest of the group. Impulsively she gave Frances a hug.

The others stood up, too. Les headed for the bedroom. Clare followed him saying, "I'll help you with that bed."

"Well," Lee said when the others had left. "You seem to be filling up your days even before you've unpacked."

Frances nodded. "I think I'm going to like it here. I won't lack for work and if I want entertainment, there are all those books of yours. I hope you won't mind if I read some of them."

"Go ahead. Read anything that appeals."

"I will. I've already been dipping into them."

"We'll turn you into a liberated woman yet," Lee joked.

"How will we do that?" Clare asked as she came back from helping Les.

"Oh, she's going to read the whole bunch of books here."

"That might do it." Clare smiled warmly at Frances. "I still haven't had time to do more than skim the surface. Who needs TV when there are all those books? Lee has a pretty wide taste in reading matter."

"I know," Frances said.

"Including," Clare added in a low confidential tone, "lesbian romances. Just like the Harlequin romances. Only girl meets girl. Girl loses girl. Girl gets girl back at the end. Who would have thought Lee would have a secret yen for such light reading matter?"

Lee looked embarrassed. "What's wrong with them? They sure beat TV."

"Yeah...you're right." Clare grinned affectionately at her. "I always suspected you had a hidden romantic streak. She's not as tough as she seems," she said to Frances.

Frances smiled. "I don't think she's so tough. She's a kind generous person and you're lucky to have her."

"Hey," Lee protested, embarrassed again.

"Yeah, I think I am, too," Clare agreed. She gave Frances a big hug. "See you later."

"Well," Lee said awkwardly. "Guess I'd better get going, too. Hope you settle in okay."

"I will. Thanks again for everything." Frances stood equally awkwardly as Lee prepared to go. Then she fought down the awkwardness and gave Lee a hug. Lee returned it in full measure.

Frances stood in the doorway of her new home and watched the two women walk together down the driveway. My new neighbors, she thought with a smile. She felt as though she had moved into a real neighborhood. There was Stella down the road and Les more than willing to spend time in the country. Her widowhood was turning out very differently than she might have imagined.

Maybe she wouldn't stay here forever. She might find work somewhere else. And she imagined someday Lee would want to sell her farm and retire. Clare would probably find a way to turn her farm over to her son if he wanted it. But for now the days held a lot of promise. She didn't think she needed to go much beyond that.

Karen Kringle lives in western Wisconsin and is a dairy farmer. She and her partner Grace Wood share their 295 acre farm with 110 Holstein cattle, 2 horses, 4 dogs and a house cat named Grubbly.

OTHER TITLES AVAILABLE FROM SPINSTERS

All The Muscle You Need, Diana McRae $8.95

Being Someone, Ann MacLeod $9.95

Cancer in Two Voices, Butler & Rosenblum $12.95

Child of Her People, Anne Cameron $8.95

Considering Parenthood, Cheri Pies $12.95

Desert Years, Cynthia Rich $7.95

Elise, Claire Kensington $7.95

Final Session, Mary Morell $9.95

High and Outside, Linnea A. Due $8.95

The Journey, Anne Cameron $9.95

The Lesbian Erotic Dance, JoAnn Loulan $12.95

Lesbian Passion, JoAnn Loulan $12.95

Lesbian Sex, JoAnn Loulan $12.95

Lesbians at Midlife, ed. by Sang, Warshow & Smith $12.95

Life Savings, Linnea Due $10.95

Look Me in the Eye, 2nd Ed., Macdonald & Rich $8.95

Love and Memory, Amy Oleson $9.95

Modern Daughters and the Outlaw West, Melissa Kwasny $9.95

Thirteen Steps, Bonita L. Swan $8.95

Vital Ties, Karen Kringle $10.95

Why Can't Sharon Kowalski Come Home?
   Thompson & Andrzejewski $10.95

Spinsters titles are available at your local booksellers, or by mail order through Spinsters Book Company. A free catalogue is available upon request.

Please include $1.50 for the first title ordered, and $ .50 for every title thereafter. Visa and Mastercard accepted.

Spinsters Book Company was founded in 1978 to produce vital books for diverse women's communities. In 1986 we merged with Aunt Lute Books to become Spinsters/Aunt Lute. In 1990, the Aunt Lute Foundation became an independent non-profit publishing program. In 1992, Spinsters moved to Minneapolis.

Spinsters is committed to publishing works outside the scope of mainstream commercial publishers: books that not only name crucial issues in women's lives, but more importantly encourage change and growth; books that help make the best in our lives more possible. We sponsor an annual Lesbian Fiction Contest for the best lesbian novel each year. And we are particularly interested in creative works by lesbians.

spinsters, p.o. box 300170, minneapolis, mn 55403